WE
BECOME
DARKNESS

WE BECOME DARKNESS

A Novel

GRACE MORROW

Books should be disposed of and recycled according to local requirements. All paper materials used are FSC compliant.

Published in the United States by Alcove Press, an imprint of The Quick Brown Fox & Company LLC.

Alcove Press and its logo are trademarks of The Quick Brown Fox & Company LLC.

Library of Congress Catalog-in-Publication data available upon request.

ISBN (hardcover): 979-8-89242-474-5
ISBN (paperback): 979-8-89242-475-2
ISBN (ebook): 979-8-89242-476-9

Cover design by Olivia Hintz

Printed in the United States.

www.alcovepress.com

Alcove Press
34 West 27th St., 10th Floor
New York, NY 10001

First Edition: April 2026

The authorized representative in the EU for product safety and compliance is eucomply OÜPärnu mnt 139b-14, 11317 Tallinn, Estonia, hello@eucompliancepartner.com, +33757690241

10 9 8 7 6 5 4 3 2 1

To anyone who thought they couldn't do it,
here's the proof you can.

VACCARIUM

Perden
Nanis
Cupisco
Sanire
Arenbis
Corithian
AGRIPA

Chapter One

"There hasn't been a new lead in six months. Not since you gutted that Vampyr in Cardin," Reina whispered.

Thalia turned, peeling her eyes from the carnage. The shadows covering the captain's dark face did little to hide her revulsion. Her armor glittered in the moonlight, although the muted gold seemed garish against the field of corpses.

"It's him," Thalia said. Her gaze roamed over the bodies peppering the land like lumps of coal—bodies that had been ripped apart and propped back together like some sort of macabre chessboard. The crops had been razed to the ground, destroyed as if some feral beast had been set loose upon them.

Reina made a face, scrubbing a hand over her short-cropped dark hair. "And you're sure it's him?"

Him.

It would have been better if it were some feral beast, not the Vampyr she sought.

Thalia clenched her jaw, ignoring the emotions rising hot in her gut. "This death reeks of him."

Reina studied her a moment longer, brown eyes flashing. "We need to head back to Corithian."

Thalia wiped the sweat from her brow. Even with night in full swing, the heat of summer worked its way down the back of her spine, itching like a pesky bug. "Why?"

"Your mother sent word."

"I'm not done here. You've seen the fields—these townsfolk won't last the next few months without their crops. They are as good as dead out here."

Reina sighed, shifting slightly. "She's the queen; her word is law even for her daughter. She's changed her mind about you going off and doing this."

"This?" Thalia's voice dropped, although they were far enough away from the ramshackle town that no one would hear them. Far enough away that no one would notice the Queen of Agripa's inner circle was in their midst. "You mean doing my duty in ensuring the townsfolk of Agripa are safe? Ensuring that they are provided enough resources that they won't starve come winter? Ensuring that *he* doesn't take any more innocent lives?"

"Listen, Princess." Reina added the last bit with enough bite that Thalia stiffened. "I do what I'm told. She said you've had your fun."

Thalia snorted, toying with the end of her light-blonde braid, ignoring the stench of decaying flesh brushing against her nose. "Fun? My duty is to the people of Agripa. I was assigned this role, and she gave me leave for this mission. To fix *my* mistake." Her mistake of allowing *him* to still breathe.

Reina leaned closer, keeping her voice soft. "I know. And I know what it means for you to do this. But your mother wasn't pleased about that stint in Cardin."

Thalia had found one of those bloodsuckers about to set fire to a granary, and she'd shoved an iron stake through its skull. But it wasn't the Vampyr she hunted. The one who kept leaving what the townsfolk were calling "the Scarecrows."

Thalia pulled her attention back, hazel eyes narrowing. "Why? It's the first lead I had since Darein. She should have been pleased I'm making headway."

Until that led to a dead end. Then another, and another.

Every city and town Thalia had traveled to had sent her on a wild-goose chase. Never close to what—to whom—she sought.

But Thalia could practically feel it, something humming through her veins, a deep sense of urgency whispering in her ear.

She was close to it. So very close to *him*.

"The Vampyr you killed was supposedly an important leader from one of the courts, did you know that?" Reina cocked her head.

"How the hell would I have known that? It's not as though the Vampyr courts have been in contact with us, not since—" Thalia choked, the image of unseeing eyes staring at hers flashing in her mind. The phantom weight of blood coated her fingers as she tried to put her sister's head back on her body after a Vampyr had ripped it off.

Maybe the Vampyr Thalia had killed belonged to the same monstrous family who'd taken her sister and father. If that was the case, important leader or not, a stake through its skull was a mercy compared to what she could have done to appease the ever-growing ache in her chest.

That thought sent the anger boiling in Thalia's bloodstream into white-hot rage. "Good. I hope it's burning in hell. I hope they all are."

Something flashed in Reina's eyes, but she quickly masked it. "Your mother needs you home."

"Tell her I'm close. That I need more time."

"To do what? You aren't going to find him."

Thalia's teeth ground together, and she looked away, unable to face the hard truth in Reina's eyes. "I will."

Only so she could stab a stake through his traitorous heart.

Reina sighed, muttering to the gods to save her. "What he did was shit." Thalia stiffened. *Shit* was the understatement of the millennium. What he'd done was unforgivable—inhuman. But she supposed he wasn't human anymore. Thalia shoved down the bile rising in her throat as Reina continued, "But your mother needs you back. There's been a new development. Something to do with the ore."

"What about it?" Thalia's interest piqued. She'd passed the fields leached of color on her way into this town. The soil that refused to be tilled and the grain that shriveled like husks, not to mention the sickness that followed in its wake. When the ore was spread across the fields, it allowed the land to become fertile—thriving. When burned, it fueled homes and mills. They needed that ore to survive, especially with the ongoing war between the humans and Vampyrs. In recent years, the human reserves had rapidly dwindled.

Reina shook her head. "I don't know. But you're needed at the castle, immediately. Now, we can either go back to the palace the easy way, or . . ." She trailed off with a smirk.

Thalia didn't take her threat seriously. Not that Reina wouldn't tie her to a horse and carry her all the way to Corithian, Agripa's capital city, if she refused. And Thalia knew she had no hope of taking her in a fight if it came to that. Reina was a good head taller than her, not to mention she knew every single one of her moves; she had taught them to Thalia herself.

Thalia forced her hands to unclench, to let go of the urgency racing through her veins. The sooner she got back to the castle, the sooner she could leave and ensure that no more townsfolk suffered because of her mistake. She'd finish her mission—for good. "Fine."

She stalked away from the field, Reina at her heels. Their horses waited on an empty dirt road, their hides gleaming in the moonlight, the summer air thick and muggy.

"We're already late," Reina said, swinging into her saddle. "I received the letter this morning; you were expected a day ago. We need to move quickly, or your mother will not be pleased."

She never was.

Thalia swung herself up onto her horse, and Reina dug her heels into her beast's side, taking off to pass through the nearly empty town.

Thalia turned to follow but froze.

Even from a distance, the Scarecrows stood out like a raised scar among the graying field. They swayed slightly in the summer breeze. Once morning came, the corpses would cook in the sun, the heat turning the remaining bits of hanging flesh into strips of leather.

Someone should take them down.

Someone *needed* to take them down.

But Thalia remained frozen, transfixed, as one particular corpse swayed harder than the others, almost as though it were curling a finger toward her in a promise.

Then a dark shadow stepped out from behind the Scarecrow.

Eyes the color of the mountain lakes stared back.

Thalia's whole body locked up, her breath coming in deep pants.

He . . . he was—

"Thalia!"

Her horse shifted and Thalia jolted, glancing over her shoulder to find Reina waiting in the distance near some old trenches dug during the start of the war.

Thalia whipped back, heart pounding in her throat. But nothing was there. No glowing eyes. No dark presence. Even the Scarecrows were gone, toppled over by that fell wind.

Thalia shook her head, forcing down the dread rising in her stomach as she spurred her horse after Reina.

She tried to push aside the image of the Scarecrows. Tried to push past the smell of decaying flesh still clinging to her nostrils, and the eyes that had seared themselves into her brain—into her heart.

But as they rode hard through the night across Agripa's dying land, she couldn't quite shake the feeling that something watched her from the shadows.

Waiting to sink their teeth in.

"You're late, Thalia."

Thalia stiffened as she glanced up at her mother's imposing figure sitting on her gilded throne.

Queen Helena Cesiaran of Agripa looked her daughter over, her features an immovable mask of marble. Her emerald eyes scanned Thalia from head to toe. Thalia was grateful she'd had time to bathe and change. Her mother was already displeased; tracking mud across the red-carpeted tile would have only served to irk her more.

"Apologies, my horse threw a shoe." The lie rolled smoothly off her tongue as she rose, her seafoam silk gown falling off her frame like water. Thalia hadn't questioned it when her handmaiden, Katrina, wrangled her into it. The gold press of her knife against her thigh echoed the coldness of her mother's face.

The queen's brows narrowed noting the lie. "You were expected days ago."

Thalia ignored the stares of her mother's scheming court. They tittered behind lace fans, their forked tongues whispering to each other, no doubt about her absence at court. "I was checking on the towns further north. They've been hit harder than most with the Scarecrows."

"I see." The queen's delicate nostrils flared as Thalia took a spot next to her. "You reek of death."

Thalia was glad her back was ramrod straight, only because it kept her from falling over. "I don't know what you're talking about."

The queen raised a well-groomed brow. The setting sun filtered in through the large-paned windows, highlighting the gold and marble of the throne room. It set her mother shining, the beams bouncing off blonde hair braided neatly into a chignon, making it glow like a halo. Thalia supposed that was how her mother wished to appear: like an angel, a savior.

"Why am I here? You know I have a duty to fulfill." Thalia steered the conversation away from the supposed scent her mother could sniff out like a bloodhound. Away from *him*.

The queen shifted on her throne, her simple crown catching the light. The two olive branches wrapped around her brow. The branches were meant to be a symbol of victory—of hope.

But hope did not shelter here. It fled when darkness came, chased out by its warring cries.

"There has been a new development with the ore," the queen said, pulling Thalia back.

"Reina said as much. Have they found something to replace it? Some new resource we may have overlooked?" Thalia's heart rate picked up.

The queen's green eyes flashed. "You know the only place to get that ore is in the mountain."

Thalia's stomach twisted like a knife. The mountain was at the very tip of their continent, accessible only to the monsters who had killed her father and sister, who hid behind an impenetrable forest. That was why the war had gone on for so long. The humans couldn't break through the forest, and the Vampyrs seemed able to send only a few of their kind at a time to target the farms.

"Has Marcus found something in the library, then?" Thalia pushed. She craned her head, trying to spot the head librarian among the courtiers, but she didn't find his curly head in the crowd.

The queen hesitated, then her face hardened. "Not quite."

"Then what—"

The throne room doors boomed open, and her mother's adviser, Kamith, strolled in. Although his hair was shot through with gray, he carried himself like a younger man. He wasn't unattractive by any means, and Thalia had learned to ignore whispers among the displeased courtiers that he was bedding the queen.

"Your Majesty." Kamith bowed before straightening. "Your guests are ready for you."

"What guests?" Thalia asked, looking between the two.

"Princess," Kamith acknowledged, sliding his guarded gaze to hers. "Potential allies."

Agripa didn't have any allies, at least here in this land. The treacherous waters around Agripa made overseas journeys from other continents more perilous than they were worth.

"I thought you had something on the ore?" Thalia glanced between the two of them, picking at the skin around her thumbs.

The queen ignored her, nodding as the last of the sun's rays fled the throne room. "Bring them in."

Reina stepped forward, flashing a warning look at Thalia before she left with a few other soldiers. Thalia had failed to note how many guards in glinting armor lined the back walls.

The queen turned suddenly to her. "You must be on your best behavior tonight."

Thalia resisted the urge to scowl. "I always am—"

"I mean it, Thalia." The queen's hand suddenly gripped her arm. "You cannot ruin this for us, for Agripa."

Everything in Thalia went on high alert. "Why?"

Her mother made another face, displeasure on her full lips. "I have brokered a mutually beneficial deal that will help both our lands—that will end this war." Thalia opened her mouth to speak, but her mother cut her off. "This deal, Thalia, will not be to your liking. But think of Agripa, think of your *duty*. You will do well to sit quietly while this plays out."

The queen released her, and Thalia's heart pounded in her chest, her thoughts racing. The courtiers all quieted as the soldiers' hands drifted nearer to their swords.

The throne room doors creaked open, the sound eerily like the closing of a coffin.

Reina reentered, her steps clipped, and bowed. "Your Majesty."

Thalia's eyes trailed past her to the guards filing in, along with five cloaked figures.

"Welcome," Kamith's voice boomed out. "On behalf of Her Majesty, Queen Helena Cesiaran of Agripa, we thank you for joining us this evening."

Thalia glanced at her mother, but she appeared stoic, unchanging, her face shifting to an unreadable mask once more.

The figure in the middle stepped forward, their hood concealing their features. "And on behalf of House Lorenzia, we want to thank you for such a . . . warm welcome." Their voice was so cold it sent a shiver down Thalia's spine. "Although we had hoped negotiations would have been concluded by now."

"I apologize on behalf of my daughter." The queen's voice nearly shook Thalia from her stupor. "She is here, as you can see."

"How excellent," the figure said, pulling back his hood.

A gasp went out, and one of the courtiers fainted, their companion catching them in a swirl of purple silk.

Thalia's stomach bottomed out.

Pale skin gleamed like cut glass, and red eyes met hers. Slicked-back blond hair was pulled away from the smooth planes of the Vampyr's face, accentuating his deadly beauty.

"Perhaps we can speed up our negotiations, then." Glimpses of sharp fangs showed behind bloodless lips.

Thalia's knees locked as her mother tilted her head. "Of course. We wouldn't wish to delay you further."

Thalia's breath seized in her lungs as soldiers stepped forward, carrying six chairs. This couldn't be happening. There were . . . there were Vampyrs in her home. There hadn't been any Vampyrs since that night over thirteen years ago. When she'd watched them rip off the head of her sister—when they'd punched a hole in her father's chest so hard his spine had splattered to the ground—

Thalia jerked, only to have a gloved hand encircle her elbow.

Reina was at her side, her features hard. "Princess." Thalia hadn't realized a chair had been placed near her mother's throne. "Sit."

Thalia couldn't.

She didn't think she could even take a breath. The remaining four figures revealed themselves, ethereal beauty exposed like the bright side of the moon. From pale ivory to deep ebony to bronzed, the faces of the Vampyrs appeared before her eyes, though Thalia couldn't quite understand what she was witnessing.

Reina helped her into her chair, her body going numb long before her mind did.

"We want to thank you again for your generous offer, Lord Damien," Kamith spoke, ever the diplomat.

The middle Vampyr, the pale one who appeared to be Lord Damien, tilted his head. The movement was much too predatory. "And of your own."

Thalia didn't know whether she wanted to scream or puke all over the marble staircase. Or better yet, fly across the floor and plunge stakes through all their monstrous skulls.

"The ore you've provided will be enough to last us a decade," Kamith continued, undeterred at the creatures before him.

A murmur broke out through the crowd.

Why was no one reacting? Why was no one screaming and wailing? These monsters had infiltrated their home, had tried to make a deal before—

"We have already broken the dams. The rivers are headed through to your forest as we speak," the queen stated. None of the Vampyrs reacted, but Thalia jerked.

"What?" Her question was too loud. It echoed around the quiet room, hitting her back in the face. Agripa had blocked off the rivers that fed the Vampyrs' sacred forest after the tentative peace between them ended over a decade ago. The dark woods allowed them to hunt during the day, and Thalia had been glad to know that the monsters' sacred forest would strangle and rot just like her heart had.

But now the river was going back to feeding them?

Her mother cast her a warning look.

"Then it seems negotiations have already been sped along," Lord Damien said, his red eyes flashing.

Thalia's nails pierced her palms, and all the Vampyrs' attention zeroed in on her.

Sweat dripped down her spine, her palms sticky with blood and water.

"We would also like to propose another offer," Thalia's mother said. It was enough to draw the attention of the Vampyrs. But Thalia still didn't breathe, not as one of them caught her stare. His ebony skin gleamed against short-cropped hair, and golden eyes glinted like two coins. It must have been a trick of the light, because she could have sworn his skin had begun to sink in, his flesh pulling taut over his skull. Thalia blinked and it was gone.

"What more could you offer?" Lord Damien tilted his head.

"We have long since been at war. While this new deal is mutually beneficial for both our peoples, my council and I fear what should happen if we fall out of favor once more."

Should one of the creatures decide to kill them as they'd done before. Thalia's lips twisted in disgust. One of the Vampyrs stared at her palm, sensing the blood smeared against her heart lines.

"And what is this proposal?" Lord Damien asked.

"A marriage between House Lorenzia and the Cesiaran line. So that no more ill blood shall be spilled on behalf of our two peoples. United, we can hope to better the lives of both our kinds."

Thalia whirled to her mother, heart pounding in her throat. "You can't."

Her sister's dead face flashed in her mind—her body cooling not ten feet from where she now sat. They'd tried this before. Tried to broker a union between human and Vampyr—

The queen ignored her daughter, focusing on Lord Damien.

The Vampyr cocked his pale head, his ruby eyes looking the princess over. "A most interesting proposition, but I'm afraid—"

The throne room doors creaked open again, and everyone turned to see the newcomer. It was then that Thalia realized one chair had remained empty.

The cloaked figure didn't walk with the fluid grace of the rest of the creatures in the room. There was almost something familiar about the way they moved, how their shoulders rolled under a velvet cloak.

"A most interesting proposition indeed." The cloaked figure stopped in the half circle of chairs.

Another shiver rocked down Thalia's spine.

"As hand to the prince, I speak on behalf of him, and I am most certain this would be advantageous to both our people. This war has gone on too long. Many have suffered, on both sides. But the time of peace is at hand, don't you think so, Lord Damien?"

"Of course, Cassius. If that is what you believe His Highness would wish."

Cassius—

Thalia jerked, stumbling to her feet, just as the Vampyr removed his hood.

Eyes bluer than the mountain lakes met hers.

She knew that sharp face. The jaw that could cut and the burnished dark-auburn hair brushing against powerful shoulders.

Not possible.

"You." The word fell from her lips, breaking apart like ash.

The nausea swirling inside her gut quickly turned to white-hot rage.

The Vampyr grinned, twin fangs gleaming as his sensual lips stretched upward. "Hello, Princess. Did you miss me?"

Thalia launched herself down the dais, knife slashing straight for the strong column of the Vampyr's throat.

Chapter Two

"I'm going to kill you!" Thalia screamed, her blade angled to cut right through his artery.

Someone grabbed her around her waist, yanking her back. Cold metal pressed against her spine as Reina wrapped a tight hand around her wrist.

"I told you to sit quietly," the queen whispered harshly.

Cassius watched her, some sort of sick delight lighting his features as Thalia snarled, "You motherfucker—"

"If you do not hold your tongue, you will be removed." The queen turned sharply to her. Thalia stiffened, Reina's sharp breath echoing in her ear. The entire throne room had quieted, a silence that suffocated her almost as much as *his* presence. "Is that understood?"

Thalia glanced at the Vampyrs once more, her fingers tightening on her dagger. Then, finally, she nodded. Reina let her go but didn't go far as Thalia stiffly sat back on the chair, blade angled.

"I apologize for my daughter. She is prone to . . . fits," her mother said, turning back to the monsters before her.

Thalia could hardly pay attention over the pounding of her heart. *He* was here.

Standing before her as though nothing had happened.

As though the last four years had never taken place—

Kamith cleared his throat, breaking the tension. "The treaty has been drawn up. All we need are the signatures before the ceremony."

Ceremony.

Thalia wasn't in her body; she was back to the night thirteen years ago when another ceremony had taken place. But instead of sitting by her mother, it had been her sister, Ariadna, she sat next to. Her sister and a Vampyr—

Thalia froze, her heart rate rising as her stomach rolled. She glanced around the room, noting the guards on the wall—guards who hadn't been able to stop the Vampyrs, who were slaughtered alongside her father and sister—

Thalia's chest seized. "This is a trap."

Her words silenced whatever Kamith was saying to the Vampyrs.

"Princess?" Kamith's brows furrowed.

Cassius was here.

Cassius who'd betrayed her. Who'd betrayed his kingdom. Who'd killed the one person who could have stopped this war long ago.

And now they were back here, under the guise of peace—

"This is a trap—" Thalia panted, her focus on *him*. The courtiers around the room murmured, unease spearing itself through the gathered crowd like oil on water. "They're going to kill us like they did last time—they're going to—"

In one blink Lord Damien was before her. He moved so fast Thalia didn't have time to raise her dagger. She sat in the chair, helpless, as the Vampyr hovering over her cocked his head.

"If we wanted to kill you, you would all be choking on your own blood at this very moment." His red eyes swept over her before he smiled at the dagger in her clenched fist.

Thalia couldn't help the shiver of fear running down her spine. She swallowed her revulsion as he leaned closer.

"Charming. You truly are a treat." The Vampyr cocked his head. "She'll make a fine bride for our prince, don't you think so, Cassius?"

He studied her a moment longer before he stepped back, leisurely returning to his companions. "The ceremony shall be within the hour. Our prince does not like to be kept waiting."

Without waiting for a dismissal, the Vampyrs all followed Lord Damien out, the guards keeping close behind them. Thalia could have sworn Cassius faltered on the threshold, but the traitor didn't look back.

Thalia didn't even realize the throne room had been cleared until her mother stood, her posture stiff.

"What ceremony?" Thalia croaked out. She couldn't believe her throat worked, let alone that her heart still pumped blood through her.

Kamith glanced at her mother, but the queen ignored her adviser. "There will be a ceremony to bind you to the prince. This marriage is part of the treaty struck between our two realms to stop the war from continuing."

Thalia jerked out of the chair. "Are you *mad*? They killed our family. Your husband—your *daughter*—" She choked on the last word. "We've tried to strike this deal before, and it ended in blood—"

"Do you think me a fool?" The queen whirled on her, speaking harshly. "To allow these creatures into our home without a plan? Without a safety net? This war has been waging for far too long. Our ore is depleted. Gone. You've seen for yourself what our towns to the north look like."

"Gone?" Thalia faltered, shaking her head. Yes, she knew the towns had run out of ore, but they still had some left in the castle's supply being rationed out. "That . . . that can't be possible. Marcus said you were close to finding something—"

"He lied." The queen's voice filled with a rare note of defeat. "Our reserves are gone, bled dry because of this war. You've already noted the devastation this has caused Agripa on your travels. The sickness in our lands that festers like a wound gone sour. The fact that our food is scarce, our people starving, dying—"

"I know," Thalia bit out, and the queen paused, cocking her head. Thalia knew the state of Agripa better than the queen did. Because she'd been slowly watching Agripa fall into ruin, despite trying to do what she could, all while she sought *him*. "You're delusional if you believe this won't end in death."

My death.

The queen stepped in front of her. "It will be different this time."

"How?" Thalia scoffed.

"Because they need our water." Kamith spoke his first words since the Vampyrs had left. "We've received word that their forest is on the brink of decay. They may live by a different set of rules, but they will uphold this treaty. They're desperate to save what is sacred to them. Ever since that night thirteen years ago, their forest has begun to die. They will not jeopardize the one source that allows them to feed without fear of the light."

"Tell that to the Vampyr who killed my sister," Thalia snarled.

The queen suddenly gripped her, fingers ice cold on Thalia's wrists. "They are leeches, Thalia, and will do anything to gorge themselves into security. They will not kill you."

The image was less than reassuring.

Thalia glanced between the two of them. "Then why even do this? Why not let their forest die? Once it's dead, we could get to the mountain, retrieve the ore ourselves."

The queen sighed, letting go of Thalia's arms. "Because we've also received word that the Vampyrs have begun looking elsewhere for allegiance."

"Elsewhere?"

Kamith shifted. "There are other Vampyr courts outside of Agripa, as you know, those who've traveled from here to different lands. If the Vampyrs somehow gain allegiance with these courts across the seas, well, Agripa is already outnumbered; we don't have the means or resources to fight a war on two fronts. We're running out of time."

Thalia swallowed. "So this is it, then? I'm to be a lamb headed to the slaughter?"

Her mother gripped her wrists once more. "Did you know that when you first came to me four years ago with the request to do more, I wanted to refuse you?" It took a moment for Thalia to catch up with the change of topic. "It was Kamith who advised me to let you, despite knowing you'd use the chance to leave these walls to also seek revenge. I know this agreement is not to your liking, but you must think of your duty to the crown."

Thalia looked away, jaw aching. She didn't want to think of her duty. How she'd ached to do more for the people of Agripa who were slowly dying from both the dwindling ore and the monsters in the north plaguing them. Then *he'd* decided to betray her, and she'd vowed to do more by killing *him*. Because he'd known what the Vampyrs had done to her family—to her—and yet he'd chosen to become one of them anyway. To prey on the innocents he'd sworn to protect. And she'd failed the only vow she'd given herself by letting him walk out of the room breathing, by letting them all walk out breathing—

Thalia slowly raised her eyes to the queen, realization dawning. "You want me to destroy them."

The queen's grip tightened. "You will be in a prime position to see the inner workings of their kingdom, to see what makes it tick. Then to pull it out from under them."

Thalia sucked in a breath. "You want me to kill their prince?" The queen nodded. "They will know of this plan. They'll suspect we'd try something after everything that's been done. *He* will suspect—"

"I know." Her mother squeezed her shoulder. "But you will have to be smarter, more cunning than they are. I know you blame yourself for the Scarecrows—for the deaths that have happened. You wish to finish your mission for good? You wish to save Agripa? This is your chance. Get close to the prince, to his court, and destroy it."

The room fell silent, the queen's words drifting between them like smoke.

But marriage?

Her mother must have sensed her hesitancy, because she straightened, her words becoming cold. "You know that alliance through marriage has always been your duty since birth, no matter the past failed attempts." Thalia didn't want to think about those failed attempts. About the night when her world had crumbled around her. "I married your father without prior knowledge of who he was. I married to save my kingdom, as you will do now."

Thalia knew the story—the alliance that her mother's and father's families brokered, two powerful kingdoms made stronger by uniting. Her own fate had been drilled into her since the moment she was born female. She'd just never thought the alliance would be with the creatures from the north. "You weren't forced to marry a monster."

Something flashed in the queen's eyes, but it passed too quickly for Thalia to decipher. "There are monsters inside us all."

"This is a solution to an issue that is long past due. If we can defeat them once and for all, as you said, we will have access to the ore in their mountain." Kamith broke the silence, as if needing to reassure Thalia of the bigger picture. "Agripa will never have to worry about our reserves depleting again. There will be no more sickness. No more death here. Agripa could thrive and be the realm it was always meant to be."

"What of the forest?" Thalia asked, her mind flashing to the impenetrable wall that separated their two worlds. The only reason they hadn't burned it down was because of the retribution the Vampyrs would seek. They were too powerful—too many.

Kamith scrubbed a hand over his jaw. "Once you've taken them out, the forest won't pose any issue. It will die, then we can burn it and move our troops through. We can set up trade along their coast, where the waters are much safer. All we must do is cut out the issue from the root."

Yet Thalia would have to live with them, figure out their secrets without getting her throat ripped out. The rational part of her brain knew this treaty was meant to save Agripa from doom, but only if she could pull it off.

But he'd be there. He'd be watching her every move.

He knew her as she knew him.

"You must swear." The queen's voice broke through her racing thoughts. "Do not do anything to revoke this alliance. To make it seem as though our intentions are not pure. You're a part of something bigger now, Thalia."

"I swear." Her words were scathing as *his* face flashed before her mind.

"On your father's bloodline, swear you will not do anything to doom us all."

Just like that, Cassius's face vanished as Thalia focused on her mother. Despite the low light, it was the first time she'd noticed how deep the lines of the queen's face were, how shadowed her eyes had become. This was the chance Thalia had been waiting for, to finish her mission, once and for all.

"I swear on my father's blood that I will do nothing to end our treaty."

The queen visibly sagged as she released her daughter. "Good." She took a step back, while Thalia remained rooted to the spot. "The ceremony to bind you to the prince will be held soon. From there, you will journey into their land."

Thalia's stomach twisted, but she pushed it aside.

"I am proud of you, Thalia." Her mother stood before her throne, Kamith near enough that they made a striking pair. "Your father would be proud."

Her words dug into Thalia's clammy skin as she left, her footsteps too loud in her daughter's ear.

Thalia might have sworn on her father's blood that she'd do nothing to ruin this treaty. But as Cassius's face flashed in her mind, she vowed that he would pay, one way or another.

Accidents happened all the time.

Chapter Three

Thalia stared at the map on her messy desk.

The onyx pieces marking certain towns to which her hunt had taken her would be of no use anymore. And it wouldn't do any good to track the darkness in the north, not with the darkness now here within their very walls. Because in a matter of minutes, she'd become a wolf dressed in a lamb's skin.

A knock on her door had Thalia turning. It was time. The ceremony to bind her to a monster. Suddenly, Thalia wasn't so sure of this plan.

Reina poked her head in, face set in a grimace, but instead of directing her to the ceremony, she said, "You have a visitor."

Thalia picked at the skin around her thumbs, a small part of her wondering if her mother had come to her senses about how precarious this treaty was.

"Send them in," she said, not allowing any sort of hope to rise in her chest.

It was a good thing she didn't.

Because that hope would have been shattered into a million pieces as Cassius entered her room.

"You—" Thalia snarled, taking a single step before Reina was in the room, blocking her.

The captain of the guard looked her in the eye. Reina didn't seem to care that her back was exposed, not as she said, "*Think*, Thalia."

Yes, think.

Think of what it would mean to kill him. To feel his blood rush over her fingers. To stab him again and again in the back, just as he'd done to her all those years ago.

"Remember your duty," Reina added, a touch lower.

Her duty had become something greater now. If she failed to carry it out, she would doom all of Agripa.

It took everything in Thalia to nod. To not give over to the anger swirling in her gut, to put her instincts to the side.

"If you don't mind, Captain, I'd like to speak to the princess . . . alone."

Just like that, Cassius's words caused her rage to spike. Her lip curled, but Reina gave her another look before stepping toward the door.

"I'll be just outside." Reina stiffened as she walked past the Vampyr.

The door shutting was louder than a thunderclap, sealing both Cassius and Thalia inside.

They stared at each other, neither moving, as if nothing had altered in the four years since his betrayal.

Cassius even looked the same, held the same arrogant posture. His face had always been one that maidens could die for, but somehow the sharpness had intensified into a sort of heightened beauty that increased the weight in her chest. He didn't hide the fact that his eyes swept her from head to toe, traveling over the white gown that Katrina had forced her into.

Finally, he met her gaze, lips curling into a smirk. "You haven't changed."

Thalia jerked, yet her slippered feet remained glued to the floor. "I wish I could say the same of you."

Cassius tilted his head, the movement much too smooth—too inhuman. "You changed the drapes."

Thalia hadn't been expecting him to say *that*. She looked to the drapes that shut out the night. The low fire in her blackened fireplace cast shadows across the deep blue.

She glanced back and nearly jolted again to find Cassius on the couch in her sitting area, not five feet away. Only a low-lying coffee table separated them, and Cassius draped his arm along the back of the velvet couch.

"Didn't throw out the rug, I see," Cassius drawled, completely at ease. As if he hadn't bled out on it after she'd tried to kill him. As if he'd never ripped out her heart, not bothering to watch how she'd bleed.

Thalia didn't need to look at the worn rug before the fireplace to know it was such a dark crimson that it hid the bloodstains that'd soaked into the fibers like spilled wine.

"I kept it," she got out.

"Oh, why?" Cassius raised a brow, crossing his ankle over one knee. It would take nothing for her to cross the distance. To grab the knife at his waist and plunge it straight into his chest.

Thalia snarled, fingers clenching at her sides. "As a reminder of what you did."

A reminder of the night four years ago when he'd appeared in her chambers. When she'd thought he was coming to bed with her as he always did. But instead, she'd woken up to find him transformed into a monster—woken up to the chaos he'd instilled by killing the human prince, Prince Darius, whom she'd been betrothed to. He would have been Agripa's shining savior. He'd come like a prince from a fairy tale, golden hair blowing in the wind, with the promise of an army to defeat the creatures of the north once and for all.

Back then, Thalia hadn't hesitated when she stabbed Cassius straight through his black heart.

She should have aimed for his head.

Cassius's eyes sparked, some of the blue seeming to glow as he said softly, "And what exactly did I do?"

"Don't play dumb, Cassius. It doesn't suit you."

Cassius smiled, although it didn't reach his eyes. "You don't know what I was forced to choose that day."

"You chose to betray your kingdom—your people—you betrayed *me* to become one of them!" She flung out her hand, her chest heaving as Cassius just sat and watched. "You chose to become a monster.

To hunger for blood like a malevolent beast. To destroy our *one* chance at hope."

Cassius met her stare, his eyes hardening like chips of ice. "You mistake me for evil, but I assure you, all I hunger for is power. Humans tend to confuse the two."

Humans. As if she were so beneath him now.

"Power?" Her lip curled as she spat, "Is that what this was all about? Because you held no power to stop this war, you joined the other side? You wished to be seen as a savior, the hero you used to talk about being when we were children?"

Cassius's eyes darkened. "You know I held no power here. No power to stop my father from beating my mother until she could barely walk. No power to stop him from fucking his way all across Agripa. I had to sit by while my father ran our name into the mud. I had to listen to the vicious whispers of your mother's court, about how the Tareino family were no more than dogs begging for any amount of scraps the royals would give them. I was helpless to do anything back then."

"Helpless? Helpless to stop the monsters preying on innocents, so you became one yourself? Did it make you feel powerful doing that?" Thalia scoffed.

A muscle in Cassius's jaw flickered. "The day my father beat my mother so badly she never woke up is the day I vowed to never sit idly by while those *innocents* suffered. You know this. Why else would I have joined the city watch all those years ago? Why else would I have worked my way up to be captain? Moving up the ranks did nothing to stop the issues happening on our doorstep. Not when those in charge are still able to dictate from their gilded thrones the lives of those below them. But now I have the power to change the world we live in."

"And what of your vow to me?" Thalia hissed, stepping toward him. "What of your vow to be by my side? To ensure that what happened to my family never happens to anyone again? You swore to help me fix Agripa—you swore to stop this war—"

"And the war has been stopped." Cassius cut her off. "And not by your hand."

His words landed, shoving straight into her gut. "Shut. Up."

Cassius smiled, a thing of deadly cruelty. "You knew this was the solution that could have saved us years of chaos. To reforge the peace between our realms and extend our hand to offer water in exchange for ore. Yet you chose to ignore it, just as your mother did. You knew the ore wouldn't last forever, and your mother did too. She was a fool and now is doing anything she can to cover up her mistake—to ensure that her reign continues unfettered. It's a good thing I have *power*, because I did what you have spent years trying and failing to do."

"Shut the *fuck* up."

Cassius tilted his head, every memory of the man he once was covered by this new creature. "I don't mean it as an insult. You've done well navigating your duties to the crown. But I know you wished to do more. Overseeing the towns, trying to be the voice of reason in your mother's court when it came to rationing out ore. But your work could only go so far."

Thalia hadn't realized she'd crossed the space until she hovered over Cassius, her hand gripping the handle of the knife in his belt. "Stop talking before I carve out your tongue and feed it to you."

Cassius smirked, his blue eyes lighting in what must be some sort of sick fascination. "How your rage has grown."

Thalia slid the dagger from his belt, and he did nothing, just watched as Thalia braced one hand on the back of the couch, leaning closer. "I have you to thank for that."

"And how has that worked out for you?"

Thalia pressed her dagger straight over Cassius's artery. If he moved a fraction of an inch, she'd slice his neck clean open. "Considering the position we're now in, I'd say it's worked."

Cassius's eyes bored into hers. But he didn't move, didn't try to disarm her. Didn't so much as flinch as she pressed deeper and a ruby droplet welled. She watched in fascination as it slid down the strong column of his throat, collecting in the crevice of his collarbone.

"If you're going to do it, at least do it right this time." Cassius's words brushed against her mouth.

She flicked her eyes up, finding his heavy, hooded gaze right on her lips.

It shouldn't have shocked her so much, but it did.

Thalia smirked, leaning closer. Close enough to count the flecks of gray in his irises. "Not yet. We have a ceremony to get to."

Cassius was a dark presence at her side as they both made their way to the castle chapel, Reina at their backs.

The chapel itself was removed from the rest of the palace, hidden in the inner courtyard among overgrown gardens. The stones had been worn away by the elements, and the stained glass appeared lackluster in the moonlight. The pointed columns and Gothic architecture only added to the eeriness as the three of them stepped up to the wooden door.

Thalia glanced up at one of the gargoyles crouching above the entrance, its pointed teeth and forked tongue twisting into a grotesque smile. Thalia kept her back straight as they entered.

The space was lit with braziers flickering over the pews, and the church was empty save at the front where the queen, Kamith, and two of the Vampyrs stood waiting.

"Princess." Kamith spotted her first, inclining his head.

Lord Damien swept his red eyes over Thalia. The other Vampyr, the one with golden eyes and dark skin, remained quiet as Lord Damien said, "Shall we begin the ceremony?"

A hesitant priest stepped forward, stammering, "Wh-where is the proxy?" He glanced at the three creatures in the church. Right, because the prince wasn't here. It wasn't as though Thalia had expected the prince to show up, given the animosity between their realms and the fact that peace had barely been achieved. He was probably content to sit in whatever dark castle he called home, draining the blood of innocent humans. The thought did little to quell her nerves.

Lord Damien stepped forward, and Thalia's stomach dropped. Oh gods, if she had to bind herself to him, out of all the Vampyrs—

"Cassius, the hand to the prince, shall stand in." The Vampyr's words echoed.

Cassius stepped into a shaft of moonlight. He glanced at Thalia, his face unreadable as he held out a hand.

Thalia had lied to herself. She would have taken Lord Damien over *him*. Because she would have to . . . to touch him.

They hadn't touched in her room; only his knife in her hand had caressed his skin. The thought of doing this—of binding herself to him after everything he'd done to her, all the false promises and lies he'd fed her just so he could turn them against her—

"Thalia." Her mother's sharp voice broke through her racing thoughts. The queen gave her a look, and Thalia swallowed. Pushing aside her rage and revulsion, she placed her hand in Cassius's.

Thalia couldn't ignore the shiver that rocked her spine as his calluses scraped against hers. The weight of her fingers in his was as familiar as the calluses along her palms.

"We—we are gathered here to witness the joining of two peoples," the priest began, his quiet, shaking voice filling the church. "This union shall be binding, by blood and earth. Two souls which shall never be parted."

Kamith stepped forward, holding a bloody ribbon.

"What's that for?" Thalia's breath spiked. The ribbon was fresh with blood, some of it still dripping onto the ground. This wasn't part of any marriage ceremony Thalia had ever witnessed.

"This is part of an ancient vow, one taken by our kind," Lord Damien slithered out. "To be bound by blood and earth to signify a bond stronger than words."

Kamith gestured for them to raise their joined hands. "It's calf's blood. Don't fret."

Thalia wanted to retort that she had plenty to fret about as the adviser bound them together, the blood cold and thick against her skin.

"You are bound by blood," the priest stated.

Thalia stared up at Cassius, ignoring the ache that came on suddenly under her breastbone. They'd once talked about doing this. Speaking a different sort of vow to each other that would bind their souls.

His words had all been lies.

"You are bound by earth," the priest continued, and the Vampyr with golden eyes stepped forward, tipping over a jar filled with dirt on their bloody hands.

Thalia bit her tongue until copper filled her mouth. Cassius's nostrils flared slightly, and she could have sworn he tensed as the priest concluded, "You are bound together, two souls entwined. May neither of you forsake the other." The priest said a few more prayers entreating some forgotten god to watch their union before bowing his head. "It's done."

"Not quite," Lord Damien said. "Our ceremony requires a bit more of a sacrifice."

Thalia glanced at the Vampyr, unease filling her gut as Kamith asked carefully, "What do you mean?"

"Marriage by proxy is one of the flimsier laws you humans have. However, we of the night believe something is required to be more binding. Something which is given in order for this entwining of souls to be seen as legitimate."

"Which is what?" Thalia asked sharply.

Lord Damien rested his gaze on her. "Blood."

Quiet fell in the church, silence like that of a tomb.

"Blood?" Thalia asked slowly. "Aren't we already bound by it?"

"Yes." Lord Damien's eyes glittered like a snake's as he inclined his head. "But it also must be consumed."

Thalia jerked but could go nowhere with her hand bound in Cassius's. "No. Absolutely not."

Lord Damien's eyes darkened. "It is customary—"

"For you," Thalia seethed, her heart rate climbing. "For you monsters who get off on violence and pain."

Lord Damien smiled, although it didn't reach his eyes. "It would be wise to uphold our traditions. Wise, also, for this treaty to be seen as legitimate."

Thalia trembled, and she wasn't sure if she was shaking from rage or fear. "Drinking his blood will turn me."

"Only if you're bitten and then feed," Lord Damien said, a knife gleaming in his hand. "But to share in this manner will do nothing but fulfill an ancient vow."

"Thalia." Her mother's voice was sharper than the blade held aloft. She would have to do this.

"I don't believe it will be necessary." Cassius spoke, his words nearly startling her.

Lord Damien's eyes flashed. "His Highness will not be pleased to know his bride did not fully complete the ceremony. With nothing tangible to bind her, she will be free to do as she wishes. This treaty could be seen as a farce—"

"The ceremony will be completed by the prince and the prince alone. I don't wish to take what is his, even if it is tradition." Cassius's words were barely audible. "Humans are bound by ink, not us. This treaty is complete."

Cassius and Lord Damien stared at each other for a moment longer before the latter inclined his head. "Of course."

Thalia didn't relax, not as the priest removed the bloody ribbon from her hands, not as she finally stepped away.

"See that the horses are ready" was all Cassius said, not glancing back as he left the chapel.

Chapter Four

Thalia didn't want to say goodbye.

Didn't want to watch as Katrina silently cried. Didn't want to look at Reina as she checked that her carriage was ready. She'd be taken by her soldiers to the border of the forest, and from there she'd enter into the Vampyr realm.

Vaccarium.

Thalia had never seen it but had heard the stories. How the land was fertile, the waters clear, their shorelines picturesque thanks to the ore within their mountain. Thalia assumed it was some sick joke from the gods that the creatures in the north got the better end of the stick while the humans below scraped by.

Then there was the forest itself, which had always been a barrier between their realms. Only the Vampyrs knew how to get through it. And before her family was all but killed, the few Vampyrs who traded with humans would guide them to and from. Back when commerce had flourished between their worlds, when the two species managed to coexist and could live side by side without fear of retaliation.

But that was before a Vampyr ripped out the throat of the king.

"Thank the gods I caught you before you left."

Thalia turned, surprised to find Marcus before her. The head librarian panted, his brown skin flushed as though he'd run all the way from the library in the heart of the dying city. "You heard?"

Marcus nodded, his curls flying, trying to catch his breath. Gods, she hadn't thought about leaving him behind, even though they'd been distant of late, both consumed by their own missions. "Everyone's heard."

Thalia swallowed, ignoring the fact that now, if she failed her mission, all of Agripa would realize she'd led to their downfall. "What's this?" She nodded to the satchel in Marcus's dark hand.

"Some books on the Vampyrs. It's not a lot; I had to dig through the archives for them. But maybe it could help." He handed her the bag. Thalia wondered if he knew or had guessed that she'd been given a new mission, one that would require far more knowledge than she'd been previously granted.

"Thank you," Thalia got out.

Marcus nodded, his attention going over her shoulder. Thalia didn't have to turn to see who drew his gaze.

Cassius was ensuring his own horse was ready, his fingers deft as they checked the buckles of its saddle.

Marcus made a face but didn't comment. The three of them had been close before Cassius's treachery. Before Cassius decided he wanted more. Before he betrayed his kingdom—betrayed them—to become a monster with power.

Marcus jerked his attention back and pulled Thalia into a tight embrace. "Don't get eaten."

She wanted to laugh, but it died in her throat.

Marcus released her just as Lord Damien stepped out from the shadows. "Princess, your new home awaits."

Thalia slid her gaze to the Vampyr, ignoring the way he watched her. She looked to the palace, but her mother hadn't appeared for her send-off. Only Kamith stood on the cracked steps, watching as the night deepened.

"It is a pity she wouldn't see you off," Lord Damien practically purred, following her gaze.

"She's the queen; she has more important things to do." Bitterness coated Thalia's words before she could stop herself. She wasn't sure why it bothered her so much. She'd never cared in the past when she'd gone to ensure Agripa was still standing. But perhaps it was this new set of circumstances placed before her Thalia wished the queen had at least *acknowledged* the shithole she was about to enter.

"Perhaps, but one should always say goodbye to family, especially those they may not see again."

Thalia stiffened, eyes narrowing. "Is that a threat, Lord Damien?"

The Vampyr cocked his head. "Hardly. Merely speaking from experience."

"Oh?"

Lord Damien forced another smile. "My brother left one day, and I didn't get a chance to say goodbye. Now I never will."

"What happened to him?"

Lord Damien's eyes seemed to glow. "You killed him."

Thalia's throat dried as he walked away, and it suddenly clicked. The Vampyr from Cardin. Reina had said he was from an important family—from one of the courts.

Shit. Shit. Shit.

"Are you ready?" Reina said, suddenly at her side.

"I killed his brother." Thalia's words were no more than a whisper.

It took only a moment before Reina cursed. "Keep your eyes open at all times; do *not* find yourself alone with him."

Thalia shook her head. "Reina, I can't—"

"You can. Because you're stronger than anyone I know. Remember what I taught you." Reina scanned her face, then pulled her into a tight embrace. "Remember your vow." Thalia nodded, and the cold metal of a stake pressed into her palm. Thalia pulled away and Reina opened the carriage door for her. "I'll see you soon enough."

Thalia nodded and took a last glimpse at the castle, but her mother still hadn't appeared.

The carriage rumbled underneath her, and Thalia tried to distract herself. But with every turn of the wheel, her mind kept flashing back to Lord Damien, the fact that she'd shoved a stake straight through his brother's skull and felt no remorse.

Gods, how many Vampyrs had she killed? How many of those creatures' families would she face once she was in their world? They would be even more inclined to kill her now. Especially Lord Damien.

She sank against the cushions, craning her neck to peer out the window, but only a starless night greeted her back. They'd have to stop at some point once the sun rose. They were still days away from the forest.

Thalia hauled the satchel to her, pulling out the first book Marcus had packed. The bound leather was worn and cracked, its cover carved in swirling spires and thorns.

She opened the page and was immediately greeted by a drawing of a Vampyr.

Thalia glanced at the windows of the carriage, but they remained dark. She flicked on a switch inside the carriage and a small light fluttered to life above her, one of the many examples of what the ore could do. At least now Agripa had access to the ore once more. Its strange power would rebless their land, making it fertile and lush.

Thalia pushed aside the thought as she studied the drawing, the fangs that were just sharp enough to draw blood. Their bites were worse than death, because if one was bitten and did not feed, one would simply decay from the inside out—flake away like paper.

The choice of either becoming a monster or being forced to die in such a gruesome way—it made sense why so many turned.

Except her.

No, she'd rather succumb to whatever dark fate awaited her than be turned into one of *them*.

Thalia scowled, turning the page, and a new drawing appeared. This one depicted an iron stake shoved straight through a Vampyr's skull.

Thalia's steel blade had done nothing to Cassius when he first turned. He'd bled out on her rug as she ran to find help. But when she returned, he was gone, nothing but a stain in his place.

The carriage rolled to a sudden stop, and Thalia jerked as the doors of her carriage were opened.

The golden-eyed Vampyr regarded her, eyes going straight to the book in her lap. She snapped it closed.

"I'm Keegan," was all he said.

"I don't care."

Keegan raised a brow. "Well, do you care to rest?"

Thalia shoved the book into the satchel. "Where?"

Keegan's lips twitched in amusement. "We have a camp. Unless you prefer the carriage, which will no doubt become an oven in the sun." Thalia would have much preferred to remain in the safety of the carriage, but the Vampyr just inclined his head. A head that was decidedly normal and not whatever grotesque trick of the light it'd been in the throne room. "Well?"

"Fine."

Thalia stumbled out of the carriage, blinking against the hazy gray of dawn.

They'd stopped off the road, no towns or cities in sight. In fact, they rested along a small, wooded area. Thalia resisted the urge to shiver as she followed Keegan to their makeshift camp. Tents had been set up with thick sides to block out the sun, which she thought must have some cooling mechanism to keep out the heat.

At least she didn't have to worry about one of them killing her during the day. They'd burn to ash if they stepped foot in the light.

She followed Keegan to a tent set up away from the others.

"Here." He lifted the flap, gesturing for her to enter.

Thalia didn't want to consider how fast this had all been set up as she glanced at the two cots in the tent.

"Who is—"

Her words died as Keegan disappeared, leaving her alone.

Thalia swallowed, glancing at one of the cots. She didn't want to admit that, after everything that'd happened in less than twenty-four hours, her body was drained.

She whirled as the tent flap opened and Cassius strode in, carrying a tray of food and a glass of water.

"What are you doing?" Thalia got out, hand going to her knife at her thigh—*his* knife. She hadn't given it back, and she wasn't inclined to either.

Cassius aimed for the empty cot and set the tray on the small stool between the beds. "Bringing you food."

"Why are you in my tent?"

"It's my tent too."

Thalia barked out a laugh until Cassius turned to her, face hard. "You can't be serious?"

"We are bound together, and as such, we are meant to go with each other everywhere until you're delivered safely to the prince."

"Get out," Thalia hissed.

Cassius raised a brow, sinking onto his cot. He pulled off his boots, a too-human movement. "Trust me, this is not ideal for me either. But the prince would have my head if he knew I wasn't following tradition."

"You didn't drink my blood; isn't that tradition?"

Cassius froze, blue eyes flicking up. "That's different."

Thalia crossed her arms over her chest. The tent began to glow faintly, a sure sign that the sun was finally rising.

"You should eat before it gets cold." He jerked his head to the tray of food, which was a simple beef stew and a hard roll. At least it wasn't blood.

Thalia knew she should eat. Because if she didn't have her strength, she stood no chance against him.

She took a sip of the soup. Cassius watched her intently as she drained the bowl, then ate the bread.

She took a long chug from the water glass—

She made a face, the liquid bitter on her tongue. Heat flooded Thalia's senses, making her lightheaded.

Something wasn't right.

Her eyes blurred, the walls of the tent shaking as the glass crashed to the ground.

"This was just to ensure you wouldn't kill us in our sleep." Cassius's voice went in and out, and she almost thought he sounded sorry.

"You prick—" Thalia couldn't finish her sentence as unconsciousness swept over her, blotting out the day.

Chapter Five

Thalia came to on the back of a horse.

She tried reorienting herself, blinking the spots from her eyes. Her head felt like day-old porridge, all muddled up and thick.

What the fuck—

She jerked and would have fallen out of the saddle if it hadn't been for a strong arm wrapped around her waist.

She craned her head and nearly fell off the horse again.

Cassius had a protective arm around her waist, her back flush against his chest. They were deep in a forest, no sign of her carriage or her soldiers that were supposed to escort her.

"What are you—" Her words were cotton in her mouth.

"Glad to see you're awake."

"Where the hell are we? Where's the carriage, the soldiers—"

"Relax, Princess. We left them near Kahgan."

Kahgan? When Thalia had left Corithian, that city near the forest was still two days away—

"You drugged me," Thalia hissed. She tried to twist in her seat, only so she could shove him right off his horse, but his arm was a band of iron.

"A precaution considering how much you hate us."

"We have a treaty, remember?"

Cassius smirked. "Yes, but I *know* you."

His words sent a shudder down her spine. He *did* know her, could guess what she would have done as soon as they'd fallen asleep. She honestly couldn't blame him or the others for their *precautions.*

But what really set her teeth on edge was Cassius's arms still wrapped around her waist.

"Let go of me."

"Believe it or not, this is not an ideal situation for me either. But orders are orders."

"Orders from who?"

"Our prince."

Thalia slightly perked up at that, trying to keep her heart rate down. "And what were his orders?"

"To deliver his new bride to him unscathed."

"And riding on this horse with you will accomplish that?"

Cassius pulled his horse to a sudden stop. The five other Vampyrs all filed past on their own mounts, their hooves muffled under a blanket of fallen leaves and moss.

"Do you know where we are?" Cassius's voice tightened to an edge.

Thalia glanced at her surroundings, fully taking in the forest now that her head had cleared.

No light broke through the thick leaves of deep purple and crimson. The trunks had faded to gray, either because of the near-absence of light or because of something else. Perhaps a lack of water as a result of the woods being blocked off from the human rivers.

But the most eerie thing about the forest was the quiet.

No birds chirped in the silver branches; no squirrels hopped along their limbs to shake down the leaves. Not even the low call of a deer could be heard among the fallen moss-covered logs. The air felt thick—heavy. As if a great weight pressed down, taking all the oxygen with it.

"What is this place?" Thalia's voice was quiet.

Cassius shifted behind her. "Chaménos."

"This is the forest that is sacred to you?" She had expected something different; the atmosphere here seemed rather gloomy.

Cassius paused. "Yes. Or it used to be."

"What do you mean?"

Cassius spurred his horse on, the silence following. "Nothing sacred lies here anymore."

Thalia's mind whirled. But perhaps the uneasiness that seemed to hang in the air like a spider from its web kept her lips sealed, as did the caution with which all the Vampyrs were now treading. If she didn't know better, she'd think they were scared. Indeed, Lord Damien and another Vampyr, one with green eyes, kept glancing at each other.

She didn't want to consider what might be in this forest if the very creatures who hunted there moved with such trepidation.

After a moment of silence, Thalia asked, "How far until we get to . . . Irenbis, isn't it?"

"Yes, the capital of House Lorenzia."

Thalia recalled the information her old governess had taught her. There were five Vampyr courts, each of which ruled a different area of Vaccarium. Each court had a leading House, run by a lord, and a capital city. She could still remember her and Ariadna giggling to each other about the names of the courts, about how important and powerful they sounded. Ariadna was so bold in proclaiming that she'd marry a Vampyr. That *she'd* be the one to bring Agripa into a time of true peace between their realms.

Just like that the memory vanished, replaced with the image of Ariadna's severed head. Her golden hair, almost the same shade as Thalia's own, soaked in crimson. Thalia had screamed, her hands slick with her sister's blood, trying to fix her torn-out throat—screamed as the entire throne room erupted in chaos and gore rained down over her as if the very sky had opened up to drown out her pain.

Thalia sucked in a breath loud enough that everyone froze. Wood snapped in the distance, and the Vampyrs tensed.

After a moment, the entourage continued on quietly. At least the strangeness pulled her from her panic. Thalia pushed down the sudden nausea rising in her gut along with the fear.

Cassius shifted behind her, taking in a sharp inhale of breath.

The bastard probably could smell her anxiety, down to the very sweat sliding down her spine. Another sickening reminder of what he now was.

"How long until we reach the realm?" she finally asked when she was sure she wouldn't vomit all over the side of Cassius's horse.

"You mean my realm?"

It seemed as though Cassius's loyalty had changed as quickly as he had. The thought sent a white-hot pang through her stomach.

"Yes, your realm," she spat a little too loudly, and the Vampyrs ahead of them all stopped short once more.

Cassius's horse paused, and he stiffened. She caught Keegan's golden stare, warning flashing in his eyes. A noise echoed deep in the forest. A sort of groaning as if the very trees were trying to break free of their roots. Thalia's stomach clenched, and the Vampyrs all lifted their chins. She could have sworn Lord Damien scented the air before they all began moving cautiously forward. Thalia swallowed.

Cassius shifted behind her, and she became acutely aware of how close they were pressed together. As if her body could still recall the way they'd lie together. How they'd sneak out of the palace when her mother's back was turned. How Cassius would spend hours showing her exactly how it felt to be alive.

But Cassius had spun a web of promises so pretty that Thalia hadn't even realized she'd been consumed by his lies until she'd nearly gotten bitten.

"In the next day or so," Cassius said quietly, picking up their conversation. "It will take a few more days of travel to reach House Lorenzia."

I'm going to marry into the House that's near the forest!

Thalia could practically hear Ariadna's voice in her head. Even though Ariadna was only three years older, she knew her duty to the crown. And she loved the woods, almost more than she loved her family. But that was before her proclamation became reality. Before she was engaged to a Vampyr. Before she'd been ripped apart.

Thalia squeezed her eyes shut, trying to suck in another sharp breath. Cassius stiffened as she got out, "What side of the continent is Irenbis on again?"

Cassius huffed out a humorless laugh, almost as though he were trying to dispel the tension in her body. "Trying to figure out its exact location to report back to your mother?"

That snapped her out of it. Thalia's spine threatened to break as she treaded carefully. "It's been a while since humans and Vampyrs have interacted. Our information is surely outdated. Shouldn't I know about the city that's to become my new home?"

"Your new home? Are you that eager to start your new life? Here I thought you resented the deal your mother forced you into."

Thalia forced herself to relax, to not stiffen further. "Considering I have no other option, what's the point of wallowing in self-pity?"

Cassius was quiet for a moment. "Indeed."

Thalia felt the rise and fall of his chest against her back, the way his thighs pressed against hers.

If she closed her eyes, she could almost pretend that nothing had happened between them. That he hadn't killed their one shot at survival. That he was still . . . human.

"What are you thinking?" Cassius's quiet voice nearly startled her from her thoughts.

"Nothing."

"You pick at the skin around your nails when something is troubling you."

Thalia hadn't realized she was doing that, not until her eyes widened and she looked down to where his hands rested against her wrists.

She immediately stopped, twisting in the saddle. "Stop it."

Cassius's brows rose. "Stop what?"

"We aren't friends. You're still a monster."

"*Monster*? Here I thought we were allies?"

Thalia stopped herself short. Shit. She needed to get away from him. Needed to stop letting her tongue loose. She needed to appear resigned—complacent.

"Get me a horse," she got out.

"Not going to happen. Especially considering you think we are monsters. I have no doubt that you'd hightail it right out of here after you'd killed us all."

"How could someone like me take on such powerful creatures? If anything, it seems as though *you're* wanting to keep me close."

"I've always wanted to keep you close."

Those words, the tone in which Cassius almost sounded earnest, had her jerking out of his grip.

"What are you—" Cassius started.

Thalia pushed herself away and half fell, half slid down the horse, landing on the moss-covered ground with a quiet thud. The ground seemed to sink down under her weight as if it were trying to slowly consume her.

"You can't be serious," Cassius said in disbelief above her.

She pushed onto her knees, glaring up. The other Vampyrs all glanced back, their stares holding nothing but lethal rage—and dread. She ignored them.

Riding in front of Cassius, she could almost forget he wasn't human. But with him staring down at her, his eyes glowing faintly and the hint of fangs peeking ever so slightly from his parted mouth, it was a sickening reminder.

Thalia needed to rethink everything, how she acted, how she spoke. And she couldn't do that with Cassius pressing so near to her. No matter that her traitorous body begged for his familiarity while her mind screamed at her to *think*.

"I'll walk, then," Thalia got out.

Cassius raised a brow. "It's a long walk."

"Then I suppose I should get moving."

Cassius's jaw flickered. His eyes flicked to the strange trees, then he shrugged, spurring his horse past. "Suit yourself."

Thalia resisted the urge to send her dagger straight through the back of his head.

But she didn't, she just followed silently after Cassius, her mind coming up empty with each step she took farther into the dark forest.

She'd lost sight of Cassius around the bend.

Thalia trudged faster, not wanting to get lost.

Scraping echoed behind her, and she froze. The hair on the back of her neck stood on end as she slowly turned to look over her shoulder.

Her eyes scanned the trees, everything in her screaming that she was being watched.

She crouched down slowly, fingers slipping through the slits of her gown to wrap around her dagger.

Something snapped in the forest, the sound like breaking bone. A flash of gleaming white appeared in her peripheral vision. She whirled, heart in her throat—

A deer lifted its head not twenty paces away, moss hanging from its lips.

Thalia relaxed slightly, straightening.

Another crunch behind her had her whirling again, dagger raised.

Keegan raised his hands, eyes wide, as the deer bolted. "Just me."

"What the fuck are you doing?" She didn't lower the blade. Suddenly, she wished she hadn't fallen so far behind Cassius.

"Cass sent me to get you."

Thalia stared at him, her stomach twisting tightly at the nickname she hadn't heard in years. *Cass.* She and Marcus used to call him that. A name he reserved for the people closest to him. Thalia didn't want to think about how close he'd gotten to the other Vampyrs if Keegan used his nickname so freely.

Thalia slid her knife back into her dress. "And he didn't think to find me himself?"

Keegan inclined his head, amusement dancing in his golden eyes. "He said you'd probably be inclined to stab him if he came after you. The camp's not far off, but we shouldn't be traveling alone."

Well, at least Cassius's caution wasn't far off.

"And why is that?" Thalia asked.

Keegan studied her again, as if debating his next words. He did a quick glance around, and she could have sworn he shuddered as he said, "This forest is dangerous to those who aren't familiar. There's a reason it acts as a barrier between our worlds."

She shook her head at his cryptic answer, stepping nearer. "Clearly."

Keegan didn't say anything more as they made their way along the quiet path.

"Did Cassius really send you to find me?" Thalia asked suddenly.

Keegan pushed aside a heavy branch cautiously, almost as though he were afraid the tree would attack him. "Yes. He didn't think you'd wish to see him."

Thalia's lip curled. He wasn't wrong.

But perhaps being away from the others loosened Keegan's tongue, because he asked, "You knew him before, didn't you?"

Thalia nearly tripped over her own feet. "Yes."

"When he was human?"

"Yes." Her heart rate pounded, images of their life before flashing through her mind. Cassius had joined the city watch thirteen years prior, right after his mother had died. It was shortly after she'd lost her own father and sister. He was sixteen while she'd been fourteen. He'd sworn to protect those who couldn't protect themselves, and she supposed he had, in a way. If only it hadn't taken becoming a monster to do so.

Keegan nodded, more to himself than to acknowledge her words. "I met him not long after he turned."

Thalia's stomach clenched. She didn't want to think about that night. Didn't want to think about how he had sold his soul to darkness to become something else.

"He spoke of you often," Keegan continued, oblivious to her growing rage.

Thalia stopped short. "What?"

Keegan regarded her, his face carefully neutral. "He spoke of a princess whom he'd fallen in love with."

"And what else did he say?"

"He said that if you ever saw him again, you'd kill him."

Chapter Six

Footsteps outside her tent had Thalia jerking upright.

Cassius hadn't appeared on the bedroll beside her, and sleep had yet to claim her. Everything beyond the tent was silent. Still.

Except a shadow passing by her tent—the figure of a woman.

Thalia eased off her bedroll, staring at the shadow before it faded away. Her heart rate quickened.

What the hell was a woman doing out here?

She moved toward the tent entrance, pushing aside the flap to peer into the camp. The Vampyrs who were asleep on their bedrolls were eerily as still as the forest around them. Thalia knew it was night only because of the slim sliver of moon filtering through the dense leaves. Strange that the Vampyrs were still asleep, seeing as night was when they roused.

The five Vampyrs who were sitting around the campfire didn't stir as she eased out of the tent.

A flash of emerald green caught the corner of her eye, and Thalia turned, only to see a figure dart around one of the silver trees.

There was something familiar about the green fabric—

Slowly, Thalia crept after the retreating figure, moving around the gray trunks and fallen logs.

The figure stopped, stepping into a shaft of moonlight, and Thalia caught sight of golden hair as familiar as her own. "Mother?"

The Queen of Agripa turned toward her, eyes wide. Her hands were bound, her mouth gagged.

"Mother—"

The queen bolted, fleeing from some unseen horror.

"Wait!" Thalia's heart leapt into her throat.

She ran after the queen's retreating form. Branches cut her face as she jumped over stones, her boots skidding in the soft mud of a stream.

"Mother! What's wrong?"

Thalia couldn't make sense of it, but something in her urged her faster. Her mother was in danger. The queen was in danger—oh gods, had the Vampyrs gone back on their treaty? Had they somehow captured the queen?

Thalia ran, not caring how far she'd ventured, only that the blind terror in her mother's face spurred her on.

"It's me! It's Thalia, let me help you!" Thalia yelled, her breath coming in deep pants.

Her mother slowed, her gown dirty and torn as if she'd escaped from someone.

The queen doubled over near an outcropping of rocks, shaking like a leaf.

"It's okay, it's me." Thalia reached for her mother, grasping her shoulder. "We need to get out of here before the Vampyrs find you again."

Her mother's wide eyes took her in, and Thalia took her knife, cutting the binds around the queen's hands, then ripped the gag off.

"What the hell happened?" Thalia asked, scanning the queen for other injuries. This would be the Vampyrs' undoing. Not only going back on their treaty but trying to kidnap the queen—

Her mother gripped Thalia's face, eyes searching hers. "You came for me."

Thalia's heart squeezed. "Of course I came, but how are you here? Are you hurt?"

The queen looked her daughter over, hands falling away. "You are so foolish to have come."

Thalia's heart stuttered. "What?"

The queen's face began to change, porcelain skin shifting into dark, hanging flesh, emerald eyes melting into milky-gray pools.

Her mother disappeared, replaced by a nightmare.

The creature was skeleton-like, with leathery skin that stretched across its frame. Arms too long for its body ended with scythe-like hands, and when it smiled, rows of razor-sharp black teeth glinted back.

The creature's lipless mouth stretched; its nostrils—no more than two slits—flared. "You shouldn't have followed me." Thalia stumbled back, her heart rate spiking as the creature crouched on its back legs. "You should *run*."

Thalia bolted.

The creature let out a strange, high-pitched screech, but Thalia didn't look back as she fled. She dodged around tree trunks, her lungs to the point of bursting as she skidded over a small stream.

She had no idea where to go, which way the camp was—

Something tackled her from behind, and Thalia screamed.

The stench of rotting flesh filled her nostrils as the creature sent her tumbling down an embankment.

The breath knocked out of her lungs as she landed on her back. The creature pressed into her from above, and she gagged. Despite its thin frame, its weight crushed her.

"Why are you not still screaming?" The creature studied her, its milky eyes unblinking. "Your screams would taste most decadent."

Thalia trembled as the creature brought its claws to her face. "Scream," it rasped, its lips stretching into a grotesque grin. "For I wish to be sated."

It leaned closer, its mouth eager to shred her flesh.

Thalia gritted her teeth and plunged her dagger into its soft side.

The creature wailed as Thalia twisted her blade. It reeled back, and Thalia scrambled out from under it.

She made it all of two feet before the creature was on her again. It flung her hard enough that her back cracked against one of the tree trunks. She let out a moan.

The creature gripped her throat, lifting her in the air. Thalia's breath stuttered as its claw tips pricked her skin.

"You should have screamed," the creature snarled, raising its free hand to gut her like a pig.

The creature froze.

Its eyes widened and it looked down just as something began protruding from its sternum.

A fist covered in black blood pushed its heart out of its chest cavity.

Thalia's eyes widened, and the creature lost its grip on her throat. She fell to the ground in a gasping heap. She stared up just as the hand disappeared and the creature's milky eyes went dark. It collapsed next to Thalia, unmoving.

Cassius stood over her, his face set in nothing but hard wrath, holding the black, shriveled heart of the creature. She scrambled backward.

"Stay back!" Thalia searched for her discarded blade. Cassius dropped the heart next to the cooling corpse.

He froze. "Thalia, it's me—"

She spotted her dagger, her fingers shaking as she gripped the handle, pointing it at Cassius. "Prove it."

Cassius paused, bloody hands upraised. He glanced down at the creature's body, then understanding flashed in his eyes. "Our first kiss was in the castle stable right after you beat up Marcus because he told me you fancied me. You were hiding in Helios's stall, too embarrassed to talk to me. I kissed you then."

Thalia's blade lowered, the adrenaline fleeing as she realized it was Cassius before her, not some creature posed to trick her.

"What was that thing?" Thalia croaked. She hadn't gotten up. In fact, she didn't think her legs worked properly.

"They're called the Nestos. They're one of the few creatures in this forest that can communicate." Cassius's face was careful. "How did it lure you?"

Thalia glanced up; her heart still hadn't returned to normal. "I saw my father."

Surprise flared, then something like deep regret flashed before it was gone in an instant. Good. She hoped he regretted his betrayal—the lie he spoke when he swore he'd fight the creatures who'd killed her father. Hoped it haunted him as much as it haunted her.

Cassius studied her a beat longer, and Thalia wondered if he knew she was lying, could hear her heart skip a beat, perhaps knew there was something deeper going on. But he didn't push as he offered her a bloody hand. "We should get back to camp. It's not safe out here."

Thalia ignored the hand, getting shakily to her feet. "How do you know the way back?" *What is he even doing out here?*

"We're taught the safe paths of the forest and which to avoid."

"*We.*" Thalia's lip curled, and she couldn't stop the sneer from twisting her features despite the death she'd just narrowly avoided.

Cassius stiffened, looking over his shoulder. "If you have any wish to survive this world, insults will not get you far."

"And you know this so well?"

Cassius whirled to her, eyes glowing faintly. "I know that your tongue will damn you quicker than your blade."

"You don't know me," Thalia gritted out.

Cassius raised a brow. "I don't *know* you?" He stalked to her, and Thalia took a step back to avoid their chests brushing. "I know you better than you know yourself."

Thalia's heart climbed as he leaned closer.

"I know that you hate honey in your tea. I know that your favorite color is blue. And not the blue of the sky—blue like the lakes in the south, where the water is so clear you can see the rocks at the bottom."

"Shut up," Thalia whispered, but Cassius kept advancing.

"I know that you would rather spend the day riding Helios than be at court. I know that you hate when Katrina sings those awful songs."

"Stop it." Her chest rose and fell, her heart beating against her rib cage.

But Cassius didn't stop. Her back pressed against a tree as he continued, speaking low, "I know that you would rather cut off your own arm than continue to see Agripa fall into ruin."

Thalia lifted her chin. "Well, perhaps I should cut it off, then, seeing as you had a hand in its suffering."

Cassius's face seemed to ripple like a pebble cast over a stream. Thalia blinked and it was gone. "I did what I had to do."

“You did nothing,” Thalia hissed. “You betrayed your kingdom, you betrayed *me*.”

“And you hate me because of it,” Cassius said lowly.

“*Hate* is not a strong enough word for what I feel for you.”

He smirked, although it didn’t reach his eyes. “When you’re ready to hear what really happened that night, I shall be glad to share it. Perhaps when you’re no longer blinded by your own rage.”

Thalia’s fingers tightened around her blade. It would take nothing to cross the distance between them and plunge it straight into his heart. “Fuck. Off.”

Cassius took a step back, cold air rushing between their bodies as he said, “You’d do well to mind your tongue when you meet His Highness. He’s far less forgiving than I.”

Then he turned his back and stalked into the night.

Chapter Seven

The entourage pulled to a stop in the courtyard of a dark castle surrounded by a forest. It wasn't the same forest they'd traveled through; these trees weren't near as menacing with their gray trunks and crimson leaves. They appeared more vibrant—less like the hollowed-out husks of Chaménos—and more lush, with full branches. The architecture of the castle featured ebony spires and flying buttresses. The large stained-glass windows making up the front of the castle didn't do much besides make for an imposing view.

No one greeted them as Thalia dismounted in the courtyard. Only two soldiers stood outside the castle doors, their armor glinting against the light of the moon.

She'd expected to feel something as they crossed into the Vampyr world. A barrier, perhaps, or some tingling to know she'd entered another realm. But the only strange thing she'd noticed about Vaccarium as they rolled through green fields, heading toward House Lorenzia, was that they didn't stop to take shelter during the day. In fact, during the day the sky was cloudy. Almost as though a summer storm were rolling in, blotting out the sun. And because the sun remained hidden, the Vampyrs weren't affected. Another strange fact to add to Thalia's ever-growing list about the Vampyrs. *Why don't they still stick to the night to hunt? Surely the clouds aren't always around to keep them safe from the light.*

"Where is everyone?" she asked Keegan, who still seemed the most reasonable out of the group. Given the fact that the Vampyrs were creatures of the night, she'd expected someone to greet her—the guards who were to protect the castle, the staff who'd now be under her charge. More importantly, she'd expected her new husband to be standing on his palace steps. But it was quiet. Unnerving. As though she and the Vampyrs she'd traveled with were the only souls on this side of their world.

The thought sent an unwanted pang of fear through her stomach.

"You'll be introduced tomorrow." Lord Damien stepped forward, aiming for the castle. "You'll be taken to your room until then, where you will be confined."

"What of the prince?" Thalia pushed, following the Vampyr up the stone steps.

"He's been detained but shall return on the morrow." Lord Damien didn't say anything more as they entered the castle. It was silent, eerily so. They passed marble busts tucked in hidden alcoves, their footsteps masked by long carpets dyed a rich burgundy. In the grand entrance, the winding onyx staircase was polished to a shine. Thalia could see her warped reflection as she followed Lord Damien into a cold wing of the palace.

It seemed the farther they walked, the colder it got. The dark-papered walls didn't hold any paintings or tapestries and were broken up only by arched windows of stained glass. The hall was decidedly bare aside from suits of armor that lined the edges and the occasional sconce casting shadows across her path.

"What is it that you do?" Thalia broke the silence. The Vampyrs hadn't seemed inclined to speak to her on their journey to Irenbis, but perhaps now that they were at the castle . . .

Lord Damien paused, cocking his head. "I am the prince's diplomat."

"To the humans?"

"To anyone he wishes to broker a deal with."

Thalia picked at her nails. "Who has he brokered deals with?"

"You are not well versed about our courts, are you?"

"I'm versed about your courts. Which one are you from?"

"I was from House Avanerius."

"Was?"

Lord Damien stared at her unblinking. "I serve the prince now. As such, I was bound to a new House, House Lorenzia."

Thalia could have sworn dark-auburn hair flashed out of the corner of her eye, but it was just her and Lord Damien in the hall. "How long have you served House Lorenzia?"

Lord Damien cocked his head. "Seven years."

Thalia tucked the information away. He had deep ties with the prince, then. Perhaps he could be of some use. "How many serve the prince?"

"All of Vaccarium serves the prince."

"Do the courts not answer to him?"

Lord Damien shifted. "They do. But that does not mean they are subjected to his rule alone."

"What does that mean?"

Lord Damien met her stare. "There are five Houses—five courts. They oversee their capital city and the surrounding territory. While the prince, and by extension House Lorenzia, technically watches over all of Vaccarium, the members of the Houses can hold votes. Can even outvote the prince if needed."

"Why would you need to outvote the prince?"

The smile Lord Damien gave didn't reach his eyes. "If the prince is ruling unfairly. If House Lorenzia is abusing its power over the other Houses." The Vampyr began walking again.

"You said you were part of House Avanerius? Who runs it?" Perhaps if she could start building trust with Lord Damien, his House would also hold some sway with the prince.

"My brother. Before you drove a stake through his skull."

Thalia tripped over her feet, slowly sliding her gaze back to Lord Damien. She swallowed, but Lord Damien did nothing, simply stared at her, emotionless.

"And now?" she asked carefully. It had been six months since that . . . incident. Surely someone would have stepped up.

"No one has been elected yet in his stead."

Thalia's throat tightened. She didn't know what to say. But she certainly wasn't going to apologize to the Vampyr. Even if she'd gutted his brother and left his entrails to be ripped apart by crows.

"How does it work, then? Choosing a ruler of a House?"

Lord Damien didn't so much as a bat an eye. "Each family who rules has a claim to their House. If you're in the bloodline, no matter how distant, you can put forth your name to be voted. Those within the House courts choose who they would like to be their next lord."

"There are no ladies?"

Lord Damien seemed to pause. "There have been a few in the past."

Her brows narrowed at that. "And the prince? Was he elected?"

Lord Damien shook his head. "No. House Lorenzia is the only house whose rule is hereditary. A true monarch compared to the elected officials of the other Houses."

Thalia chewed the inside of her cheek. It was similar to what she was used to. While her mother governed and Agripa's rule was passed down through her bloodline, there were those on the queen's council—those who ran certain cities—who were elected by the people. The way the Vampyrs ran their courts felt too . . . human.

"Why has no one stepped forward in your House, then?" she pushed.

Lord Damien stared at her. "It is not a task to be taken lightly. Running a House comes with its own set of challenges."

"Like what?" Thalia's interest piqued. Maybe those *challenges* could be used to bring the courts down.

Lord Damien smiled, but it didn't reach his red eyes. "Challenges every court suffers from. Some wish to see the realm run in one manner while others wish to see it led differently. Surely, as princess of Agripa, you know what sorts of challenges a ruler might face."

A nonanswer. Thalia didn't think she'd get anything more from Lord Damien, but speaking about the courts had given her an idea. If there was a court without a ruler, perhaps she could use that to her advantage to further destabilize an already unstable House.

She'd need to confirm court loyalties, study the books Marcus had given her to find out who was more inclined to push back against the prince's rules—

She sucked in a sharp breath. She hadn't seen those books since the night they'd left Corithian.

"Everything all right, Princess?" Lord Damien looked her over, the sconces in the hall casting shadows over his features.

Thalia forced herself not to panic at the thought that the knowledge she needed was lost. "If I am to meet the prince tomorrow, is there anything I should know about House Lorenzia?"

Surprise flared in his red eyes. "Why are you asking me?"

She waved a hand. "I'll admit that my memory of what we were taught is hazy. You are a diplomat for a reason, and you come from an important House, meaning you know about the other Vampyr courts. If I am to be joined to this House, I'd like my first impression not to appear weak."

Lord Damien smirked, and she had a sinking feeling he'd like to have her look weak, only so the Vampyrs could tear her apart. "What would you like to know, Princess?"

"How long has House Lorenzia been around?"

Lord Damien cocked his head. "Since the beginning."

"What do you mean, the beginning?"

"The Vampyrs have been around since the dawn of this world. When the pockets of magic were plentiful."

Thalia's mind briefly flashed to the story she'd been told as a child. There were beings of great power—Mages—who could manipulate magic into whatever they wished. "So the story about the Mages creating you is true?"

"Yes. What do you know about them?"

"The Mages?" Lord Damien nodded, and Thalia chewed on her lip. "You were formed from those pockets of magic by the Mages to be personal soldiers—until they realized you couldn't be controlled and instead began to kill those around you for sport."

Lord Damien's eyes flashed, and Thalia slipped her hand into the slit of her dress, feeling the iron stake Reina had given her next to her knife. "Control is an interesting thing. Your story may allude to us being controlled, yet for the Vampyrs, we were no better than their slaves. They cursed us to fear the sun, then created iron so they might protect themselves against their own creations."

"What happened after?"

Lord Damien didn't even blink as he said, "There was a great war between the Vampyrs and the Mages. Humans seem to have forgotten about it, for it was before even you were called out of the magic." Thalia refused to dwell on *that* information. "Eventually, peace was forged. The Houses rose to ensure protection for Vaccarium and protection for the Vampyrs against the Mages."

"Where are the Mages now?"

Lord Damien flashed a guarded look. "The Mages are of no concern to you." His robe billowed as they moved deeper into the castle.

"What about the prince?" Thalia said when they stopped before closed oak doors.

Lord Damien slid his ruby eyes to her. "What of him?"

"What is my new husband like?"

"You didn't seem inclined to find out much about him once your mother sealed your fate."

Thalia picked at the nails around her thumbs. "I was . . . resigning myself to that fact. But political alliances are as old as this world. I have accepted the fact that this treaty is something that will help *both* our peoples."

"Indeed." Lord Damien paused. "The prince is often away from court."

Interesting. Her mother never left court. What sort of troubles could plague the Vampyr world that would cause even their prince to disappear?

Thalia kept picking at her nails, the skin pulling, pulling, pulling—

She hissed as she picked too deep, a ruby droplet welling.

Thalia froze, slowly lifting her gaze to Lord Damien, his attention straight on the blood on her finger.

Shit. Shit. Shit.

He glanced at her, his face carefully blank—unresponsive. She waited for him to transform, to lunge at her, but he did nothing. "If you think a small droplet of blood is enough to tempt me into ripping out your throat, then you know very little about the self-control we have to master."

Thalia swallowed as the Vampyr inclined his head. "Your bedchambers. You shall remain here until someone summons you in the morning. The courts are eager to meet their new princess."

Thalia glanced at the closed doors, then back at the Vampyr. "Are there to be guards?" None had been lining the halls, something that immediately put her on edge. In Agripa she couldn't go two feet without a patrol walking by, ensuring all was well.

Lord Damien cocked his head. "You shall have Cassius."

Thalia stiffened as Cassius seemed to step out of the shadows, his face hard.

Where he'd appeared from, she had no idea, but his preternatural silence was unnerving.

"He's fulfilled his duty, hasn't he? I am here, am I not? Delivered unscathed? Surely I don't need a proxy anymore."

"Until you're presented before His Highness and a true ceremony takes place, you're still bound as law. Cassius will remain with you and ensure no harm befalls you in the meantime."

"What sort of harm?"

Lord Damien didn't answer. "Rest well, Princess."

Then he seemed to glide down the hall, not glancing back.

Thalia looked to the closed doors again, then to Cassius, who stood in the dark hallway, arms crossed over his chest. "Well?" he said, nodding to the door.

Thalia gritted her teeth, the dagger and stake strapped to her thigh her only comfort. But the sooner she went to bed, the sooner she could wake up and meet the prince, which meant the sooner she could be unbound to the traitor constantly at her back.

And the sooner she could kill him—kill all of them. Time was not her ally, and that thought alone had her shoving open the door, only to stop short as she took in the bedroom.

The damask-covered walls were black, although a touch lighter to reveal the designs in the paper. In fact, everything was decorated in shades of either black or crimson. The room opened to a sitting area with settees and a table set before a roaring fire. To her right was a large bed with crimson drapes swept aside to reveal silk sheets. On her left was an open door that Thalia assumed was the bathing chamber, based on the short glimpse she'd caught of a luxurious tub.

The only problem? Cassius was still in the room with her.

"Get out." She whirled to him as he closed the door.

"Can't do that, Princess. We're bound until His Highness appears."

"Then sleep outside."

"And what if something goes bump in the night?" He turned to her, a smirk riding his sensual lips.

"The only bump will be your head when I sever it from your body. Get. *Out.*"

Cassius ignored her, aiming for the bathing chamber. "It's not as though we've never shared a room before."

Thalia's teeth ground together. "That was different."

"Right, as you like to keep reminding me."

"What is your game?" she hissed, trailing after him.

The bathing chamber was bedecked in the same colors as the rest of the room. A large black tub took up most of the back wall, big enough to fit at least four.

Then she watched in horror as Cassius slung his tunic over his head.

What the fuck—

He ignored her as he let his dirty clothes fall to the cold marble floor. A surge of satisfaction went through Thalia at the sight of the jagged scar right between his shoulder blades—from where her knife had stabbed him in the back.

"You're staring," he drawled, and Thalia jerked her gaze to his.

"Does it hurt?" she crooned.

Cassius met her smug stare in the mirror. "Hardly."

"Shame. I should have severed your spine."

"A hairsbreadth to the left and you would have."

"A true shame, then."

"Indeed."

They stared at each other, and Thalia refused to study him closer. To see what other scars marked his torso, new or old.

"I'm going to bed," she finally got out.

"Fine."

"If you so much as come near me, I'll put my dagger through your skull."

"I wouldn't dream of it, then." Cassius started unbuckling his pants.

Thalia stormed back into the bedroom before his trousers hit the floor.

She didn't bother to change as she pulled the curtains of the bed closed and tried to shut out the world.

Chapter Eight

You haven't changed a bit. Cassius murmured low, and the weight of him settled around her—over her. *Gods, the sounds you used to make for me.*

Thalia felt it then, barely the brush of his lips against the sensitive underside of her jaw. She arched into him, biting back the moan that gathered in the back of her throat. She felt his heat, his strength.

Cassius's nose nudged near her ear, and she let out a breathless gasp when his teeth nipped at her skin. "I've missed you. Missed hearing those little noises," Cassius chuckled softly, his bare chest vibrating against hers.

Thalia knew she should pull away. Should take the dagger hidden under her pillow and plunge it straight into his neck, then grab the stake she'd placed under the mattress and finish him. But she did nothing as his lips trailed over her shoulder, his body familiar to her—comforting.

"Aren't you at all curious what it would be like again?" His words were rough, near guttural.

Thalia swallowed her tongue as Cassius's callused hands were suddenly on the hem of her dress, his fingertips touching her skin. They trailed upward, slowly, torturously. Thalia's breath stuttered as his fingers paused near the inner part of her thighs.

"Aren't you at all curious if it would feel as good as it did then?" Cassius pressed his lips right into her neck, and Thalia's pulse fluttered.

She gasped when his other hand grasped her breast, his fingers playing over her hardened nipple.

"Tell me that you want this," he whispered, his breath hot against her ear. Thalia shifted, aching for his fingers to keep going up. To finally sink inside her—

"Look at me, Thalia. Tell me that you want me. Tell me that you want a *monster*."

Thalia forced her heavy lids open.

Red, glowing eyes stared back from sunken flesh.

Thalia tried to scream, but nothing came out as Cassius sank his teeth right into her throat and ripped—

Thalia jerked awake, snagging the dagger tucked under her pillow, and lunged at the person looming above her.

The person yelped as Thalia grabbed them, twisting to pin them to the bed beneath her.

"Fuck's sake!" the person barked. Golden eyes widened with fear at the blade pressed against her lifeblood.

Thalia blinked down at the woman under her. She couldn't be much older than she was, with ebony skin and curly black hair. "Who the fuck are you?" Thalia practically panted out. Her heart was a riotous beat in her chest, her skin covered in cold, clammy sweat.

The woman swallowed, the knife wavering with the movement. "Camilla. I'm to oversee you while you're here."

"Says who?"

Camilla's golden eyes narrowed, and she brazenly placed her hand over Thalia's, pulling the dagger away with more strength than Thalia expected. "Says His Highness."

At the mention of the prince, everything came flooding back, including the night before and finally arriving in Irenbis. Thalia's eyes flew to the sitting area, but Cassius was nowhere to be found. In fact, he wasn't even in the room.

Thalia's heart rate still hadn't returned to normal, but she eased off the woman. "And what exactly do you do for the prince?"

Camilla got up, casting her a glare as she rubbed her neck. "I'm one of his advisers. I'm on his council."

Thalia raised a brow at that. "Oh? And what do you advise him on?"

"Well, I would have advised him not to take a human wife if he was here," Camilla snapped.

Thalia's brow only quirked further, but something caught her attention. Or the lack thereof. She gasped. "You're not—you're not a Vampyr." Indeed, no sharp canines peeked from behind the woman's full lips.

Camilla placed her hands on her hips. The ruby gown she wore was corseted and cinched, highlighting her lithe figure. "I'm not."

Thalia sat up, her hands trembling. "How is it—I mean, how are you—are you human?" For some reason, the thought of another human in this world of monsters gave her a sick sort of comfort.

Camilla barked out a laugh, the sound high and brassy. "Gods, no."

Not human? Then what the hell was she?

Thalia's eyes narrowed. "Get out."

Camilla shook her head, curls flying. "I'm here to ensure that you are properly introduced to the courts this afternoon."

Thalia faltered. Her poor heart couldn't take all this starting and stopping. She'd known the introduction was coming, yet still she had to force the dread from her face. She crossed her arms over her chest and tried to say as neutrally as possible, "Where is Cassius?"

Camilla gave her a look, as if noting the way her breath had hitched. Thalia couldn't stop the heat from flooding her cheeks. But she couldn't ignore the feeling of how his teeth had sunk into her flesh—the pain as he tried to rip her throat out, dream or not.

Camilla finally inclined her head. Something about it seemed almost animal-like. Not in the way of the Vampyrs but something . . . else. "He's probably off being the good little hand to the prince that he is."

Something oily squirmed in Thalia's gut at the words, at the tone. There was a fondness in the way Camilla spoke, no indication of bitterness despite her words. Then the words hit Thalia—the knowledge that this truly was Cassius's kingdom now. He served the very creatures who'd sent those other Vampyrs to her home thirteen years ago, the creatures who'd taken her family. White-hot rage slammed into her so hard that she choked.

"Do you want me to find him?" Camilla added after a moment.

Thalia uncurled her fists, forcing a sharp exhale, only so that she didn't shatter something. She picked at her thumbs. "No."

Camilla looked at her like she didn't believe her. But before the strange woman could question her further, Thalia stormed to the bathing chamber.

"What are you doing?" the woman demanded at her heels.

Thalia turned the water on in the large tub. "Becoming presentable."

Camilla watched her from the doorway, arms crossed. "You could have a servant do that."

"There are servants here?"

Camilla snorted. "Of course there's servants; it's a castle and you're the princess."

Thalia stared at the water rising in the black tub. Another perk of the ore—having access to clean water sent straight into your home. But Camilla's words stuck. Yes. Yes she was going to be the princess of a realm that meant to ruin her. That she needed to destroy instead of allowing her fear to take over. She needed to think, needed to figure out a new plan. And she couldn't very well do that with Camilla watching her like a hawk.

She turned suddenly to the woman. "Can you bring me a breakfast tray?"

Camilla's brows rose. "I said there were servants here. Not saying *I'm* a servant."

Thalia bit down on her rising annoyance. "I know that. But can you ring for them?" *For anyone, really. Anyone except you.* "You said I'm to be presented to the courts this afternoon. I should get ready."

Camilla's eyes narrowed at her as if trying to sense the lie. Finally, she stiffly went back into the room to do as she was asked.

Thalia locked the door of the bathing room chamber, her body already weary and strung out, though she'd been awake for less than ten minutes.

She stared at the tub again. It was still heating, given its size, but something caught the corner of her eye—she'd almost missed the scrap of a shirt hanging out of the laundry chute.

His shirt.

Thalia pulled it out. It was dirty and sweat stained, but she could still smell him under it. Smell the way the wind always seemed to cling to him and how he used to worship the sun, lying in the fields with her when the first stalks of grass sprang up from the earth. Yet underneath it all, she smelled blood. That cloying stench of rot as he left the Scarecrows for her to find like some sort of fucked-up bread trail.

Thalia shoved the shirt into the chute. She shut her mind to her growing rage as she switched the running water to ice cold.

"I can't breathe," Thalia gritted out as one of the servants Camilla had been referring to pulled at the laces on her dress.

Camilla rolled her eyes from where she watched the servants tend to their new princess. Thalia had been lathered and plucked and pinched into what she guessed was perfection. It was almost worse than when Katrina tended to her.

The thought of her handmaiden sent another pang of sadness through her. She pushed it aside. She had a job to do.

"The Vampyr courts are adamant about appearance," Camilla tutted, pulling Thalia from her thoughts. "If you can't breathe, you can't say something that will offend them."

Thalia held back the insult poised on her tongue that would surely offend Camilla. But she wasn't surprised to hear of the Vampyrs' preferences. Given the way they seemed to idolize elegance and their own ethereal beauty, vanity must run deep.

"And if I pass out? Will you or anyone stop the courts from feasting on my blood?"

The servant tightening her dress faltered. Thalia couldn't tell if the three who attended to her were Vampyrs or whatever mysterious thing Camilla was. They hadn't spoken at all to reveal their canines.

"Are you always this dramatic?" Camilla raised a well-groomed brow. Yes, appearances must be important, because somewhere between the time Thalia had gotten out of her freezing bath and the time the servants finished making her up like a porcelain doll, the woman had changed. She wore a silk gown of such a deep violet that it was nearly black, the sleeves three-quarter length with lace trim. Black diamonds dripped from her throat and ears.

Thalia didn't comment as the servant finally stepped back and she had a chance to look in the mirror.

Her gown was similar in fashion to Camilla's, only a rich crimson color that reminded her of dried blood. A stiff piece of red lace wrapped around the back of her neck; it was scalloped, with tiny droplets of black diamonds sewn into the rigid fabric, and flared slightly in a small half-moon.

Thalia's hair had been curled and pinned up, ruby clips holding the strands in place. Her lashes had been darkened and lengthened, her cheeks painted to bring out a natural blush. While she couldn't deny that at least she did look good, like a princess, she wanted to laugh at the pomp of it all—it was far more ostentatious than when her mother held court. But she didn't. She kept her face carefully blank as a servant handed her a black silk fan.

The cold press of her dagger against her thigh was her only comfort as she faced Camilla. Neither she nor the servants had seen her slip it under her dress when their backs were turned.

Camilla looked her over, nodding once. "This will have to do."

Thalia bit her tongue as Camilla pulled something out of her dress pocket and held out her arm. "Here."

Thalia looked at the cream letter and a small velvet pouch dangling from Camilla's fingers. "What's that?"

"From His Highness."

His Highness.

Thalia swallowed as she tentatively took the items, cracking open the thick seal of the letter to read the contents.

Princess,

I hope your journey into Vaccarium was uneventful. Please accept this token as a symbol of our everlasting union and the beginning of true peace.

His Royal Highness

"Not one for words," Thalia muttered, and she could have sworn Camilla snorted. Thalia opened the pouch, spilling the contents into her palm.

A ring with a blood-red ruby stared at her. The band consisted of silver spires that twisted to hold the ruby in the middle, almost like a rose covered by thorns.

Camilla whistled. "Got the family jewels."

Thalia glanced up, but the woman's face was serious. She looked back at the ring. A part of her wanted to throw it into the fire—to watch it melt and crack under pressure.

But she needed to think of her mission.

Thalia slipped the ring onto her left hand, ignoring the weight and coldness of the metal against her skin.

Camilla nodded, then inclined her head. "Shall we?"

Chapter Nine

Camilla led her down the shining staircase and toward the right wing of the palace, which was void of Vampyrs.

Thalia's footsteps echoed, and the back of her neck prickled, urging her to turn around, although she knew no one followed her. Camilla, her curls bouncing with each step, occasionally glanced back to hiss at Thalia to keep up.

And like the good princess she'd decided to be, Thalia did as she was told.

Because Thalia wouldn't be able to take them all down if she continued to act a fool. She'd been born a princess, been raised as such, despite some of the more dangerous escapades her mother had let her indulge in of late. If the Vampyr courts insisted on appearance, so be it.

Thalia kept her back straight as they came to a set of double doors, the black wood smooth like glass. At least here there were two guards posted.

Camilla didn't give a warning as she pushed past them and into an expansive throne room.

Sweat gathered along Thalia's palms as the entire room turned its attention on *her.*

The throne room was surprisingly well decorated. A long red carpet ran the length of the room, ending on an empty throne made entirely of obsidian. A floral applique of silver and black covered the walls, and a huge shimmering chandelier hung in the middle of the room, its crystals winking in and out like dying stars.

Spread around the room were representatives of the five Vampyr Houses, made known by their standard bearer holding their House emblem. Thalia met the Vampyrs' stares, their eyes varying from red to gold to green and the occasional brown. Then blue eyes caught her attention near the empty throne.

Cassius looked her over.

Even from afar, she felt the weight of his stare. He'd cleaned up, perhaps to also make an *appearance.* He wore a cutting doublet of black and silver that molded to his body. He'd even managed to tame his hair, which was brushed and half pulled away from his face, accentuating the sharpness of his jawline.

He stood under a banner, no doubt House Lorenzia's, which bore the symbol of a raven with three eyes; the same image was embroidered in identical silver thread on Cassius's tunic. Next to him were Lord Damien and Keegan.

The raven on the banner seemed to watch her as she stepped farther into the room.

"Well, aren't you all looking good enough to bite," Camilla drawled as she made her way to the front of the throne room, toward the seat of House Lorenzia. "You may all bow to your new princess." She gestured behind her to where Thalia still hadn't moved from her spot not far from the threshold.

The Vampyrs studied her like she was a field mouse set before a barn cat. If she bolted, they'd all pounce, shredding her into bloody ribbons. *Where the hell is the prince?*

Thalia forced a trained smile, inclining her own head. "So you're the courts I've heard so much about." Cassius smirked as she moved toward the front of the room, feeling the weighted stares of the Vampyrs between her shoulder blades. "And where is His Royal Highness?"

Cassius stepped forward, and she automatically stiffened. "His Highness was called away late this afternoon and unfortunately will not return for a fortnight."

A few murmurings ensued from the courts, but Thalia faltered, her eyes whipping to Cassius's. A fortnight? That meant she'd be bound to him for another two weeks—

She glanced down at the ring on her finger. The ruby seemed to darken, almost like it was drawing in the shadows of the room.

"Princess, it seems that our realm is already suiting you." Thalia resisted the urge to shudder as Lord Damien stepped forward. He bowed low. Far lower than she'd anticipated. "On behalf of House Lorenzia, we welcome you to Irenbis."

Thalia inclined her head as Lord Damien stepped back. She'd caught sight of a few other pale-blond Vampyrs with red eyes standing under a black banner, onto which a ram's head with four twisting horns had been stitched in red. Most likely House Avanerius, his old House. She wondered if any of them knew she'd killed their lord. She pushed aside the sudden fear rising in her gut.

Camilla found her a chair, setting it to the left of the throne. Thalia sank into it, graceful as any of them.

"The Queen of Agripa would like to extend her appreciation of the ore that is being provided to our world," Thalia began, careful of her words. "In turn, I hope that this union between our two peoples will strengthen your realm as well."

The Vampyrs all studied her a beat longer before one of them stepped forward. His dark skin and golden eyes matched Keegan's, although he stood below a banner bearing the royal-blue image of an ampithere. "Princess, Lord Amadeus of House Santorien. Forgive my boldness, but without our prince present, how do we know that you humans have held up your end of the treaty?"

She straightened even further, looking him in the eyes. "My mother's word is her bond. Before we left, the water from our rivers had already been diverted to feed your forest. The prince's . . . hand"—she nearly choked over the word, and Cassius stiffened—"can attest to that information himself."

"That's it?" the Vampyr scoffed. "What of the issue in our forest?"

Thalia's interest rose at that. "What issue?"

Cassius seemed to be resisting the urge to fly down the steps to silence the golden-eyed Vampyr, but he remained at her side.

"Perhaps this conversation should wait until the House meeting." Lord Damien swept in.

Lord Amadeus's face twisted. "This issue grows more pressing by the day. Waiting while this madness grows would be unwise."

Thalia's mind whirled. What other issue could there be? Agripa had already unblocked the rivers; the waters surely would have reached the Vampyrs' sacred springs by now. She racked her mind, trying to remember anything she might have heard back in Corithian. Were they facing famine? That didn't make sense; their lands had appeared fertile as she passed through them. Perhaps something with trade—

"I agree with Lord Amadeus." Another Vampyr stepped forward. His black hair fell nearly to his waist, and his eyes matched the banner he stood before, this one embroidered in forest green with the symbol of an eight-legged stag. "This issue is near reaching a breaking point. If the prince were to see for himself—"

"The prince is not here, though, Lord Adrian." Cassius suddenly spoke from Thalia's side, his nearness so acute she almost jumped in her seat. "He is attending to matters up north, which is why I've been seeing to that issue."

Lord Adrian sneered, and Thalia caught the eye of another Vampyr standing under the same banner, one with green eyes similar to those of the apparent lord. In fact, she recognized him from traveling in their entourage.

"It seems rather convenient that the prince was called away, and to the north, of all places. Just as his bride was to be presented to him," Lord Adrian said, sharp fangs poking out behind thin lips. "Perhaps he's trying to find a different solution. One that doesn't require . . . humans."

The lord's stare landed right on hers.

Sweat slid down the back of her spine, working its way under her too-tight corset. She clenched her fingers in her lap, only so she wouldn't pick at her skin, drawing blood.

Cassius stepped in front of her. "Bold of you to threaten the princess in her own home, Lord Adrian."

Lord Adrian's lip curled. "This is *not* her home."

A dissonance of murmurs echoed. If she were in her mother's court, he would have been hauled away for treason. But this wasn't her mother's court, and she was far from the castle she had once called home.

Tension stretched around the room, each strand a web waiting to spring.

Lord Adrian stared at her. Some sort of humming filled the back of her mind as though a mosquito buzzed in her ear. The Vampyr's face began to ripple, his flesh starting to sink into his skull—

"You're right," Thalia blurted out. Collective surprise swept through the crowd as she stood. "This isn't my home."

Cassius turned to her, his own surprise quickly replaced by annoyance. He flashed her a warning look, but she ignored him. Thalia took a step away from the throne.

"But this treaty was made in the hope that both our homes could thrive," she said. Thalia's ring caught the light, and Lord Adrian's eyes narrowed on the ruby, his lips pulling into a sneer. "It was made to stop this ceaseless bloodshed between our two realms."

"And what do you know of bloodshed?" Lord Adrian said lowly.

Thalia resisted the urge to look at House Avanerius, to the banner that had no lord. The image of a staked Vampyr flashed before her eyes. "I know enough."

"She used to kill us." The Vampyr whose eyes matched Lord Adrian's stepped forward, his face hardened in contempt. "I heard it from Lord Damien himself."

Thalia glanced over her shoulder at the red-eyed Vampyr. But he remained motionless, unwavering.

"Is this true?" a Vampyr asked from beneath a banner featuring a grinning orange fox with multiple teeth.

"I—" Thalia faltered. Every Vampyr seemed to still. A sort of preternatural quiet descended that had everything in her screaming to *run*.

"Does it appear that she could do any harm?" Cassius stepped in front of her, and despite the apparent danger in the room, Thalia bristled. "She's a human."

"Indeed," Lord Damien said from behind her, and Thalia's fingers clenched. "The likelihood of this woman taking down any of our brethren is abysmal at best."

Thalia whirled on her heel, heart pounding. Lord Damien stared at her, and if she hadn't been so locked in on him, she would have missed the barely noticeable dip of his chin. For whatever reason, he was protecting her.

Both Lord Damien and Cassius were.

Cassius drawled, "It seems to me, Julian, that you're eager to stir up trouble. Seeing as how the last few months have gone for House Gallinus, I would have thought you wiser than that."

The green-eyed Vampyr, Julian, bared his fangs, his skin sinking into his skull.

Cassius snorted at the obvious display of posturing. "If that is all, I do believe the festivities should commence, unless you all wish to see true bloodshed."

Cassius's back was to her, but from the sudden shift in the crowd, he must have . . . changed.

Camilla clapped her hands, startling Thalia. "Lord Amadeus, perhaps you'd do us the honor of leading our Houses into the great hall. We shall celebrate this new treaty, which will greatly aid in the vitality of Vaccarium."

Lord Amadeus stiffened, bowing. "Of course."

Doors opened to an adjoining room and the courts filed out, although it seemed a few of the House members stayed behind, including Lord Adrian.

"I wish to discuss an urgent matter," Lord Adrian bit out. Apparently, he either didn't take Cassius as a threat or was incredibly stupid. Thalia had a feeling it was the latter. "Seeing as you're in charge now as hand"—he spat the word with as much hatred as he could muster—"perhaps you can help."

Indeed, the way Cassius was nearly vibrating with ire, the Vampyr must have been desperate if he wished to continue his insult by standing there. "It cannot wait until the next House council meeting?"

"I'm afraid not."

Thalia stared at the Vampyr, her slippers suddenly fused to the ground.

"It will have to wait until tomorrow, then. We have a celebration to attend."

"Lord Cassius—" Lord Adrian growled, but Cassius ignored him, stepping in front of Thalia.

To her horror, he held out a scarred hand. "Princess?" Thalia stared at it, very much wishing that damned servant hadn't made her laces so tight. "Shall we?" Cassius's face was hard, but his eyes were open, the blue scanning her. It almost seemed like he was pleading with her to take his hand. To get them out of whatever news Lord Adrian wished to discuss.

Thalia offered a cruel smile, and Cassius immediately stiffened. "I would like to hear about this urgent matter."

"This matter does not concern you, *Princess*," Cassius bit out, a hint of fangs showing, eyes now hardened into chips of glass.

Thalia smirked, staring up at him. "If this is something that's so important that the prince's *hand* must be informed, then it surely must be important enough for his wife to hear as well."

While Lord Adrian seemed inclined to rip her throat out, she weathered the contempt in his gaze as she said, "I would assume that women can partake in matters of state, given Camilla's own role as adviser to the prince." Thalia glanced over her shoulder to where Camilla had disappeared into the great hall with Lord Damien and Keegan. She turned around. "Given my new position, I would like to know. I aim to do the best I can as your princess. This shall be my home now, and I hope that I can acclimate quickly to this court so I might better aid any matters that the Houses bring to the prince's attention."

"Unfortunately, Princess, as a human, you do not have any position with this court and matters of state besides one of formality," Cassius cut in.

Thalia's rage spiked as he stared down at her, some sick, twisted sort of delight flashing in his eyes as he watched her seethe.

"Is this something that the prince has decreed?" she bit out.

"Something that the prince's council voted on before your arrival."

Lord Adrian snickered, causing Thalia's rage to spike further. If only she had her stake so could embed it in his skull.

"And was the prince part of this vote?" Thalia countered. A muscle in Cassius's jaw flickered, but he said nothing. She picked at the skin around her thumbs, gritting out, "There is to be a House council meeting soon. When is it?"

Cassius met her burning stare. "A fortnight."

No doubt when the prince finally returned to the castle after concluding whatever business he had up north.

"And I take it that even though I am not on the prince's council as a member of House Lorenzia, I can bring forth matters to the Houses? Is that not the law? That members of the Houses can bring forth matters for other Houses to vote on?"

Finally, he gritted out, "Yes."

Thalia would have crowed in triumph if it weren't for the deadly glares of the Vampyrs boring into her. "Then this is something that I shall bring up in the next House meeting. That despite the fact that I am human, as His Highness's *wife* I should be allowed to speak and be a part of all matters in this realm."

Then Thalia swept past Cassius and headed straight into the great hall and the gathering crowd of monsters.

"You really pissed him off." Camilla's light voice appeared behind her.

Thalia turned from where she'd been watching the court of Vampyrs. Musicians played a haunting tune that wove itself into the dark ceiling. But no one danced. Or even ate. They all stood around in clumps, speaking too quietly for her to hear and holding silver goblets she knew contained blood, if the sharp metallic scent in the air said anything.

"I don't care," Thalia said. She knew Camilla was speaking about Cassius, but her head had begun to feel a bit light, which felt more urgent. Whether it was from the lack of food and water provided or from the corset, which threatened to squeeze the breath out of her, she couldn't say. Perhaps all of the above.

"You should care, Princess," Camilla said, coming into her line of sight. "He is hand to the prince. He holds sway and power. His Highness listens to him far more than even his council."

"Who is on the prince's council?" Thalia cut in. His position still grated on her nerves. Lying, traitorous prick.

Camilla's pretty face flashed in surprise before she said, "Cassius. Me, obviously. Lord Damien, and Lord Keegan."

"Lord Keegan?"

Camilla nodded to where Keegan stood speaking with some members of House Santorien. Surprise drifted through her. She hadn't realized three of the prince's council had traveled into the human realm to broker a deal. Thalia wouldn't have pegged Keegan as someone who'd be on the prince's council, given his quiet nature. But perhaps that was why. His personality offered a contrast to Camilla's loud nature and Cassius's sharp one.

"Why did Lord Damien lie for me?" Thalia whispered. Camilla was no doubt privy to what she'd been doing before the treaty, given her position on the prince's council.

"You may not be a Vampyr, but you're still part of House Lorenzia," Camilla said, equally quiet. "Despite whatever you did, you're part of something greater now. Lord Damien wouldn't jeopardize the treaty out of spite."

"But what of Lord Adrian?" Thalia asked, her eyes glued on the Vampyrs who stood near the banner depicting a stag with eight legs. House Gallinus, if her deductions were correct.

Camilla made a face. "Lord Adrian and his son are pissed that they got booted off the prince's council."

Thalia turned in surprise. "What?"

Camilla ignored the passing servants carrying silver goblets. "Their House, House Gallinus, has been . . . difficult to work with recently. The last lord was a sadist, to say the least. Not to mention Lord Adrian and his son, Julian, are hotheaded. Much more inclined to bite first and ask questions later." She nodded to the two Vampyrs. It made sense that they were related, given their appearance and personality. "Eventually, the prince realized they'd both be of better service elsewhere."

"Yet he's still a lord?"

Camilla pursed her lips. “It was a way to appease him. Lord Adrian has served House Lorenzia for decades. He has sway with many of the other Houses. If the prince banished him entirely, well . . .” She trailed off.

Thalia swallowed. Great. Here was another Vampyr who might be able to provide her more insight on the prince, yet he seemed the most inclined to kill her without a second thought.

“Where did His Highness go?” Thalia hedged. There were too many questions floating in her head, all jumbled together like wooden blocks.

Camilla shook her head, huffing out a laugh. “You really don’t let up, do you?” When Thalia refused to break, Camilla said, “There’s a small town up north that’s been hit badly by some storms. He went to check the damage to see what could be done.”

Thalia didn’t know why the knowledge didn’t settle her. Perhaps because the Vampyrs seemed more civilized than she had anticipated. Not even her mother would have gone to other parts of Agripa if something as damaging as a storm came through. No, that duty had been left to her. And she was glad to take it, if only because it made her feel better to try to help the people of Agripa . . . although what had she really done? Made note of which towns to send more food to? Tried to stop the growing attacks, to no avail? The thought sent a note of bitterness across her tongue.

Thalia brushed it aside, picking at her thumbs. “What about the forest?”

Camilla glanced at her. “What about it?”

“Is there something wrong with it?”

Camilla offered a smile though it seemed forced. “No. Lord Amadeus just worries about the springs. He claims we’ll all fall into madness if we don’t attend them.”

Thalia could sense the woman holding back. But Camilla’s eyes became guarded, and Thalia had a feeling that no matter how hard she pried, the woman wouldn’t divulge anything on this matter.

“I’d like to retire,” Thalia said.

The room spun slightly, but she ignored it as Camilla led her quietly back through the castle to her room and left her without a glance or word between them.

Thalia didn't care. Too many things had happened. There were too many missing pieces, too many locks that had no key.

She couldn't breathe. She needed to get this damned dress off.

Thalia shoved into her room, tugging at the ties on the back of her gown, but that damned servant had knotted them. Thalia's breaths came out in short puffs as she wrestled to get herself out of the dress suffocating her.

She hissed, looking around to see if there was a bell or pulley that might signal a maid. The movement caused dots to dance across her eyes. Thalia swayed, her hand gripping the back of the settee as she willed the spots from her vision.

Thalia scrabbled to grab the dagger strapped to her thigh under the swaths of fabric, her world spinning.

"Did you think it would make you look powerful? Bold? To be so brazen in a court you're sorely unfamiliar with?" Cassius's voice growled behind her. She hadn't even heard him enter. Not that she would have noticed, given the way the room danced a quadrille.

"Thalia, these courts are not what you think. The position you're in as a *human*—what's wrong?" Cassius came up beside her.

"What is wrong?" he growled again.

Thalia shook her head, jerking back. The movement caused her nausea to surge, but she managed to fight down the bile. "Go. Away."

"Not until you tell me what's wrong."

Thalia's hand shook as she held her dagger. At least she'd gotten it out of her dress. Now she needed to figure out how to move her arm to cut the ties.

He let out a disbelieving laugh. "Are you going to try and stab me?"

Thalia shook her head, more spots dancing. "This. Dress."

Cassius's gaze traveled from her wan, sweaty skin to the dress, which cinched her waist and pushed her breasts to an unnatural height. "Turn around."

Despite her weakened state, Thalia managed a disbelieving laugh. "No."

"Don't be a stubborn ass; turn around so I can undo you."

"I'd rather cut off my own *arm* than let you untie my dress," she seethed, finding the strength to throw as much hatred and disgust into her glare as she could muster.

Cassius raised a brow, arms crossed over his chest. It was only because of lack of oxygen that the thought of how beautiful he looked flashed briefly in her mind.

"You'd rather pass out?"

"Yes."

Cassius rolled his eyes, stepping nearer. She raised her dagger feebly, but he took it from her hand easily, turning her around. "You're still such a bad liar," he muttered.

Thalia couldn't even bite back a retort, not as darkness crept to the edges of her vision.

"Fuck, who tied this?" Cassius grumbled out.

Thalia didn't know, couldn't speak as Cassius tugged at the ties of her dress. Slowly but surely, air slipped down into her lungs.

But apparently he couldn't get it untied either, because he let out another curse. Then Cassius ripped her dress in half. Thalia gasped as oxygen burrowed into her lungs like a fox in a hole.

She leaned against the settee, breathing deeply, letting her world return to normal now that she could inhale again.

Once the world had stopped spinning, she whirled to Cassius. "You ripped my dress!" Indeed, the back had been ripped clean open, cold air rushing over her heated skin. It hung awkwardly off her shoulders, nearly slipping off from her turning.

Cassius stared at her in disbelief. "You were going to pass out, and *this* is what you're mad about?"

"You could have untied it!"

Cassius's face darkened. "You are truly unbelievable."

Thalia surged forward.

She didn't have her knife, but she still had nails and her fists.

Cassius easily outmaneuvered her, appearing at her back. "You're also incredibly predictable."

She spun, tripping over the swaths of her gown as she stumbled after him. "I'm going to kill you."

"Aren't you getting tired of this, Thalia? I certainly know I am," Cassius drawled as she swung again and he moved out of the way like mist dissipating.

She panted, raising her fists again, but suddenly Cassius clamped his hands around her wrists. Thalia let out a squawk of surprise as he twisted her arms behind her. His chest brushed against her bare back as he said low, "We could work together, you know. These courts are deadly, full of vipers. I could help you navigate them. Help you figure out how to handle the other lords."

"Fuck. Off."

He chuckled, his lips brushing the shell of her ear and caused an unwanted shiver to cascade down her spine. "That dirty mouth of yours is going to get you in trouble one day. Perhaps you need a lesson in manners."

"And are you going to be the one to teach me?" Her voice dropped.

She felt Cassius's shock at the change in her tone, the way she'd deepened it into an almost seductive curl, the words seeming to have come from nowhere.

She leaned her head back against his chest, feeling the rise and fall of it. He wasn't even winded. Prick.

"Shall you fuck those foul words right out of my mouth, then? That would surely teach me manners." Her words curled again. A small, traitorous part of her remembered what it felt like to be fucked by him. Her whole body heated at the thought, and Cassius whirled her around to face him.

His chest rose and fell rapidly, his pupils so wide they nearly devoured the blue of his irises.

"Shall we start our lessons right now?" Her words were a silk sheet wrapped around a dagger, full of wicked promise. That depraved heat in her chest traveled lower, pooling into her belly.

Cassius's heated gaze flicked to her parted mouth. Their bodies were pressed so tightly together that his arousal pushed against her stomach, heating her treasonous core further.

Then his gaze went straight to the pulse fluttering in her throat, and his irises turned impossible dark.

Everything in her froze at the look. At the *hunger*.

Her core clenched, her body locking up at his gaze. Fear like she'd never known threw itself against her rib cage.

Cassius noted the change immediately.

He jerked his head back, grip loosening. "Thalia—"

"Let go of me. Let go of me right now." Thalia couldn't keep the panic from her voice. Her whole body started trembling uncontrollably.

Cassius let go, taking a step back as Thalia shrank against the bed. "What happened?"

"Leave," Thalia choked out.

"Thalia—"

"Leave!"

Cassius stared at her, too many emotions flashing across his face for her to decipher. But, finally, he left, closing the door behind him.

Thalia sank to the ground, pulling her knees up to her chest as the image of Cassius ripping out her throat flashed over and over in her mind.

She did not move for some time.

Chapter Ten

"Good morning," Thalia said as she entered a drawing room in the west wing of the castle.

Cassius, Camilla, Lord Damien, and Keegan all sat around a small breakfast table with stacks of what must be reports strewn about the dark surface. A few empty silver goblets stood next to them, their contents drained yet the interiors still stained red.

Thalia sank down into an empty wingback chair, the wood groaning as she looked at the three of them. "Am I interrupting anything?"

Keegan and Camilla both glanced at Cassius, who leaned back in his seat, fiddling with the quill in his fingers. "You're up early," he said cautiously.

Thalia forced herself to shrug as a servant appeared with her breakfast tray. They removed the lid. Thalia was surprised the food wasn't bland, given the circumstances. She dug into her porridge, ripe with honey and berries.

"You didn't wish to take breakfast in your room?" he added.

Thalia glanced up.

She could practically see the memories replaying in his mind. How she'd have a servant send up a tray so she could eat quickly and be gone from the castle before her mother had even roused. That or she'd find a way to have breakfast while he was on duty. They'd find themselves in the guards' barracks with Reina—Marcus joining them when he could escape the library. She had a feeling her tray would have been sent up, no doubt ordered by Cassius himself. But she had other plans in mind for the day other than hiding in her room.

"Should I not greet the day with the prince's council? Seems more productive than lying around waiting for something to happen." The Vampyrs and Camilla all watched with various degrees of unease as she took a long sip from her herbal tea.

"Speaking of, any news on my husband?" Thalia said, and the words immediately soured the berries in her stomach.

The four exchanged a glance, but it was Lord Damien who cleared his throat. "He is still holed up in the north, but he sent these." The pale Vampyr slid over a cream letter similar to the one Camilla had given her the day before, along with a rectangular box wrapped with silver string.

Thalia felt the weight of their stares as she popped open the seal, this time noting the emblem on the wax crest was a raven with three eyes.

Princess,

I have heard you are an admirer of beautiful, deadly things.

His Royal Highness

Thalia frowned before opening the gift.

A jeweled dagger lay on top of a red velvet cushion. The handle was silver swirls, almost mimicking the swirls of her ring, and encrusted with rubies and black sapphires, matching the scabbard it came in. The blade sang as she unsheathed it, the point sharp and gleaming.

"Perhaps you might give me my knife back now," Cassius drawled, breaking the silence.

The knife she'd taken in Agripa, which was currently strapped to her thigh.

In the past, she might have suggested that if he wanted it back so badly, he could take it from her. And given the way he watched her, something flashing in his blue eyes, maybe he was thinking the same thing.

But that memory vanished as the sounds of her sister's last gurgling breath whispered in her ears.

Cassius had betrayed her, cut a wound so deep there was no recovering from it. His knife wasn't the only thing she'd take from him. A castle didn't just crumble overnight, and she'd start chipping away at his, removing pieces brick by brick. Thalia sheathed the dagger, setting it to the side.

"I thought it would be wise to get to know more about my new home," Thalia said, ignoring his comment. "I think it would be good to see what the capital is like, to introduce myself to the people."

Cassius watched her, his face unreadable as she stabbed her fork in the eggs atop her rich, buttery, golden toast.

"So you want to go into the city?" he said, watching as she swallowed her food before downing the rest of her tea.

Thalia daintily wiped her mouth. "Yes. Unless that is forbidden." She frowned at the spot of tea that'd fallen onto her chest. She patted away the spot, taking extra care to wipe her napkin across her cleavage, which was on special display thanks to the dark-green gown she wore.

She glanced at Cassius, whose jaw flickered. "It's not forbidden," he finally said.

Thalia raised her brow. "Then I'd like to go. I'm sure it is customary in your world for fanfare when a royal makes an appearance, but I have no need. I'd rather be seen as . . . me." The last part came out awkwardly, and Cassius noted it with a flare of his nostrils.

"You'll need an escort," Cassius bit out.

"Of course," Thalia practically purred. She turned to Keegan. "Are you busy this afternoon?"

Camilla choked as she drank from her goblet.

Keegan glanced at Cassius, but Thalia ignored the latter. "I'm afraid I have other duties to attend to."

Thalia kept her grin fixed, not letting it slip as she turned to Camilla, who hid her laugh behind her cup. "Shall you escort me?"

Camilla shook her head, trying and failing to hide her smirk. "I have other duties to attend to as well."

Fine, Lord Damien, then, even if being around him still set her on edge. But before she could open her mouth, the red-eyed Vampyr said smoothly, "I'm afraid I also have duties, Princess. But Lord Cassius shall be of service."

Thalia slowly slid her gaze to Cassius, who glared at Lord Damien with so much ire she was surprised the Vampyr didn't catch flame. "And will you escort me?"

Having Cassius accompany her was less than ideal, not with him watching her every move. But sacrifices needed to be made if she had any hope of learning more about the Vampyr realm and how she might gut them all.

Cassius toyed with the black quill, his fingers twisting so hard it nearly snapped. Finally, he said, "I have a few things to get to, but yes. We can leave in an hour."

Thalia felt a surge of satisfaction go through her as she stood, her chair scraping back with the movement. "Then I look forward to it."

Being out of the castle during the day was a shock to the senses.

The sun remained firmly behind the clouds, the sky gray and dreary as if waiting to rain. It cast the whole courtyard in a sort of gloom that seemed to wait for Thalia as she stood on the castle steps.

A few guards were stationed at her back, keeping watch. Thalia ensured that both Cassius's knife and the prince's gift were strapped to her waist. She'd also changed into pants and a tight-fitting tunic, practical clothes in case something should go south—like a Vampyr deciding they didn't take too kindly to a human now serving as their princess.

Thalia craned her head as Cassius led two horses through an archway from what must have been the direction of the stables. She really needed to get a map of the castle. Given its vastness and quiet halls, gods knew what might be lurking around unsuspecting corners.

"I get my own horse?" Thalia asked.

Cassius raised a brow, adjusting the stirrups of the horse she'd ride. The dapple gray mare dipped her head, and Thalia scratched her forelock. "You seem disappointed."

Thalia let the horse snuffle her fingers. "Not disappointed but surprised. What's her name?"

Cassius paused. "Feryena."

A pang of sadness swept through her as she thought of her own stallion, Helios. She'd spent hours riding him before her whole world went to shit. And often Cassius would be riding right beside her.

That was before his betrayal.

Before he decided he wanted power instead of her.

Then it was just her and Helios as she tracked him across Agripa.

"Should I be worried about you riding alone?" Cassius's voice broke through her thoughts.

Thalia met his stare, his blue eyes intent on hers. He must have seen the shift in her emotions, because he straightened as she said, "I've told you, this is my home now. To do something that would jeopardize the fragile treaty between our people would be foolish. I'm here to make the best of my circumstances."

Cassius gave her another look before he gestured her forward. "Leg up."

Thalia had barely lifted her leg when Cassius boosted her into the saddle. She squawked, not having expected him to lift her so high. She tangled with the reins, her body nearly pitching over the side before Cassius grabbed her waist, steadying her. His other hand was on her thigh, his palm searing into her skin below the fabric.

"What the hell was that?" Thalia hissed, heat rising to her face as Cassius stared up at her.

"It seems like someone wasn't prepared," he said matter-of-factly before going to his own gelding.

Thalia resisted the urge to flip him off. She had the feeling the prick had done it on purpose.

They didn't speak as they rode through the inner courtyard, an area dotted with thick trees. They reminded her a lot of the trees in the Vampyrs' sacred forest. A forest that was supposed to be their only protection for hunting during the day—

Thalia jerked, sickening realization dawning as she twisted in her saddle. "Why do you really need the water from our rivers?"

Cassius raised a brow as they passed through the gilded gates of the palace, entering a broad expanse of forest. "What?"

Thalia shook her head, focusing on guiding her horse as opposed to staring at Cassius, but her heart pounded. "You—we were told that you needed our river to feed your sacred forest. It's the only place you can hunt safely during the day. But since being here, you all have been able to hunt because of the cloud cover—"

"Have you seen us hunt?" Cassius cut her off.

Thalia's mouth opened and closed. No, she hadn't. But the prick knew that. "How is it possible for it to be so overcast all the time? Wouldn't you be . . . worried to be out if the clouds suddenly parted?"

Cassius ducked to avoid a branch. "A Mage cast a spell over this territory."

"I thought Mages and Vampyrs didn't like each other," Thalia said, recalling the story Lord Damien had shared.

"They used to not, but this act was a way to atone for the wrong the Mages committed against our kind. Not every place in Vaccarium is like this. There are many that still face the consequences when they step into the light."

"So the forest is, what? A lie to get our rivers? Why?"

"It wasn't a lie. The treaty we made with your mother was true. Our forest is dying; there are streams and pools there that are sacred to us Vampyrs—it's where the Mages first created us. It's now used as the location when two Vampyrs are joined together; you'll finish your vows there when the prince returns. Besides, what does it matter? You all needed our ore if you had any hope of surviving."

Thalia's mind whirled, too many questions on the tip of her tongue. Perhaps Cassius was partly telling the truth; if the forest was dying, it made sense that they needed the rivers to be diverted. However, that didn't explain why they'd lied about being able to hunt during the day. Although, if they could live freely during the day without the wrath of the sun, it made sense that their habits had changed from being solely nocturnal. But they'd withheld mention of whatever sort of magic the Mages could use that allowed the sky to darken and fester like an old wound.

"Are there really pockets of magic here?"

Cassius pulled his horse to a stop, and her horse automatically stopped next to his. They stood on a leaf-strewn path. Sounds of the forest reached her, the twittering of birds in their nests, the scurry of squirrels along branches. This forest, at least, was alive, unlike the one that separated their two worlds, despite them appearing the same.

"Yes," Cassius finally said after a moment, breaking through her thoughts. "At least a few are still left."

"How are they used?"

Cassius paused, contemplating. "From what I was told, the Mages were able to use that raw magic and shape it into something solid."

"Like the Vampyrs?"

Cassius's face darkened, but he nodded.

"What else did they make?"

"Other beings."

"Like?"

Maybe Cassius saw the genuine interest in Thalia's face, or perhaps he didn't see the harm in sharing. "The shifters."

"What are they?"

"Beings that were created to fight against the Vampyrs. They can shift into beasts."

Thalia chewed on the inside of her cheek. "Is . . . is Camilla a shifter?"

Cassius raised a brow in what might have been silent pride at her deduction. It caused something in her chest to tighten. She cleared her throat. "How do we—how do humans not know about this? We were taught about the creation of the Vampyrs, but the shifters? These pockets of magic? Why is this not part of our history?"

Cassius studied her a beat longer. "History has a way of changing depending on who is telling the story."

The words held far more meaning than Thalia cared to admit. She shook her head, nudging Feryena on, and Cassius had no choice but to follow. "Where are the Mages?" Thalia asked.

"They mainly reside in Lorceium with the shifters," Cassius said. "It's the mountain at the tip of our continent where the ore is found. It holds the city of Perden, the capital of House Olvectus."

"Why couldn't the Mages just use the pockets of magic to cast all of Vaccarium in shadow?"

"There's only a handful of Mages left, and the pockets of magic have been drained. They only have what is left in their reserves in Lorceium."

"So you really did need this treaty, then?"

Cassius nodded. "As the Mages' magic grows weaker with time, so does the barrier that keeps the light away. Once that magic fades, we will have to hide from the sun as we first did."

"When will that happen?"

Cassius shook his head. "We don't know, but it's gotten worse. There's a reason the courts went to Agripa thirteen years ago. It's when the first cracks in the Mages' shield began to materialize; they were hoping to find an answer in Agripa's library."

Thirteen years ago. When her father and sister were brutally killed. When the marriage meant to bind the two realms turned the palace into a charnel house.

Rage rose so hard in Thalia's stomach that white spotted her vision.

I'm going to marry into the House that's near the forest!

"Thalia?" Cassius's concerned words broke through her rage.

She took a sharp inhale, pushing Ariadna's voice aside. "Is that the issue that Lord Adrian was so pressed about?"

Cassius stiffened, then relaxed almost immediately. "Yes. There's a new crack near Cupisco, the capital of House Gallinus, which he rules."

"And what's the solution to this problem?" Thalia asked.

Cassius glanced at her. "That's something the prince is trying to find out."

"And the forest? Lord Amadeus seemed adamant that something else was going on with it."

Cassius stared at her, and she could have sworn that his eyes began to glow. "The forest is fine. Lord Amadeus was worried the rivers wouldn't reach the springs in time."

They continued on in silence, and Thalia had the distinct feeling she was being lied to.

Chapter Eleven

Irenbis was a few miles from the castle, and the forest opened to rolling green hills with the capital nestled among them. The spacious city sprawled over the rich landscape.

Thalia glanced over her shoulder as they left the tree line, finding the castle's dark spires in the distance. She quickly turned back as Cassius urged his horse to the road.

Cobblestones echoed under their horses' hooves as they passed the city's watchmen. The Vampyrs all nodded to Cassius, a few whispering to each other when they caught her stare.

She didn't know what to make of it. Nor did she know what to make of the city itself. It was laid out like an eight-pointed star, the roads and homes forming a grid-like pattern, all merging into what appeared to be a vast city center.

Thalia kept her jaw from dropping as they moved deeper, passing homes with ivy-covered walls and open storefronts, the scent of freshly spiced meat tickling her nose. The smells made her mouth water, and her stomach grumbled. Thalia didn't think it was very loud, but Cassius looked over his shoulder with a smirk.

Thalia scowled as he turned back around.

But despite the richness that seemed to bleed from the buildings and the opulence of everything she saw, attesting to the full coffers of House Lorenzia, something was off.

No Vampyr was out in the city. No one shouted their wares; no children ran underfoot with their toys. It was quiet—still. Like someone had frozen the place and forgotten about it, leaving it to collect cobwebs and dust like an ivy-covered tomb.

"Where is everyone?" Thalia asked. She hadn't whispered the words, but she felt as though she should have.

"Days like this are quiet in the afternoon; most don't venture out until the night," Cassius replied, stopping in the middle of the city center. A large fountain bubbled, the only noise as he dismounted.

"But there's no sun."

Cassius patted his gelding. "That doesn't stop one's instincts."

Thalia glanced around. Shop fronts opened into the city center, and she could have sworn she caught someone peeking out behind curtains. She blinked and the shadow was gone.

Thalia dismounted, leading her horse next to Cassius's. "So what does this city do?"

Cassius tilted his head. "What do you mean?"

"I mean, there's no ocean, or even river, from what I've seen. What are its exports?"

Cassius raised a brow. "Did you actually listen to all those lessons Domina Tullia taught you?"

Thalia rolled her eyes at the mention of her governess growing up. In fact, Cassius used to sneak Thalia out of lessons when the crone's back was turned. They'd go off hunting wolves in the woods. Thalia never would have guessed that she should have been hunting Vampyrs instead.

"She did teach some rather important things." Thalia crossed her arms over her chest. "Besides, it's not as though I did nothing in my mother's court." Yet Agripa's exports were far and few between, given the dangers of their shores.

Cassius smirked, also crossing his arms over his chest. Finally, he relented. "Irenbis has a number of exports."

"Like?"

"Wine, and wool. Meat and grain from farms."

Thalia's eyes narrowed. "Who do you export to?"

"Other territories in Vaccarium, that and some continents across the sea. Our wine is particularly popular in Sula."

Thalia knew of the small island to the east. The humans there had been the first to refuse aid to Agripa when her family was murdered. But the other territories . . . those could be the ones the Vampyrs were trying to ally with.

Thalia chewed the inside of her cheek, letting the information settle over her. Trying not to let the rage festering inside her gut take over. Agripa had tried for years to set up trade with the bordering continents. It was no wonder they hadn't been successful, considering those continents profited from the very creatures Agripa was plagued by.

Thalia picked at the skin around her thumbs but stopped when she caught Cassius's stare. "Why meat? I smelled something cooking earlier. Don't you all drink . . . ?" She waved a hand.

"Blood?" Cassius's eyebrow quirked further.

"Yes, blood," Thalia gritted out.

Cassius shook his head. "Did you not read any of the books Marcus gave you?"

It took a moment for his words to register. "*You* took my books?"

Cassius shrugged, flicking a speck of dirt off his leather doublet. "You weren't looking after them. Considering I hauled them all the way from Agripa to the castle, you should be thanking me."

Thalia stepped forward, her anger spiking. "Thanking you? For stealing *my* books? Where the hell are they?"

"In our room. I would have given them to you if you'd asked. Although some of the information needs to be amended. But I can't fault Marcus for that. It seems no one has updated the information since before our treaty fell."

Thalia pushed the image of the night aside. Her sister's unseeing eyes, her mother kneeling in a pool of her father's blood. She didn't realize she stood toe to toe with Cassius until she had to tilt her head back to see him clearly. "What information?"

Cassius cocked his head. "Be specific."

"You're a prick."

"Now, that *is* specific."

"How can you eat meat—food?"

"Because blood isn't our sole source of nutrients. It's like how you eat meat and drink water. We eat meat and drink blood. Same concept." That would explain why her breakfast hadn't tasted like shit. But that didn't explain why she hadn't seen any of the Vampyrs eat anything since being in their realm.

"How long can you go without consuming blood?" she pushed.

Cassius shrugged. "A few days."

"Do you have to drink blood from the source?"

"No. Another fact Marcus's books got wrong. And before you ask"—Cassius interrupted as Thalia opened her mouth again—"it doesn't have to be human. Believe it or not, Vampyrs never lived off the blood of humans as a sole source. Sheep's blood works just as well."

"Then what about the Scarecrows? Why suck out their blood if you had other sources? Tell me, did you all draw sticks on who got to terrorize the farmers? Who got to slice them up and peel their skin until they were strips of leather? Was the war between our worlds, the fact that our ore was dwindling, not enough for you?" Thalia wished she weren't standing so close to him, if only so she could kick dirt onto his boots now. "Or is it just you who was assigned that honor?"

Cassius's jaw flickered. "You must think me quite capable to cause that much damage all over Agripa."

"I know it was you."

"How so?"

Thalia scanned his eyes. "I tracked you."

Surprise flared in Cassius's face before he quickly masked it. "Of course you did."

Thalia's anger rose. "Did you really think I'd let you go? That I wouldn't try to find you?"

"I didn't realize you wanted me dead so badly."

Thalia's lips twisted into a cruel grin. "Considering what you did, the fact that after your betrayal you began hunting innocent humans, death would be a kindness."

"And why would I have needed to hunt humans?"

"I don't know. I guess I'd take a look in the mirror."

Cassius's face darkened. "Did it ever occur to you that I didn't do it?"

Thalia scoffed. "Who else would have done it?"

"Do you really think me capable of such a horror?" Anger filled Cassius's voice, his words a near-inaudible growl. "Do you really think that the man I am could be so easily given over to my bloodlust? I may be a Vampyr, but the man inside me is still alive. If you really think I could do something as heinous as what was done to those farmers, then you truly don't know me at all."

Thalia swallowed, but she didn't let his anger faze her as she lifted her chin. "Then who else would have done it?" she repeated.

Something in Cassius's eyes flashed too quickly for Thalia to decipher it. "It was probably a different creature from the forest."

"A different creature?" Thalia's mind flashed back to the Nestos. Its scythe-like hands were perfect for dicing up flesh. But she'd never even heard of that sort of creature before traveling to Vaccarium. Not to mention she had been deep in the forest when it appeared. Thalia would have received word from someone, anyone, if there were other creatures leaving the Scarecrows.

Either Cassius didn't know, or he was lying. And Thalia had a sense that it was the latter. For some reason, the thought of him lying sent a sour note through her stomach. He didn't owe her any truths, and gods knew she was lying to him too. There was too much betrayal between them, too much anger and hurt.

Before Thalia could ask anything more, her stomach grumbled loud enough that Feryena jerked her head up from where she'd been drinking her fill.

Cassius glanced at her stomach, then back to her face. Anger still lined his blue eyes, but he just handed her his horse's reins. "I'll find us something to eat."

He didn't glance back as he walked back down the path that led to the area where she'd first smelled the cooking meat.

Thalia huffed out a breath, pushing aside the hair from her face. Fine. If he wanted to be an ass, so be it.

The sound of a door creaking open in the quiet center had Thalia's head perking up. She didn't see anything as she scanned the area, the storefronts quiet, their curtains drawn. Then, there—

A shadow moved down an alleyway.

Thalia glanced at the horses, then to the retreating figure. After a split second's hesitation, she dropped the reins. She moved on silent feet, heading after the figure who seemed so eager to remain unnoticed, and she intended to find out why. Perhaps she could figure out what sorts of secrets the Vampyrs were hiding in their capital city so she could report back to her mother.

With no sun to chase her, the gloomy sky tracked her as she slunk down the alleyway, keeping at a safe distance. She drew Cassius's dagger from her hip, the worn hilt comforting as she followed after the creature.

The shops gave way to homes, and Thalia journeyed deeper into Irenbis. Yet the Vampyr she stalked kept going, occasionally glancing over its shoulder, a satchel gripped tightly in their hands. They moved with an urgency that bordered on panic.

Finally, after what felt like eternity, the Vampyr stopped at an unmarked house on the very outskirts of the town. The homes were a bit more run-down than those near the center, though nothing like those in the slums of Corithian.

Thalia watched from the shadows of an abandoned store as the Vampyr gave the wooden door a few quick knocks. It opened into darkness, and the Vampyr slipped inside.

Thalia counted to thirty in her head before she peeled off the building, sneaking to the door. The windows of the home were boarded up, but the glass must have been removed, because she heard soft murmuring from within.

Thalia pressed against the building, her ear against the wood.

"This won't help him!" someone inside exclaimed, followed by a loud crash of glass.

"This is all we have!" another voice whispered harshly.

"Well, it's not fucking good enough," responded the first person—a female. Her voice cracked.

"It's the prince's fault," the second voice snarled.

"You can't speak like that, Julian," the female pleaded.

Julian.

Thalia's eyes widened. What the hell was Lord Adrian's son doing all the way out here?

"I can do whatever the fuck I want, Francesca," Julian growled. "If His Highness wasn't so set on marrying that human bitch to try to cover up this whole mess, then we wouldn't be in this position."

Thalia flinched at the words, at the disgust coating Julian's tone.

"He's looking for a cure." Francesca tried to placate him.

Another soft crash echoed. "Bullshit. He's doing nothing while we have to suffer. While we have to watch our loved ones succumb to this madness."

Madness?

Thalia's brow furrowed, and she pushed closer. But the two of them seemed to be moving deeper into the house, their voices drifting away.

She pulled away, her mind spinning. Lord Amadeus had mentioned something about madness in the forest. But that didn't make any sense. They must have been talking about the Mages' wards failing. But that didn't make any sense either. *Does being in sunlight cause Vampyrs to become mad?*

Too many questions spun in Thalia's mind, but right now, she needed to get back before Cassius realized she was gone—

The hair on Thalia's neck prickled and she whirled, dagger drawn.

Only to find Cassius not six feet away, his arms crossed and his face livid.

"What the fuck are you doing out here?" Cassius growled out, eyes bright with anger.

Thalia knew better than to glance at the house she'd just been eavesdropping on. Not that it mattered, considering how quiet it'd become.

"I thought I saw something," she said, casually tucking her dagger away.

"What?" Cassius snapped.

Thalia's annoyance rose. "Nothing, apparently. Why does it even matter?"

She made to move past him, but his arm snaked out, grabbing her wrist.

"It matters"—Cassius pulled her to him, his voice low—"because you're a human."

"So you keep reminding me." Thalia struggled to shrug out of his grip, but he kept hold of her firmly.

"Just because you're married to the prince doesn't mean everyone is pleased with this treaty between the humans."

"I know," Thalia snapped, raising her eyes to his. As if her introduction to the courts hadn't made this obvious enough. She matched the anger whirling in his irises. "I thought I saw a dog with a rope stuck around its neck. I went to try and help it, but it disappeared."

Cassius studied her, his gaze so intense that Thalia was surprised she didn't catch flame. She refused to look away, to swallow past her dry tongue. To do anything that would show him she was lying. To allow any sort of sweat to dot her brow that he could scent.

"We don't have dogs in Irenbis," Cassius said after a moment.

"Well, I saw *something*," Thalia insisted.

A muscle in Cassius's jaw flickered, but he released her, taking a step away. "We should head back. We've lingered too long."

Thalia didn't falter or glance back as she moved ahead of him. Yet even when they'd gotten on their horses and were making their way back to the castle, she could have sworn more faces peeked out of the closed homes, casting their hateful gaze right on her.

Chapter Twelve

Cassius didn't question her further. Didn't call her out on her lie.

Which was fine by her.

As soon as they were back in the castle, Cassius disappeared, leaving her to fend for herself. She managed to find the books Marcus had given her, tucked in a drawer in their shared bedroom.

Thalia scowled as she pulled out the tomes, then shoved them into one of the nightstands by her bed. She'd look into them more later. Perhaps they had some sort of clue about whatever madness the Vampyrs had been discussing. But first she had a letter to write.

Thalia stared at the blank sheet of paper on her writing desk. It wasn't like correspondence had been forbidden. But she also had no doubt her letters would be read by whatever Vampyr sent them off. Which meant she'd have to be careful of how she worded her message.

Thalia dipped her quill into the ink pot, the point hovering over the page.

She set the pen down.

Thalia couldn't ever recall a time she'd written to her mother. Ever. Not even when she'd trekked halfway around Agripa on her mission. She'd never traveled far when she was a child, certainly never long enough to warrant correspondence. Thalia didn't even know how to start a letter to the queen. Did she address it *Mother*? Or should it be more formal? Would the Vampyrs suspect anything if she didn't know how to write a letter to her own blood and kin?

Your Majesty,

I am pleased to say that I've integrated myself quite nicely with the ~~monsters~~ Vampyrs here in House Lorenzia. I have yet to be introduced to my new husband, as he's been called away to the north to attend to some damage caused by storms. The courts themselves are ~~terrifying~~ foreboding and no one will tell me shit about anything. But they are for sure hiding something—

Thalia made a face, ripping up the paper before she tossed it aside and grabbing a fresh sheet.

She dipped the quill again, the ink dripping onto the wood of her desk.

Mother,

I hope things are running smoothly in Agripa now that the ore has been provided to our people. I've acclimated myself nicely into House Lorenzia. The castle is far more opulent than I was anticipating, as are the courts—

Thalia paused, making a mental note to try to figure out more of the castle layout in the morning.

—although I've yet to meet my new husband, as he was called away to the north to deal with a bad storm that hit. I truly am surprised at his willingness and the kind-hearted soul my new husband appears to have—

Thalia made a face. Was she saying too much? Would the Vampyrs even send the letter if she mentioned that the prince was away from his court? Should she try risking it anyway?

She crumpled the paper up, staining her fingers with wet ink, before she went back at it again.

Thalia hadn't realized how long she'd labored over writing the letter until the clock above the fireplace chimed the eleventh hour.

She glanced up, her eyes blurry from staring at the words on the page. They'd begun to jumble together, like a mixed bag of nuts. Thalia sighed, leaning back in her chair, and closed her eyes. She pinched the bridge of her nose, willing her sudden headache away.

The creaking of her bedchamber door had Thalia lifting her tired head. She didn't have to turn to know who had just entered.

"Can I help you?" Thalia's voice dripped with ire.

Cassius eased in, shutting the door behind him. They hadn't spoken since their outing, which had been hours ago, although it might as well have been days.

"With His Highness still gone, I am still meant to act as proxy." Cassius finally broke the silence.

Thalia's lip curled, but she knew it would be useless to fight him. Perhaps at the House meeting, she could call a vote to bypass the proxy laws, if only so she could get away from him and finally sleep in peace.

He glanced at her position at the writing desk, then to the ink dotting the surface like raindrops. "What are you doing?"

Thalia's jaw ached. "Writing a letter to my mother."

"And it's taken you all night?" He gave a pointed look at the still-full tray left by a servant for her dinner, then at the scattered, crumpled-up pieces of paper.

A retort formed on the tip of Thalia's tongue, but she shoved it aside. "I don't—I mean, I've never written my mother a letter before."

"I see."

Thalia glanced at him. He still stood by the door, the top of his doublet unbuttoned to expose the strong column of his throat. She looked away.

"Do you need help?" Cassius asked.

Thalia stiffened, her cheeks heating with embarrassment, but she forced herself to nod. *Be nice.*

Cassius came up beside her, his presence nearly engulfing her as he picked up her current letter.

She picked at her thumbs as he scanned the contents before reading them out loud. "'Mother, I hope things are well in Agripa. House Lorenzia has welcomed me with open arms, although I have yet to be introduced to my husband, as he is dealing with matters outside his court—'"

Cassius paused, and Thalia felt her chest hitch. But then he continued, "'The courts are all just as glittering and opulent as one would expect. The capital here is also just as beautiful, although I do feel as though I must do more to win the people of Irenbis over—to show them that as their new princess, despite the fact that I am human, I wish the best for both our realms. I cannot blame them for their wariness, though, nor can I blame the courts for their hesitancy in sharing their world with me. I hope to continue to earn the trust of House Lorenzia so I might better aid in the issues that this realm faces. Please give my regards to those in the castle. I hope to continue to make Agripa proud. Yours, Thalia.'"

Finally, he handed it back to her. "Why are you worried? It seems fine to me."

Thalia huffed out a laugh. "Because I don't know *how* she's going to receive it."

"She's your mother; she'll be glad to know you're safe."

Or livid that her daughter hadn't yet taken out the Vampyr courts. But at least Cassius hadn't seemed wary of any of the information she was sending. A small mercy.

Thalia chewed the inside of her cheek as Cassius moved to the bathing chamber. The sound of water running drew her in; she knew he'd turned on the sink, no doubt getting ready for bed.

Honestly, the whole proxy thing was ridiculous. Especially considering that half the prince's court wasn't even present. Thalia made a mental note to ask Camilla about that in the morning.

Thalia found herself going to the bathing chamber, stopping on the threshold. Cassius stood before the sink, his shirt off. Water ran down his face and neck, pooling into the crevices of his sculpted stomach.

"Can you send it for me tomorrow? Well, two letters—I don't know how," Thalia blurted out.

Cassius met her gaze in the mirror. "Two?"

"I wrote one for Katrina." The mention of her handmaiden sent a pang of loneliness through her stomach. She'd been a bit more honest in that letter. Well, at least about how horrible it was to be near Cassius again. How she hadn't managed to find a . . . friend to confide in. Gods, maybe she shouldn't send that letter; it bordered on pathetic.

"You don't know how to send a letter?" Cassius interrupted her thoughts.

She rolled her eyes. "Not here I don't."

Cassius snorted but nodded, going back to what he was doing. It took Thalia a moment to realize he was applying ointment to a cut on his arm.

She started. "What happened?"

Cassius glanced up at her again. "Nothing."

Thalia was already across the bathing chamber. "That looks like it's barely healing; it's not *nothing*. When did this happen?"

Cassius applied more ointment to the cut. "Yesterday."

"How?"

Cassius sighed, muttering to himself before he turned to her, his eyes flashing in annoyance. "A dog."

"You said there aren't dogs here—"

"Exactly."

It took Thalia a moment to realize what he'd said. "Oh, I get it, is this because of what happened earlier?"

Cassius washed his hands meticulously.

"Really, Cassius? What are we, twelve?"

He turned off the water, drying his hands on a towel. "Considering that you don't trust me enough to share information, why should I share anything with you?"

Oh, the prick was *hurt*. Thalia would have laughed if she weren't so pissed off.

Cassius moved into the bedroom, aiming for the settee.

She trailed after him. "I told you I saw *something*."

He sank onto the couch, facing her. "And I've told you, you're a bad liar." Thalia's jaw ached from clenching it so hard as Cassius grabbed a discarded blanket. "Good night, Thalia."

Then he turned over, pulling the blanket up to his chin.

Prick.

Her annoyance only grew as she got ready for bed, turned out the lights, and crawled between the sheets. But she kept the curtains open, only so she could see Cassius's form on the settee, his back to her.

She knew he wasn't asleep. And maybe because darkness concealed them and her mind still hummed with questions, she asked, "How did you become hand to the prince?"

Cassius shifted to face her. "Because the prince knew what I'd done before."

Yes. He'd been captain of the guard, and he was the one who'd trained Reina and the rest of the soldiers in the palace. He had talked with her about how they might defeat the enemy in the north. Cassius, who'd promised to be by her side till the end. Even when an offer of marriage came from a human prince in a far-off territory with the promise of armies, he understood. Because her duty—her need to see her father's and sister's deaths avenged—came first. Even though it very nearly killed her to accept that marriage proposal.

But Cassius hadn't understood after all.

Because the night he'd turned, he'd come to the castle and killed the very man who would have saved Agripa.

"And he trusted you that readily?" Thalia pushed aside the emotions clogging her throat, the rage that was as dark as the room.

"I couldn't stay in the human realm after it happened. I think the prince realized I had nothing left to lose."

Because even if he hadn't committed such a heinous crime, he didn't have any family left. He had nothing left in Agripa, except her. She'd thought she was his family. She and Marcus and Reina.

But apparently the gods had decided the sentiment was a joke. Because her true family would never have done what he did. Would never have betrayed her so readily.

She still couldn't stomach asking him how it happened, how he'd even come upon a Vampyr in Agripa and gotten turned. Instead, she said, "Is that couch comfortable?"

Cassius grunted. "No. It's like sleeping on a hard plank."

Thalia couldn't help the smile that quirked her lips. "A shame we're still bound and you have to sleep in here."

"A shame considering I still have two weeks on this thing."

"The prince won't return sooner?"

"I haven't gotten word that he will. Trust me, as soon as he's back, this will all be over."

Thalia picked at her nails under the covers, her mind churning and churning. The prince wouldn't return anytime soon. Which left her with nothing. No way to figure out how to get closer to the very creatures who mistrusted her as much as she mistrusted them. And how could she destroy the courts if she couldn't get close to them? Unless . . .

A terrible, twisted, partially selfish plan began to form in her mind. One that might just allow her to learn more about this world and complete her mission—to stir up discourse and cause the Vampyrs to turn on one another.

"Well, two weeks on a plank doesn't seem like it's going to do anyone any favors," she finally said.

"What do you mean?"

Thalia rolled her eyes, even though he couldn't see her. "You sleeping so poorly explains a lot. It's no wonder you've been such a prick."

"*I've* been a prick?"

"Yes you have."

"Then I apologize, Princess. I'll try to be less of a prick while sleeping on this bed of nails."

More shuffling ensued, as if Cassius was trying to get comfortable. Thalia took a deep breath, then blurted out. "You can sleep here."

The silence felt too deafening, and she suddenly wished she hadn't even suggested it. Shit, this was a terrible plan.

"Sleep with you?" Cassius's voice echoed.

"We're stuck together for two weeks. I'd rather deal with a rested, happy Cassius than a prick. Besides, it's not like proxies don't share a bed. In fact, I think it's encouraged, considering the binding oath we've taken."

More silence followed, and Thalia thought Cassius would simply refuse her until soft footsteps padded toward her.

She didn't move, didn't turn to watch as he slid into the bed beside her, the mattress dipping slightly.

"Still sleeping on the right side," Cassius said after he'd settled beside her.

Thalia's heart rate climbed at his nearness, the scent of him enveloping her, as did the heat of his body. Fuck, she'd forgotten he'd gone to bed shirtless.

"Still being a prick," she snapped.

Cassius chuckled low. "My apologies, Princess."

Thalia swallowed, the sound audible. Carefully, she hedged, "What else is going on with the Houses? What other sort of issues does the prince need to know about but can't since he isn't here?"

"Why are you so keen to know?" Cassius said cautiously.

"Because this is going to be my home, and I want to know the affairs of my kingdom."

Cassius chuckled. "You've been quick to step into the role of princess."

"Camilla's been a wonderful help."

"Camilla needs to learn to keep her mouth shut."

"What do you have against her?"

"Nothing, but she schemes as much as you do, and I'm already spread thin as it is."

"How hard it must be for you as hand to the prince," Thalia mocked.

"You have no idea, Princess." Cassius's words brushed against her lips. Thalia's eyes widened, her heart rate spiking for a different reason. Cassius stared at her as if he didn't have a care in the world. As if he didn't realize how close they lay, where one tilt of Thalia's head would bring her lips to his.

"You should get some sleep," he finally murmured, the sound as dark and deep as the shadows gathered in the corners of the room. Cassius pulled away, turning his back to her.

Silence pressed in, and Thalia nearly flew out of her skin when Cassius closed his hand over hers.

"Stop," he said. Thalia turned, finding his attention on her. She'd been picking at her skin, the flesh snagging as she dug deep.

His eyes glowed softly in the night, his dark hair falling across his sharp cheekbones. He gave her hand a squeeze. "Sleep, Thalia."

She swallowed as he gently squeezed her hand again, letting go. He turned his back to her, somehow falling asleep quicker than she'd anticipated, his chest rising and falling in deep slumber.

Something about the image caused tears to spring to Thalia's eyes and she looked away, blinking rapidly so they wouldn't fall.

But she didn't sleep.

When morning came, her thumbs were a mangled mess.

Chapter Thirteen

"What can you tell me about each House?" Thalia asked Camilla. The woman watched her as she dug through the castle library.

As soon as Thalia had woken the next morning, she'd rung for a servant, who'd directed her to the castle library, the space boasting large aisles and hidden nooks filled with old tomes and rolled-up scrolls.

She'd just found a map of the inner workings of the castle and snuck it into her pocket when Camilla found her.

"What do you want to know?" Camilla asked, studying her. She sat at one of the desks, dressed in a black velvet gown. She lounged in the chair like a cat, the desk next to her laden with all sorts of books and other paraphernalia.

"What do the symbols mean for each House?"

Camilla raised a well-groomed brow. "You weren't taught about them?"

Thalia paused, looking up from where she'd pulled out a book from a bookcase. "We were. But I was young when the treaty between our people fell. I'll admit, after what happened—" Thalia strangled the anger rising in her gut. The sudden image of her father and sister cooling on the throne room floor. "I didn't care to keep up with my knowledge of this realm."

Thalia just prayed it wouldn't be her downfall. If she'd known where she'd land—in a marriage to a Vampyr prince—she wouldn't have let her rage brush aside valuable information.

Camilla's long nails ticked on the wooden desk, but she didn't respond, so Thalia added, "I should know what the symbol of my own House means."

Camilla finally stopping her tapping. "The raven with three eyes represents unity and stability."

Thalia chewed the inside of her cheek. It made sense, given that House Lorenzia oversaw all the rest of the courts. "And the others?"

Camilla rose, gesturing for her to follow. Thalia trailed after the woman, the darkness of the aisles deepening as they walked farther into the library until they came upon the back wall. A large tapestry took up almost the whole expanse of it, depicting the emblems of the five Vampyr Houses stitched in their respective colors.

The raven with three eyes embroidered in silver seemed to watch her with keen interest.

"House Avanerius," Camilla said, her dark hand pointing to the ram's head with four horns. "Represents strength and protection." Indeed, Lord Damien seemed surprisingly eager to ensure his world was protected. "House Santorien"—Camilla gestured toward the blue ampithere—"represents balance and harmony. You'll find they're the more . . . level-headed of the courts, eager to keep everyone on good terms."

Thalia tucked the information away.

"And the other two?" Thalia asked.

"House Gallinus represents power and freedom, and House Olvectus"—Camilla paused, staring at the fox with multiple teeth stitched in orange—"represents transformation."

Thalia turned to her. "When were you going to tell me you're a shifter?"

Camilla raised an approving brow. "Figured out what I am finally?" She nodded. "Does that information disturb you?"

Thalia shrugged. "It's not like I had prior knowledge about what you were before this. Can't say I've really dwelled on it."

Camilla snorted.

"How close are the Houses with each other?" Thalia asked. "I mean, Cassius told me that the shifters were made by the Mages. I assume, giving you reside in Lorceium, the shifters are a part of House Olvectus."

Camilla crossed her arms over her chest. "It seems Cassius told you a lot."

Thalia's brows narrowed at that. "He was surprisingly helpful when I had questions about my new kingdom."

Camilla still didn't seem to trust her, and fine, Thalia couldn't blame her. But the shifter seemed to realize that Thalia was her princess now, because she relented. "It depends on the House. Some are on better terms than the others. But they all answer to House Lorenzia."

Thalia knew as much from her conversation with Lord Damien. But if the Vampyr courts were anything like the humans', there was always some manner of discord. Perhaps she could use that to her advantage . . .

"And given the history between the shifters and the Vampyrs, there's not any . . . bad blood?"

Camilla cast her a wary look. "No. Not anymore. The shifters and Vampyrs have coexisted for hundreds of years, since the rise of the Houses."

Thalia let it go, it would do no good to keep prodding, given the expression on Camilla's face. She changed topics. "Any word on His Highness?"

"I don't know. You'd have to ask Cassius."

"But aren't you on the prince's council? Shouldn't you know?"

"He tends to keep a lot of the communication between him and Cassius," Camilla admitted.

Thalia couldn't keep the scowl from her face. Yes, it did seem that way. In fact, before she'd gone to the library, she'd found a note from Cassius informing her that the letter and gift on her desk were from the prince. This time she'd received a beautiful bridle for Feryena. Perhaps Cassius had informed the prince of her love of riding.

Cassius had the power that he'd always seemed so desperately to crave, given that he practically ran House Lorenzia in the prince's absence. A part of her felt his betrayal even now. She knew he'd been angry with the queen before, regarding her lack of action against the war and the dwindling ore. He'd watched his father abuse his mother, had been forced to try to dig his family's name out of the mud, to be seen as something other than a minor lord's son . . . but did he have to go to these extremes? Her stomach twisted.

Camilla noted the change in her mood. "You knew Cassius before, didn't you?"

Thalia's fingernails pierced her palms. "I did."

"I take it that him turning into a Vampyr was not expected."

Thalia let out a bitter laugh. "No."

Camilla studied her a beat longer. "Cassius might be an ass on occasion, but he doesn't do anything without cause."

"And you know him so well?" Thalia snapped. Her mind flashed to how fondly Camilla had spoken of him in her room. There was no denying that Camilla was beautiful, alluring. And she had power, given her status on the prince's council. She and Cassius were equals. All Thalia had ever been able to give him was a spot in the shadows. Because even if she'd married that prince back in Agripa, she would have found a way to still be with Cassius—to make him her lover.

Perhaps he'd finally gotten sick of standing on the sidelines.

Camilla's face flashed in surprise before turning hard. "I have been working closely with him for four years. Everything he has done, as asinine as it is, is meant to help our prince and the people of Vaccarium."

Thalia's lip curled, and she stepped into the shifter's space. "And I knew him for *years*. He served *me*. And what he did was without cause."

Camilla's golden eyes burned with some sort of fire as the two women faced off. "Perhaps you should ask Cassius what the price was in betraying you."

"I don't care what his price was," Thalia seethed.

Camilla's face became stone. "Everyone who lives in this world pays a price. Even you."

"Is that a threat?"

Camilla didn't back down. "Call it council."

Thalia's jaw ached. "I wish to hold court."

Camilla blinked. "What?"

"Court. I wish to hold court. Does the prince not do this when he's here?"

Camilla's eyes narrowed. "We hold court. Are you sure you want to do this?"

"If I wanted your *council*, I would have asked. Summon House Lorenzia."

"Where is the rest of House Lorenzia?" Thalia asked. She and Camilla stood in the great hall, watching the other members of House Lorenzia mill about. "Is this everyone?"

Camilla at least had done her job in summoning the court, although it had taken the rest of the afternoon to do so. But with the lack of Vampyrs, maybe a few had decided to ignore the summons.

"House Lorenzia has always kept a small court. The prince has never liked to have that many Vampyrs around—prefers to keep things small and quiet," Camilla answered, pulling Thalia from her thoughts.

Well, at least they'd deigned to heed the request of their new princess. Indeed, it seemed only a few members from the other Houses were even present. Thalia noted Lord Damien along with Keegan, which wasn't surprising considering they were part of the prince's council. But she also saw Lord Adrian, the lord of House Gallinus. He seemed to have lingered in Irenbis even after their altercation. Perhaps he hadn't gotten help from Cassius like he wished.

"Where do they all stay?" Thalia asked, taking a sip from her goblet. It had taken her a few moments to try the liquid, but when she had, she was glad to find it was wine, not blood—although she was sure the rest of the Vampyrs present didn't share the sentiment. At least food had been cobbled together and distributed about the space, including steaming braised ducks and tureens full of jewel-like fruit.

"They have their own residences outside the castle. Not many like to stay here."

"I'm surprised they haven't fallen for its homely charm," Thalia commented.

Camilla snorted, taking a drink from her own glass.

"I don't think most like staying here."

"Why is that?"

Camilla shrugged. "The castle is cold."

Thalia didn't think that was half of it, but she spotted one sole member of House Olvectus, judging by the orange fox with multiple teeth stitched onto their doublet. The shifters and Vampyrs might be on good terms now, but maybe Thalia could find some buried discord still among them.

Everyone pays a price.

Despite the tension between her and Camilla having eased since the library, the shifter's words festered in Thalia's gut.

What was Thalia's price?

To be sold off and bound to the very man who'd betrayed everything he'd ever said he loved and fought for. To be tasked with the impossible mission of taking down the creatures that could kill her in seconds. And this mysterious prince she was married to conveniently being called away didn't help matters.

"When will the prince return?" Thalia got out.

Camilla didn't bat an eye. "I don't know. He's still trying to find a solution for the drought in the east."

Thalia's heart stuttered. "I thought he was up north."

Camilla stiffened, sliding her gaze to hers. "Yes, he was up north, but he moved east. Another storm came in."

Thalia forced her face to remain neutral, even though her heart pounded in her throat. Camilla had just lied to her face. Something else was going on with the prince. Thalia set her goblet down on one of the banquet tables. "Does any of this have to do with what's going on?"

Camilla glanced at her cautiously. "What do you mean?"

Thalia looked around the room. The courts were quiet, and she hadn't spotted Cassius the whole evening. In fact, he'd been missing the entire day. "About the barrier?"

Camilla stared at her a moment longer. Her eyes shifted. "You'll have to ask Cassius."

The prince wasn't dealing with a storm, that much was certain. But Thalia let it go, tucking the information away just as a Vampyr with a blue ampithere stitched on his chest walked past.

"Lord Amadeus," Thalia said, and the lord of House Santorien faltered. He turned on his heel to face her, a silver goblet in hand.

"Princess." The Vampyr inclined his dark head. "You summoned court." It wasn't really a question.

Thalia forced a smile. "In Agripa, my mother holds court weekly. I thought it would be a nice way to show the merging of our kingdoms, especially with the prince still away."

Lord Amadeus seemed to wince at the thought. "Indeed."

But the Vampyr wasn't running away, and Camilla had been pulled into a conversation with a servant asking where to put the roasted boar, so Thalia took a step nearer to him. "I do hope your concerns were eased about the forest."

Lord Amadeus's golden eyes flashed. "Has a solution been achieved, then?"

Thalia's heart hammered in her throat. She willed her nerves to calm, to slow her heartbeat so the Vampyr wouldn't suspect anything. "The rivers would have reached your springs by now; there is no need to worry about the forest dying."

"Oh . . . yes, that matter." Lord Amadeus shifted, eyes glancing around the room.

"Is there something else that's wrong with the forest?" Thalia pushed. But his attention wasn't on her; it was on Lord Adrian staring at them from across the hall. "Lord Amadeus?"

Lord Amadeus jerked his attention back to hers. "Forgive me." Then he bowed and walked away.

"What was that?" Camilla's voice sounded loudly behind her.

Thalia shrugged, taking a sip of her goblet only so her hands wouldn't shake. "Nothing. Just reassuring him that Agripa released the waters for the forest."

Camilla gave her an odd look, but before the shifter could question her, Thalia nodded to where Lord Adrian had been pulled into a conversation with Julian and a female with red eyes and long dark hair. "Who's that?"

Camilla followed her eyeline. "Francesca. She's from House Avanerius. Julian's lover."

Julian, who was hiding something in that house in Irenbis.

The green-eyed Vampyr caught her stare. His brows narrowed at her attention, his jaw clenching. They hadn't spoken since her introduction to the courts. Given the death glare he cast at her, she didn't think they'd be speaking anytime soon. But he was hiding something. They all were—something suspicious enough that her mother would probably kill to find out what.

And Thalia was tired of not knowing what they were keeping from her. She winced suddenly, pressing a hand to her temple.

"Are you all right?" Camilla asked, brows knotting.

Thalia shook her head. "If you'll excuse me, I-I seem to have a headache. I think I'll lie down for a bit."

Camilla frowned, but nodded her acknowledgment as Thalia slipped from the great hall. But instead of aiming toward her room, Thalia went in search of the stables.

Chapter Fourteen

Thalia crept through the quiet city of Irenbis, the hood of her cloak drawn up to mask her features.

Cassius had lied about its citizens coming out after dark. Because it was just as dead quiet in the moonlight as when she'd gone in the afternoon.

Another lie to add to her ever-growing list.

The homes were all shut, no lights shining into the cobblestone streets. It was thoroughly silent and still. Her only company was the moon as she crept to the boarded-up house.

Thalia glanced over her shoulder, but nothing prickled at the back of her neck like she was being watched. She didn't think Julian or Francesca would be in the house. When she'd left the great hall, they'd been thoroughly engrossed with whatever the courts were discussing.

Thalia eased up to the door, pressing her ear against the worn wood. Silence echoed. She slipped the knife out of her boot, placing it into the crack of the doorframe, then she pushed.

The lock broke and the door creaked open, swinging inward to reveal an empty living area. Thalia took a moment, counting in her head to see if anyone would come and investigate. When nothing jumped at her from the shadows, she slipped inside.

The room she entered was bare save for a few broken pieces of wood and littered glass shards. A worn rug had been thrown over a spot in the back of the room with a rickety table set on top of it. It was a small space with the remnants of a kitchen off to her left, and there was a closed door at the back—the only door in the room.

Thalia took a breath, keeping her grip loose as she tiptoed on silent feet to the closed door. Once more she pressed her ear to the wood but was met with quiet. She pushed open the door.

The room was just as bare as the rest of the house, although it seemed someone had dumped a sack of grain in the corner and its contents had spilled onto the floor. A bed with its mattress fallen through, its springs and stuffing exposed, was the only piece of furniture. A family of mice seemed to have made their home in the decaying cloth, because they all startled at her approach.

Thalia bit down on her tongue as they all bolted past, scurrying over her boots in the process.

She willed her heart rate to slow as she looked around. There was nothing here. Not even a dresser or desk. She scowled. There had been a third person in the house, she knew it. Someone who needed help based on the Vampyrs' previous conversation. Something to do with *madness*.

Thalia stalked back into the main room to see if she'd missed something, but there was nothing. No other room, no other furniture.

A high-pitched squeak echoed, and Thalia ducked as something dark flew near her head.

"Fuck," she hissed, dropping her knife as the bat who'd been nesting in the rafters let out another strange pitch. Her knife had fallen near the crumbling table. She moved to pick it up, and froze.

The corner of the rug had been lifted, revealing wooden planks that didn't match the stone floor of the house.

Thalia shoved the table to the side, flipping back the rug. Her heart pounded in her throat at the trapdoor staring back at her.

Thalia carefully eased it open, and musky, dank air floated up to her. The opening revealed a set of stone steps leading down into pitch black.

She cursed again, looking around to see if there was anything to light her way. Nothing. Not even a torch.

Thalia stared into the dark, willing her eyes to adjust. She could have sworn that at the very bottom of the steps, there was a gray haze of light. Against her better judgment, she took a step down.

Thalia kept one hand on the wall as she slowly crept down the staircase. The musky, wet smell intensified, and Thalia resisted the urge to gag as something rotten hit her nose, like the stench of decaying meat. But a soft glow lit the bottom of the stairs. Her eyes took a moment to adjust to the dim light.

The space she entered was much larger than the house above her. But unlike the house, it wasn't bare.

An empty metal cage stood at the back of the room. The bars looked as though they'd been ripped off their hinges, and chains lay discarded inside. The sole source of light came from an odd lamp against the wall. It glowed faintly, like a drop of moonlight had been captured and placed within the glass.

Lumpy sacks were piled up in the other corner. A substance oozed from the bottoms of them, coating the dirt ground like oil, and a figure was hunched over the sacks.

The smell worsened as Thalia stepped deeper into the room, trying to make sense of what she saw.

The figure—a person—was rummaging around the sacks, pale fingers flying over them before discarding them without care.

Thalia covered her mouth against the smell. Squelching and slurping sounds echoed from around the person.

What are they doing here? Are they being held hostage by the Vampyrs?

Everything in her screamed to get out, but Thalia took another step forward, and her boot scuffed against something she hadn't seen in the shadows. She slowly looked down, bile rising to her throat.

It was a leg. A skinned leg ending in a hoof, the tendons hanging off the bone like strips of cloth.

The slurping stopped.

Thalia's eyes jerked up as the figure kneeling slowly rose. The person was naked, their fingertips dripping in blood as they turned.

Thalia's stomach bottomed out as the Vampyr's hazy gaze met hers. Sores covered his entire body, as though his own nails had scrabbled at his flesh until it ripped apart. His mouth was a gory mess, bits of meat hanging from his bloody lips, and his nostrils flared once. Then twice.

Thalia's heart beat so hard she feared her chest would cleave open.

The Vampyr smiled through the mangled mess of his mouth, revealing sharp fangs—

Thalia bolted.

The Vampyr let out an eerie screech, his scream rattling the room.

Thalia flew up the stairs two at a time, ignoring the way her shins barked as they slammed against stone.

Her palms slickened as she dragged herself to the top, whirling to grab the trapdoor. She slammed it down just as the Vampyr's upper body broke the surface.

It screamed as it scrambled to pull itself out from the wooden planks.

The Vampyr's hand wrapped around her boot, fingernails biting even through the thickness of the leather. The creature snarled, foaming blood flying from its mouth.

Thalia placed all her weight on the planks, trying to get the thing back into the hidden room. The wood groaned under her weight, splinters biting into her palms.

Shit. Shit. Shit.

Thalia kicked the leg the Vampyr gripped, hoping to dislodge the creature. Its teeth gnashed, bringing her leg ever closer to its mouth.

Thalia screamed, picking up the trapdoor and slamming it as hard as she could on the Vampyr's back.

The wood splintered, but the Vampyr didn't let go.

Thalia sobbed, slamming the wood down again and again on the creature's spine. The Vampyr didn't even seem to feel the blows.

It yanked on her leg—hard.

The world slipped out from under her feet. Thalia's head slammed against the hard floor. The weight on her leg sent pure panic racing through her bloodstream. She used her free leg to kick the Vampyr in its face.

It wailed, blood spurting from its broken nose and its mashed-in mouth. Then it pulled Thalia, yanking her across the ground.

Thalia tried to twist, but its grip was iron. It latched on to her boot with both hands. Thalia watched in horror as the Vampyr brought its mouth to her leathered sole.

Thalia kicked it again, and her foot slipped out of its boot. The Vampyr reeled back at the lack of weight in its hands, and Thalia scrambled backward.

The Vampyr discarded her boot, staring at her as it crawled on all fours out of the stairwell.

Thalia's heart jumped like a hare, nausea mixing with the growing panic in her veins.

She didn't know where her knife was, what had happened to it in the scuffle—

The Vampyr's broken face smiled again as it scuttled ever closer.

Thalia whimpered, frozen in terror, as the Vampyr inched over her cowering body.

Its smile was a thing of grotesque beauty. Its red-tipped fingers trailed over her face, leaving a path of blood in its place.

"*Hunger*," the Vampyr rasped. Thalia trembled as its fingers gripped her throat. "*Hunger!*" it roared. Then it reared back, clutching its head. "*Hunger!*" the Vampyr screamed, ripping at its hair. It scrabbled at its flesh, tearing more holes into its skin, as if its very bones were liquifying.

"*Hunger—*"

Blood sprayed over Thalia as a dagger embedded in the Vampyr's open mouth.

Thalia jerked back as Cassius appeared, his sword drawn and an iron stake in hand—her iron stake.

The Vampyr touched the dagger in its mouth, its hazy eyes wide. Then Cassius shoved the stake right through the Vampyr's skull. The creature crumbled to the ground like a broken marionette, its skin turning to ash.

"You killed him!" someone screamed behind her, and Thalia twisted just as two other figures appeared in the doorway of the house.

Thalia managed to scramble out of the way as Francesca stumbled into the home, Julian at her heels.

Cassius said nothing as he withdrew the stake, his gaze harsh. Tears ran down Francesca's cheeks, but she faltered as Cassius faced her, his features holding nothing but lethal rage.

"How long?" Cassius got out.

Francesca swallowed, paling, but she said nothing.

"Don't make me ask again," Cassius snarled.

Julian came up to Francesca's side. "Near two weeks."

Cassius let out a dark chuckle, one Thalia had never heard before. "Do you know what you risked? What you allowed by keeping him alive?"

"We were hoping to find a cure." Francesca's voice trembled.

"The *prince*," Julian spat, disgust evident in his tone, "is taking too long."

Cassius's eyes darkened as he stepped near them, his face an unbreakable mask of granite. Francesca shook and Julian stiffened, but Cassius brushed past them. Thalia was still sprawled on the ground, and Cassius sank onto his heels at her side.

"Did he bite you?" Again there was that lethal voice.

Thalia shook her head no.

Cassius stood, turning his back to the two Vampyrs. "What you have done is treason. You have endangered the life of not only the prince's bride—and through her risked the treaty with the humans—but also you have put every single Vampyr in this city at risk. Get out of here. And if you ever step foot in Vaccarium again, your lives will be forfeit."

Chapter Fifteen

Cassius pulled her into their bathing chamber.

He shut the door, his back to her, dirty fingers splayed out against the surface. Blood crusted under his nails.

Thalia didn't want to look in the mirror to see how she fared.

Cassius jerked his chin to the tub, an indication for her to sit. She did as he asked.

He grabbed a rag, wetting it before coming before her. He knelt, his face harsh, and took her hands in his. Thalia swallowed as he began to clean the blood and dirt from her fingers.

"What was that thing?" Thalia croaked, breaking the silence that'd fallen. Cassius didn't look up, swiping the rag over her palms. "Cassius?"

Maybe it was the slight plea in her tone that had his gaze meeting hers. "A sick Vampyr."

Thalia stared at him. "What do you mean, sick?"

"Vampyrs get sick just as humans do."

Thalia couldn't interpret his words. "That doesn't make sense. That—that thing was insane."

Cassius shook his head, his dark hair sliding with the movement. He broke her gaze, his attention returning to her hands. He began to dig out the slivers of splinters from her flesh as he said quietly but not weakly, "There's a sickness that's been spreading. But we've kept it contained."

"Have you?" She hissed in pain as he dug out a particularly large sliver.

Cassius paused his ministrations, and Thalia glanced at him. "The sickness spreads easily amongst our kind. Which is why those who are found sick are removed from society until they are better. This sickness is not one that concerns you."

"It should concern me considering that thing nearly killed me!"

He didn't answer, just wrapped a strip of bandage around her palms, quickly and efficiently.

"Are there more who are sick?" Thalia asked when he still refused to speak.

"A few, but it is being handled." Cassius tied the bandage tight, and Thalia hissed again. "What the fuck were you doing out there?"

Thalia lifted her chin, cradling her bandaged hand to her chest. "I told you before, I saw something. Since no one was inclined to tell me anything, I went to go see for myself."

"And you didn't think there was a reason we aren't telling you things?" Cassius sneered.

"Fuck. You."

She stormed out of the bathing chamber, her anger as palpable as the creature Cassius had killed.

"Oh no you don't." Cassius grabbed her arm, halting her in her tracks before she could leave the room. "You don't get to storm away just because you're pissed off."

"Let go of me before I put my dagger through your heart. Again."

"You mean my dagger?"

"If you want it so badly, feel free to take it," she crooned.

Cassius smirked. "If you think I'd disarm you so readily, you mistake me greatly."

"Mistake you?" Thalia scoffed. "I don't think I've mistaken you, not for a moment." She jerked out of his grip.

She moved to the door, but Cassius was there, hand splayed out on the wood. Damn him and his speed. "You're not leaving this room."

Rage bridled her tongue. "Oh no? And are you going to stop me?"

Cassius flashed a cruel smirk. "It won't be hard."

Thalia stormed over to him. "Move out of the way."

"No."

"I outrank *you*. Considering how much you care about your position on the prince's council, it would be unwise to refuse me."

"Your rank means nothing when you put yourself in danger."

"Danger?" she scoffed. "I decided to leave the castle, as I am free to do as *princess* of this House."

"You decided," Cassius snarled, "to nearly get yourself killed."

"Then you should have let that creature do it. I'm sure it would have saved you the headache."

Cassius's eyes darkened. "The prince will return soon, and I'd rather not be the one to get staked because you got bored."

"Bored?" Thalia gawked. "Have you ever thought about what it's like for me? To be here? To be surrounded by monsters who'd rather see me dead? Who no doubt picture ripping out my throat every waking moment?"

"So why did you seek one of us out?"

"So I could escape you!" Thalia screamed. "So I could get a moment's peace away from *you*."

Cassius's face was stone, his fingertips digging so hard into the door the wood groaned.

"When will you accept the fact that I'm still me and not some monster you've conjured up?"

Thalia stared at him in shock. "Still . . . *you*?" The muscle in Cassius's jaw flickered as she took a step closer. "You are nothing like the man I knew."

"And the man you loved?"

Thalia's heart twisted as if he'd just shoved his dagger into it. "He died on the rug in my bedroom."

Cassius's eyes roved over her face, the blue so stark it faintly glowed. He took a step closer to her. "Do you want to finally know what happened that day?"

Thalia's rage spiked. She shut it down. Shoved it under the sea of whirling regret in her stomach. "I know what happened."

Surprise flared in Cassius's eyes before it was gone. "What happened?"

She tilted her head. "You chose the coward's path."

Cassius shook his head, his burnished hair brushing against his shoulders. "I chose to *live*."

Thalia's face twisted. "Live? As this?"

Cassius's face darkened. "It was either that or dying."

"Then you should have died!" Thalia's chest heaved. She knew she should be quiet. Should be cautious of the other Vampyrs in the castle who could no doubt hear her, but emotions bombarded her senses, overwhelming her nerves as she stared at the man who'd ruined himself. "You are pathetic. A worthless, immoral creature who should have done the honorable thing and died before turning into one of *them*. But you were a coward. A weak, dishonest piece of shit who should have just turned his blade toward his own heart—"

He moved so fast Thalia didn't realize what was happening until slight pressure on her throat made her freeze.

Cassius had pinned her against the door, his blood-crusted hands gripping her arms as his teeth pressed against her artery. Not enough to draw blood, but with enough force that she couldn't move.

Her heart was a riotous beat in her chest. Her pulse fluttered like a bird caught in a cage. She could barely think as Cassius slowly released the pressure on her throat, but he didn't move.

Didn't so much as shift backward as he said lowly, "Pathetic? Worthless?" Thalia swallowed, and Cassius's lips trailed her throat. "An immoral creature?"

Thalia began to tremble. She wasn't sure if it was from fear or from his nearness. His very presence consumed her, engulfing her like a flame. She wished she had air in her lungs, only so she could gasp as his nose skimmed the sensitive skin of her jaw.

"I have morals, Princess." He let out a dark chuckle. "Should we talk about them? Do you know what my morals tell me? They tell me to ignore all the wicked things that I imagine in my head."

His hand traveled up her arm, scorching her collarbone as he brushed a strand of hair from her neck. "My morals tell me that I shouldn't give in," he said lowly. "That despite the fact that I can *feel* your blood as it runs through your veins, I have to ignore it. But it calls to me like a song. It begs for me to get a taste. Your heart *beats* for me. And being in your presence, the idea of tasting your flesh again, it's driving me insane."

Thalia gripped his arms, hardly breathing as he tilted his head. "Do you know what else my morals say?"

She couldn't speak, could barely give an acknowledgment as his lips brushed ever so slightly against the place he'd bitten.

"My morals tell me to let you go. That you are now bound to someone else. That you belong to *him*."

"I belong to no one." Her words were breathless; they didn't hold the weight she intended. Cassius pulled back, his burning eyes going straight to her parted mouth.

"You have no idea what it's like to be near you. To feel your hatred. To burn in it."

And she did hate him. But the words to shred him apart didn't form on her tongue. Not as the burning in his eyes deepened, his gaze flicking to the bruised spot on her neck.

Something flashed in Cassius's eyes. He let go of her suddenly, cold air rushing between them.

Cassius ran a hand through his hair, seeming to compose himself, his change in behavior more shocking than being doused in ice. "You are to stay in the castle until further notice. You may outrank me, but as hand, I speak on behalf of His Highness, who outranks *you*." He met her blazing stare. "This world is a dangerous place, Thalia. You'd be wise to heed its warnings."

Chapter Sixteen

"There's an informal council meeting today," Camilla said, watching as Thalia got dressed the next morning.

Thalia looked up from where she was getting wrangled into a gown. "Oh?"

Camilla nodded, noting the dark smudges that had appeared under Thalia's eyes. "Not all the Houses will be present, but House Avanerius wanted to discuss who will be the next lord. Would you like to attend?"

Yes, that had been her plan all along. To attend council meetings so she might better begin building connections within the court. So she might find a weakness among the Houses and exploit them.

"Will I even be welcomed, considering my position is merely a formality?" *Not to mention the prince still isn't here?*

Camilla shrugged. "You may be a human, but you are the princess. Whether the other courts like it or not, you are now part of House Lorenzia."

Thalia chewed the inside of her cheek, debating. On one hand, it would be a prime time to learn more about the Houses. On the other hand . . . Cassius would be there.

She hadn't spoken to him since he'd pinned her against the door. Annoyance pulsed in her stomach in time with the throbbing in her neck from the bruise that marred her throat.

"Well?" Camilla asked, breaking through her thoughts.

Thalia nodded as the servant stepped back. "Yes, I would like to attend."

Camilla gave a half smile. "I should warn you . . . these council meetings can get rather intense."

"So can humans'."

Camilla raised a well-groomed brow, smoothing her hands over her purple satin gown. "Are you on the human council?"

Thalia nodded. "Yes, but my mother likes to keep her circle small. She only has a few advisers, and she relies on one more than the others." Thalia's mind flashed to Kamith. She resisted making a face as she continued, "But even if she had more, I'm not sure if she'd listen to them."

"Why is that?"

Thalia fiddled with the brocade of her own dress, the gown dripping in gold applique over black satin. "I don't know. She hasn't had it easy being queen. Too many men have already tried to usurp her. Better to keep her circle close." She shut her mouth. Talking to Camilla had started slipping dangerously close to being . . . friendly. And she couldn't allow that.

Camilla pursed her lips, not seeming to notice Thalia's sudden silence. The shifter shrugged. "Well, prepare for a lot of usurping today, because despite what you've seen with a human council, there is something far more dangerous about a Vampyrs'."

Thalia expected to be whisked away to the council room, the only room she hadn't acquainted herself with, but instead they gathered in the great hall. A circle of chairs had been placed in the middle of the room, and the back walls were lined with silver goblets of blood and glittering fruit.

Thalia braced herself to face Cassius, but to her surprise, the prick wasn't there. In fact, the only Vampyrs on the prince's council who were present were Camilla and Lord Damien.

"Princess." Lord Damien inclined his head. Thalia resisted the urge to shiver at his red eyes. "Welcome."

"Where's Cassius?" Thalia said, and immediately regretted it when Camilla raised a brow.

"The prince has him dealing with another matter," the lord said smoothly.

She made a face at that, but she remained quiet as she took a spot in the circle of chairs next to Camilla. More Vampyrs trickled in, and Thalia braced herself when Lord Adrian appeared. As soon as the lord saw her, his lip curled, sharp fangs exposed.

Thalia didn't allow herself to cower.

"Welcome," Lord Damien said as the Vampyrs took their seats. "We appreciate you all for coming. House Avanerius has called this meeting to discuss the current seat which is up."

Thalia felt the stares of the Vampyrs searing her face. She ignored them.

"Well?" Lord Adrian said, his annoyance already evident. "Let's hurry this along so we can end this meeting."

"You seem to have more pressing things to attend to," Camilla said dryly.

Lord Adrian's lip curled again. It was surprising that his face hadn't frozen like that. "You know I do."

Interesting.

Lord Damien cleared his throat, drawing the attention of the room. "My father was voted by the rest of House Avanerius to take up the role of lord."

Thalia glanced up at the Vampyr who stepped forward. He looked nearly the same as his son, although a touch of age graced his smooth face. He must have traveled from his capital city, Sanire, if Thalia's faded memory of what she'd been taught as a child served her. She didn't recognize him from when she had first been introduced to the courts.

"Congratulations, Lord Calphis," Camilla said. "I know that the prince would approve of this choice. Your experience in politics will strengthen House Avanerius, I have no doubt."

The new lord bowed his head, red eyes flashing to Thalia before he took his seat once more.

"Are we done here?" Lord Adrian stood. "I have business to attend to."

"What sort of business?" Thalia spoke.

The room stilled.

Lord Adrian's eyes seemed to burn. "None that concerns you."

Thalia kept her back ramrod straight. "Seeing as I aim to help the Houses as princess, I would like to know the affairs of my kingdom."

"Except that the Houses don't answer to you," Lord Adrian sneered. "You think that attending a singular meeting means you are entitled to know the affairs of all Houses? You might have married into House Lorenzia, but you are a far ways from running it."

Thalia bit the inside of her cheek, the Vampyr's words slapping her across her face. "Do the other Houses not answer to House Lorenzia? Is it not part of your law that while you, Lord Adrian, run House Gallinus, House Lorenzia presides over all?" Lord Adrian's eyes blazed as she continued, "Does that not mean that your House still answers to mine?"

The tension in the room stretched. Lord Adrian's face rippled, his flesh sinking into his skull. Thalia wasn't scared. "So, I will ask this again, what sort of *business* do you have to attend to?"

Lord Damien and Camilla stilled beside her.

But before Lord Adrian could open his mouth, Lord Amadeus spoke. "We are having issues with exportation, Princess."

The room shifted and Lord Adrian scowled, but his face didn't return to normal; it remained emaciated, his green eyes nearly black.

Thalia made a face. "What sort of issues?"

"Vaccarium exports multiple goods to other territories," Lord Amadeus said. "Recently, the price of exportation has increased as the demand for certain goods like timber has lessened. House Gallinus is the sole exporter of timber due to their capital being so rich with wood."

"And you are facing . . . financial crisis because of this?" Thalia turned to Lord Adrian. At least he was sitting down, but his face kept rippling as though he were trying to get his transformation under control. But financial strain . . . yes, that could work. Depending on how badly House Gallinus needed money for its city—

Lord Adrian's eyes darkened. "Call it what you like."

"No other House will help?" Thalia pushed.

Lord Adrian scoffed. "House Lorenzia could. Your coffers are full."

Thalia's heart thudded. She willed it to calm. "Have you brought this up to the prince? I'm sure money could be spared if your city is in need."

"The prince"—Lord Adrian bared his fangs—"appears to have more pressing business than overseeing the Houses he was meant to help."

"I could find the funds," Thalia said.

Lord Adrian stiffened, his skin warping. "I didn't ask for your help—"

"House Lorenzia would be glad to discuss financial issues, Lord Adrian," Camilla said smoothly. "We are always eager to help our fellow Houses, especially if this matter affects the people of Vaccarium. We wouldn't want to see any more issues arise with House Gallinus."

Lord Adrian seemed near bursting, but it was Lord Amadeus who swept in. "Thank you, Princess. That is most generous."

Thalia nodded, even as Lord Adrian stood, the other members of his House standing as well. "Excuse me, *Princess*," he spat, but no one made to stop him as he and his entourage filed out.

But before the doors of the great hall closed, Keegan slipped in. His steps were clipped as he crossed the floor, coming up to Lord Damien's side. Camilla perked up, but Keegan spoke too low for Thalia to hear. Lord Damien stilled before tilting his chin.

Keegan stepped back, surprise flaring slightly when he noticed Thalia, but he didn't comment.

Lord Damien stood. "I'm afraid the prince's council is needed elsewhere. Any other House needs will be discussed at the House meeting when the prince returns. If you'll excuse us." He nodded to Camilla, who also stood.

Thalia rose to follow the prince's council, but Lord Damien shook his head. "I'm afraid you cannot come."

"Why not?" Thalia knew she wasn't on the prince's council officially, but surely attending this meeting was a step in the right direction—

"The hand's orders."

Thalia scowled, but Camilla and Keegan merely passed her and headed out of the room. The other Vampyrs also trickled out. But Thalia had more questions.

"Lord Amadeus," she called, before the lord could leave with his entourage. "A moment, if you please."

The Vampyr turned, surprise on his dark face, before he made his way back to her. Even though it was now just them in the room, Thalia wasn't frightened. He seemed to be the only Vampyr who wasn't eager to see her bleed. At least for now.

"Yes?" the lord said.

"I'm sorry to keep you, but I have some questions, if you don't mind."

The lord tilted his head, golden eyes wary. "About what?"

Thalia gestured for him to take a seat once more as she did the same. "House Gallinus seems to be . . . struggling. Are the Houses not all beholden to aid each other in times of need? Surely there are funds outside of House Lorenzia that could help House Gallinus maintain their city."

Lord Amadeus scrubbed a hand over his jaw. "The Houses do aid each other. But we are not beholden. The only House we are sworn to uphold and protect is House Lorenzia, because the prince watches over us all."

Thalia tucked this kernel of information away; her mother would be very interested to hear it. Because if the Houses didn't *need* to help each other, then surely there must be something she could use to turn them against one another.

"But just because we aren't sworn to help doesn't mean we aren't allies," Lord Amadeus said, as if reading her thoughts. "At the end of the day, the vitality and sanctity of Vaccarium is what matters. No matter what sort of . . . disagreements the Houses might have with each other. We all must work together for the good of Vaccarium."

Thalia picked at the skin of her thumbs. "How is House Santorien?"

Lord Amadeus seemed surprised at her question. "It is well."

"I heard that your House keeps the peace between Houses."

The Vampyr raised a dark brow. "House Santorien prefers peace over strife. Surely, as a ruler, you also feel the same."

Thalia felt her stomach tighten, but she forced a smile. "Of course. That is why I'm here—to ensure that peace continues, not only with the humans but also here, in Vaccarium."

Lord Amadeus smiled, although it seemed more like a grimace. "Is there anything else, Princess?"

Yes, what sort of secrets are you all hiding so I might exploit them?

Thalia's cheeks stretched farther into a near-painful smile. "Please do inform me of anything I might help with. I know I haven't earned the Houses' trust yet, but I do wish to do my part in helping rule alongside the prince."

Lord Amadeus hesitated before nodding. "Of course."

He left, and Thalia was left alone in the great hall. She picked at the skin around her thumbs which snagged, but she ignored the pain.

She needed to think. Too many things had transpired in less than twenty-four hours—from finding the strange Vampyr who was sick to learning that House Gallinus was facing exportation issues. She had more questions than answers, and she was beginning to feel like her head was going to explode.

She rose, her gown swishing at her heels.

She might not have answers, but she could get some fresh air.

And a ride on Feryena sounded like just the remedy.

Chapter Seventeen

Fresh air was what she needed. The only problem? Cassius had been serious about her staying in the castle.

She'd tried to go to the stables, only to be turned away by the guards at the door.

"Let me through." Thalia lifted her gaze to the two guards. She couldn't very well see their features behind their onyx helmets.

"Orders are for you to stay indoors," the one on the right said.

Thalia's lip curled. She was well aware of who'd implemented *those* orders. "Do you know where the prince's council is?" They'd been called away for whatever reason *she* wasn't allowed to know of.

"They are busy in the throne room and are not to be disturbed," the guard on the left said.

Fine. Despite wanting to cool off with a ride on Feryena, maybe she could find more answers in the library without Camilla watching her like a hawk, now that the council was distracted.

Thalia didn't run into any other Vampyr as she hurried through the castle, passing the strange armor and bare walls.

She needed to do two things when she got to the library. The first was researching sickness. Cassius had said the Vampyr who'd nearly killed her was sick, but she'd never seen such a sickness before. Not to mention Julian and Francesca had said they were holding out for a cure.

The second was to pen another letter to her mother. Thalia silently cursed; she should have ensured that Cassius had sent out the first one and not assumed he would. She pushed the thought to the side. For now, she made a mental note to get a map of Irenbis and Vaccarium. At least that would help her figure out where exactly the other Houses were.

Thalia slowed when she reached the wing of the palace that led to the library. But instead of taking the right hall, her feet turned left, venturing to a part she'd yet to explore.

The hallway stretched with blood-red carpets, and sconces on the walls cast eerie shadows. But walking had helped clear her head.

Thalia slowed again as she came to a set of double doors.

She frowned. She knew the library wasn't behind it, but without thinking, she pushed open the door.

She blinked, trying to adjust her eyes to the darkness of the room.

The bedchamber she'd entered was empty, and Thalia flicked on the lights. The ore in the glass lamps flickered, and Thalia's eyes widened.

The bedchamber was massive, at least twice the size of hers, though the red wallpaper was similar to the damask wall coverings of her own room. The bed was a behemoth made of black onyx, with sheets the color of dying rose petals.

"What the hell?" Thalia whispered, journeying farther into the room. She moved to the drapes, tugging them aside to allow more light to filter in. Dust motes hung in the air before floating like snowflakes to the ground.

Thalia frowned as she took in the items of the room. There was a sitting area to her right, same as in her room, but larger. No adornments sat atop the marble fireplace mantel, although the fireplace itself was large enough she could crawl inside it.

She moved to the dresser. A thin layer of dust covered a bottle of cologne and a jeweled box carelessly arranged on the top. She opened the drawers, rifling around the pressed silk shirts and trousers.

Thalia's stomach clenched as she glanced at the bed. Given the size of it along with the ornateness of the room, she had a sinking feeling she knew exactly whose room she was snooping in.

Without making a sound, she hurried to a door that opened into a study. The space was just as ostentatious as the bedroom, with a dark desk taking up the middle of the room. Floor-to-ceiling bookcases lined the back wall, and an arched window allowed the strangely overcast sky's light to filter in.

Well, at least she had a map.

A map of all of Vaccarium stretched over the desk's dark surface. Thalia took it all in.

It seemed that each capital city was marked by its House's symbol. House Lorenzia, indicated by the raven with three eyes, presided over the territory on the east side of the continent, just north of the forest that separated Agripa from Vaccarium. To the west of House Lorenzia was House Avanerius, with its ram's head with four horns; north of that was House Santorien and its ampithere. At the tip of the continent was a fox with multiple teeth, identifying Perden, the capital of House Olvectus, along with the mountain it resided by. Finally, above House Lorenzia was House Gallinus, marked by the stag with eight legs. Its capital city, Cupisco, was situated deep in the heart of a dense forest—

I'm going to marry into the House that's near the forest!

The breath knocked out of her, and she caught herself, spilling a pot of ink that bled all over the desk.

The black ink spread, blotting out House Gallinus in the process.

It—it couldn't be possible. She would have connected the dots sooner. Oh gods, House Gallinus exported timber because of their woods—

Thalia took a sharp inhale through her nose, trying to calm her racing heart. There was . . . there was no way that House Gallinus was the House her sister had been engaged to.

Her mind whirled, trying to remember that night her sister had been murdered. Trying to recall the details of the Vampyrs who came—

Thalia squeezed her eyes so tight that spots danced. All she saw was Ariadna's unseeing eyes; her neck, jagged and ripped open like an unstuffed doll.

Sweat beaded along her brow, and she pushed aside the bile gathering in her throat as the memory of that night hit her in full force.

"No, no, no," Thalia screamed. Her hands were slick with her sister's blood. It gushed over her fingers, making them slippery as she tried to reattach Ariadna's head. Her beautiful golden hair, which had been braided with flowers, was soaked in viscous fluid.

"Get the queen out!" someone else screamed—maybe her father.

Too much was happening. The throne room erupted in chaos. Guards were trying to fight off the Vampyrs—the ones who'd fully given over to their bloodlust and were preying on the courtiers gathered for the wedding.

"We need to go." Someone gripped her arm, a guard whose name she didn't recall.

"Save her!" Thalia sobbed, tears mixing with the blood on her hands.

"Get them out!" another roared.

Thalia was hauled to her feet, her silk slippers soaked in the rising gore, her hem ruined and stained brighter than wine. Ariadna had picked out the gown herself.

"Get the queen and princess out!" It was her father, screaming at the guards as the Vampyr who would have been her sister's husband faced him. The guards were trying to get the royal family out of the throne room, trying to seal the Vampyrs inside even though there were still innocents there.

The queen joined Thalia, her crown lost, eyes white with fear. She grabbed Thalia hard enough to bruise.

"Ariadna!" Thalia yelled until her vocal chords shredded. She turned, trying to get back into the room, trying to get to her sister.

But all she saw beyond the guards forming rank around the two of them was her father.

Her father, whose eyes widened as he stared down at his chest—at the hand protruding from it.

Then his spine splattered to the floor, and he collapsed.

"No!" the queen screamed.

The doors to the throne room closed, leaving only chaos trapped inside—

"I've been looking everywhere for you." Camilla's bright voice appeared behind her, far too cheerful for the misery hanging over Thalia's neck like an axe. "A servant said they saw you heading to the library, but this clearly isn't the library, so what are you—" The shifter's words died as Thalia slowly raised her head.

She hadn't even realized tears were streaming down her cheeks until the water landed on her curled fists. "Who were they?" she got out.

Camilla's face flashed. "Who was who?"

"Don't play dumb," Thalia snarled. "Who were the Vampyrs that came thirteen years ago to Agripa? Which House were they a part of?"

Camilla froze, glancing at the ruined map on the desk. "Do you really want to know?"

"If you do not tell me this second, I will carve it out of you." Thalia jerked away from the desk, her hands sticky with ink—with the phantom weight of blood. "Who were they?"

The shifter didn't back down as Thalia stopped before her. Camilla's eyes hardened. "House Gallinus."

Thalia felt the words land, punching deeper than a blade. She turned, the walls spinning and warping like the dirty edges of a mirror.

"Thalia?" Camilla's words came in and out, the shifter's voice garbled as if she spoke underwater. "Thalia?"

Thalia bolted.

She ran out of the room, her boots skidding across the stone. Her anger fueled her, each footfall reverberating up her leg, filling her lungs with white-hot rage. She skidded around the corner, her shoulder barking as she slammed into the wall with enough force the sconces shook.

No one stood watch outside the throne room. But Thalia didn't care, not as she burst through the doors and her eyes landed on the one Vampyr she sought.

"You." Thalia locked eyes on Lord Adrian. The leader of House Gallinus stood off to the side, watching something that was going on in the middle of the room.

Thalia didn't care.

She'd gut the lord from head to navel, pulling out his intestines for the vultures to pick at. Then she'd sever his head and spike it on the castle wall for all to see what her wrath had brought.

She'd taken one step toward the Vampyr when someone blocked her.

"Get out of my way," Thalia growled at Cassius.

"What is the meaning of this?" Lord Adrian hissed in outrage. It only stoked the fire inside Thalia more.

"I don't know what happened," Cassius said lowly, all memory of their heated exchange the night before forgotten. "But come with me and you can tell me. I can fix it."

"Fix it?" Thalia barked, her laughter acidic on her tongue. "The only way to *fix* it is to kill him." She flung out a finger, her hand shaking so badly it wavered like the edge of a knife.

"Trust me, I would like nothing more than to kill him too, Princess. Unfortunately killing a lord would cause chaos in the courts."

"I don't care." Thalia's eyes burned, her arm dropping to the side. "Kill him."

Cassius took a step closer, the scent of his skin breaking through her rage. He still smelled like the sun and earth. "Tell me what happened, and maybe we can come up with something else that won't cause civil war."

"He was—he killed—" Thalia choked, her eyes blurring so hard she could hardly see the Vampyr who'd damned her family.

"Cassius." Keegan's cautious voice spoke somewhere in the room. Shuffling echoed, and a deep grunt that Thalia couldn't place.

"I don't know who he killed, but I can guess," Cassius said softly, gently taking her arm. "But you can't be in here."

At Cassius's words, Thalia finally took in the room.

All the prince's council except Camilla were there, along with Lord Adrian and . . . another Vampyr.

This one knelt in the middle of the room, and Lord Damien stood above them. The red-eyed Vampyr had transformed, his skin sunken in and ashy. Veins ran beneath his thin flesh, his fangs exposed, as he stared at the Vampyr on their knees.

"What's going on?" Thalia got out.

"You need to go," Cassius said again in that same gentle tone, trying to guide her out.

"What the hell is going on?" Thalia jerked out of his grip, stumbling past him. She hadn't noticed that the Vampyr on the ground was hunched over, his left hand splayed out on the ground. His hand was broken, each finger twisted and bent at an odd angle, and blood was pooling, soaking the throne room floor. In his right hand was a hammer.

"Get her out!" Lord Adrian hissed again. "Lord Damien, finish this."

Thalia watched in horror as Lord Damien's face rippled and the Vampyr on the ground raised the hammer before smashing it onto his already broken hand.

The Vampyr groaned, tears streaking down his face as he raised the hammer again and brought it down with a sickening crunch.

"Stop this," Thalia whispered, frozen as the Vampyr continued to ruin his hand. He had no control of his movements. No control to stop whatever torture he was under. Just like she'd had no control when that Vampyr killed her sister. "Stop this now."

"You wished to be a part of this world? To be ruler?" Lord Adrian said between the sounds of bones shattering. "You wished to call this place your home?" Lord Adrian flashed a snake smile, his own features rippling. "Welcome to it."

"Thalia, please." Cassius grabbed her arm, tugging lightly. His face was pained, but something else flashed in his irises—deep-rooted anger. She didn't know if it was directed at her or at someone else in the room.

All the fight left her as Cassius began to lead her out.

"Now, where did you see the bitten?" Keegan's voice was soft, almost like he felt sorry for what was being done. But she didn't hear the other Vampyr's reply as the throne room doors shut, sealing the prince's council inside.

Chapter Eighteen

Thalia stared out her window.

Night was falling, the clouds slowly dispersing like mist as the moon's glow replaced them.

She hadn't moved from her spot in hours. Not after she'd written another letter to her mother. She wasn't even sure that what she'd said made sense. She'd tried to inform the queen about the Houses. How there were issues going on within them. But every time she lifted her quill, watching the ink drip from its tip, all she'd been able to see was the blood of Adriana leaking from her ripped-out throat. All she wanted to do was ask her mother *Did you know?*

Did the queen know that the House responsible for the horror of her husband's and daughter's murders was still standing?

Thalia's nausea spiked.

And here she was, knowing that the lord who'd no doubt had a hand in her family's butchery was still alive and that she couldn't just go and put a stake through his head unless she wanted her whole mission to unravel at her feet.

Thalia pinched the bridge of her nose, ignoring the sudden ache coming on in her skull. Killing the lord without cause would start an internal war, that much was clear. She wasn't strong enough to do it alone, not unless she wanted her own heart pulled from her chest.

There had to be some other recourse, something that could be done to get someone else to do it for her. While Santorien seemed to be the peacekeeping House, they weren't jumping at the chance to help House Gallinus with their financial issues. Lord Amadeus seemed the easiest Vampyr to get on her side, or at least, he seemed more inclined to listen to her. Perhaps she could plant some seeds in his head, turn him against House Gallinus. Maybe she could figure out how to wield him and his House like puppets, like Lord Damien had done with that Vampyr.

Thalia shuddered, glancing down at the ring on her finger. She hadn't forgotten what had happened in the throne room. How Lord Damien had seemed to compel that Vampyr to ruin his hand.

There was more to it than just the prince's absence. Something to do with madness and sickness and whatever "bitten" thing Keegan had asked before Cassius escorted her out of the throne room.

The Vampyrs seemed desperate for something—angry. And anger often led to fear. Fear could be more lethal than any bite. If she could just figure out all these damn secrets they were keeping—

Movement in the woods caught her attention.

Thalia straightened, shuffling closer to the paned window. A flash of white hide flickered among the crimson leaves, nearly glowing against the moon hanging low overhead.

A shiver traveled down her spine as whatever was in the forest moved again, rustling the branches as it went.

The door creaking open had her whirling, hand going to her thigh where she kept her dagger strapped under her nightdress.

Cassius looked surprised to find her awake.

"What do you want?" Thalia's voice was cold.

Cassius eased in, shutting the door behind him. He leaned against the wood, hands clasped behind his back. They hadn't spoken since the throne room. Since he'd so gently taken her arm and led her from whatever mess she'd stumbled upon.

"I came to see if you were all right." Cassius finally broke the silence.

Thalia's lip curled. "All right? Do I seem *all right* to you?"

"I don't want to fight you, Thalia." Cassius sighed, the sound tightening her stomach further. "Something happened today. I want to know what it was. Believe it or not, I'm not trying to be your enemy."

Enemy.

Thalia felt the retort on her tongue. The fact that he already was, based on his choices.

Maybe it was the shadows gathering in the corners, or the fact that the memories of that night thirteen years ago haunted her as much as his face did, that had her saying, "It was House Gallinus."

Cassius's brows knotted in understanding. "How did you figure it out?"

Thalia shook her head, pushing past the tightness in her throat. "It doesn't matter." She slowly lifted her gaze.

Cassius studied her, not in a lust-filled manner but as if he was searching for something amiss. Almost like he was concerned for her. The thought sent her stomach twisting further.

"Thirteen years ago," Cassius said, "The prince's father ruled—King Valeran. When the cracks first appeared in the Mages' spell, the Houses thought that if they couldn't find an answer in Agripa's library, perhaps a union between the Vampyrs and humans could be used."

"In what manner?" Thalia bit out.

"I don't know. Perhaps to expand the forest so there would be a greater area for us to live without the fear of the light. But the forest would cut into Agripa's own land. The prince was opposed to this idea. The humans and Vampyrs had always interacted tentatively. There was already tension rising between the two realms. So, since the prince wouldn't offer his own hand, House Gallinus stepped in."

Thalia fisted her hands, trying to ignore the image of Lord Adrian's hateful face mocking hers.

"It wasn't Lord Adrian's idea," Cassius continued, "although the Vampyr is brash enough to do it. It was his father's."

Thalia sucked in a sharp breath, rage blanketing her mind like a cloud.

"His father hated humans, thought them to be a mistake the Mages created. He believed humans to be less than the Vampyrs and were taking up land that rightfully should be Vaccarium's. He concocted a plan to try and kill the Cesarian line. To force your territory under the Vampyrs' rule."

"He nearly succeeded," Thalia got out.

Deep regret speared itself across Cassius's handsome features. "When they returned after the failed mission, Lord Adrian's father was executed, staked right in front of his own family. The prince offered Lord Adrian a deal: He, and his son Julian, could either quell the grumblings of House Gallinus, or he would meet the same fate as his father."

"I see."

"The prince should have killed him," Cassius said bluntly. "Lord Adrian may not have had a part in what happened to your family, but he didn't stop his father. Even when word got out about what the lord planned to do."

Thalia's lip curled again. "And that was all his punishment? To be removed and set up as a lord? Did you know this?" she hissed, stepping away from the window. "Did you know what he did to my family?"

Cassius's face darkened. "I knew the day I arrived here."

Thalia felt as though he'd struck her. "And yet you so willingly work with him?"

"I don't willingly do anything," Cassius snarled, stalking toward her. "As soon as I became hand, I removed both him and Julian from the prince's council."

His words stopped her. "What?"

"Do you really think I could ever willingly work with someone like them? To know how horribly depraved they are to want humans dead—to want you dead?" Cassius's eyes glowed, a thin sliver of blue barely visible around the black of his irises. "I wanted to rip his throat out—both of them. I still do. And I would have if the prince hadn't stopped me. This was the only option I could take."

Thalia couldn't face the emotions in Cassius's face—didn't want to dwell on the truth laid out like a map. She'd told him that he should have died. He'd ruined himself, cut a wound so deep she still bled from it. It didn't make sense how he could be so ready to avenge her family, yet chose to betray her and turn into one of the very creatures she'd sworn to fight.

Too many things hung in the air between them. The threads that stretched between them tightened. At any moment, one of them would snap and send them both down the path of darkness.

Thalia turned away, wiping at her face. "I have another letter to send in the morning."

Cassius's eyes lingered on the desk where the letter to her mother sat. The wax seal seemed to suck in the moonlight. "All right."

"Did you send the other one?" Thalia asked, turning back. Cassius nodded. She studied him, wondering if he was lying. But tiredness wrapped around her shoulders, and maybe she didn't want to fight with him either. She struggled with her next words. "Did I—have I received anything from home?"

"No."

Just like that, her stomach twisted. It had been days since she'd arrived in Vaccarium. And her mother hadn't even cared to see how she was? To see if she was still alive? She pushed past the burning gathering in her throat.

"Were you expecting something?" Cassius asked softly.

She didn't want to hear the softness in his voice. To see the quiet understanding of her pain at not hearing from her mother. It shouldn't bother her so much. She had a duty to keep. A vow she'd made. Feelings had no place in her mission.

She forcibly cleared her throat. "What's the prince's name?"

Cassius shifted at the change in topic. "Prince Aeneas of House Lorenzia, why?"

"He sent me another gift today." She nodded to the seating area, where a black marble chess set sat on the low-lying table before the fire. "He never signs his name. Why?" She turned to Cassius, finding his face carefully guarded.

"Dramatics, I'd assume," Cassius finally said.

Despite the bleak horror she'd uncovered about her family's murder, Thalia snorted. The sound made Cassius's lips quirk. "Did you tell him I liked to play?"

Cassius hesitated before nodding. "Do you hate me for that?"

Hate.

Thalia swallowed, looking away. Because she was supposed to hate him. But after his reveal—the way he'd handled Lord Adrian—that hate seemed to flicker ever so slightly.

"No. No, I don't hate you for that," Thalia said softly. She focused on the chess set so she wouldn't have to see the relief in his eyes. "Do you want to play?" She glanced back, and Cassius gave a slow nod.

Before she lost her nerve, she moved to the sitting area, sinking onto one of the velvet armchairs.

After a moment, Cassius followed, taking a spot across from her on the settee. Silence mounted, the cracking of the logs in the fire the only sound.

"Well?" Thalia asked, finally glancing at him. He seemed tense, and he watched her with so much intensity that she was surprised she didn't catch flame. "Are you ready?"

"I'm always ready for you, Princess."

Thalia swallowed the sudden heat in her stomach, taking a pawn and moving it two squares.

They didn't speak as they played, the marble clinking as they exchanged pieces.

"You've gotten better," Cassius said as Thalia took out his queen with her rook.

Thalia raised a brow. "I've always been better than you."

Cassius smirked, his eyes lighting as he moved his bishop out of her queen's way. "Maybe, but I've learned a few things since our time together."

Together.

Thalia moved another pawn, trying to block his bishop's path to the king. "Like what?"

"Distraction, for example." Cassius's callused fingers moved a knight, taking out her pawn.

"Distraction?" Thalia glanced up, finding him leaning forward, his arms resting between his knees. The fire cast shadows over his cheekbones, highlighting the sharp facets of his face. The flames turned his hair into burnt amber, glinting in deep shades of red and gold.

Cassius smiled, a hint of fangs showing. "Check."

Thalia scowled, glancing down at the knight poised to take out her king. She moved the king out of harm's way. "You aren't distracting."

"Oh no?" Cassius leaned even closer. "A true shame. I'll have to work harder, then. Check."

Thalia's scowl deepened at the bishop facing her king. "What was going on in the throne room today?" She moved her rook before the bishop, protecting the king. Cassius took out the rook, and Thalia claimed his bishop. "Did it have something to do with the sickness?"

Cassius paused, his eyes flicking up for a brief moment. "Yes."

"What was Lord Damien—what was he doing?"

Cassius moved his other knight back to the starting line. "He was using compulsion."

"Compulsion?"

Cassius nodded. "A full-blooded Vampyr, like Lord Damien, has the ability to sway others to do their bidding."

"What do you mean, full-blooded?"

"Vampyrs with red eyes are full-blooded—born of pure Vampyric blood." Like Lord Damien. "Golden eyes belong to Vampyrs born of pure blood and turned; they're known as half-bloods. But they can also have green eyes as well, not just gold."

"Why is that?"

Cassius shrugged. "Something to do with the way the Mages created them. When the Vampyrs started turning humans, it changed the way the magic was written in their blood and how it presented itself. Kind of like when a wolf breeds with a house dog, their offspring look different. Vampyrs and humans were never meant to . . . intermingle."

"But they did."

Cassius shifted, his eyes flashing. "That only happened after the human had turned and became a Vampyr themself."

Thalia didn't believe that. She would bet all the remaining ore in Agripa that there were more humans who'd been . . . forced to do other things besides turn. After all, humans were prey to Vampyrs.

Thalia chewed her lip, mulling over the information. Cassius tracked the movement. She stopped. "And what of the others? Your eyes are blue and always have been." Granted, the blue of Cassius's eyes had intensified, almost like they'd been sharpened with a whetstone.

"Any humans who were turned by a Vampyr, regardless of their status as pure or half-blood, their eye color remains the same as when they were human. You'll find there aren't as many as you'd think."

"And do you all transform?" She couldn't keep the image of Lord Damien's shrunken skull from her mind.

"Yes, when a Vampyr has a strong urge or uses their power, they can transform. Many can control it, but others choose to embrace it."

Thalia shuddered, then horror twisted her stomach. "Have I been compelled?"

Cassius's face softened. "No. That ring you wear, it was spelled by a Mage. It stops the effects of compulsion."

Thalia stared down at the blood-red ruby, noted how it seemed to suck in the light. "Someone tried to compel me in the throne room when I was introduced."

"What?" Cassius's words turned lethal.

She shook her head. "I thought Lord Adrian was doing something, but if only full-blooded Vampyrs can . . ." Cassius's face darkened, but Thalia asked, "What of you? Have you been compelled?"

The thought had her stomach twisting in knots.

"No. It is harder to compel a turned. The fact we were once human but are now something else makes the Vampyrs' influence become confused. Even then, we are trained to fight against it. Lord Damien is powerful; the Vampyr that was brought before us was weak."

"What were you trying to find out? Francesca . . ." Thalia's mind flashed to Julian's lover. "She mentioned trying to find a cure." She moved another chess piece.

Cassius moved a piece without looking at the board. "Yes, it was about the cure."

"And there are no leads to it? Surely there must be something to help them get better."

Cassius moved his bishop, exposing his king, although Thalia didn't think he realized it. "The prince's council is seeing to it."

That wasn't an answer, but given the guarded expression now crossing Cassius's features, she didn't think she'd get any more from him.

Thalia moved her queen. "Checkmate."

Cassius raised a brow in surprise, then huffed out a laugh. "Seems I was the one distracted."

Thalia smirked, stretching her neck, then winced at the sharp pain coming from her throat. She touched the bruise that marred her neck from where Cassius had bitten her the night before.

"I am sorry," Cassius said, his voice quiet but not weak.

Thalia glanced at him. "For what?"

Cassius's throat bobbed. "For my behavior last night."

His eyes were on her neck, slightly glowing against the heat of the fire. His gaze wasn't full of hunger but rather remorse.

"It was a brutish thing to do. Something that I should have had better control of. You have every right to"—he looked at the bruise, and indeed, there was deep regret and shame flashing in his blue eyes—"to not wish me to touch you."

Thalia wasn't sure which surprised her more: his apology, or the anguish with which he'd said the last words. "What are you talking about?"

Cassius swallowed, nodding toward the end of the bed. "The day you were introduced to the courts, I held you and you flinched."

Thalia glanced at the foot of the bed. The memory of when he'd torn her dress so she didn't pass out surfaced. "I didn't flinch because you held me."

Cassius's face flashed in surprise, the look so human it almost made Thalia laugh—until his eyes seemed to brighten further. "Why did you flinch, then?"

Thalia looked away, her fingers picking at the skin of her thumbs. Cassius didn't push. Didn't even tell her to stop before she finally got out, "I had a dream that night. About you."

At Cassius's nod to go on, she added, "You ripped out my throat."

Too many emotions flashed in Cassius's features for her to decipher before he finally said low, "I see."

"When you—when you held me that day, you looked at my neck."

"And that's why you flinched?"

"Yes. I saw the hunger in your eyes." Bile rose in her throat at the image flashing in her mind, but she pushed it aside.

Cassius stared at her a moment longer, his gaze dark. "Do you know what that hunger is?"

"No. But I assume it's your incessant need to be sated by blood?"

Cassius huffed out a laugh, leaning back on the couch. He shook his head, something like amusement dancing across his face. "No."

Surprise speared itself through her. "No?"

Cassius shifted. "When a Vampyr drinks blood from the source, particularly that of a human or another Vampyr, it's . . . pleasurable."

Thalia suddenly didn't know what to do or where to look. And she certainly couldn't explain the odd flush that traveled over her skin. "What do you mean, it's pleasurable?"

Cassius raised a brow. "I mean that it's an aphrodisiac."

"Oh." She felt the heat of Cassius's stare sweep over her face. She hoped that sitting so near the fire could be blamed for the redness creeping over her cheeks. "Is that why you refused to share blood at the ceremony?"

"Partially, yes. Although, that pleasure wouldn't be as strong, because I wouldn't have actually bitten you, just tasted it as it dripped from the cut. But I meant it when I said I wouldn't take what isn't mine." Just like that, the heat inside Thalia died, quickly replaced by anger. "But if I had bitten you to drink your blood, as a human, it would have caused you excruciating pain. It would have triggered the process of you turning."

Thalia's stomach knotted, nausea rolling alongside. "So it's true your bite causes pain?"

"To a human, yes. It's why most who are bitten turn in the end. The pain is worse than death."

Thalia didn't realize she'd shifted closer until she knocked over a chess piece. "But it doesn't cause pain to another Vampyr?"

Cassius stared down at her, unblinking. "No. Sharing blood between Vampyr and Vampyr is pleasurable to both parties."

Something oily filled her stomach, along with a bitterness she couldn't quite place. "So the reason you've been staring at my neck since the moment you laid eyes on me is because you want to get off?"

Cassius smirked, not taking the bait. "Trust me, I have no issue getting off." Thalia's heart rate quickened as he leaned closer. "My issue is that I've never wanted to do it before."

"What do you mean? You said it was pleasurable."

Cassius shrugged, his dark-auburn hair rising with the movement. "So I've heard. I've never tried it."

It'd been four years since he'd turned into a Vampyr. Four years—

"Have you fucked anyone?" Thalia blurted out.

Cassius raised a brow. "Have you?"

"You didn't answer my question."

"No, I haven't."

Thalia scanned his face, but all she saw was the truth laid out. "Why not?"

"Why haven't you?"

"I guess I've been too busy hunting you across Agripa," she snapped.

Cassius's smirk grew. "Then I guess I've been too busy running from you."

But Cassius leaving the Scarecrows in Agripa didn't make sense anymore. Not with the way he held himself now. Not with the duties he carried as hand to the prince. Not with who *he* was.

The clock above the fireplace chimed, and they both startled, having lost track of the time they'd spent together.

Cassius stood suddenly. "It's late. I have some things to attend to." He aimed for the door but stopped with his hand on the doorknob. "I missed this," he said softly.

"Missed what?" Thalia's words were too breathless.

There was an invisible string that kept pulling them together. No matter how she fought it, somehow she always found she had no choice but to be tugged along.

A ghost of a smile flickered on Cassius's lips. "Sparring with you."

"You think this was sparring? Please, this was barely a warm-up."

He chuckled, the sounds traveling straight to her toes. "Then I look forward to actually sparring with you soon." He didn't glance back as he left.

Thalia felt her warm cheeks with the backs of her hands, swallowing hard. Her eyes were drawn down to the chessboard, her queen taking out his king.

But Thalia didn't feel like she'd won at all.

Chapter Nineteen

"*Hunger.*"

A chill ran down Thalia's spine at the word spoken low in her ear.

"*Hunger.*"

She didn't want to open her eyes, didn't want to see the sick Vampyr hovering above her.

"*I hunger for you.*"

A cold finger pressed into her cheek, leaving a trail of wetness in its wake.

"*Hunger—*"

Thalia woke, gasping for air.

She twisted in the sheets, trying to untangle herself from where they were wrapped around her throat like a noose.

"Thalia—" Cassius's voice was a beacon in the dark as she finally flung the sheets off her. "What's wrong?"

She felt a warm hand on her bare shoulder. She hadn't heard him slip into bed after he'd finished whatever he'd attended to. Thalia jerked, her feet finding the floor as she stood, pacing away from the bed.

"What's wrong?" Cassius's words were sterner now, but she couldn't look at him. She shook her head, arms wrapping around her middle as she walked to the window, trying to get air into her lungs.

"Talk to me."

She turned, making out Cassius's form at the end of the bed, his bare torso gleaming despite the lack of light. He looked like she remembered him. Back before he'd betrayed her, before she'd stabbed him. Before this whole mess got dumped in her lap. He didn't even seem to have been affected by their time together earlier that evening. After his confession about missing her had sent fire straight into her bloodstream and she couldn't tell whether she burned from rage or something else.

"Thalia?" Cassius's face was open, his brow knotted in concern.

She wished he would stop saying her name. Wished he would stop looking at her as though he cared. Because how could he care as . . . as *that*? As a monster? As a creature meant to drink blood, not water? How could he still feel human?

Thalia's throat tightened.

"I'm here." Cassius's words broke through her racing thoughts.

She stared at him, her throat tightening further.

He's a monster. He's who you've sworn to destroy. Her mother's voice seemed to whisper like a snake in her ear. And yes. He was a monster. Her plan to use him to get close to the prince was the only one she had. But even that thought sent an oily feeling through her stomach.

Because he was . . . Cass.

Cass who'd bandaged her arm when she'd fallen off Helios and scraped it against a sharp rock when she was fourteen.

Cass who'd rescued her from her first ball when all her mother wanted was to parade her before the court—yet he'd snuck her out so they could go walk in the garden instead.

Cass who'd promised to be by her side no matter what. No matter if she married someone else. No matter if she had to live in a different kingdom.

He'd vowed to be with her until the end.

And maybe it was the fear still pulsing through her blood from the nightmare, or the memories that chased her almost as much as she'd chased him, but she craved some semblance of comfort—of something she knew after being thrust into a world she so sorely didn't understand.

Thalia moved across the floor and Cassius stiffened, no doubt bracing for an attack, but Thalia just grabbed his face, hauling her mouth to his.

He grunted against her lips, surprise sharp and tangy on her tongue. Thalia wound her arms around his neck, pulling her body flush against his, her nightgown doing nothing to mask the feel of his hard body against hers.

She kissed him deeper, willing him to kiss her back. Willing him to let go of whatever restraint he kept for himself.

Please, her lips seemed to beg his. *Please.*

Cassius gripped her shoulders, pushing her back. His eyes glowed brighter than the moon. "What are you doing?" he rasped.

Thalia shook her head. "I- I need you," she got out, closing the distance between them. His lips formed perfectly against hers, a key fitting into a lock.

Cassius tore his mouth away, his chest rising and falling rapidly. "Thalia, this is not—we aren't—we aren't going to do this."

She gripped his wrists, feeling the strength of his muscles. "You said you missed me," she whispered. His hands loosened slightly, and she was able to press herself against him. "Was that another lie?"

Cassius's throat bobbed. "No. No it wasn't a lie."

"You said you wanted to taste my flesh again." She ran her tongue up the strong column of his neck, his heated skin burning beneath her mouth. Cassius groaned, his fingers tightening once more on her shoulders. "That it's driving you insane."

Cassius suddenly gripped her face with one hand, tilting her head back with the other, his fingertips tangling in her blonde hair. Hunger marked his features, his mouth parted slightly to reveal sharp-pointed fangs. But the sight didn't scare her. In fact, it sent a pang of awareness straight into her belly.

"You're married," he finally got out. "To the man I serve."

"It can be our secret," she whispered. She didn't even care that suddenly this didn't feel like seduction. Didn't care that the traitorous heat in her chest had traveled right to her core, making her ache. "It's not as though monarchs don't take other lovers. It's not as though we've never talked about doing just that."

Because even when she'd been engaged to that human prince, the plan was always to have *him*.

His gaze darkened, his head tilting slightly until they shared a breath. "What happened, Thalia?"

She snapped her gaze to his, frustration blooming alongside her desire. "I don't want to talk."

"We should talk."

Thalia jerked back. "Talk about what, Cassius? There's nothing to discuss. Do you want to fuck me or not?"

A muscle in Cassius's jaw flickered. Then he let go of her face and took a step back. Cold air brushed between them, stretching like a shoreline.

"What are you doing?" she practically growled out, her fingers curling as though she could still feel his strength beneath them.

"We aren't doing this."

"Why the fuck not?"

"Because when we fuck, it's because we *both* want it. Not because one of us is trying to escape something. And it certainly won't be a secret." Thalia's body went numb as Cassius grabbed the blanket at the end of the bed. "I'll sleep on the settee."

Just like that, the fire inside her died, leaving nothing but a pile of ash in its wake.

Chapter Twenty

"Why are your eyes gold?" Thalia asked.

She'd finally made it to the library the next morning. Camilla had stumbled upon her there a few hours later and made a comment about reading for the afternoon. But Thalia had the sense Camilla was keeping an eye on her. She couldn't say why, but every so often she'd feel Camilla's eyes on her shoulder blades as she searched the shelves for books on sickness.

"That's a strange question," Camilla said, marking the spot in her book with her finger.

Thalia shrugged. "We were talking about eye color last night—"

Cassius's words from the night before rang unbidden in her ear. *Because when we fuck, it's because we* both *want it. And it certainly won't be a secret.*

She hadn't spoken to him since he'd thoroughly shut down whatever was happening between them. And when she'd woken, he was already gone. White-hot anger pulsed in her stomach. She'd made a fool of herself, and her cheeks still burned with embarrassment every time she thought about it.

There would be no fucking anytime soon, that was for certain.

Camilla gave her an odd look, and Thalia cleared her throat. "Cassius explained what your eye colors mean. The whole pure-blood and half-blood thing. But you're not a Vampyr, so why are your eyes gold?"

Camilla set her book aside. Thalia wasn't sure what she was reading, but the title sounded like some sort of erotica. Thalia resisted the urge to snort.

"You know about the pockets of magic, yes?" Thalia nodded as Camilla went on. "We were formed from those pockets of magic but also of the earth. The gold represents the minerals in the earth's crust."

"Really?" Thalia breathed. Every time those pockets of magic were mentioned, her mind spun.

Camilla smirked, laughing slightly. "No, but you should see your face right now."

Thalia scowled, shoving a book back on the shelf. "Ha-ha. Very funny. I was being serious."

Camilla sobered. "The gold was a way to identify us as shifters. Just like you can identify a bird based on their feathers."

"But the Vampyrs also have gold eyes."

"Their gold isn't as pure."

"Is it because they're half-bloods?"

Camilla nodded. "If you look at Keegan's eyes, they aren't as gold as they seem; they have almost a copper hue."

Thalia stared at the shifter, and indeed, her irises were nearly yellow because of how bright the gold was.

Thalia chewed the inside of her cheek. "Can you also . . . smell?"

Camilla raised a well-groomed brow. "If you're asking if I can scent things like a human, the answer is no. But I can smell and hear things you can't, just like the Vampyrs can."

"What can you smell exactly?"

Camilla tilted her head, her delicate nostrils flaring slightly. "You used a jasmine soap last night for your bath." Thalia raised an approving brow. She couldn't even smell the soap she'd used. "I can also smell Cassius on you."

Thalia's pulse jumped, but she forced herself to breathe to bring her heart rate back down. Yes, Camilla probably smelled the desperation Thalia had felt when she practically threw herself at him. "Can you smell emotions? Like fear and—" *Arousal.* Thalia pushed the thought aside.

But Camilla must have sensed where her mind was going, because she smirked. "Yes. Anything that heightens the emotions, both shifters and Vampyrs can smell."

Great.

"Can you smell anger?"

Camilla tilted her head, making a face. "Sometimes. Anger is an emotion that, while powerful, doesn't have as strong of a scent. Fear and arousal—those emotions cause your body to react physically, and it's easier to pick up on that."

Well, at least Thalia had that going for her. Although she would like Cassius to choke on her anger next time he saw her.

"Is House Gallinus really facing financial issues?" Thalia changed the subject. Maybe she needed to work on her subtlety. But at this point, subtlety wasn't getting her anywhere.

Camilla sighed. "Yes and no. Their exports have slowed immensely within the last six months. But that isn't making them destitute. They have other resources that could be set up to trade with other continents. Lord Adrian is just stubborn."

"How are the other continents in dealing with Vampyrs?" Thalia pushed.

"What do you mean?"

"I mean . . ." Thalia paused, trying to word things carefully. "There are humans on other continents. Sula, for example, has no Vampyrs. They aren't . . . worried about dealing with you all?"

Camilla's eyes seemed to sharpen. "Only Agripa has ever had issues with Vampyrs."

Thalia felt her rage spike. "With good reason."

Camilla's face softened ever so slightly. "I don't agree with what happened between our two worlds. Believe it or not, other Houses don't agree either. But things are different now. We have a chance to coexist once more, to set up trade between our realms and better the lives of both our peoples."

Thalia swallowed.

Wasn't that what she'd been trying to do too? Better the lives of the people of Agripa by killing the Vampyrs?

But being here . . . hearing the way Camilla talked, as though she wanted the same thing, to ensure that her people not only survived but thrived . . .

Thalia cleared her throat. "I'm surprised that Lord Calphis didn't try and kill me."

"Because you killed his son?"

Thalia's stomach twisted, the image of a staked Vampyr flashing. "Yes."

Camilla leaned back in her seat. "Lord Calphis and his family have always been loyal to House Lorenzia."

So they'd be of no use to her.

"How is Lord Damien a lord? He's not a ruler of any court."

"That is the prince's doing," Camilla said. "Anyone who is on the prince's council rises in rank."

"So you're a lady?"

Camilla nodded, gesturing to herself. "Can't you tell?"

Thalia snorted. "Are there any other ladies of the Houses? Lord Damien mentioned that there have been some in the past . . ."

"Yes, a lady currently runs House Olvectus."

Thalia was surprised by that, but also a bit impressed that the ruler of the House that included the shifters but also dealt with the ore was a woman. "Was she at the court introduction?"

Camilla shook her curly head. "No, she had to stay in Lorceium."

"Why?"

Camilla's long nails clicked on the arms of her chair. "Someone had to ensure that the ore was being sent to Agripa."

Thalia chewed the inside of her cheek. She hadn't even realized she'd gone back to searching the bookshelves when Camilla asked, "What are you looking for, anyway?"

Thalia's pulse spiked, but she pushed it aside. "Nothing, really."

Camilla's eyes narrowed. "You've been in here for hours."

Thalia sighed, staring at the shifter. She would probably smell it if Thalia lied, but also, Camilla had most likely heard about what had happened in Irenbis.

"Cassius said there was a sickness that affect Vampyrs. There isn't a cure that they know of, but I figured it couldn't hurt to look and try to help," she said.

Camilla gave her a wary look. "I see."

"I thought it would help to show the courts that I aim to do my job as princess," Thalia got out.

Camilla stiffened. "You're trying to earn their trust."

Thalia nodded, although it hadn't been a question. "It would be more helpful if they weren't so afraid to voice what was going on in their Houses," she muttered. She turned her back, continuing her search, although Camilla's stare seared her shoulder blades.

"I sent your letter, by the way."

Camilla's words had Thalia's head jerking up. "What?"

"Cassius was busy this morning, but I sent it. Just wanted to let you know."

"Thank you." The thought should have settled her. After all, she'd told her mother in not so many words that the courts weren't as strong as they appeared, how the prince being away was causing strain. But she hadn't mentioned the sickness, not yet. Not until she figured out how that all tied in.

But for some reason, it didn't calm her nerves.

Camilla didn't say anything more, and silence stretched as Thalia went deeper into the library.

When the door to the library creaked open, Thalia craned her neck around a bookshelf.

Keegan strode in, urgency lacing his footsteps. "The meeting has been moved up," he said to Camilla, the shifter having gone back to reading.

Camilla set the book aside, rising. "To when?"

Keegan glanced behind him. "Right now."

Camilla cursed, looking around until she spotted Thalia. "Are you wanting to join?"

Thalia's fingers tightened on the book she held. "No."

Both of Camilla's brows rose, and even Keegan seemed surprised at her answer. "No? Weren't you pushing to meet with all the Houses?"

Thalia forced herself to not react, to not allow her body to give away any scent that would indicate her lie. “I was . . . but is the prince here?”

Keegan shared a look with Camilla before shaking his head. “No, he’s still away.”

Thalia shrugged, feigning nonchalance. “Then the meeting must not be too urgent if it was moved up and he’s still away. I’m sure you can fill me in on anything I miss, but I want to keep researching. I think I might have found something.”

The Vampyr and shifter shared another look.

“All right,” Camilla finally said, taking a step toward the door. “I’ll find you after, then.”

Thalia forced a smile, waving the book in her hand. “I’ll be here.”

The two left, closing the library door behind them. Thalia waited, counting in her head. When five minutes had passed, she tiptoed to the library door, pressing her ear against the wood, but she heard nothing on the other side.

Heart pounding in her throat, she pulled out the map of the castle from her dress pocket. She’d found it when visiting the library days ago, and now was the perfect opportunity to put it to use.

She stared at the drawing, then glanced around the library until her focus landed on the tapestry in the back with the different courts stitched on the surface.

Thalia hurried over to it, lifting up the tapestry to stare at the cold stone beneath it. She glanced down at the map, then back at the wall. There—a small emblem of a raven with three eyes appeared carved in the corner of one stone.

“There you are,” she whispered, pressing her hand against the stone.

The wall gave away with a groan and Thalia froze, glancing back to the door, but no one came to investigate.

Thalia counted to thirty in her head before glancing into the secret passageway. Cold, musty air floated to her.

Taking a deep breath, she steeled her spine.

Thalia didn’t look back as she stepped into the dark.

Chapter Twenty-One

Thalia dodged cobwebs thick with dust, trying to push aside the thought of spiders crawling into her dress. The cold stone soaked through the soles of her slippers, the dirt leaving footprints in her wake marked by the shafts of lights spilling above her from vents high in the castle walls.

She knew that if she were there in the council meeting, they wouldn't actually share what was going on. Spying on them seemed like a better idea.

Eventually, Thalia stopped before a marked wall, the brick worn with use. Thalia glanced at the map. Behind the wall was the council room, a place Thalia hadn't ventured to yet. She tucked the map under her arm and pushed.

The stone moved and Thalia held her breath, peeking through the crack. She nearly sagged with relief when she realized the wall was hidden by a large tapestry, no doubt put there to ensure no one realized someone was listening in. Despite the tapestry being in place, it was thin enough that Thalia could see through the threads of the woven fabric.

It seemed that all the leaders of the Houses were present.

They sat around a large, circular oak table in high-backed chairs. The banners behind them indicated the Houses they belonged to.

Cassius sat at what would have been the head of the table, speaking quietly with Keegan on his left, while Lord Damien was to the right of Cassius. Camilla was seated on the lord's other side next to a woman whose dark skin and features matched the shifter's—perhaps a distant relative?

Cassius's head jerked up suddenly, his nostrils flaring. Thalia tensed, holding her breath. Shit. He looked around the room, his eyes settling on Camilla for a second. Thalia prayed her scent could be attributed to spending the afternoon with the shifter.

After a moment, he shook his head and went back to speaking with Keegan.

Thalia let out a sigh of relief. She squared her shoulders, leaning closer to hear.

Lord Damien cleared his throat, drawing the attention of the room. "Members of the Houses, welcome. On behalf of His Highness, we want to thank you all for traveling such a great distance to discuss the matters of Vaccarium. While His Highness isn't here, he is represented by his own inner circle."

Lord Adrian sneered, but Lord Damien ignored him, continuing. "As you are all aware, the humans have kept their end of the treaty. We received word just this morning that the springs are fully filled. We are hopeful that in the next few months our forest will again be thriving.

"In turn, the humans have received the ore from our mountain. Labor has been slow due to unforeseen circumstances. The humans' reserves were far more depleted than we thought, and they are pushing to receive more ore soon. Given the amount of effort and the tentative peace we have with them, House Lorenzia turns to you all to see what men might be spared to go into Lorceium to harvest more."

Her mother had been in contact with the Vampyrs? Had Cassius lied to her? The news had her stomach twisting. She didn't want to consider that the queen might have ignored her letters.

Thalia picked at the nails around her thumbs. The knowledge sent a pang of hurt spearing through her. No, it seemed evident that her mother had been talking to the Vampyrs this whole time and hadn't even bothered to see how her daughter was faring. If she even still breathed.

Thalia suddenly regretted sending word to her mother at all. If only out of spite.

"House Olvectus is closest to the mountain; why can't they be used?" someone from House Santorien asked.

"Because we are currently dealing with the *other* situation happening at our borders," the woman next to Camilla said.

"Oh yes, Lady Decima," Lord Adrian sneered. It clicked that this was the leader of House Olvectus, the only female leader in the room. "You and the Mages, I'm sure." His green eyes flashed, much like his son's. Thalia wondered if the leader of House Gallinus knew what his son had done and that he'd been banished by Cassius.

"Yes," Camilla snapped, butting in, her golden eyes blazing. "You yourself have witnessed this blight upon your own lands. It is of the utmost importance."

"But so is keeping the humans appeased." Lord Amadeus spoke. The leader of House Santorien nodded to Cassius. "Our forest has gone too long without nutrients. Our springs were nearly dried. What happens if the rivers are cut off once more? What happens once the trees are dead? When the creatures who live within its shadowed border cannot find enough food? Then they will come out of hiding—they will come for our homes, our people. We'll be fighting more than just one blight at that point."

What blight are they talking about?

"And the prince continues to ignore this problem." Lord Adrian directed his hateful gaze at Cassius.

Cassius leaned back in his chair, the portrait of arrogant grace. "The prince is well aware of the problem at hand. He is working up north with the Mages as we speak."

Lord Adrian's lip curled. "Those damn Mages aren't doing shit against the blight." Both Camilla and Lady Decima stiffened as he plowed ahead. "He has done nothing as his people have succumbed to this madness. He has disappeared, despite you trying to cover for him. He's probably fucking and drinking his way across Vaccarium while we all suffer. While you"—Lord Adrian pointed an accusing finger—"do just the same thing."

Cassius raised a brow, letting the insults fall at his feet. "I can assure you, we are doing everything in our power to stop this madness."

"Are you?" Lord Adrian snarled. "It seems that you all have become more distracted of late. Especially you, *Hand*. In fact, I'd say that human bitch is why you've all done nothing as the blight against our kind grows."

"Be careful how you speak about the prince's bride," Keegan said softly. "She is part of House Lorenzia now. Any insult you make of her is an insult cast on us all."

"The human princess," Cassius bit out, "is none of your concern. She has no idea about the creature in our woods, no idea about the madness it causes."

Thalia sucked in a sharp breath, but with so much tension rising in the room, no one heard her.

A creature in the woods . . . madness.

Thalia's mind flashed to the Vampyr in the cellar, how utterly deranged it had acted, as though it had gone mad. Then to the conversation she'd first heard when she was introduced to the courts, and Lord Amadeus's own concerns about something continuing to fester in the forest . . .

"No idea?" Lord Adrian growled, his chair scraping as he stood. "She was the one who discovered the bitten in Irenbis! She's the reason my son is *banished*."

"Your son is banished," Cassius growled, his face rippling, "because he was foolish in bringing a bitten into the city. He put countless lives at risk, all for his own selfishness."

"You wish to speak of selfishness, Lord Cassius?" Lord Adrian's words dropped, his own face rippling. "Was not that human princess your own lover? Was she not who your heart sang for? Yet the prince was called away that day you brought her back, and has remained absent from his court while his bride remains here."

Cassius didn't take the bait, although his face darkened.

"He is trying to find a cure," Camilla said, eyes livid. "You would know that if you ever took your head out of your ass."

"Is he?" Lord Adrian challenged.

"Yes," Lady Decima spoke, her voice firm and unwavering.

"Which is more than can be said of you and your family," Camilla commented.

"And what is that supposed to mean?" Lord Adrian's eyes narrowed.

"Your own son was harboring a bitten," the shifter said. "Considering the fact that another creature was spotted near Cupisco, when you *swore* your borders were secured, I wouldn't be surprised if there were more bitten being harbored."

"Are you accusing me of something, shifter?" Lord Adrian asked.

Awkward silence stretched as the rest of the leaders of the Houses all looked at each other

"If you were harboring bitten"—Cassius's voice turned deadly serious—"then there would be no choice but to banish you and all of your House members."

Lord Adrian's lip curled, but he said nothing.

Lord Damien cleared his throat, turning to Lord Amadeus. "House Santorien is near Olvectus. Do you have laborers that can be sent to Lorceium?"

Lord Amadeus nodded slowly, glancing at Cassius. "Yes. I shall send twenty men within the week."

"Fifty," Cassius cut in.

Lord Amadeus shifted. "I don't have more men to spare."

"Find them." Cassius's words were final. Lord Amadeus's jaw flickered, but he gave a stiff nod.

Lord Damien glanced around the room. "The blight grows stronger as the days go on. It is becoming more difficult to go through the forest to bring the ore to the humans. While we have our ships to bring the ore by sea, we have always struggled to find a safe place to port." The Vampyr turned to Cassius. "Do you know of a safe dock where we might get ore to the people?"

Cassius's fingers clenched on the table, his face unreadable.

Why the hell has he never shared where our ports are?

Granted, not that the ports would do much good. Only the most skilled sailor could ever hope to safely land in Agripa. But Thalia couldn't make sense of the fact that Cassius had never provided the Houses with this information. Certainly not given his seemingly new devotion to the Vampyrs. The fact that he'd never told the Vampyrs where they might enter, as though he were protecting Agripa, sent another piece of the hazy puzzle scattering.

"Perhaps," Keegan said tentatively, "Thalia would know."

Lord Adrian sneered again. "She'd be more inclined to show us the opposite. To watch our people drown as their ships were smashed upon the rocks."

"Do not speak about her as if you know her." Cassius's voice was lethally quiet.

"No, but I am sure you know her well enough. Better, considering all those cold, lonely nights alone together. Given your history together, I wouldn't put it past you if this plan was yours in the making."

"What exactly are you accusing me of, Lord Adrian?" Cassius said softly.

"That you brought the human here for a purpose. That perhaps you wished to seduce her, to win her to your side so you might overthrow the prince together. So you might rule House Lorenzia officially. Is that not what you've always wanted, to restore your family name, given what happened?" the green-eyed Vampyr spat.

"What I've always wanted," Cassius said in the same lethally quiet voice as his face shifted, flesh sinking into his skull, sunken cheekbones highlighting the sharp planes of his face, "is to keep my people safe. That is what I am doing as hand, what the prince is also trying to do."

"And what is there to show for it?" Lord Adrian snarled again. "I don't see you going out into the forest to try and find a cure. I don't see the prince either. It's no wonder the blight is getting worse. When you pick and choose his own people to be sent out as lambs for the slaughter—adding more fuel to the fire."

Cassius stared at the lord, not refuting the claim, his jaw tense.

Was that why House Lorenzia was so empty? They were being sent out to find a cure for the sickness? What was taking them out?

"Perhaps it's time for a new hand," Lord Adrian said, and the attention of the room shifted to him. "Perhaps one who might be willing to do whatever it takes to stop this once and for all."

"And what would it take?" Cassius growled out.

Lord Adrian smirked. "It would start with ending the treaty with the humans. It would start by killing—" Thalia stepped back, her boots kicking some pebbles on the ground. Lord Adrian's nostrils flared, eyes widening in surprise, then rage. "Someone is here."

Before she could turn and run, Lord Adrian ripped down the tapestry, flinging open the hidden door to expose her.

Chapter Twenty-Two

"You," Lord Adrian snarled.

Thalia trembled, snatching the blade at her side, but not fast enough. Lord Adrian grabbed her, twisting her arm hard enough behind her back that she yelped.

Everyone stood, the Vampyrs in various shades of transforming as Lord Adrian pushed her into the room.

Cassius's face had turned stone cold.

"This is what we get from the humans." Lord Adrian's unwanted breath was hot in her ear. "We cannot trust them. We cannot trust this treaty."

"Think about what you're doing," Lord Damien said softly, his red eyes moving between them. "You toe the line of treason, Lord Adrian. The prince will not stand for it once he hears of how you threatened his bride."

"If only the prince were here," Lord Adrian hissed. He wrenched Thalia's arm higher and she whimpered, but she didn't drop her blade.

"Let her go." Cassius's words were hardly a whisper.

"Or what?" Lord Adrian snarled.

Cassius's face hadn't changed back. If anything, his cheeks had sunk in deeper, black veins running beneath his skin. "Julian wasn't just banished."

Lord Adrian stiffened, but his grip remained iron. "What do you mean?"

Cassius smirked, a thing of deadly cruelty. "I had a feeling you might react poorly when you heard of what he'd done. So, before he left Vaccarium, he was taken."

"Where?"

"Let the princess go, and I'll tell you."

Lord Adrian faltered. "You're lying."

"Am I?" Cassius growled. "A single word from me and he will meet a fate more gruesome than death—a fate we've all been trying to avoid." Lord Adrian's grip loosened slightly. "So I suggest, Lord Adrian, you let Thalia go. Unless you wish to see your son turn into a crazed beast and let loose upon your own House."

Thalia's shoulder twinged in pain, another whimper escaping her lips before the Vampyr pushed her forward hard enough that she stumbled.

Cassius caught her immediately before shoving her behind his back. Keegan and Camilla were at her sides, Lord Damien at her back, each closing rank around her.

Lord Adrian cast him a scathing look, nothing but hardened hatred in his eyes. He looked at the other lords. "You all are complicit in this." Then the Vampyr fled, the few in his entourage scattering with him.

"This meeting is over. Everyone get out. Now," Cassius rumbled.

All the lords shuffled out, along with their companions. But Lady Decima remained, either oblivious to the rage shaking Cassius or not caring.

"Did you need something, Lady Decima?" Keegan asked softly.

The lady inclined her head, her gaze on Thalia. "I know this isn't an ideal time"—Cassius snarled, and Lady Decima continued undeterred—"but I must share before I head back to Perden."

"What is it?" Cassius snapped.

"The Mages have had setbacks," Lady Decima said.

Cassius stiffened, some of his rage leaving. "By how long?"

"Months."

Camilla sucked in a sharp breath, and Keegan cursed.

Cassius finally looked at Thalia. He seemed to have gotten his transformation under control, although his face still rippled, turning ashy, then full of color.

His wariness set her anger spiking. He didn't trust her with whatever information Lady Decima wanted to share. Cassius's face darkened as he looked away. "Thank you, Lady Decima. I'll be in touch shortly."

The leader of House Olvectus inclined her head, then she left.

Thalia glanced around at the remaining members of the prince's inner circle. "What did you ask of her?" She directed her question at Cassius, wariness be damned.

He flicked his gaze to her, his blue eyes iced over. The rage was back, but this time it was aimed at her. "Do you want to tell me what the fuck you were doing listening in?"

Thalia lifted her chin, ignoring the twinge in her shoulder as she sheathed her blade. "I heard the council meeting had been moved up, and I knew the courts wouldn't share anything if I was in the room."

"You could have gotten killed," he said lowly.

"And I could have gotten killed when I faced that crazed Vampyr," Thalia countered. "What the hell was that thing? And don't you dare tell me that it was just sick. There's something else going on. Something that has to do with the forest and . . . and some creature?"

The four of them glanced at each other but said nothing.

"If you don't tell me, I'll just go into the forest and figure it out myself," Thalia hissed.

"You do that, and you really have a death wish," Cassius growled.

Thalia lifted her chin, refusing to back down.

"Cass," Keegan said softly. "We should tell her."

"I agree," Lord Damien said, sinking into one of the chairs. It was the first time the pale Vampyr seemed almost tired. "Whether you like it or not, she's part of this world now. To keep her in the dark further could only endanger her more."

"Tell me what?" Thalia looked around.

Cassius finally met her gaze. "There's a reason you were able to track me through Agripa."

Thalia stared at him, unsure why he was bringing it up now. "What was the reason?"

"I was hunting those who'd turned."

Thalia couldn't interpret his words. "You were hunting other Vampyrs?"

Cassius shook his head, his auburn hair sliding with the movement. "Those things are not Vampyrs. Not anymore."

"What are they?"

"They've been turned by something else. A half-crazed animal whose hunger is insatiable. They are the ones who have been causing the Scarecrows in Agripa."

Thalia's throat bobbed, her mind flashing to the cellar and the Vampyr who was eating lambs and skinning them. "What is turning them?"

Cassius paused, and Lord Damien supplied, "A creature. Something more terrible than even the Nestos or anything you might have encountered here."

Thalia flicked her gaze to each member of the prince's council. "And it dwells in the forest?"

Cassius hesitated, then nodded slowly. "It seemed to have spawned from Chaménos, but with Lucarius having been bitten here . . ."

Lucarius must have been the sick Vampyr he'd killed. "That's why you were all so worried, traveling through the forest, why you were so adamant about being quiet?"

"The creature likes to hide in the forest. It makes it near impossible to find. Even our best trackers have difficulty pinning its exact location, and it seems to have a particular fondness for the environment," Keegan said miserably.

"Can't you stop it?"

Cassius shook his head. "We have tried, but when we have managed to stumble upon it, it is not easily killed. And those who've gone up against it . . ."

"Are they turned?"

Cassius met her stare. "Its bite causes Vampyrs to go mad. They become rabid, not knowing who or what they are, only that they must feed. But whatever is in the creature's bite, once it's in a Vampyr's system, they can spread it to others."

"That's why you said that Julian and Francesca had endangered your people," Thalia breathed out. "And why Lord Adrian let me go at the thought that his son would be turned into one."

Cassius's face hardened. "And it was a good thing he bought the lie."

Thalia swallowed, her stomach twisting at the thought of what could have happened if the lord hadn't believed Cassius. "Francesca said they were trying to find a cure. Is there one?"

The muscle in Cassius's jaw flickered. "Not that we know of."

Thalia shook her head, her mind whirling with too many questions. "You said the prince was looking for a cure up north with the Mages. Was the story about the barrier cracking even true?"

Cassius met her gaze, something like regret flashing over his features before it was gone. "A Mage *did* cast a spell to allow us to roam during the day, but no. The shield in place is fine."

Thalia thought she'd be angry at Cassius for lying yet again, but only curiosity filled her stomach.

"You can't kill the creature?" Thalia asked.

"Its hide is near impenetrable," Keegan got out bitterly. "It uses the forest as its own personal battleground. But that's not the worst we're now facing."

"What do you mean?"

Cassius finally sank down onto a chair. Heaviness lay around his shoulders, as if great millstones were wrapped around his neck. "It seems the creature has discovered a way to breed."

Thalia's stomach knotted. "Breed?"

"It has birthed or spawned two more of its kind. One was spotted near Cupisco," Keegan supplied. "The one near Cupisco was small; a number of Vampyrs were able to bring it down, but not before a handful were bitten."

Good gods.

"What happened to those who were bitten?" Thalia was almost afraid to ask.

Cassius met her gaze. "They were killed."

Thalia's heart stuttered, and she closed her eyes. When she finally opened them, Cassius studied her. "And there is no cure, truly?" she asked.

"The water from our sacred springs in Chaménos seems to slow the madness down. At least push off the inevitable for a few months," Lord Damien said, his own frustration lacing his otherwise stoic demeanor.

"That's why you really needed our rivers," Thalia stated.

"Yes," Cassius sighed. "The springs are the only thing that is giving us some hope that there might be a cure out there. If they dried up, the Vampyrs who've been bitten would succumb to their madness sooner and could very well spread it to others quicker."

"Then why didn't you tell my mother all this?"

"You of all people should know how the humans in Agripa feel about the Vampyrs." Cassius's face flashed in wariness.

Indeed. Given the information the prince's council had shared, Thalia could send word right to her mother to have her stop the rivers. Once the springs dried up in the forest, it would only be a matter of time before the creature bit more Vampyrs and its poison spread among them. They could effectively wipe out the entire Vampyr population without so much as lifting a finger. Given Cassius's guarded expression, Thalia had a feeling he thought she'd run right home to the queen to give her the information. This was what she'd been waiting to uncover—the key that would unravel the Vampyr courts and bring them to their knees. And yet . . .

Thalia's mind flashed to the conversation she'd had with Camilla. The fact that not every House agreed with what had happened between the humans and Vampyrs all those years ago. How she hoped that the lives of her people could be better—

Thalia shook her head. "Those Vampyrs I stumbled upon in Agripa, the ones who weren't bitten, what were they doing there, then?"

Cassius straightened. "They were sent to take out the Vampyrs who'd turned. That and see if there is any cure outside of Vaccarium."

Thalia glanced at Lord Damien. The red-eyed Vampyr stared at her unblinking. She'd killed his brother—killed him without remorse.

Some sort of regret festered in her stomach. He hadn't been the one who'd left the Scarecrows, and neither had Cassius. All they had been trying to do was stop the spread of poison from further digging its roots in.

"No wonder the prince isn't around," Thalia said quietly.

Cassius nodded. "He is trying to find anything that might stop these creatures from killing more of his people."

"Lord Adrian sounded bitter about it."

Cassius sighed again, running a hand through his long hair. "The people aren't happy about what's going on. They are terrified of even stepping out of their homes and running into a creature or one that has been bitten." No wonder Irenbis seemed so deserted. Did those Vampyrs holed up in their homes deserve this grim fate? "They don't believe that the prince truly has their best interests at heart."

"Why is that?"

"Because the prince has not always been a just or fair ruler. This creature has been in the woods for years. Been allowed to grow and feed on other monsters—to grow stronger. There were reports of something strange brewing in Chaménos five years ago, but the prince ignored it."

"Why would he do that?"

"He believed the reports were rumors started by the humans to stir up discord amongst the Vampyr courts," Lord Damien said.

Thalia chewed the inside of her cheek, studying Cassius. Everything was beginning to make sense now. Why the treaty had been struck and why the prince was always gone. Suddenly, the validity of her mission seemed to waver.

"And I fear," Lord Damien continued, "that the blight of the bitten will only grow stronger. Julian may not have been the only one hiding loved ones who've been bitten."

Cassius's face darkened. "What do you mean?"

"My father discovered a group of bitten in a barn just outside Sanire, the capital of House Avanerius." Thalia guessed he had added that last bit for her sake. "A whole family except one had been turned. They were trying to keep it a secret so they wouldn't all be killed."

"They're becoming desperate," Keegan murmured.

Cassius's face became a granite mask. "The more Vampyrs that are bitten, the more they'll do anything to keep their loved ones alive. Including hiding those who've turned . . ." He looked to Camilla. "I need you to go to Lorceium. We don't have months. Figure out what can be done to speed things along."

Camilla nodded. "On it." She went to the window, throwing it open before she stepped onto the ledge.

"What are you—" Thalia started, but Camilla didn't look back as she jumped.

Then something shot past the window, a cry echoing. Thalia's eyes widened at the retreating form of a falcon in the distance.

"I need a unit of men who can sweep through the cities, especially those near the border of the forest, to look for anyone who may be harboring a bitten. Can you do that?" Cassius turned to Lord Damien.

The Vampyr inclined his head. "It will be done." He left, leaving only Keegan as the remaining member.

"What about the prince?" Thalia blurted out.

The two Vampyrs glanced at each other.

"What about him?" Cassius got out.

Thalia met his intense stare. "Isn't he supposed to be back soon? Surely he can't expect you all to deal with this and the courts on your own? I mean, you aren't all the rulers of House Lorenzia. The prince can't really expect his people to follow his councilors' orders alone."

A muscle flickered in Cassius's jaw. "No, we aren't the rulers. But the prince sends his orders, and we see that they are fulfilled. This is nothing we haven't already dealt with."

"But you shouldn't have to deal with it."

"What are you getting at, Thalia?" Cassius scanned her face.

"You are not the prince; you're his hand. He should be the one here, giving orders directly—telling his advisers and his courts what to do. Instead, he's doing what? Looking for a cure? But how? My mother sent out people on her behalf to try and find a solution to the ore—"

"The prince is not your mother," Cassius snarled out, surprising Thalia with his vehemence. "And the prince likes to see things done by his hand."

"So he can appear to be a savior after neglecting his realm?"

"If that is the case, it doesn't matter. Nor does it concern you."

"I think it should concern me, considering the man I am married to isn't even around! Is our marriage even binding? Legal? Given the fact we haven't consummated it?"

Cassius stilled, his gaze slowly lifting to hers. "Are you so eager to consummate this union?"

Thalia lifted her chin. "I thought Vampyrs cared about customs."

Cassius's lips twisted into a smile, although it didn't reach his eyes. "We do. Which is why I am still your proxy."

"Then, as a proxy, I am sure you'll be more than willing to step aside once the prince returns."

Cassius raised a brow. "I'll be happy to offer my own room for you to consummate your marriage."

Thalia bared her teeth in a resemblance of a smile. "How generous."

Cassius tilted his head. "Anything else you wish to discuss?"

"Nope."

"Good. I have business to attend to." Cassius rose, aiming for the door. He paused, looking over his shoulder. "Oh, I'll refrain from telling the prince that his wife threw herself at me while he was away. I'm sure that would be an embarrassment on your behalf."

Chapter Twenty-Three

Prick. Prick. Prick.

Thalia stewed in the bathtub, the bubbles long having disappeared. She wished she had something to strangle. Perhaps Cassius himself.

Thalia pressed the heels of her palms into her eyes, trying to stanch the growing ache behind them. Her shoulder twinged in pain. At least Lord Adrian was gone from court; at least she didn't have to worry about him ripping her throat out . . . for now.

Things were getting worse. The bites were spreading, especially if those who'd been bitten were being protected by their loved ones. It would be so easy to write her mother. To tell her that the Vampyrs were on the cusp of collapse.

But Thalia knew her mother wouldn't be pleased to sit back and wait for the inevitable. She'd want it to move faster. She'd want Thalia to move faster—to set things in motion so that their demise happened swiftly.

So why the hell wasn't she acting?

She'd tried to write another letter, this one with more intel, hints that something was amiss in Vaccarium—that the Vampyrs were acting strangely, many having gotten ill with some mysterious disease. But she'd left it half written on her desk.

If only the damn prince would return so she could set things in motion. Yes. Yes that was the reason for her hesitation. Because if the prince were here, she could get the animosity between House Gallinus and House Lorenzia to boil over. When she was sure the courts would turn on each other. Then, once they were fighting among themselves and the fear of the creature took hold, *then* she would write to the queen and Agripa could sweep in for victory.

The thought set her stomach turning uncomfortably.

Thalia swallowed the burning in her throat. But none of it mattered, because she was effectively screwed. The courts had left, they didn't trust her, and seducing the hand to the prince was going less well than expected.

Thalia's lip curled as Cassius flashed in her mind. The heat in his eyes before he'd shut her down the night before.

Prick. Prick. Prick.

The door of her room opened, the sound reaching her through the cracked opening of the bathing chamber.

Thalia craned her head to find Cassius in the bedroom. She sank back in the tub, scowling.

Cassius didn't seem to realize she was in there, because he shuffled about the room before slinging off his tunic as he aimed for the bathing chamber. His hands went to the buckle of his belt, snapping it off as he pushed open the door and froze.

Thalia raised a brow as he slowly took her in. "Were you going to take a bath?" she asked, smirking.

Cassius jerked his eyes to hers. "No."

Thalia shrugged, her fingertips trailing in the water. "Shame. It's been a tense last few twenty-four hours. I was going to suggest you join me."

The muscle in Cassius's jaw flickered, then he caught the gleam in her eye and he quickly relaxed, leaning against the doorframe. He crossed his arms over his chest. "Shall I add this to the list of things to not tell the prince when he returns?"

"If you like." Thalia met his gaze, and he seemed to take extra care to stare at her face. "Oh please, Cassius. It's not like you've never seen me naked before."

"That was different."

"How?"

"You weren't married to someone else."

"That thought didn't seem to stop you last night."

Cassius raised a brow in challenge. Then he slowly looked her over, the little bits of suds left in the tub doing nothing to hide her body. Each sweep of his heated gaze set her skin on fire, and she was grateful for the steam gathering along the mirror—that her face was already flushed because of it.

"I suppose old habits die hard," he finally said, meeting her gaze once more.

Thalia's anger spiked. "Is that what I am to you? An old habit?"

"Am I not yours?"

Thalia barked out a laugh, standing. Water sloshed off her body and Cassius straightened. She ignored him as she grabbed her silk dressing robe. But she didn't put it on as she got out of the tub. She walked toward him, dressing gown in hand, leaving a trail of water in her wake. "Do you want to know why I kissed you last night?" she asked low, stopping before him.

Cassius didn't move, his eyes once more glued on hers. Every hard line of his body was taut, a bow threatening to snap. "Why?" he got out.

Thalia trailed her fingers up his arm, leaving droplets of water along his hot skin. "I had an itch that needed to be scratched."

"Clearly."

Thalia smirked, her fingers drawing down across his pectorals to the line of his stomach. She flicked her gaze up, finding his attention on her hand as it traveled lower.

"But frankly, I would have done that with anyone. You just happened to be the only person in the room."

Cassius slowly raised his gaze to hers. "Is that so?"

"Mm-hmm," Thalia hummed, her nails scratching lightly against the skin of his lower abs. "But that itch has been dealt with, so no need to worry about adding more incidents to your list."

Cassius's eyes flared. "By who?"

Thalia's grin stretched, delight spearing through her at his sudden interest. She pressed closer, the tips of her breasts nearly brushing against his chest. "Wouldn't it kill you to know?"

Cassius's jaw flickered, once, then twice. "You should get dressed. You'll catch cold." He brushed past her, aiming for the sink. "And I'd be careful of your shoulder; you wouldn't want to further injure yourself."

Thalia nearly crowed in triumph as his back stiffened. But she kept her lips sealed moving into the bedroom and didn't bother to get dressed.

Cassius didn't come to bed that night.

He didn't even sleep on the settee, and Thalia slept poorly because of it. When morning came, there was no indication that he'd even be there at all.

Thalia didn't want to admit that a small part of her worried she'd done too much—pushed him too far.

Cassius didn't appear for breakfast, nor later that afternoon. It was nearing evening when Thalia finally found a servant.

"Have you seen Cass—Lord Cassius?" she asked. The servant just shook their head, scurrying off to fulfill whatever task held their attention.

Thalia walked around the quiet castle. It wasn't like she could ask Camilla, and there was no sign of Keegan, although she wasn't sure if he even stayed in the castle.

Thalia managed to sneak past the guards at the front and found herself in the stables, the smell of hay drifting to her nostrils. A stable hand mucked out a stall and looked up in surprise when she appeared.

"Have you seen the hand to the prince?" she asked, her fingers picking around the skin of her thumbs.

The stable hand shook his head, glancing at her hands. Thalia stopped and the boy swallowed, meeting her gaze. "He—he took his horse out late last night. He hasn't returned."

Thalia's stomach tightened. "What about Lord Keegan?"

The stable hand just shook his head, confused. "I don't know."

"Where did Cassius go?"

The stable hand ran a shaky hand through his hair. "The forest on the east side of town."

The forest.

Thalia's heart pounded as she instructed the boy to get Feryena ready. *It could be nothing,* she told herself as she spurred her horse out of the castle grounds. Cassius had probably gone into Irenbis to ensure no more bitten were being hidden.

But the forest . . .

Thalia tried to keep the panic from her veins.

The creature causing the madness seemed to stay in Chaménos, but it had managed to breed, and one of its offsprings had been found in a forest far from the one that bordered the realm. Meaning the spawn could travel anywhere. And even the spawn could be just as deadly.

Thalia urged Feryena faster, breaking through the woods that surrounded the castle, and looked toward Irenbis. Then, there—to the east was another set of trees, ones that looked like they'd sprouted from Chaménos itself.

She kicked her horse, and Feryena took off, dirt flying from her hooves.

Thalia only slowed once she'd reached the edge of the trees.

She silently cursed. She should have asked the stable hand where exactly in the forest Cassius said he was going to. Thalia scanned the landscape until she spotted a small trail leading into the woods. She pushed her horse on, slowing as she entered.

The trunks of the trees rose close together like the strings of a harp, the branches laden with thick, crimson leaves. Thalia's heart pounded, but she willed herself to breathe and think.

Whatever Cassius was doing in the forest, tramping through in a panic would no doubt ruin it, or piss him off further. Thalia took a deep breath.

Feryena moved along the path, and Thalia searched for anything amiss. It wasn't until she'd gone at least a mile into the forest that she saw something strange.

Deep gouges appeared in some of the tree trunks, branches and underbrush broken from something being dragged.

Thalia grabbed the dagger in her boot, silently cursing herself again for not taking more weapons.

She halted her horse, ears straining. She heard nothing, and the trail of broken ground was old. The hair on the back of her neck prickled, and she slowly looked over her shoulder, glancing between the trunks.

Feryena swished her tail, ears flicking back and forth. There was nothing. Not even the scurrying of squirrels above her—

A screech broke through the trees, the sound startling her horse. Thalia fumbled with the reins as Feryena spooked.

She didn't have time to scream as something slammed into her side and she was knocked clean out of the saddle.

She rolled as she hit the ground, trying to get her feet under her, fighting for breath in her lungs. Whatever had knocked her off had been sent flying a few paces away, and she whirled, dagger drawn.

The blood drained from her face.

The creature that rose from the brush was the size of a dog, its body lithe and muscular. It was covered in a slick white leathery skin, its strange handlike paws ending in sharp claws. Its face was oval shaped, but with a long snout like a hound's. It had no eyes, but its mouth had come unhinged, revealing rows of pointed teeth all dripping with green saliva.

Its nostrils flared, its mouth widening as it let out another screech.

Thalia flung her dagger right into its open jaws.

The creature screamed, head shaking at the embedded knife. Thalia didn't look back as she ran.

Her arms pumped as she fled, branches cutting into her face and arms. She should have grabbed another weapon—

The creature roared behind her, and she ducked around a trunk. The sound of the tree breaking as the creature slammed into it echoed. She dodged and weaved behind trunks, trying to slow the thing down.

A stitch speared itself up her side, and Thalia gasped. She pushed past the pain, her lungs to the point of breaking.

She just needed to get out of the forest.

A pang of fear speared through her. She couldn't go to the city. Not if this was one of the spawned creatures—it could bite the Vampyrs, spreading its poison—

In a split-second decision, Thalia changed course. She flew between the densely packed trees, her body scraping against the tight spaces. The creature chased her, but she led it deeper into the forest, away from Irenbis.

But she couldn't outrun the thing forever; already her body was to the point of giving out—

Thalia screamed, ducking as something sailed overhead. The creature appeared before her and lunged.

Thalia's back hit the ground and she managed to catch the creature by the throat. Its jaws snapped at her, saliva flying. Her dagger was still embedded in the back of its throat, the blade doing nothing to stop it.

Thalia gritted her teeth, struggling against the weight of the animal and its jaws inches from her face.

A roar sounded off to her left, and Thalia's heart sank—there were two creatures.

This was it, how she was going to die.

Something slammed into the creature's side. The creature was a blur of white as a figure with auburn hair tackled it.

Thalia gasped, her chest heaving as she struggled to get up.

Cassius.

Cassius flung the creature aside, its back cracking against one of the trees. He pulled out his sword. The creature's maw opened, shooting toward Cassius. He rolled, narrowly avoiding its snapping jaws. Cassius swung his sword, the blade barely cutting through its leatherlike skin.

The creature whirled again, lunging. Cassius grunted, the front of his chest shredding against its claws.

Thalia screamed.

Cassius turned, but not fast enough as it attacked a third time. The creature knocked him aside, jaws at his throat.

Thalia surged forward, her knife finally having fallen from the creature's mouth. She gripped the slick handle, flying toward the creature.

She screamed again as she brought her blade down, aiming straight for its side. It was like cutting through thick mud. The force of her downward swing reverberated up her arm.

It distracted the creature enough to turn to her.

Thalia expected it to lunge at her, but it merely bared its teeth, nostrils flaring in her direction, almost like it was inhaling her scent for the first time. It must have been too set on killing her to really take note when it'd knocked her from her saddle.

She froze, stunned by its reaction. It flared its nostrils again, a low sound chortling in its throat. It took a step away from Cassius's fallen body, and Thalia retreated.

The creature kept scenting the air, chuffing as it advanced slowly on her. Thalia's limbs shook as she backed away until her spine pressed against a trunk.

The creature paused, lifting its head. Its nostrils flared a third time, and then its strange snout touched her chest.

Thalia trembled as it shifted backward—

It let out a screech as Cassius's sword embedded in its neck.

Cassius grunted, the sword sticking halfway through, the creature somehow still alive. Its cries spurred Thalia, and she surged toward Cassius. Her hands wrapped around his own and together they used all their strength to push the sword down.

Two arrows thwacked the creature's body, and Thalia knew Keegan was there only by a blur of gold in her peripheral vision.

Finally, after three more arrows and a last push from Cassius, the sword slid through bone and sinew. The creature's headless body stumbled backward before falling over in a heap, its limbs twitching.

"Fuck, are you all right?" Keegan panted, racing over.

Thalia turned to Cassius. Bright red stained the front of his shirt. She gripped him as he fell to his knees, fresh panic entering her veins.

"Did it bite you?" she rasped as Keegan came to Cassius's side, whipping off his cloak to try to staunch the bleeding.

"Cassius, did it bite you—" She hadn't realized how tightly she clutched him until one of his hands squeezed her wrist.

"No. No it didn't," Cassius got out.

Thalia's relief was short-lived. Blood was soaking through the fabric of the cloak now. "We need to get you back to the castle." Her eyes met his. "Now."

Chapter Twenty-Four

Cassius's blood soaked the back of Thalia's cloak.

She gritted her teeth, trying to push aside the image of that creature's claws digging into his chest like butter.

Keegan rode hard in front of her, the dead creature tied to his horse's flank, its head resting in a knapsack.

They were almost to the castle, but Cassius's grip was starting to slacken around her waist. He grunted behind her, and Thalia gripped one of his hands.

"Almost there," she murmured, spotting the castle spires through the trees. But Thalia didn't breathe a sigh of relief as they broke into the inner courtyard.

Keegan dismounted, immediately going to grab Cassius as he half slid, half fell off his horse.

Thalia was right behind, looping his arm around her shoulders and they both helped Cassius up the castle steps.

The only sound was the dripping of blood from Cassius's chest as they traveled through the dark castle. Thalia didn't know where to go, but Keegan aimed for the back wing, the sconces flickering as they passed under them.

After what felt like eternity, they entered the infirmary.

It wasn't a large space, with a few cots and a back wall covered in a stone fireplace with a cauldron hovering over a stack of wood inside it. Cubbies lined the right wall, filled with dried herbs and glass jars of liquid. A large worktable sat smack in the middle of the room, and both Keegan and Thalia helped Cassius onto the table.

Thalia immediately pulled off Keegan's cloak that'd been staunching the blood and sucked in a gasp.

Cassius's chest was a mangled mess of flesh. The claws had cut much deeper than she'd thought, and bits of his rib cage were visible between the torn muscle.

Thalia shoved the bile out of her throat, turning to Keegan. "What do we do?" Keegan's face was hard as he rolled up the sleeves of his shirt. "Keegan? What do we do?" Panic laced her words. Cassius's breaths came out in wet pants, his teeth stained with his own blood. His normally tan skin had paled, turning a grayish-green color.

He can't die, she thought. *He can't die.* Because he was a Vampyr, the only way to kill him was to stab him with an iron stake through his skull.

But Thalia had never seen an injury like this.

"Keegan—" Thalia's voice was on the verge of hysteria as Keegan shoved her aside.

"Stop us when it's done." Keegan's words were firm.

"When what's done—?" Thalia cut off as Keegan brought his dark wrist to his mouth, cutting into his own flesh. Then he brought his arm to Cassius's bloodless lips.

Thalia didn't think Cassius had any strength left in him, but as soon as Keegan pressed his wrist to his mouth, he lunged. Cassius grabbed Keegan's hand, his sharp canines sinking straight into the tender underside of Keegan's wrist.

Keegan grunted as Cassius pulled the other Vampyr's arm closer, his fingers gripping Keegan's arm like a lifeline. Cassius's throat worked as he took long pulls from the Vampyr's veins.

Thalia's eyes flew to Cassius's chest. His flesh was knitting back together, muscle snapping back into place, his skin inching slowly closed. Thalia glanced back at the two of them. Cassius's eyes were closed, his face relaxing, yet his mouth still worked. Keegan's eyes were closed too, his face just as relaxed as Cassius's, almost like both of them were experiencing pure bliss.

Her cheeks heated as she realized they were.

Keegan gripped Cassius's neck, allowing him to drink his blood. Neither of them seemed inclined to slow anytime soon.

Thalia snapped back into focus. *Stop us when it's done.* Because, given the way they were both entranced in whatever pleasure they were experiencing from Cassius's bite, Cassius wouldn't stop until he'd bled his friend dry.

Thalia focused on Cassius's chest, the skin slowly sealing itself back together. After another few seconds, nothing but smooth skin stared back at her.

Thalia jerked, shaking Keegan's arm. "Keegan?"

The golden-eyed Vampyr didn't move, didn't so much as open his lids.

"Keegan," she said more firmly, gripping his bicep and shaking. "Snap out of it. It's done."

A low sound came out of Cassius's throat, one that sent awareness right to her toes. She ignored him, shaking Keegan harder.

"Keegan!" she yelled.

He moaned, but he couldn't pull himself out of his pleasure-induced trance. His skin had taken on a waxy sheen as Cassius continued to gorge himself.

Thalia looked around the room, heart pounding. She spotted a small knife near a cubby full of herbs. She raced over, fingers gripping the handle before she turned to the Vampyrs.

Keegan swayed slightly, and she didn't think twice as she cut her palm. She fisted her hand, letting the blood gather between her fingers before it dripped out, plinking onto the cold ground.

Keegan's head jerked up. He turned, sluggishly looking over his shoulder, his golden gaze hazy. Thalia held up her fist, letting him see the droplets of blood.

His nostrils flared, once, then twice. Then he looked back down at his own arm. That seemed to pull him out of whatever stupor he was in.

Keegan shook his head, then pushed down on Cassius's now-healed chest. "That's enough, Cass." Cassius's eyes opened slightly, and he let out another low sound in the back of his throat, his fingers tight enough to bruise Keegan's arm. "You're healed; let go." Keegan tried again, pushing harder.

"Cass?" Thalia said.

Cassius stiffened, then slowly looked at her.

Thalia didn't balk at his gaze, his irises glowing as Keegan's blood dripped down his throat. She took a step toward him.

"I wouldn't do that—" Keegan warned, his voice much clearer now.

Thalia ignored him, coming up to Cassius's side. "Let go," she said. Cassius's eyes flared as she brought her uninjured hand to his. She gently pried his fingers off of Keegan's wrist. "Let go, and I'll give you something."

Cassius cocked his head at that. His pupils were so blown out they nearly devoured the rings of his irises.

"Let go, and we can finish what we started the other night."

Cassius's throat bobbed, his nostrils flaring, then he released Keegan's arm. The golden-eyed Vampyr sagged, his shoulders light with relief.

Cassius stared at her, his lips bloodied. Thalia thought he'd lunge at her next, but then he blinked. He took a deep, shuddering breath, squeezing his eyes tight. He lowered his head back down on the table, his eyes still shut as he murmured, "Are you hurt?"

Thalia shook her head, then realized he couldn't see her. "No."

"I smell blood."

"I-I think that's Keegan's."

Cassius cracked open an eye, staring at his friend. "Thanks," he rasped.

Keegan nodded, the color returning to his face. The bite marks on his wrist were already clotting. "I'm going to see about that creature." He flashed a relieved look at Cassius before nodding to Thalia. Then he left, leaving them alone.

"Are you all right?" Thalia whispered.

Cassius swallowed, his words low. "It feels like my chest was cleaved open."

Despite the circumstances, Thalia's lips quirked. "It basically was."

Cassius relaxed against the table, his breathing slowing. Thalia's chest squeezed. She made to move away, but his hand snaked out, gripping her injured one. "Stay."

She swallowed, ignoring the pain in her hand. But Cassius must have sensed the injury, because he cracked open both eyes, his brows furrowing. "You said you weren't hurt."

Thalia shook her head, finding a small wooden stool under the table and pulling it out, still holding on to Cassius's hand. "I'm not."

Cassius made a face, but his lids were growing heavier by the minute. He brought her wrist to his mouth and Thalia had a sudden pang of fear that he'd bite her, but he simply pressed his lips to her cut heart line.

"Thank you," he murmured, before sleep claimed him hard and fast.

Thalia stared down at their entwined hands now resting on Cassius's chest. Her eyes watered, and she blinked the tears away as she rested her chin on her other arm. She watched the rise and fall of his chest, ensuring he still breathed. Until the fear and adrenaline finally wore off and sleep claimed her too.

Something rustled above Thalia's head, and she jerked, blinking the sleep out of her eyes. It took her a moment to adjust to the dim light cast by the fire in the room.

She relaxed when she realized it was Cassius shifting on the table.

As if her eyes snapping open had made a noise, Cassius opened his own. He blinked, his blue gaze bright but not glowing.

He swallowed, his brow furrowing slightly. "You stayed." Thalia nodded, not able to break away. Then his brow furrowed more. "You're hurt."

Her face twisted in confusion, and she nearly startled as Cassius's hand gripped her face.

She winced as he ran his thumb lightly over her cheekbone. She hadn't realized the branches had cut her face when she fled the creature.

Cassius suddenly sat up, and Thalia started. "Should you be doing that?" she asked as he swung his legs over the side of the table.

"I'm fine," he said, standing.

"Hours ago your chest was hanging open." Thalia twisted in her seat, watching as Cassius rummaged around the cubbies.

"Keegan's blood did the work. If I wasn't fine, I'd rest." He turned to look over his shoulder, then jerked his chin at the table.

Thalia made a face, but she managed to hop onto the surface, a groan of protest escaping her lips. She hadn't realized how sore she was. Her body ached, and her skin was bruised from fleeing the creature.

Cassius kept his back to her as he mixed herbs and other tinctures in a mortar, grinding them together before he added liquid to make a paste. He grabbed some rags and a bowl of water, then turned back.

Thalia swallowed as he set the things down next to her, stepping between her dangling legs.

He gripped her chin lightly, turning it back and forth in the light, his eyes playing over her features. Then he dipped the rag in the water, squeezing out the excess, the drops plinking down before he gently dabbed the cut along her cheek.

She winced again, and his touch softened even more, as did his features as he went back to his ministrations.

Thalia's throat bobbed, and she said lowly, "Are you sure you're all right?"

Cassius nodded, attending to a cut near her hairline that she hadn't noticed. "When a Vampyr drinks another's blood, it allows them to heal at a much faster rate than a human. But only if you drink from the source. There's a reason we don't share blood over an injury unless it's grave."

"Is it because of what happens when Vampyrs drink blood from another?"

Cassius met her gaze, but he didn't seem embarrassed as he swiped the rag down her neck. "Drinking from another is an intimate moment. There's a level of trust that goes into it, because no matter how much you love that person, there's always a risk of overindulging."

"That's why Keegan asked me to stop you."

Cassius nodded, moving to the poultice he'd made. He dipped his fingers in, the paste sticking between his fingers. Thalia swallowed again. "If you hadn't stopped us—stopped me—I would have drained him of all his blood."

"I thought Vampyrs can only be killed by shoving a stake through its skull."

Cassius swiped his finger over the cuts on her face. "It's true. But when a Vampyr drains another of their blood, we go into a coma-like state. The only way to bring us out is to refill the blood that's been taken."

"So that Vampyr would have to drain another?" Thalia asked.

Cassius nodded, his fingers going again to the cut at her hairline. "It's a vicious cycle when that happens."

Thalia stared at him, studying the way his eyes roved over her face. The way he worked thoroughly and efficiently, like he always had.

When he was satisfied with his work, he moved to her hand. He didn't speak as he cleaned the blood off her fingers. She hissed when he cleaned the cut.

"Sorry," he murmured, his brows knotting. "How did this happen?" Cassius must not have recalled through his haze.

"I-I cut myself—to snap Keegan out of it."

"Smart."

"There was no other way to pull him out. Even shaking him didn't work," Thalia rambled.

Cassius tipped his chin. "That's not uncommon. Especially if there's a lot of damage and a lot of blood is required. If we were both at our prime, it wouldn't have taken you cutting yourself to snap one of us out of it." He wrapped a length of gauze around her hand, tying it off before stepping back.

Thalia suddenly craved his nearness as he went about putting away the things he'd used. She stared at her covered palm, the sounds of clinking ceramics echoing.

Finally, she asked, "That was one of the creature's spawn, wasn't it?"

Cassius finished drying off one of the bowls. "Yes. We got word late last night that one was spotted near Irenbis."

"And you went by yourself?"

Cassius shrugged. "Better to stop it before it could get to the city."

"You could have been killed." Or worse, bitten.

Cassius turned to her, ire suddenly washing over his features. "And you could have been too. Tell me, Thalia, why the hell were you in those woods?"

Thalia crossed her arms over her chest, lifting her chin. "Same as you."

He raised an unimpressed brow. "You went to hunt the creature?"

"I went to find you."

Cassius blinked, something flashing over his features before ire replaced it once more. "And why the fuck would you do that? I told you to stay in the castle."

Thalia threw her hands up. "Yeah, well, maybe it's because you didn't come to bed last night!"

Cassius's brow rose farther. "And you were worried?"

Thalia bit the inside of her cheek, annoyance replacing her concern. "You're an asshole."

She hopped down from the table, aiming for the door, but Cassius stopped her. His hand gripped her arm, pulling her back toward him.

"I'm not being an asshole," he said, eyes scanning hers. "I'm asking you if you were worried."

Thalia weighed her words and wished she were better at lying. Wished he weren't able to tell when she was. "Yes. I was worried. Happy now?"

Cassius's brows knotted. "Why is being worried a bad thing?" Thalia looked away, her throat suddenly knotting like his brows. He gripped her chin with his free hand, turning her face back to his.

"Because being worried about you means I care," she got out.

"And what's so bad about caring?" His thumb stroked alongside the curve of her jaw. She resisted the urge to lean in. To lean into *him*.

Yes, she was starting to care. Starting to feel the cracks in her mission. Her reaction to him almost dying was evidence enough of her impending failure. Thalia willed her mission to become clear. For her mother's desire to stop the Vampyrs once and for all to root itself in her heart—willed the image of her sister's shredded throat to appear.

But all she could see was Cassius's chest being ripped open.

All that flashed in her mind was the way his lips felt against hers. The strength of his arms when he held her. The fact that maybe . . . maybe he wasn't the monster she'd believed him to be.

"I—"

Scuffing on the threshold had them both turning. Cassius's hand fell away as Keegan appeared, his eyes bright as he said, "You're going to want to see this."

Chapter Twenty-Five

The three of them gathered in what must have been the cells of the castle. Or perhaps a torture chamber, given the sharp, wicked-looking devices along the walls and the chains dangling from the ceiling. The creature's body was splayed out on a steel table, its head next to it.

"What are we looking at?" Cassius asked, eyeing the dead thing. At least he'd put a shirt on, which did nothing to hide his physique as he crossed his arms over his chest. He'd cleaned the blood from his face too.

Keegan moved to the table. Various instruments littered the top, as if waiting to dissect it. Thalia resisted the urge to shiver.

"This thing is dead, right?" Keegan asked, and Cassius and Thalia exchanged a glance.

"Yes," Cassius said, eyes narrowing.

"But watch this." Keegan moved the head closer to the severed neck.

As soon as they were a hairbreadth apart, the muscle and tendons shot out like little vines. Thalia started as the separate pieces of flesh began to reach for each other, almost stitching themselves together the same way Cassius's skin had stitched itself.

"What the fuck?" Thalia breathed as Keegan ripped the head away, the tendons and muscles falling flat against the table, shriveled up like dried worms.

"Do you think it can come back to life?" Cassius asked, stepping deeper into the room.

Keegan placed the head a good distance away from the creature's body. "I don't know, but given the fact it did *that*, anything is possible."

"You said it was near impossible to kill, at least the mother. What happened to the spawn near Cupisco?" Thalia eyed the creature.

Cassius looked to Keegan, who shook his head, saying, "They burned it to ash." Cassius seemed to relax slightly at the information. Keegan went on, "I sent word to Lord Damien about this spawn. We need to be more vigilant in combing the forest. At least catching them young, we have some sort of chance in killing them."

But it wouldn't matter, not if the mother was still breeding in Chaménos.

Thalia shuddered, but she pushed aside Cassius's sudden concern as she moved closer. Up close, and without the fear of being maimed, Thalia studied the creature. It was already as big as a dog; she couldn't fathom how big the mother must be. At least the size of a horse. And given the difficulty in killing it . . .

She pressed her fingers against its flesh, surprised to find it cold and slimy. "Have you figured out what it is?"

Out of the corner of her eye, she saw Keegan shake his head. "This is the first one we've been able to kill and keep the remains of."

She pursed her lips, and Cassius cut in, "Send word to Camilla. She'll know more than anyone what sort of creature this could be. And clear out the castle, if this thing still poses a threat . . ."

"Both are already done," Keegan replied.

Thalia ran her hand over its hide, feeling the strange musculature, avoiding its claws, which were as sharp as blades. She moved around the table until she came to the head.

Its mouth was closed, the tendons of its neck hanging like strips of ribbon. Where eyes would have been, there were merely indentations in its skull, meaning it relied solely on smell. Given its long snout, that wasn't surprising.

"What about its teeth?" Thalia asked, turning to the two Vampyrs.

"What about them?" Keegan's lips pursed.

"Its bite causes madness, right?" The two Vampyrs nodded. "What if there was a way to extract the poison so you can test out potential cures?"

Cassius raised an approving brow as Keegan shook his head. "I tried prying the mouth open, but it won't budge."

"What do you mean?"

Keegan went to the wall, grabbing a pair of metal pliers. He tried shoving them between the creature's lips, but he couldn't pry its jaws apart. It was if the creature's mouth had been fused together.

"Let me try." Cassius stepped in. But even with their combined strength, its mouth wouldn't open.

They stopped only when the pliers snapped in half.

"Well, that didn't work," Thalia said as Cassius chucked the pliers into the corner.

He cast her an annoyed look. "I didn't see you stepping in to help."

She rolled her eyes, nudging him out of the way so she could get a better peek at its head. Thalia crouched down so she was at eye level, placing her hand on top of its smooth skull. "Why won't you open?"

The creature's jaw popped open, its tongue unfurling. Thalia yelped, jumping back and hitting the hard planes of Cassius's chest.

"How did you do that?" Keegan asked from across the table, his blade drawn. Thalia shook her head, just as confused as them.

Cassius kept hold of her waist, leaning closer. "The poison is still in the teeth."

Indeed, a greenish sheen seemed to glow within the creature's sharp rows of canines. He reached out a hand, but Thalia stopped him.

"You shouldn't touch it." She gave him a look, then glanced at Keegan. "Neither of you. If the poison is still in its teeth, that means there's still a chance that if it gets in you, you'll go mad."

Cassius pulled back his hand. "When will Camilla get here?"

"I sent a raven an hour ago. But given the flight from Perden, probably two days," Keegan said.

Cassius cursed, scrubbing a hand over his jaw. "We need to get it extracted now. Only so it can be ready for her when she arrives."

Both Vampyrs stared at the creature. It seemed they would have to pull straws of hay to see who got the task.

"I'll do it," Thalia blurted out.

Cassius turned to her. "What?"

"I'll do it. If its teeth somehow cut me, I'm not a Vampyr; it won't affect me."

"We don't know what it will do to a human," Cassius said lowly. "The poison could still affect you, just in a different manner."

Thalia shook her head. "I don't think so."

"What do you mean?" Keegan asked, curiosity lighting his handsome features.

"In the forest, there was a moment where it had me cornered but it didn't attack me," Thalia said, thinking back to when the creature had pressed its snout against her chest. Almost like it recognized her in some manner.

Cassius crossed his arms over his chest. "I don't like it."

"You don't have to like it. But I'm doing it; it's less of a risk."

They glared at each other, tension rising.

Finally, Keegan broke the silence. "Thalia is right, Cass. It's less of a risk if she does it. Once those teeth are out, we can at least burn the head. Then Camilla can do what she needs to with the teeth and body."

A muscle flickered in Cassius's jaw before he finally tipped his chin. "Fine."

Thalia turned back to the creature, its mouth open and gleaming. "So where do we start?"

Thalia meticulously pulled the teeth out of the creature's jaw, putting them in glass jars. It had rows of teeth, on both its top and bottom jaws, and Thalia had to be careful not to let anything prick her. While she didn't think the poison would affect her as a human, she wasn't particularly keen on discovering whether she was wrong.

Thalia wiped the sweat off her brow, plunking another tooth into the jar. Cassius watched her intently, his eyes near glowing.

Thalia blew a strand of hair that'd fallen into her face. The strand wouldn't budge. She made a face, blowing harder as she tried to swipe the hair with her arm.

"Do you—" Cassius started, but Thalia cast him a sharp look. He raised his hands in surrender. "Never mind."

Finally, Thalia managed to get the damn hair out of her face and focused back on the creature's mouth.

"Your hair is the longest I've seen it," Cassius said from his spot on the stairs.

Thalia glanced up. They hadn't said much since she'd begun, but she'd heard the occasional scrape of his whetstone against his blade between the plinking of teeth. He'd sent Keegan away to rest. The golden-eyed Vampyr had seemed reluctant, until Cassius reminded him that not only had they been up half the night tramping after the creature, but he'd also given him his blood. Keegan finally relented, with the promise to return to switch shifts.

"I started growing it out." Thalia didn't add that she started growing it out the minute he'd left. Because she'd always had short hair when she'd been with Cassius, the strands barely brushing her collarbone. Now it hung at least to her waist when she left it down.

"I like it," Cassius said.

Thalia tried to ignore him, working to extract another tooth. The small pliers she held scraped as she wiggled it out of the creature's gums.

"What else has changed?" Cassius broke the silence.

"What do you mean?" Thalia's brows furrowed. This damn tooth—

"Back home."

Home.

Thalia jerked, pulling the tooth with her. She dropped it into the jar, trying to ignore the emotions rising in her chest.

She worked her jaw, unsure whether or not to share, but at this point, what harm could there be? "Reina is captain now."

"I know," Cassius said, and Thalia glanced up at the fondness in his tone. Of course he knew. He'd been to the damn castle and had seen her himself. Reina had always wanted to move up. The castle guard wasn't an easy role, and during Thalia's father's reign, women weren't expected or asked to join. But Cassius had seen her on the city watch and invited her to join the royal guard, and she'd worked her way up from there.

Thalia swallowed, pushing aside the tightness in her throat. "Marcus is head librarian."

Cassius chuckled softly. "I know that too. It's about damn time." Once more there was a kind of pride in his voice that had Thalia's chest aching.

"Then I suppose you know everything that's new," Thalia got out, turning back to the creature.

"What about you?" Cassius said quietly.

"What about me?"

"What changed besides the hair?"

Thalia straightened, eyeing him, debating whether or not he was messing with her. But there was genuine openness in his face. It reminded her of what it had been like when they were together. When Thalia would complain and gripe about Agripa and her mother's lack of care over her people. And Cassius would listen, not judging or pushing, merely being the person Thalia could go to with any problem, any grievance, no matter how small.

Thalia cleared her throat. "Nothing."

She turned back to the head, pulling out more teeth. She'd made it through the top jaw and now was starting on the bottom.

"You seem calmer," Cassius said.

Thalia made a face, yanking out a canine with more force than necessary. "Do I?"

Cassius snorted. "Maybe *calmer* isn't the word. But more . . . grounded. Older, more mature."

Thalia looked up at him, exasperation dancing on the tip of her tongue. "No shit. That's what happens when you're forced to grow up. When you're forced to deal with betrayal." She stared at him, now finding his gaze guarded, if not a bit pained. She let out a bitter laugh. "What are we doing here, Cassius?"

"I'm trying to have a conversation with you—"

"No, you're not," Thalia cut in. She set the pliers down with a harsh clink. "What is it you want? Do you want to be friends again? Is that it?"

"Yes," Cassius said without missing a beat.

"Why?"

"Because I miss you," he said softly. "I miss talking with you. I miss being in your presence. I miss the smell of your jasmine perfume, and the way your nose quirks right before you laugh. I miss how you'd tease Marcus whenever he showed us some new information he'd found lost in the library. I miss watching you train with Reina. I miss how you used to look at me. Not with hatred but with something else. I miss *you*."

Thalia met his open stare, the pain and regret etching itself across his handsome features like lines in the sand. "Then stop."

She watched her words land, and Cassius didn't react. Didn't so much as flinch. But something guttered in his irises. Something so raw it was as if she'd plunged her dagger straight into his heart.

"We are not friends, Cassius. You chose *this*. And once the prince returns, this"—she gestured between the two of them—"won't be of consequence anymore."

Cassius's throat bobbed, and he stiffly stood, gathering his blades in hand. He looked over his shoulder at the top of the stairs. "I told you that I don't regret my decision in turning, but I do regret one thing."

Thalia swallowed. "And what is that?"

Cassius met her gaze. "I regret that it's caused you so much pain. I know you're not ready to hear what happened, and I respect that—hell." He huffed out a laugh, looking to the ceiling. "It's one of the reasons I fell in love with you. That tenacious fierceness you have when you've made your mind up about something."

He met her gaze once more. "I still love you. I don't say this because I want anything from you. Friendship or otherwise. You can hate me for the rest of your life, but that love hasn't changed, and it never will."

He opened the door, the coldness of the castle seeping in. "I came to you that night four years ago not to betray you, but because I wanted to say goodbye. I knew you'd try to kill me once you saw what I'd become, but I wanted you to know that I still loved you. Even as this."

Thalia's throat had tightened with near unspeakable pain as Cassius quietly left, leaving her stuck with the dead creature and the poison festering on the table.

Chapter Twenty-Six

Thalia's eyes were blurring by the time she finally dropped the last tooth in a jar. They now had three jars filled with the creature's sharp teeth, and already the bottoms of the glasses were filled with a slimy, green liquid.

Thalia stepped back, setting the pliers down. Her fingers cramped, but she still checked to make sure there weren't any nicks or scratches on her arms or hands. Satisfied that there was none, she sank down onto a wooden stool.

"That took forever," Keegan said.

The golden-eyed Vampyr had come in soon after Cassius left. But unlike Cassius, these were the first words he'd spoken to her.

"Tell me about it," Thalia grumbled. Her back ached, not only from being plowed over by the creature but from bending over the table so long. "What are you going to do with it?"

Keegan stretched, his golden eyes bright. Either his rest had restored him or perhaps he'd had some blood along the way, Thalia didn't care to ask. "I'll get rid of the head. At least then we don't have to worry about it somehow coming back to life."

Thalia grunted, staring at the toothless beast. A part of her almost felt bad. Without its teeth, it seemed so helpless. Until the memory of it shredding apart Cassius's chest quickly pushed the image aside.

"What's Camilla going to do with it?" Thalia stretched her neck.

"Camilla has some affinity with magic." When Thalia opened her mouth, Keegan cut in, smiling. "I don't know what that means. Her family line had deep connections with serving the Mages, and they blessed her ancestors with it."

"Can Camilla shift into more than just a falcon?"

Keegan cracked another smile. "She won't tell us. Cass and I have tried to get her to spill her secrets of shifting for years, but she's never broken." Thalia offered a tight smile at his response. Keegan was too keen for his own good, it seemed, because he noticed the subtle change. "Does it bother you that I call him Cass?"

Thalia huffed out a laugh. "It's . . . odd." She made a face, trying to gather her thoughts. "We—I mean Marcus and Reina and I—we were the only ones who called him that."

"Marcus is the head librarian at Agripa, and Reina the captain?"

Thalia nodded, chewing her lip. "It's just that by using it, by hearing someone other than one of us say it, it solidifies the fact that this is his home now. That he chose this."

Keegan studied her. "Cass saved my life. In more ways and more times than I can count. I know that it's only been four years since he turned, but living here, his role as hand, has put us into some very dangerous positions. I wouldn't be here right now if Cassius hadn't turned."

"What do you mean?" Thalia asked, curiosity poking its head out.

Keegan sank back down onto the steps of the chamber, getting comfortable. "It was around a month after he'd turned. I was told to go to the border of House Santorien up the coastline; there was a bad storm rolling in, and they needed all the help they could get. Cassius had just joined the prince's council and convinced the prince to send him along too. When we got there, the storm came in full force. I was out by the docks, securing boats, when it hit—crept up on us like a thief in the night. The wind was so strong it sent a beam from one of the ships at me, knocking me clean into the water." Keegan ran a hand through his short hair, almost like he was picturing the impact. "I was too far from shore for anyone to see except Cassius. He knew that I'd been at the docks. When everyone ran to take shelter, he went into the storm. I don't know how he figured it out." Keegan huffed a laugh. "But he dove into the water to save me and dragged me to shore. If it wasn't for him, I'd be at the bottom of the sea having to experience a living death over and over."

Thalia's throat constricted more and more the longer Keegan talked. She pushed past the tightness, getting out, "Cassius has always wanted to help. He was too young to save his mother from his father's fists. That's why he joined the city guard when he came of age, so he could help."

Keegan looked up in surprise, then his face shifted into something like quiet understanding. "Did he tell you what happened that night?"

Thalia shook her head, too many emotions bubbling up to name. She shut them all down. Closed them one by one until she had them under a thick padlock of iron. "No."

Keegan nodded in understanding, then said softly, "My mother was human."

Thalia looked up in shock. "What?"

Keegan offered a sad smile. "My father was from House Lorenzia, a full-blooded Vampyr. My mother was mortal." That explained his golden eyes. "He forced her to turn."

Thalia sucked in a sharp breath, anger rearing its head. "What was done about it?"

"Nothing. He died ten years ago, ran his mouth long enough that someone finally tore it out."

Thalia didn't flinch at the gruesomeness. "And your mother?"

Keegan's smile softened. "She's well. Has a house up north near the border of House Lorenzia." His smile slipped, meeting Thalia's gaze. "But she tells me about it, what it was like being a human."

"Where was she from?"

"Sula. Have you heard of it?" Thalia nodded. "They've been in contact with the Vampyrs for quite some time and have a trade route going. Anyway, my father was on one of the boats that went there to trade."

"He took her?" Thalia didn't hide her shock.

Keegan shook his head. "No. Not forcefully, at least. My mother came from a situation which wasn't kind to her either. My father offered her sanctuary in Vaccarium. Yet when they arrived, he failed to mention that humans didn't survive in our world. That's when he turned her.

"But she tells me that even though her situation in Sula was dire, there are pieces of her that don't fit in here. She was not born a Vampyr. And even though I am half-blooded, my blood is still Vampyric. Her blood was turned—twisted to fit a new mold. She says it's like walking around with a phantom limb. Even now, decades later, she'll move too fast or find herself hearing something from a great distance away and realize those aren't human qualities but Vampyric."

Thalia met Keegan's stare. "Are you telling me this so I'll somehow find myself sympathetic to Cassius?"

Keegan stood, going to the table. He carefully grabbed the head, placing it into a burlap sack, before he finally said, "I am telling you this because even though it's only been four years, the man you know is still in there. The foundation, that intrinsic imprint of him, is still Cassius."

He headed for the door, turning to look over his shoulder. "My mother used to tell me that in those initial years, she wished she could turn back time and redo it. But she spent too many years living in the what-ifs, too many years resenting what had happened to her as opposed to taking control of her own life."

"Is this about me or Cassius?"

Keegan cocked a smile. "A bit of both."

Cassius was propped on the settee by the time Thalia had bathed and gotten ready for bed. She didn't even know what time it was, only that the moon remained tucked behind the clouds.

Thalia aimed for the bed, aware that Cassius watched her. But when she glanced at him, he looked away, staring into the dead fireplace.

She climbed under the covers, pulling her knees up to her chin. "How are you feeling?" She broke the silence stretching between them.

Cassius had his profile to her, but he slid his gaze to hers. "Fine."

She nodded, chewing the inside of her cheek.

"How are you?" he asked, cautiously.

"Sore."

He huffed out a laugh. "Yeah. Being knocked off your horse will do that to you."

Thalia's lips twitched into a smirk. She swallowed, the sound audible, before she got out, "You can sleep here if you want. I won't try and throw myself at you or anything."

Cassius's mouth tilted upward.

She thought he'd make some excuse, but to her surprise he groaned, standing up. He stiffly headed toward the bed, his bare torso gleaming softly, no hint of scarring in place. He didn't move as if he were reluctant to get in bed, more like his body was just as sore as hers.

"Thank the gods," he said, practically sinking into the mattress. "Here I thought you were trying to seduce me with that red nightdress because you remembered it was my favorite color."

Thalia flushed, glad for the darkness that hid her flaming cheeks. She had remembered it was his favorite color but hadn't put much thought into choosing the silk gown. "That would be a rather good tactic, but alas, my choice of nightwear is purely out of comfort."

She met his stare in the dark, his irises glowing faintly. A soft smile splayed out across his sensual lips. "It does look comfortable."

"Do you want to wear it?"

Cassius snorted, pulling his legs up to slide under the sheets. "You know I don't wear clothes to bed."

Thalia flushed harder. Yes, that image certainly hadn't left her mind, even after four years. "You're wearing pants now."

"I didn't want you to think I was trying to seduce *you* if I took them off."

Thalia arched a brow. "I think it would take a lot more than that to seduce me."

Cassius raised his own in challenge. "And what would it take?"

Thalia's whole body heated in awareness as Cassius shifted, the sheets around his waist slipping, revealing every hard-earned muscle.

Thalia's tongue peeked out to moisten her lips. Cassius's eyes latched on to the movement, his pupils growing wide.

"What do you think it would take?" Thalia finally got out, her voice much lower and more tense than she'd wanted.

Cassius didn't pull his gaze from her mouth, his voice dropping. "I would get you flowers."

"Flowers?" Thalia hadn't expected him to say *that.*

He finally smiled, flicking his gaze to hers. "Not just any flowers—bluebells and poppies. And you would absolutely hate the gesture." Thalia resisted the urge to cross her arms over her chest. Cassius's lips stretched even more at her scowl. "But you would secretly like it. Because even though you'd think it to be trivial, no one has ever done it before. At least not in a way that matters. Not because they simply want to see the joy on your face when you realize they were hand-picked for you."

Cassius scanned her face. "I'd tell you to weave those flowers into your long hair, then I'd take you to a pool up near Nanis, the capital of House Santorien. There's hundreds of pools all tucked away into caves. They glow like starlight, and the caverns are covered with thousands of glowworms. It feels as though you've stepped into the cosmos."

"Then what?" Thalia whispered, her words barely pushing past her lips.

Cassius's gaze landed right on her parted mouth, his words turning rough. "Then I would take out each and every one of those flowers you'd so meticulously woven into your hair. I'd lay them out on the rocks so they wouldn't get ruined. Then I'd lay you out." Thalia swallowed, the sound audible. Cassius's dark gaze went straight to her throat. But it didn't scare her; it sent a white-hot pang of awareness straight to her belly. "And I'd worship you. First with my fingers, then with my tongue, and only when you'd been spent would I bury my cock inside you until all that consumed you was me. Until you could think of nothing—scream nothing—but my name."

Cassius slowly met Thalia's eyes, his pupils near devouring the twin moons of his irises.

Thalia had never felt his presence so acutely as she did now. Never been struck with such burning desire.

She swallowed, forcing her tongue to unstick itself from the roof of her mouth. "Then I suppose it's a good thing you aren't trying to seduce me."

"Indeed."

They stared at each other a moment longer, tension stretching and warping like the edges of a mirror.

Thalia forced herself to not give in to the sudden craving ghosting her tongue. To not give in to the insatiable desire dangling before her like sweet candy—to shut out the image of exactly what he'd do to her. If he so much as touched her, she'd give in, and she could not allow that.

She turned her back, scooting as far away from him as possible. "Good night, Cassius."

"Good night."

Chapter Twenty-Seven

Something heavy pressed into Thalia's chest—a weight that nearly crushed her rib cage.

Her breath stuttered as something pricked her collarbone like sharp needles. Thalia's lids peeled open.

A headless creature hovered above her, tendons and muscles twisting to replace the face that'd been cut off.

Thalia screamed, trying to escape the creature, which was very much alive.

The creature raised its stubby neck, the muscles coiling like snakes to reform its head—

Cassius slammed a dagger into the creature's side. It fell backward off the bed, writhing on the ground. Cassius grabbed another dagger from his nightstand, moving faster than she could blink, and shoved it into its side.

The creature's body convulsed, twitching, as he pulled out his blades. He whirled to her, eyes bright. "Are you hurt?"

Thalia shook her head, too stunned to speak. Small pinpricks of blood patterned her chest, soaking into the red of her gown.

A flicker of light caught the corner of her eye the same moment it caught Cassius's. He jerked to the window, his jaw tightening as he looked out the paned glass.

Lights were moving through the trees of the forest surrounding the castle. Not just any lights—torches speared their flames into the night sky, illuminating the gathering crowd in the castle's inner courtyard.

"Fuck," Cassius said.

Thalia scrambled to his side, getting a better view. The entire courtyard was filled with Vampyrs, each holding a light as though they'd burn the place to the ground.

"That's Julian," Thalia gasped, catching sight of the dark-haired Vampyr with green eyes. He led the pack, his gaze rising to their window. "And Lord Adrian." Apparently, Julian's father had found his banished son. As soon as Lord Adrian spotted them in the window, he pointed.

Cassius grabbed Thalia's arm, yanking her out of the way just as an arrow pierced the glass, shattering it.

"Fuck," Cassius growled again, shoving Thalia away from the window.

"What is he doing?" She whirled as shouts drifted through the broken window.

"Making a point." Cassius grabbed his clothes, shoving himself into his boots before strapping on his sword, which he'd propped against the fireplace. "We need to get out of here. Now."

Thalia didn't have to be told twice. She found her own clothes, shoving on whatever she could find before she and Cassius crept to the door. He eased it open, peeking his head out into the quiet hall.

Nothing.

But deep within the castle, pounding echoed, wood groaning as if the mob of Vampyrs was trying to break down the doors.

Cassius's hand slipped into hers as they left their room and quietly ran through the castle. They turned the corner and stumbled into a group of five Vampyrs, their weapons drawn.

"Go!" Cassius roared, pushing her behind him.

Thalia stumbled, turning just as he plunged his sword into the belly of one of the Vampyrs. His other hand plunged into the spine of another, and Thalia only caught a glimpse of severed vertebrae before she bolted.

Thalia's heart pounded as she skidded around the castle halls. She had no idea where to go. Which way would lead out—

She slammed into the hard panes of someone's chest.

Immediately she reared back, drawing her dagger.

"Hey! It's me!" Keegan held up his hands, eyes wide.

She clutched his arms, pointing a shaking finger behind him. "Cass—"

Keegan's eyes went past her, to the shouting echoing down the hall. "Get to the stables. Keep following this hall and go through the kitchens and out the back. There are horses waiting. If we aren't there in five minutes, you leave."

"But Cass—"

"Would want you to get the fuck out of here," Keegan finished. He drew his own sword, heading for the hall Thalia had just fled. His footsteps echoed as loud as the shouting.

Thalia stared at his disappearing form, then made it all of two steps before she gasped—the teeth.

She didn't want to think about what would happen if Lord Adrian or Julian discovered the poisoned barbs in the chamber or how they might use them to whatever advantage they hoped to obtain.

Thalia's eyes snagged on a brick with a three-eyed raven carved into it. Making a split-second decision, she ran toward it, shoving open a secret passageway. She didn't want to think about what Cassius and Keegan were facing in the halls. Gods, there must be at least thirty Vampyrs that Lord Adrian and Julian had gathered. Apparently, the lord's hatred for the prince and his council—and his sway with the other Vampyrs—had won over the other Houses over in the end.

Her mind formed a map of the passageway, and she was silently grateful she'd taken the time to actually study the drawing before Camilla found her in the library. She flew over old stone, choking on the dust motes in the air.

She followed the twist and turns, praying she was right, until she came to the end of the passageway.

Thalia shoved against the stone, and the wall gave way. She burst into the torture chamber, the wall closing behind her.

The teeth were still on the table, glowing a faint greenish color.

She carefully wrapped each jar in a different part of her cloak before she shoved them into a satchel she'd taken from her room before fleeing.

She heard a scraping sound and whirled, faltering.

Julian stood in the doorway, his green eyes blazing as he took her in.

"You don't have to do this," Thalia got out, raising her dagger. The blade looked like a pitiful needle compared to the double-headed axe the Vampyr wielded.

"The prince has been ignoring our blight for too long," Julian snarled, stepping further into the room. "Banishing us for trying to save those we love."

"And what? You think burning down his home will get him to listen to you?"

Already she could smell the smoke in the air; the Vampyrs hadn't wasted any time putting their torches to use. They'd burn them alive if they didn't make it out. Her insides trembled.

"No, but killing you might," Julian got out.

Thalia let out a laugh, trying to figure out how she might pass him. He blocked the only exit. "The prince hasn't even met me. The only thing I am is part of a treaty. One that, if you ruin, will affect my mother far more than the prince."

"You're right," Julian said, his axe lowering a fraction of an inch. Thalia almost breathed a sigh of relief. "The prince won't care about some human's death, but his hand will."

Thalia jerked, blade posed. "I mean nothing to Cassius."

"Lies. I'd like to see his face when he realizes he couldn't save the one he loved. When he has to watch his lover die!"

Thalia paled as Julian raised his axe. But it wasn't because of the imminent death looming before her—it was the death hovering behind the Vampyr.

Julian tensed, slowly turning over his shoulder, and let out a scream.

The headless creature launched itself at the Vampyr, taking him out in a tangle of limbs and steel. Thalia didn't stop to see how much of its head had reformed, but its claws still worked. She bolted up the stairs, heart in her throat, as Julian's screams followed her.

Her arms pumped as she flew down the halls; the smoke had spread. Her eyes burned from the hot air, her lungs near to the point of breaking as she half fell down the stairs into the kitchens. Cassius caught her before she could land face-first on the stone floors.

"Where the fuck have you been?" Cassius snarled.

The edge of his sleeve was torn, an angry line bleeding under it. His face was splattered with blood that didn't appear to be his.

"Julian," Thalia gasped, trying to get clean air into her lungs. But the fire had spread; they needed to get out. Now. Cassius's face darkened into the edge of a blade. He made to move past her, but Thalia clutched him harder. "Creature."

It took a split second for Cassius to register her words between her pants. Then he grabbed her hand, pulling her out the back door. Thalia sucked in a sharp breath of clean air.

Two Vampyrs found them in the inner courtyard, but they didn't stand a chance as Cassius swung his sword, lopping off the head of one as his free hand plunged into the chest of the other. Keegan appeared on a horse, Feryena prancing at his side.

"Cassius!" Keegan yelled.

Cassius nodded to Thalia. "Go!"

Thalia ran, scrambling onto her horse just as Cassius pulled the heart out of the second Vampyr. He let it fall to the ground in a splatter.

"Cassius!" A voice bellowed behind them, and the three turned to find Lord Adrian, his face set in a snarl.

Cassius ignored him, running up to Feryena. He swung himself up behind Thalia, and Keegan spurred his beast towards the castle gates.

"You can run and hide," Lord Adrian shouted, the castle crackling and burning behind him. "But your prince won't save you. Not this time."

They didn't wait to hear the rest of the words as they broke into the forest, the castle of House Lorenzia crumbling in their wake.

Chapter Twenty-Eight

They rode hard through the forest, skirting the edge of Irenbis. Even in the night-covered sky, Thalia could have sworn she saw the smoke coming from the castle—saw the light from the fires as they cracked the infrastructure of the palace.

Their horses didn't slow until they'd put enough distance between themselves and the castle that both Keegan and Cassius relaxed.

"Why the fuck would they do that?" Thalia asked. Her words came out in a sharp whisper. They were deep in another part of the forest, the leaves thick and droopy. She didn't want to think about what sorts of creatures stalked through the night or if any more creatures had somehow spawned.

"I knew Lord Adrian was already angry, but the council meeting must have pushed him over the edge," Cassius said behind her. Despite the blood covering his hands, they were a comfort she allowed a small part of herself to indulge in as they wrapped around the reins.

"He's a fool," Keegan said ahead of him. "Burning the castle will only anger the prince. It's a grievance that won't go unnoticed."

"What's going to happen?" Thalia pushed. Keegan looked at Cassius, and while she couldn't see his face, she had a feeling he clenched his jaw.

"There's only been one other uprising before," Cassius finally said. "When Vampyrs pitted themselves against each other."

"When was this?"

"Long ago. It was an uprising between the pure-blooded and half-blooded. But the courts reformed themselves to ensure no Vampyr could take control," Keegan supplied.

"The courts have been rocky since the creature emerged," Cassius rumbled, his chest brushing against her back. "Lord Adrian has been unhappy. It was his men who were sent out the most into the forest to search for a cure outside of House Lorenzia." Thalia swallowed, and Cassius squeezed one of her hands. "House Lorenzia is all but gone. With the prince's absence, I don't know how long the other courts will be content to sit by and watch."

"I'd say considering tonight, that time has come," Keegan said dryly.

"Aren't the courts supposed to support House Lorenzia?" Thalia turned in her seat.

Cassius focused on the path, but he glanced down to meet her gaze. "Yes, the courts are all pledged to the prince. But with any rule, there are always usurpers."

"Surely there must be some courts who are aligned with House Lorenzia still?"

"House Olvectus," Keegan said, twisting in his saddle. "They've always supported the prince. No matter what."

"What of House Avanerius?" Thalia asked, thinking of Lord Damien. "Camilla said they have always been aligned with House Lorenzia."

Cassius shook his head. "They have been. But I fear if the courts start turning on House Lorenzia, they would side with House Gallinus only so they wouldn't find themselves pitted against them all. While the pure-bloods have always been more apathetic when it comes to matters of state and have served the prince, Lord Adrian's influence has spread deep."

"Even though Lord Damien is on the prince's council?" Thalia said.

"Even then," Cassius admitted. "Regardless, House Lorenzia was beginning to crack. We'd hoped that the treaty with Agripa would staunch some of the grumblings, that it would show the people that we are trying to find a cure. We'd hope the rivers replenishing the springs would be taken as that."

"Fear breeds distrust," Thalia murmured.

Cassius cursed. "I should have thought of this sooner. I should have known that Lord Adrian would try to force a coup."

Thalia heard the bitter regret coating his words and turned to face him. She squeezed his arm, forcing him to meet her eyes. "This isn't your fault." Cassius's eyes flashed, something she couldn't quite pinpoint in his gaze. "What Lord Adrian did was because of his own desperate sense of self-righteousness. This would have happened regardless of whether the prince was here or not."

"She's right," Keegan said over his shoulder. "Lord Adrian has always been brash. He wasn't happy when you came along and joined the prince's council. Less happy once you booted him off, not to mention this treaty between the humans. It was only a matter of time before he did something."

Cassius didn't relax, and Thalia squeezed his arm once more. He stared down at her, and she nodded, just once, to show she understood why he felt the way he did. His sense of duty, of honor, still bled even under a different set of skin. And when she leaned her head back against her chest, it was also a message. One that conveyed that she was there if he needed to talk, whenever that was.

"Where do we go from here?" Thalia asked. Cassius relaxed slightly as they navigated deeper into the forest.

"We should go back to the humans," Keegan said.

Thalia stiffened. "No."

"Why not?" The golden-eyed Vampyr turned over his shoulder.

Thalia swallowed, her throat suddenly sticking to the roof of her mouth. "My mother won't care; she won't help. She's gotten the ore. Despite what still needs to be mined in the mountain, Agripa will have enough to last ten years or more."

"Surely she'd care about her daughter?" Keegan's brows narrowed in confusion.

Thalia felt it then, a mere brush of Cassius's thumb running along the back of her hand—a quiet understanding and reassurance. It gave her the courage to say, "My mother and I have had our difficulties in the past. And frankly, given the tension between our two worlds, even if she did care about my safety in being returned to Agripa, she wouldn't help you."

"So we're on our own?" Keegan's words were bitter.

"Not quite," Thalia said.

The two Vampyrs exchanged a glance before Cassius's chin grazed the side of her head. "What do you mean?"

Thalia shifted, pulling the satchel still strapped around her shoulders into her lap. She opened it, revealing the three sets of jars and poisoned teeth nestled inside.

"What is it?" Keegan asked, too far ahead to see what she carried.

"You went back for that?" Cassius's words were a sharp exhale.

Thalia stiffened, closing up the satchel. "Yes."

"I thought Keegan told you to get to the stables," Cassius gritted out.

"I didn't know what Lord Adrian or Julian would do if they found them," Thalia snapped, suddenly wishing his arms weren't wrapped around her waist. She didn't want to dwell on the fact that her first thought in the moment hadn't been for herself but on what would happen to the Vampyrs if Lord Adrian got the poison.

"Julian," Keegan sneered. "If I see that prick again, I'll rip his heart out myself."

"I don't think he's going to be a problem anymore," Thalia got out.

"What do you mean?" Keegan asked.

Thalia swallowed, already feeling Cassius tense behind her. "When I was leaving the chamber, Julian found me."

Cassius tightened the reins hard enough that Feryena's head jerked up. Thalia scowled, prying his fingers off the reins, only to save her poor horse. But that meant his viselike grip went to her waist.

Thalia ignored the shiver rocking down her spine. Now certainly wasn't the time.

"And you killed him?" Keegan said in disbelief.

"No, I didn't. But I think the creature did."

"What creature?" Keegan shook his head in confusion.

Cassius sucked in a sharp breath. "It found you down there?"

Thalia nodded, and at Keegan's exasperated face, she quietly explained how she woke up with the beast on her chest, its neck trying to re-form into a head.

Keegan looked like he was going to be sick. Granted, after sharing everything, Thalia felt her own nausea rise in her stomach.

"I burned the head," Keegan said. "Right after you extracted all the teeth."

"Well, it somehow is able to re-form," Thalia countered, trying and failing to push aside the image of its skin twisting like vines.

"It would make sense, then, why it's so hard to kill. It's regenerating." Cassius spoke.

"Which means that you have to burn everything for it to remain dead," Thalia finished.

"Well, let's hope it died in the fire, along with Julian," Keegan muttered.

Thalia nodded her agreement. She didn't want to think about how it had somehow found her, even in the midst of the chaos. The fact that it'd touched its nose to her chest in Irenbis, almost like it was taking in her scent—marking her.

"You said that Camilla can somehow use the teeth?" Thalia asked, and Keegan nodded. "Then we go to her. Maybe see if those Mages can do something about it."

"Having the shifters on our side if it does come to the courts turning fully wouldn't be bad," Keegan mused.

Thalia swallowed. A war between the Vampyr courts would be exactly the type of intel her mother would kill to have. Her stomach twisted, her mission flickering like a candle about to burn out. "Isn't the prince there anyways?"

Cassius stiffened behind her, the movement so subtle she wouldn't have noticed if she hadn't been leaning against him. "Yes."

"Then we kill two birds with one stone. Take the teeth to Camilla, see if she can use them for something, maybe an antidote?" She'd heard stories from farmers who'd been bitten by snakes, how the venom used to poison them had also been used to cure them.

"So we head to Perden." Keegan nodded.

Perden.

Thalia didn't know what to expect from House Olvectus, but she had a feeling she'd discover a lot more than just shifters.

"Where are we?" Thalia squinted at the run-down inn before them. A light drizzle had started, the air hanging with a thick mist as they dismounted at the muddy outpost.

"Arein," Cassius said, pulling his hood over his head. "Twenty miles from Irenbis."

Thalia didn't like that they were still so close to the capital, but given that both Cassius and Keegan seemed ready to fall off their horses, it would have to do.

"I'll see to the horses," Keegan said, grabbing the reins to lead them into the stable around the back.

Thalia stared up at the inn. Its roof sagged and the sounds of drunken laughter spilled out onto the street.

Cassius's hand materialized on her lower back. "Stay close to me."

Thalia nodded as they moved inside. Immediately the smell of sour beer and sweat slapped her across the face. At least her hood covered the face she made as Cassius stalked to the counter.

The innkeeper was a half-blood Vampyr, with dull golden eyes and a permanent scowl. "What do you want?"

"A room," Cassius growled out.

The innkeeper raised a brow. "Just the two of you?"

"Three. And two horses that need tending to."

The innkeeper's scowl seemed to deepen. Until Cassius set a bag of coins on the counter and the contents jingled. "For your troubles, and your silence."

The innkeeper glanced between the bag of coins and them. Finally, he pulled out an old key.

"Fifth door on the second floor. There isn't any breakfast, and only one common bathroom. Don't hog it."

Thalia's lip curled. As if she'd spend a second longer than necessary in what was no doubt a shitty bathing room.

Cassius nodded, his fingers closing over the key. They didn't speak as they made it to the stairs, climbing up the rickety worn steps until they got to their room. Cassius pushed inside, stepping aside for Thalia to squeeze in.

At least the room had two beds. Albeit tiny, worn beds that would barely fit one, let alone two.

Thalia's scowl matched the innkeeper's downstairs as she pushed back her hood.

Cassius caught her stare. "At least we have a roof over our heads."

"I didn't say anything."

Cassius gave her a knowing look. Thalia forced herself to shrug, taking off her cloak. She folded it over the end of one of the beds. A small fireplace sat against the wall, which would probably only aid in smoking them out, and a washstand with a rickety wooden chair in the corner completed the space.

The door behind her creaked open and they both whirled, blades drawn. But it was just Keegan.

He shoved back his hood, face wet. He took a look around the room. "Cozy."

Thalia snorted, turning back to the two beds. There was no way the two Vampyrs could share. Not a chance.

"I'll take the chair," Cassius said, moving toward it.

"It's fine," Thalia blurted out. At his confused look, she gestured to the bed with her cloak. "It's not like we haven't shared a bed for days now." *Or in the past.*

Cassius stared at her, his jaw flickering. But Keegan cut in, breaking through the tension. "Well, I'm not going to complain if I get my own bed."

He moved between them, shucking off his cloak and boots, and took off the outer portion of his clothing to dry. He wore the same kind of linen pants that Cassius wore to bed. Granted, they'd all been pulled from their sleep, so it was no wonder he still had them on. He promptly pulled back the covers and went straight to sleep.

Thalia stared at him in shock.

"He does that," Cassius got out.

"Weird."

"I know."

The corners of her lips twitched.

"The bathroom should be up here somewhere," Cassius continued. "You can go freshen up. Do you want anything to eat?"

Thalia shook her head. "No."

Cassius nodded, and Thalia left only to see to her needs in the gross common bathing room before scampering back.

Cassius excused himself to do the same thing, leaving her alone with sleeping Keegan, who snored softly.

If he kept it up, she'd have to hit him with a pillow.

Thalia peeled off her boots, placing them near the fire, then she tugged off her shirt and pants. Part of her was glad she'd kept on her nightdress, only so the rest of her clothes could dry.

But another part screamed with embarrassment, especially at the thought of Keegan rolling over and seeing her. Thalia inched to the hearth, adding a few logs to try to start a fire. Even though it was the height of summer, the rain had added a bit of cold, which she was more than a little aware of given her lack of clothing. It took a few tries to get the fire started, but eventually the logs cracked, the sparks catching.

The door creaked open, and she stood hastily, wiping her hands off on her nightdress.

Thalia's embarrassment only grew as Cassius froze, looking her over. His shirt was off, and the cut on his arm was clean.

Thalia crossed her arms over her chest. "It's the only thing I had on under my clothes."

"I didn't say anything."

Cassius moved to the chair, setting down his shirt. The muscles in his back rippled as he tugged off his boots, setting them near the fire along with his pants. It seemed he'd kept his linen ones on. Which was fine by her. She didn't think she could handle his nudity, dire situation or not.

Thalia hopped into the bed, ignoring the scratchy wool of the blanket. Cassius took a few more minutes to ensure Keegan's clothes and boots were near the fire as well, then he headed for their tiny mattress.

Thalia did her best to scoot to the very edge, but the bed was hardly meant for two people. As soon as he lay down, his arm pressed against her bare back.

"Your elbow is digging into me," she whispered harshly.

"It's not like I have a lot of room," Cassius bit back.

Annoyance flared, heating her more than the fire. "Then make room."

"And how do you suggest I do that?"

Thalia chewed the inside of her cheek. "I don't know. Figure it out."

Maybe sharing a bed with him was a mistake. Gods, she'd rather take Keegan snoring in her ear than Cassius, whose presence threatened to engulf her.

"Do not stab me for this," Cassius muttered.

Confusion flashed before Cassius shifted, and Thalia nearly yelped as his arm suddenly banded around her waist, pulling her flush against him.

Shit. Shit. Shit.

Cassius slipped his other arm around her chest, his hips pressing against her backside.

Fuck.

Thalia swallowed, suddenly wishing she hadn't built a fire, not with how hot she burned.

"Is this okay?" Cassius's words brushed the shell of her ear.

Thalia nodded, not trusting herself to speak.

"Try to rest."

Thalia nodded again. But even when his breathing became slow and steady behind her, his arms relaxing, Thalia's lids refused to close, her heart pounding long into the night.

Chapter Twenty-Nine

"What's this?" Thalia asked as the three of them broke through the tree line. A half-forgotten manor rose before them, its walls covered in thick ivy and growing moss. They'd spent three days traveling, the forest slowly shifting from trees with silver trunks and crimson leaves to more brownish and green hues.

"This is one of the prince's safe houses, to either use himself or for his advisers. Only his personal council know of this place. We'll be safe here," Cassius rumbled, nudging Feryena over a small stream.

Thalia relaxed against him as they got to the manor, which was tucked away into the forest like a hidden gem. Behind the house was a glittering lake with thick pine trees framing it, the water crystal even from a distance.

"I'll send word to Camilla to expect us," Keegan said, dismounting in the small courtyard.

Cassius nodded, and Thalia didn't protest as he helped her down. Her knees nearly buckled with relief, and she was glad Cassius kept hold of her until she'd steadied.

He led her into the manor. The walls were covered in colorful tapestries and paintings, the polar opposite of the castle in Irenbis. Cassius led her to a bedroom bedecked in shades of soft brown and sage green, the smell of rose and crisp linen tickling her nose.

"You can freshen up here. I need to check in on Keegan and take care of a few things. The manor is safe to explore, just don't go down into the lower levels."

Thalia made a face at that. "What's down there?"

Cassius's eyes flickered, but he ignored her question. "The grounds are warded; they wrap all around the lake. Just don't go past the tree line and you'll be fine."

"Warded? How?"

Cassius shrugged. "Camilla managed to erect a barrier years ago. It keeps unwanted guests from venturing in."

Or unwanted creatures, Thalia thought.

She shuddered, not able to push the image of the creature from her mind. Her collarbone had scabbed from where it'd dug its claws into her chest.

"Anything else?" Thalia said, focusing on him once again.

Cassius studied her. "The bathing chamber is through that door." He pointed to a closed door at the back of the room. "And the kitchens are stocked if you get hungry."

Thalia nodded.

Cassius opened and closed his mouth. "I'll be back later."

Thalia didn't comment on his strange behavior. She was just grateful for the bathing chamber, which sported a porcelain claw-foot tub, set against a wide-paned window overlooking what must have been the manor's back courtyard. An overgrown garden stretched before a small stone wall, and behind it was the glittering lake. The trees surrounding the lake didn't look as ominous as the forests she'd been accustomed to in Vaccarium. In the distance, a snowcapped mountain poked through the overcast skyline.

Lorceium.

Thalia swallowed, not having realized how close they were to the mountain—to the ore that provided the humans their shot at surviving, and whatever other secrets the Mages and shifters held within its heart.

Thalia quickly bathed before digging in the armoire for something to wear. She didn't know whose clothes lined the dresser, maybe Camilla's, although the attire seemed less daring and dramatic than what the shifter normally wore.

Thalia grabbed a dressing gown, feeling that to be the safest option, given that the other dresses seemed too small for her to squeeze into. She pushed aside the thought that another woman she didn't know about was part of the prince's inner council. If there was some other female who was close to Cassius . . .

She tied the dressing gown tightly before she opened the door, slipping out of the room.

Despite the quietness of the old manor, Thalia didn't feel the hair on the back of her neck rise as she moved through the halls, noting that the upper floor had only a few rooms. She moved down the stairs, glancing to her left and spotting a formal dining room. To the right, she found a small music room with a worn pianoforte, an equally small library, and a sitting room.

Thalia paused at the top of a small stairwell, which descended into the lower levels of the manor. She didn't see much besides a solid oak door. But Cassius's warning rang low in her head. *Don't go into the lower levels.*

Part of her wanted to ignore his warning. But that other part, the part that didn't actually want to fight with him, heeded his words, and she went to the very back of the house where the kitchen sat.

She grabbed an apple before pushing through the door into the back courtyard. A garden overflowing with ripe fruit and vegetables greeted her along with a small pen containing goats and chickens, the birds' clucking making Thalia's lip twitch. It was all peaceful. Surprisingly ordinary. A place she would never expect a royal to take refuge in.

Thalia wandered through the back gate, moving toward the glittering lake. The air was crisp, biting at her cheeks, but not cold enough for her to flee inside.

She stopped at the shores of the lake, the water lapping at her toes. Her feet sank into the soft mud, and she took a deep breath, letting the pine-scented air ground her.

Movement across the lake caught her eye.

Thalia's gaze sharpened, trying to see what was flashing among the trees or if it was just a trick of the light reflecting off the waters of the lake.

Then, there—another flash of white.

Her throat dried, but she couldn't quite seem to focus on whatever was at the tree line. Whatever it was, it didn't move closer.

Thalia shivered, the wind picking up, and she hurried back into the manor, praying that whatever she'd seen in the forest was nothing more than a curious creature.

Chapter Thirty

Thalia had found a quiet library to read in until a noise had her lifting her head.

She glanced out the window.

The sky was beginning to darken, the strange clouds starting to disperse, indicating that the moon would rise and night would soon fall.

Perhaps Cassius and Keegan had returned from wherever they'd been off to. Thalia set her book down; the romance she'd found was too dramatic even for her taste, although Camilla might like it. The thought of the shifter sent a strange warmth through her chest.

Thalia wrapped her dressing gown tighter around herself, padding to the door. She poked her head into the hall, shadows starting to make tracks along the floor.

"Cassius?" she called, walking farther.

No answer. Thalia frowned.

Odd. Perhaps she'd misheard something, or maybe the noise had been outside. One of the chickens or goats no doubt bumping into something.

A knock sounded, and Thalia turned toward the front door. But the knocking wasn't coming from there; it was coming from behind her.

Thalia swallowed, following the sound, her footsteps too loud in her ears.

"Hello?" she called.

The knocking grew insistent, and she hurried down the hall. *Maybe someone's at the back door?*

Thalia faltered when she got to a set of stairs that led down into the lower levels—the knocking was coming from a door at the base.

Maybe Cassius or Keegan had locked themselves in accidentally?

"Cassius?" Thalia called, taking a step into the stairwell.

The knocking stopped.

Thalia swallowed, sure she'd imagined it, until a muffled voice floated from under the threshold.

"Help."

Thalia took another step down the stairs, her heart pounding. "Is someone in there?"

The door rattled slightly as another muffled word escaped. "Help."

Thalia made it to the base of the stairs before she realized she'd even moved.

The door handle jiggled, and Thalia placed her hand on it. "Are you stuck?"

"Help," a distinctly female voice said.

Thalia's stomach clenched. Maybe it was the same woman whose room she'd been in. *How the hell has she locked herself in there?*

"Hang on," Thalia called. She tried the handle, but it wouldn't budge. Thalia cursed. "Give me a second."

Thalia didn't hear the woman's reply as she took the stairs two at a time, heading into the kitchen until she spotted a butter knife.

She grabbed it before running back to the door, which now rattled with intensity.

"I'm here," Thalia said breathlessly. She jammed the knife into the keyhole, wiggling it around. "Almost there—" The lock clicked, and Thalia breathed a sigh of relief, swinging the door open. "How did you—"

Her words died in her throat.

A woman stood on the other side of the threshold. Long auburn hair fell to her waist in a tangled mess. She wore only a simple nightdress, the fabric tattered and dirty. Her golden eyes widened, the irises hazy as she took Thalia in.

But it was the foaming droplets falling from the woman's torn lips that had Thalia stepping back. The droplets splattered onto her dress, leaving tracks in their wake.

Thalia's heart started to climb, and the Vampyr's nostrils flared. Once. Then twice.

"Help," the bitten Vampyr said, revealing her canines.

Thalia ran.

She made it to the top of the stairs before hands grasped her shoulders.

The Vampyr slammed her back into the wall hard enough that Thalia's bones groaned.

Thalia didn't have time to scream before the Vampyr turned her head and sank her teeth straight into Thalia's neck.

Pain like Thalia had never felt coursed through her body. Her veins boiled, her organs screaming as the Vampyr took long pulls of blood, drinking from her like she was the finest of wines.

Thalia jerked, trying to dislodge the Vampyr, but she held fast. Her fingers dug into Thalia's wrists with enough force that her skin bruised.

Thalia's heart threw itself against her chest in panic.

The Vampyr pressed into her, making low moans in the back of her throat.

The pain in Thalia's body spread as her lifeblood flowed right into the Vampyr's mouth.

Thalia's eyes grew heavy, her heart stopping and stuttering.

She couldn't stop the Vampyr. Could do nothing—

A dark form appeared before her, and Thalia caught a glimpse of golden eyes before Keegan swung a wooden board the size of his forearm. It hit the back of the Vampyr's head hard enough that it splintered. The Vampyr's teeth ripped out of Thalia's neck, and she crumpled.

Thalia's breath came out in wet pants as Keegan stared at the unconscious Vampyr at his feet.

Skidding sounded, and Thalia lifted her weak head.

Cassius rounded the corner, his chest rising as heavily as Thalia's. His blue eyes glanced to the Vampyr at Keegan's feet, then to Thalia's neck. His face morphed into a mixture of horror, then downright fear.

Blood ran down the side of her throat, soaking into the dressing gown.

Thalia only made it one step before she realized her feet weren't working, and neither were her eyes.

Darkness bled at the corners of her vision. All she saw was Cassius lunging toward her before she fainted.

Chapter Thirty-One

Thalia woke with her hands chained on either side of the bed.

She started but immediately regretted it, as fire erupted all over her body.

Thalia moaned, her head lolling into the pillows. The fabric scratched her—skin tingling with a deep-rooted burn.

"Is she secure?" She heard Cassius somewhere in the room.

A slight tug on the chains around her wrists sent another wave of pain spreading through her. "Yes."

"Are you sure?" Cassius growled.

"Yes," Keegan replied, his voice low.

Thalia managed to peel open her lids.

Cassius and Keegan were at the foot of the bed, the latter with his arms crossed, face set in hard determination. Cassius, on the other hand . . .

He couldn't stop running his fingers through his hair, pacing as though he'd wear the carpet bare.

"Cassius?" Thalia managed to work her throat, despite the pain it caused. Her neck felt as though it hung by a thread, a throbbing pulse echoing from the bite marks.

He stopped pacing, turning to her immediately. He was at her side in an instant. "I'm here."

Thalia tried to move her arms but cried out, pain flaring along her bones. "It hurts," she said, tears leaking from her eyes.

Cassius didn't touch her, but his fingers curled as if aching to. "I know. I know."

"What's happening?" Thalia groaned. The hairs along the backs of her arms stood on end, causing needle-like pricks to echo in their wake.

"Your body is in the process of trying to change," Keegan said gently.

Thalia tried shaking her head, but her neck refused to work. "I don't—"

A deep stabbing flared in her stomach, cutting off her words. Thalia cried out, her body arching.

Her muscles spasmed, pain racking her system, before she collapsed onto the mattress.

"Cass," Thalia whimpered.

"I know," Cassius murmured, his face so pained it was though he were experiencing the burning in her body instead of her. "But this is the only way."

Thalia's eyes blurred as another wave of agony swept through her. The chains tightened around her wrists.

"Your body is trying to fight the Vampyr bite," Cassius said, his voice near guttural. "It will fight it until it works its way out of your system."

Thalia's limbs trembled as her organs turned over in her abdomen.

"Make it stop," Thalia cried, twisting in the chains.

"We can't," Cassius gasped. Hands pressed into her legs, and she cried out once more. The grip felt as though daggers were slicing into her shins, each press against her heated skin cutting deep into the muscle. "You have to fight the pain."

Thalia shook her head, the muscles in her neck straining. Her throat tightened, closing until she choked.

She screamed as wave after wave racked her body. She was a practice dummy, the Vampyr's bite spearing arrow after arrow into her swollen flesh.

She was being flayed from the inside out. Her organs were being taken out and roasted on a spit before being shoved back into place, still flaming.

Her tears burned the sides of her face as they fell—each nerve ending frayed at the edges, making her whole body spasm and tighten.

Then, through the pain, something dangerous hit her tongue.

An insatiable hunger that had her arching off the bed, the chains the only thing keeping her in place.

"I'm so hungry," Thalia sobbed, that desire intensifying as she somehow managed to focus on Cassius.

His brows were narrowed, his jaw clenched tight enough to snap. "I know."

"I need it," she got out.

She didn't know what she needed. Only that her senses were being overwhelmed with the sharp tang of blood—her own blood.

Her head jerked, eyes landing on Keegan, who held her legs down. Her eyes went straight to the pulse fluttering in his throat. "I need it," she got out again, her mouth nearly salivating.

Then another wave hit her and she closed her eyes, biting through her tongue as she cried. Each bone in her body snapped in half before being glued back together in jagged spikes.

"Maybe we should let her feed." Keegan's tentative voice broke through the wave of pain.

"No," Cassius growled out. "I can't."

"If it saves her, we should." Keegan's voice sharpened.

"She will never forgive me," Cassius snapped back. "And she was bitten by Sybil. If she turns, then she'll become one of them too."

"Cassius, she is dying! The pain is killing her!" Keegan yelled.

Dying? Was that what was happening to her? Her insides felt as though they'd been lit on fire, sizzling and peeling until everything in her was stripped away, leaving only a bloody pulp in its wake.

A hand pressed into her face, and Thalia groaned, peeling her lids open to find Cassius hovering above her. "You need to fight it," he whispered, his eyes scanning hers. "You need to."

Thalia tried to nod, but the pain was so great she arched, screaming. The headboard behind her cracked, her arms straining against her bounds—

The chains ripped from the wood.

"Fuck." Cassius lunged, grasping her arms just as Thalia tried to surge upward.

"Cassius, you need to decide," Keegan ground out behind him.

Thalia could barely think. Not with her brain melting into a soup. Not with the scent of Cassius's own blood flowing beneath his veins.

"Thalia." Cassius gritted his teeth.

Thalia thrashed, sobbing through the pain. "I don't want to die—"

Cassius's eyes guttered, his fingers still tight on her biceps. But he was lost, his eyes flashing in deep fear, as if he could feel her dying slowly, painfully, beneath him.

"Cassius," Keegan cautioned.

"I know." His voice shook. He swallowed, eyes scanning her face. "Thalia. Thalia, can you hear me?"

Thalia trembled, her muscles seizing like tightened ropes. His words broke through the haze of her pain.

"There is something we can try," he said lowly. "To maybe get you past the pain." Thalia moaned, her body weakening with each heartbeat. "But I need you to agree. I need you to understand what is going on."

Thalia shook her head, her tears like acid. "I don't want to die."

"I know, I know, my love," Cassius murmured. "The pain is what will kill you. That is why so many of us turn. But we can try to find a different stimulus, one that will override the pain. Do you know what I'm saying?"

The waves of agony threatened to drown her. Thalia panted, the veins in her neck bulging. Yet somehow she understood. A stronger stimulus could get rid of this pain. "Yes."

Regret speared itself through Cassius's face, his hesitation palpable.

Thalia whimpered, latching on to his face. "I don't want to die."

Cassius's face hardened. "Switch places with me."

She didn't know who he was talking to, only that one moment her arms were free, then warm hands clamped on them.

Through the haze of her pain, she saw Keegan above her. He stared at her, holding her down as her body thrashed uncontrollably. She screamed until her vocal chords shredded.

Then hands clamped onto her legs once more.

Thalia managed to open her eyes, her chest cracking in half, to find Cassius at the foot of the bed, his hands wrapped around her ankles.

She sobbed as her body trembled, bile rising in her throat at the pain. The insatiable hunger deepened. Keegan's blood pulsed just out of reach above her. Yet through the hunger, darkness hummed along the edges of her vision. Pain blinded her, making her arch until her spine groaned.

Cassius stared at her, his face a mixture of guilt and trepidation.

"Cassius," Keegan warned as Thalia slumped, her poor body lying useless like a broken doll.

"Give me a minute."

Thalia wasn't sure if she had a minute. But then Cassius knelt, his hands drifting up her legs.

"Do you remember our first coupling?" Cassius said quietly. Another wave of pain hovered on the edge of her vision, but she latched on to Cassius's words. Latched on to his fingers, which were slowly inching up her thighs—tried to zero in on the sensation instead of the building agony. "It was right after you'd told off Lord Vincent's son before the whole court."

Thalia's muscles bunched, shrinking and warping, begging her to succumb to the pain.

"You told him that you'd rather marry one of the horses in the stables than him. Your mother was furious, so angry that you'd embarrassed her before her court. But you didn't care. You just held your head high, claiming that if you were going to marry anyone, it would be for the good of Agripa. Not just because your mother was trying to appease her simpering council."

Thalia's arms strained, but Keegan's weight kept her firmly pressed against the mattress.

"I remember your mother dismissed you from her court entirely then. And you just looked at her and smiled, sketching a bow before you swept out of the room."

Cassius's fingers set tiny fires in their wake, the pad of his thumb sweeping up the inner part of her thigh. Pain reared its head, and Thalia couldn't stop it as it hit her.

"I remember you got to your room, and I followed you inside. You slammed the door hard enough it rattled on the hinges. Then you turned to me." Cassius's words brought her back. He paused, his fingers pausing with him. "And your eyes blazed with such annoyance, with such anger, it sent my own blood sparking. Do you remember what you said to me?"

Thalia couldn't speak, not with the pain still wrapping tightly around her throat. Cassius continued, "You told me to get out. That you couldn't bear to hear a lecture from me regarding your behavior at court—about how you should have behaved better."

Thalia's mind flashed only briefly. The image was hazy. She remembered screaming at him to leave. Because she'd come to care for him far more than she'd realized. And the thought of him being disappointed in her was worse than the banishment from her mother's court.

But he hadn't left.

He'd stayed.

Crossing the floor until his lips had collided with hers.

"I think about that look on your face," Cassius murmured, his fingers parting the folds of her dressing gown, pushing the fabric aside despite it already being twisted around her from her thrashing. "That blaze in your eyes—that defiance when you told your mother how poorly she was running her realm."

Thalia shuddered, her breath hitching.

"And that look on your face is all I picture when I wrap my hand around my cock."

Thalia's body arched as his fingers finally found her. Pain speared through her, but it was quickly chased away by Cassius sliding his finger inside her.

Thalia groaned, her nerve endings sparking, as if trying to tie themselves back together after they'd been frayed raw.

"And I think about every coupling we've ever had," Cassius continued, his thumb swirling over the bundle at the apex of her thighs. "I think about when we fucked in the stables." He added another finger in. Thalia panted, her body twisting. "I think about when we fucked on your mother's throne." His fingers pumped inside her. "I think about when you used to take me inside your mouth so hard you'd choke."

Pain flared along her limbs, but she pushed it aside, fighting to find that growing ache now burning deep inside her. Her hips arched, her breath sawing out through her teeth.

"You are all that consumes me. Every thought. Every moment. Waking up beside you every day is torture."

Thalia groaned as he added a third finger.

"And then you wear those little nightgowns. The red one is particularly wicked."

His finger curled, just as his thumb pressed hard on her bundle of nerves.

Thalia cried out, her back arching as pleasure pulsed through her. She let the wave lap against the pain. Let it wash some of the agony away.

The wave passed, but the pain persisted.

Thalia shook, gooseflesh pebbling her skin. She peeled open her eyes, finding Cassius still hovering over her.

His brows narrowed at her body, which still twitched with sharp, aching stabs.

"I can do this all night," he whispered, his fingers starting to pump once more. "I can do this until my hand falls off."

Thalia moaned, clenching around him. Her hips bucked and Cassius cursed.

Her arms strained to grasp her breast, but Keegan wouldn't let go. She sobbed, trying to get any sort of friction that wasn't the fabric of the dressing gown. Writhing, she finally felt the gown slip over her shoulder. Cold air ghosted over her peaked nipple.

Her heavy lids latched on to Cassius, who watched her, pupils near devouring the ring of his irises. Without removing his fingers, he leaned over, his nose trailing up the center of her stomach before his mouth closed over her breast.

Thalia hissed as his teeth scraped her skin, tugging her nipple between them. His free hand came up to grasp her other breast, squeezing hard enough that Thalia cried out.

Her hips rolled, trying to get him deeper. Trying to appease that ache that hovered above the pain. A low chuckle echoed from his throat. "Fuck my hand like you mean it."

Heat flooded Thalia, pushing the pain back even more. Her hips moved in earnest, just as his teeth tugged at her nipple—

Pleasure exploded through her, and Thalia nearly wept.

Her skin tingled, the pain no more than a buzz now spreading through her body, but it still hummed on the edges of her mind.

"Cassius," she moaned, her throat sore.

The pressure left her shoulders, leaving her trembling arms free.

He removed his fingers, and Thalia nearly cried out again until her body was tugged to the edge of the bed.

Her eyes flew open, and she only caught sight of Cassius's dark stare before he lowered his mouth to her aching core.

Thalia groaned, fingers twisting in the sheets as Cassius's tongue slid between the folds of her sex.

He moved her legs, placing them over his shoulders, and Thalia panted, his tongue plunging into her with just as much fervor as his fingers.

She could barely think over the feeling of him between her legs. His tongue worshiped her sex until it throbbed and pulsed. One hand tangled in his hair, pressing his face into her.

"Cass," Thalia ground out, her pleasure building.

Then his fingers slipped inside just as he took her clit between his teeth.

Thalia screamed as she came, his tongue chasing away the last of the pain that racked her body.

It felt as though a lifetime passed before the waves slowed, and his fingers slipped out.

Thalia slumped against the mattress, the pain ebbing away like water along the shore.

Cassius pressed his lips to the soft inside of her thigh.

"Cass?" she mumbled. Already her lids were growing heavy, tiredness wringing her out as thoroughly as his tongue had.

"Yes?"

But whatever she was going to say didn't come. Not as exhaustion swept her away in its current, his name still posed on her lips.

Chapter Thirty-Two

Thalia took a deep breath, her eyelids fluttering open.

She blinked, taking in the grayish dawn bleeding into the room. Birds chirped outside her window. Had it all been a dream?

Thalia shifted and sucked in a sharp breath. The dull twinge coming from her neck said otherwise, as did the pleasant ache between her thighs. She rolled over and her heart squeezed.

Cassius sat in one of the armchairs in the room, his head propped in his fist. His chest rose and fell deeply, although his brow was still furrowed, even in sleep.

The sight made the back of her throat tighten.

As if she'd swallowed too loudly, his eyes flew open, and he sat up, suddenly alert. Then his gaze settled on hers.

They stared at each for a moment. Some thread stretched between them, pulling taut. Thalia swallowed once more, blinking her eyes rapidly. She pushed herself to a sitting position and groaned.

Cassius was immediately there, propping up a pillow behind her back. "Easy," he said, his voice soft. "Your body will need to rest."

Thalia stared up at him as he finished adjusting the pillows, then stepped back. She didn't know what to say, how to act.

Cassius watched her with a wary expression. Finally, he said, "Do you remember last night?"

Even though pain had muddled her memory, she still recalled the sharp torment of the Vampyr's bite, then the agony coursing through her burning body until Cassius offered a different solution. One that had the ache between her legs throbbing.

"Yes."

Cassius's face was guarded, but he sank back onto the chair, watching. "I want to apologize."

Thalia lifted her head in shock. "For what?"

Cassius scrubbed a hand over his jaw. "For what I had to do."

Too many emotions bubbled in Thalia's stomach. "You did what you had to in order to save my life. You don't need to apologize for it."

"I know but—" Cassius cut himself off, his eyes suddenly full of regret and guilt. "But it shouldn't have happened at all."

Thalia's heart sank, and she was suddenly unsure why his adamancy that he shouldn't be intimate with her set her stomach churning. "Well, it's done now."

She swung her legs to the floor, wincing at every part of her body that hurt. It felt as though she'd been run over by a carriage repeatedly, then thrown down an embankment for good measure.

She hobbled to the bathing room, taking a sharp breath as she tried bending to turn on the tub.

A hand appeared, turning the water on for her. She didn't comment as Cassius added an assortment of soaps and oils to the clawfoot tub. As if his guilt drove him to do it. Thalia gritted her teeth, ignoring the ache in her jaw.

"You don't have to do that," she got out when he went so far as to set extra soap along the window's edge.

He turned to her, his eyes still guttering. "Thalia—"

"Is this some sort of self-righteous act to make you feel better about fucking me with your mouth and fingers? Is this supposed to—"

"I'm the reason that Vampyr bit you!" Cassius's harsh words stopped her.

"What?"

Cassius shut off the water in the tub, running a shaking hand through his hair. "Do you really think what I did last night is the reason for my guilt? Sybil—she—she is here because of me."

Sybil. The name rang through Thalia's hazy memory. Cassius had said something about her turning into one of them because of it—

Thalia sucked in a sharp breath, the image of Sybil's foaming mouth flashing. "You're harboring a bitten."

Cassius raised his devastated gaze to hers. Thalia took a step back, her body shaking as the image of Sybil flashed in her mind. The feeling of her canines sinking into her flesh, as she *drank* from her.

"Let me explain—" Cassius reached for her, but Thalia kept stepping back. Her heart pounded in her throat as she retreated into the bedroom.

"You—you let this happen—" Thalia's fingers shook. "You said they are supposed to be killed—"

"She's my sister."

Thalia faltered. "What?"

Cassius looked as though he'd ripped out his own heart as he rasped, "My half sister. I didn't know she existed until I was turned."

Thalia's knees hit the back of the bed. She hadn't even realized how far she'd withdrawn until she sank onto the mattress. "Your sister? How?"

"My father," Cassius stumbled. "You know what he was like. I don't know how or even when it happened, but he met a Vampyr. I only knew because Sybil sent me a letter."

Thalia stared at him in shock. "How did she even know about you?"

"Her mother was favored by the prince. Sybil's mother wasn't a lady at first, but the prince ended up accepting her onto his council—accepting Sybil. Her mother was bitten and killed. It was then that the prince told her of her human sire and . . . me."

Thalia ran a hand over her face, unable to imagine what Cassius must have felt when he read the letter. Because humans had always been taught to fear the monsters to the north. And to know that one of them was his own kin?

"I went searching for her four years ago." Cassius's words broke through her thoughts.

She sucked in a sharp breath. Four years ago . . .

"What happened?" she finally asked. The question she'd avoided for so long finally needed to be brought to light.

Cassius sank onto one of the armchairs, his shoulders heavy. "I heard rumors that there were a few Vampyrs who'd be willing to talk to humans. After the treaty failed over a decade ago, and given the war between our two worlds, I knew it was a risk. But I needed to find her—to see her. So I had Marcus find me an old map of our world." Thalia felt a sudden sting of betrayal from her friend back home. "And I looked for the Vampyr ports. I took a boat, knowing that despite the rocky waters, I could navigate them as opposed to trying to go through the forest. I landed in a little town not far from Irenbis.

"The Vampyrs have been dealing with other humans for as long as they can remember. It was only Agripa they cut off all connection to, so finding me on their shores wasn't a great surprise. I managed to make my way to House Lorenzia. Sybil had already been serving on the prince's council, same as Camilla and Keegan. It was then I learned about the first rumors of the bitten, the blight which was threatening the Vampyr world. I left with the promise to try and see if Agripa would be willing to aid them. But when I left to return home, I ran into a rogue Vampyr."

Thalia swallowed, watching Cassius's eyes shift. "The Vampyr didn't have the self-control as one should. He was still young. He smelled my blood, and I could do nothing to stop him before he bit me."

"How did I not know you were going to find her?" Thalia whispered.

"It was right when the Scarecrows began to appear. Your mother sent me away often to try and figure out what was going on." That was around the same time Thalia had accepted the marriage proposal meant to save her world. The growing Vampyr attacks had urged her to finally accept the human prince's treaty.

"You lied to me?"

"What would you have done if you'd known?" Cassius said softly.

Thalia looked away, suddenly ashamed to realize she would have refused to allow him to find his sister. Because at the end of the day, Sybil was a Vampyr.

"Damien found me, right on the border of Vaccarium. I begged him to make the pain stop, so he let me feed. Then he took me back to the prince's council, where I've stayed ever since."

Everything was falling into place. The reason Cassius was so intent on helping the Vampyrs—it wasn't just because he was now one of them but also because of his sister.

"What happened after?" Thalia asked.

Cassius took a shuddering breath. "I recovered from the bite, and I—I went back to Agripa. To find you." He met her stare. "When I finally got to the castle, I discovered that Prince Darius was planning to attack Agripa—to take it by force in whatever way necessary so he could have a better foothold to attack the Vampyrs in Vaccarium."

"That's why you killed him?" Thalia felt the breath punch out of her.

"Yes," Cassius got out. "I couldn't—I couldn't let him live. Not knowing he had plans to kill you and your mother."

Thalia's world faltered, the truth baring itself brighter than the sun shining on a darkened bay. Guilt whirled in Thalia's gut as Cassius continued. "After I got back, I joined the prince's council officially. The rumors of the creature were spreading, along with the bitten, who began leaving Scarecrows in Agripa. We needed to search for a cure and to try and stop the bitten. I spent three and a half years doing that."

"What about Sybil? What happened to her?" Thalia met his stare.

The muscle in Cassius's jaw flickered. "Six months ago, there was a rumor that the creature had been wounded in the forest. Me and Keegan were away dealing with the Mages in Lorceium, but Sybil got word and took it upon herself to try and stop it. She was bitten."

Thalia sucked in a breath, and Cassius leaned back in his seat. "I-I couldn't do it. I couldn't kill her once I found her. She hadn't yet gone mad, but the poison in her bloodstream was spreading. We—Keegan,

Camilla, and I—we brought her here. Warded the place so no one would venture in but also so she couldn't escape."

"Is this place really one of the prince's estates?" Thalia asked.

Cassius nodded. "Yes. He gave it to his council. I didn't lie about that. Camilla and Sybil stayed here the most. This was her room."

Thalia's heart twisted as she glanced around the space. The soft decor was the polar opposite of the crazed Vampyr who'd bitten her. "Where is she now?"

Cassius swallowed. Hard. "She's been dealt with."

Thalia jerked. "You killed her?"

Cassius looked away, his eyes filling with too many emotions to name. "No. But I asked Keegan to drain her blood. She's in a comatose state now."

Which meant she was as good as dead. Sybil would only come out of her suspended state if she drained the blood of another. Then the vicious cycle would continue—

"Why would you do that?" Thalia gasped. "Why would you—"

"Because I cannot bear the thought of you getting hurt," Cassius snapped. His eyes glowed as he gripped the arms of his chair, his face rippling slightly. "Because it makes me sick to my fucking stomach thinking that I almost lost you last night. To know that it was my own mistake—my own foolish, selfish desire in keeping Sybil alive in hopes we find a cure—that allowed you to get in harm's way. I am no better than Julian. No better than any of the other Vampyrs trying to keep their loved ones alive for a little longer."

Thalia swallowed as Cassius's chest rose and fell, his anger at himself washing over his features like slashes on a dartboard.

She rose, her feet padding across the floor until she stood before him. Cassius looked at her, his eyes shining with such deep regret and devastation that it made her own heart crack.

"You are not Julian," she said. His face twisted, but she placed a hand on his cheek, feeling the rough stubble under her palms. "And you are not like any other Vampyr. You took her away when you found out she was bitten. You ensured that no one would stumble upon her or that she would get out and cause harm. You did not just leave her so anyone could find her."

Cassius's throat bobbed, his eyes shining. "But she still found *you*."

Thalia gripped his face in her hands. She moved, finding herself straddling his lap. Cassius didn't say anything, but his hands immediately found the curve of her waist, holding tight.

"I was stupid," Thalia whispered, running a thumb along his sharp cheekbone. "I heard her crying for help and thought a woman had locked herself down there. I was foolish, and didn't listen when you told me to avoid the lower levels. If I had, none of this would have happened."

Cassius swallowed. Hard. His fingers clenched around her waist. "You could have died last night. And I would have never forgiven myself."

Thalia's own throat bobbed. "But I didn't." She grasped one of his hands, bringing it to her chest—to her heart, a steady beat under his palms. "I'm right here."

Cassius scanned her, blue eyes bright. "Thalia—"

She silenced him with her lips.

Cassius pressed his fingers into her chest, his hand burning as if needing the reassurance that she was alive.

His lips answered her own, a thread wrapping between them, fusing them together like two halves of a mirror. All sense of fear and decorum fled as Thalia nipped at his lips, her teeth snagging on his flesh, and Cassius groaned. His kiss turned fervent. Heated.

He gripped her face with one hand, tilting her head back farther so he could devour her. His tongue slipped into her mouth, and she made a sound in the back of her throat, her body going loose and tight all at once.

Cassius smiled against her lips. "I've missed those little noises." His hand over her heart drifted to her breast. "I missed the taste of you."

Thalia kissed him deeper, her arms winding around his neck. She felt his hard length right against the soft, aching part of her. She arched against it, needing to feel the friction between them.

"Fuck," he growled, fingers digging into her flesh.

Cassius's lips left hers, but he didn't go far as he tilted his jaw, his hot mouth meeting her neck. Thalia tilted her head back, and his lips traveled down to her collarbone.

Thalia rolled her hips against him, needing to appease the ache in her core—

Pain flared through her body. Thalia let out a hiss, pulling away.

"What? What happened?" Cassius's brows pulled, immediately stopping.

Thalia shook her head, pushing the pain aside. "Nothing." She leaned back in to capture his mouth and groaned, the muscles in her back twinging.

Cassius shifted. "Maybe we shouldn't do this."

Thalia's eyes narrowed. "No. I'm fine. It's fine."

Cassius caught her chin between his fingers, his eyes shining now for a different reason. "As much as I'd like to continue this, I don't think your body can handle it."

Thalia would have argued had the muscle in her calf not begun to cramp. She groaned again, and Cassius stood, picking her up in the same movement.

And she didn't protest as he plunked her into the tub, the warm water soothing the aches and pain in both her body and heart.

Chapter Thirty-Three

"So what do you think?" Cassius asked. His face remained neutral, although Thalia heard the barest hint of hope in his voice.

Thalia, Cassius, and Keegan all stood around the table in the small dining room in the manor, watching as Camilla held up the jars of teeth to a light.

"I'll have to test it out," Camilla said, setting the jar down with a clink. "It's possible, but don't get your hopes up."

Cassius nodded, his face still carefully blank, although his shoulders tensed.

"Can you test it out here?" Thalia asked.

Camilla shook her head, curly hair flying. "Not here. I need to go to Perden. Decima can help." Thalia shuffled the information to the side as the shifter turned to Cassius. "You'll want to come too. The Mages have found something."

Cassius straightened. "What is it?"

Camilla just shook her head. "They can explain more. But we might have a different solution to what you've asked."

Thalia glanced between the two and caught Keegan's gaze. At her confused stare, he shook his head.

Camilla shoved the teeth into the satchel. "I can take these back to start testing, and I'll inform the Mages you're on your way."

Cassius nodded. "Thank you."

Camilla smiled, slinging the satchel over her shoulder. She stared at Thalia, noting the bruise on her throat. "It's good to see you, Thalia."

Then she was gone.

"What is the solution the Mages are trying to come up with?" Thalia blurted out as soon as the three of them were alone. Lady Decima had mentioned a similar thing at the council meeting with the other Houses.

Keegan slid his eyes to Cassius, raising a brow as if to say *You take this.*

She'd thought there'd be awkward tension between her and the golden-eyed Vampyr, given the state he'd last seen her in. But Keegan didn't seem to care, which put her at ease.

Cassius sighed, running a hand through his long hair. Thalia pushed aside the image of her own fingers running through the strands. "We'd hoped when the creature first emerged that they'd know of a way to stop it. Or the very least, how to find a cure." Thalia waved a hand for him to get to the point. Cassius gave her a look before continuing. "When that failed, we started thinking of a different solution for the issue."

"Like what?"

"Creating a place for Vampyrs to go if things turned south."

"Like a sanctuary?" Thalia's brows pinched in confusion.

"In a way . . . the mountain—Lorceium—doesn't just provide the ore which Agripa uses as fuel. There are pockets of magic in the mountain, the last of the Mages' reserves. They've been trying to see if those pockets can be harnessed to use as protection."

"Like the wards around this place," Thalia murmured.

Cassius nodded. "The wards here are strong but not lasting. They'll eventually fade in the coming years, and not even Camilla's magic can replace them. But the magic in the mountain is far greater. Strong enough to withstand hundreds of years."

"So all the Vampyrs would move into the mountain? It would save you from getting bitten?" Thalia said.

Cassius sighed, scrubbing a hand over his jaw. "Yes. But the problem we are running into is that there isn't enough room to bring all the Vampyrs of Vaccarium into Lorceium. The pockets of magic are small, some not much bigger than this room. The Mages are trying to find a way to grow those small pockets."

Thalia swallowed, realization dawning. "But what happens if the Vampyrs retreat into the mountain? No one will be able to fulfill the treaty with the humans. What happens if the creature turns to Agripa when there's nothing left for them here?"

Cassius's eyes darkened. "This is a last resort. One we don't wish to implement unless it's necessary."

Thalia shut her eyes, pushing past her sudden panic about the creature entering the human realm. The humans didn't stand a chance against the bitten Vampyrs; there was no way in hell they'd stand against the creature that had infected them.

Resolve suddenly filled Thalia's gut. The Vampyrs needed a cure, not just for themselves but for the whole of their world. "When do we leave for Perden?"

Thalia rode in front of Cassius, the rocking of their horse sending her more forcefully back against his chest.

Thalia chided herself as they made their way through the forest. Now certainly wasn't the time to think about the steady reassurance of Cassius's arms around her.

"What are the Mages like?" she asked suddenly.

Keegan had moved a ways ahead, his shoulders at ease. Despite leaving the safety of the wards, at least the Vampyrs seemed relaxed as they traveled.

"What do you mean?" Cassius said.

"Are they . . . old?"

Cassius chuckled, his breath stirring a strand of her hair that had slipped from its braid. "Some are. Others are younger than us."

"Really?"

Cassius nodded, his cheek brushing against her head. "I've only met a few. Decima is one of them. There's a few others; Larellia is head of the Mages. She's the one who's been actively looking for a cure."

Thalia chewed the inside of her cheek. "And there's really no way to defeat the creature? Kill it instead? Maybe find a way to incapacitate it so it can be burned?"

Cassius's hands tightened on the reins. "We could try. But trying to fight it in the forest has always ended badly, with more losses than it's worth. The amount of Vampyrs it would take to bring the creature down, to try and burn it in the forest with such tight quarters . . ."

"What about trying to lure it out? Maybe if it was out in the open, you could do something."

Cassius shook his head. "We've tried. The thing won't leave the forest line, and given that its offspring can regenerate, I have a feeling that the mother can too."

Which made sense as to why they'd been fighting it for years, but something didn't sit right with her. "Where did the creature come from anyway?"

"We don't know. The forest has bred many strange things. Some believe that Chaménos has pockets of magic, much like the mountain. But the magic in the forest is wild, unpredictable."

Thalia made a face at that. "Huh."

"What?"

She sighed, leaning her head back against his chest. "This world is so strange." Cassius snorted, and Thalia's lips twitched upward. "I mean, in Agripa, you know our lack of knowledge. I don't recall ever learning about the specific creatures living in your forest. Marcus would have a heyday if he was here. He'd probably explode with excitement trying to write it all down despite the imminent danger he'd be in."

Cassius's chuckle rumbled against her back. "Yes, he would be rather keen on getting to know this world."

Thalia's heart sank, suddenly missing her friend back home. She cleared her throat. "What of the prince?"

"What of him?

"Will I finally meet him in Perden?" The thought should have excited her. Finally, she was about to meet the man she'd been betrothed to—the Vampyr whose House she was trying to usurp.

But none of it . . . none of it felt right.

Not being with the prince, nor using his House against him.

And if she finally joined with him, what then? The thought of . . . coupling with him, even if he wasn't the monstrous Vampyr she'd painted him out to be, didn't sit well with her. Especially not with everything that'd transpired between her and Cassius. And where did Cass fit into her life? When she was officially joined with House Lorenzia, would the prince allow her to take a lover? Would Cass—would Cassius even want to? Given his loyalty to the prince?

"He's gone to try and gain some semblance of his House." Cassius's words pulled her from her thoughts.

Thalia twisted in the seat. "What?"

Cassius kept his gaze focused on the path. "The Vampyrs are still grumbling. He's trying to figure out a solution with House Gallinus."

Thalia shook her head. "That doesn't make any sense. His council is here—"

"Camilla said he was insistent on getting back, on making things right."

"What about me?"

"What about you?"

Thalia twisted again. "Does he not care that his wife is tramping across his realm?"

Cassius's jaw flickered. "He is aware you are with me."

"And how does he feel about that?"

"What do you mean?"

"He knows of our history?"

Cassius met her stare, brows furrowing. "Yes."

"And he's not jealous?"

Cassius pulled their horse to a stop. "Do you want him to be?"

Thalia felt her annoyance rising. "I want him to actually show up. I want to actually meet the man I've uprooted my whole life for."

"You will."

"When?" Thalia's voice rose. "When will I meet him? It's beginning to feel as though he doesn't exist at all."

Cassius stared at her a moment longer before he nudged Feryena on. "The prince has not forgotten you, and you will meet him. Sooner than you expect."

Thalia had a sinking feeling Cassius was lying.

They set up camp in a small glen. Flowers swayed gently in the breeze as they configured their bedrolls. Keegan had gone to tend to the horses, and Thalia watched as Cassius started a fire, the sparks rising with the smoke.

The moon watched her through the leaves as she settled down.

"What are you thinking?" Cassius's words pulled her from her stare.

She realized she was picking at her nails and stopped. She didn't know if she could voice her concern, her dismay at the idea of not being with Cassius even after everything that had happened—

"Do you miss it?" Thalia blurted out.

Cassius met her gaze across the fire. "Miss what?"

"The sun?"

Cassius's brows furrowed. "Sometimes." Thalia waited, watching, as emotions flickered in his eyes, too fast for her to decipher. "Sometimes I miss the feel of the warmth on my face. When I could look skywards and know no matter how cold I was, I knew where to find the light."

"Are you still cold now?"

"Yes."

"You're hot, though." Cassius raised an amused brow, and Thalia's cheeks heated. "I mean, your body temperature. I still feel your heat."

Cassius shrugged, moving around the fire. He grabbed a water skin and took a swig before handing it to her. "My body heat may feel that way, but my insides don't."

Thalia made a face but drank as well. Cassius watched her swallow. She wiped her mouth with the back of her hand. She was glad she didn't know what that type of cold felt like, that she'd been saved from having to find out.

Cassius settled down on his bedroll next to hers. Thalia lay down, pulling her blanket up to her chin. They had a foot of distance between them, and Cassius grabbed his own blanket, trying to get comfortable on the hard ground.

"We'll arrive in Perden tomorrow," he said softly. Vaguely, Thalia heard Keegan returning, settling onto his own bedroll on the opposite side of the fire.

Thalia nodded, tucking her arm under her head.

Tension stretched between them, the fire suddenly feeling much too hot.

Thalia flipped off her blanket, and Cassius raised a brow. "Everything all right?"

"It's too hot," Thalia whispered. Her heart rate rose, and she couldn't say why. Maybe it was the fact that Cassius's eyes had gone to her throat. "Are you . . . are you still cold?"

Cassius offered a small smile. "I told you, my body may be hot, but my insides always feel as though they're coated in ice."

Thalia made a face. "What stops it?"

Cassius's eyes darkened. She barely breathed as his hand reached out, brushing a strand of her hair from her neck. "Usually I can get warmed up if I think about something . . . arousing."

"Like what?" Thalia whispered.

Cassius's fingers didn't leave her neck. "Like thinking of you."

Thalia shifted closer, the heat of his body transferring to her. "And what do you think about?"

Cassius smirked, his fingers trailing down her neck to her arm. "I think about what it would be like to make love to you now. How four years may have changed a lot of things, but the way we were together never will."

Thalia closed her eyes, the image of him thrusting inside her making her burn.

"I think about those little noises you make," he said quietly. "How you gasp every time I put my mouth around your breast. The way you clench when my fingers are inside you."

Thalia shuddered, imagining the feel of his teeth scraping against her nipple.

"You have no idea what it's like, Thalia." He let out a low chuckle. "How your jasmine perfume makes me feel feral. Makes me want to peel those tight pants off you and worship every inch of you."

Thalia opened her lids, finding his stare dark. His hand hadn't left her arm, but she trembled, need filling her with such desire that she nearly cried.

"And when you look at me like that," Cassius got out, his eyes slowly lifting to hers, "it takes everything in me not to take you right here. To fuck you until we both forget who we are and what we're doing."

Thalia swallowed, the growing ache between her legs so great she had to clamp her thighs together.

"I beg you, please don't."

Thalia jerked, all sense of heat dying as Keegan's words floated across the fire. Mortification speared through her as she realized what she and Cassius had been doing—the words they'd been speaking.

Cassius cast a glare across the fire even as he chuckled. "Prick." He turned back to Thalia, his features now dancing with amusement. His features softened at her embarrassment. "Keegan's just jealous that he doesn't have a pretty face to stare at."

"I have a mirror for that," Keegan said over his shoulder.

Cassius snickered and Thalia's lip twitched as she lay back down, pulling the blanket up once more.

Cassius settled down beside her. He reached across the space, his fingers entwining with hers. "Get some sleep," he said, his voice low.

Thalia nodded, forcing her lids to close, Cassius's hand a steady weight in her palm.

Chapter Thirty-Four

Perden shone like a lost jewel hidden among shadows.

It stood on the precipice of a waterfall, a citadel rising high against the mountainside—an entire kingdom, really—as if it had been stuck there by some giant hand. A bridge spanned the waterfall, the water flowing under it until it disappeared into a misty basin.

"Holy gods," Thalia murmured as Cassius nudged Feryena onward.

The stone bridge stretched at least six wagon-widths across, and mist met her face despite how high they were.

"Is this the only way to get to the city?" Thalia asked, the roar of water humming in her ears.

"There's three entrances into Perden," Cassius rumbled. "This is one. One down in the basin, although you have to climb thousands of stairs to reach the top. And then one that leads from the other side of the mountain to the sea."

Thalia tried to take it all in, the mountain looming larger the closer they got to the stone city built into its side. She caught sight of little blobs flying into and out of open windows.

"What are those?" she asked, pointing.

"Shifters," Cassius replied.

Thalia stared in awe as the distant shapes continued to enter and exit the citadel. The trio slowed their horses when they came to a closed gate, its wood gleaming with moisture. All sorts of whorls and designs that Thalia couldn't decipher had been carved into its surface.

One of the guards standing watch stepped forward. He nodded. "Lord Cassius, Lord Keegan, we've been expecting you."

The gates swung open on their own, and Cassius nodded his thanks as they rode into Perden.

The city was laid out on cobblestone streets, all winding up the mountain, each level grander than the last. Various shops and cafés lined the streets at the bottom, the scent of crisp apples and roasted honey drifting into Thalia's nose. The second level held homes and other, nicer storefronts. Thalia's lips twitched as a group of children ran by pushing a hoop on a stick, their laughter chasing her as she and her companions climbed through the city.

They finally stopped when they got to the very top of the citadel. The castle's courtyard was made of stone and fossilized tree trunks. Cassius dismounted before the entrance, helping her down. She turned, sucking in a deep breath at the view.

They were high enough to see the expanse of the horizon. She squinted, and though she knew she was too far away, she could have sworn she saw the forest bordering their worlds.

She shivered, a crisp breeze tugging at the strands of her hair.

Thalia turned back just as Camilla and Lady Decima greeted them.

"Lord Cassius." Lady Decima inclined her head. "I hope the journey was uneventful."

Thalia resisted the urge to snort as Cassius replied, "You could say that."

Lady Decima gestured for them to follow her inside. Thalia glanced at Camilla, but the shifter just smirked, trailing after them.

The inside of the castle was carved into the mountain itself, and covered hallways and arches bled to different areas. They all followed after Lady Decima, heading deeper.

Cold air nipped at Thalia's cheeks, even though the wind off the mountain couldn't reach them here. Carvings of various creatures, ones Thalia didn't recognize, covered the walls. Strange beings that seemed to dance in starlight.

She shivered, and Cassius glanced over his shoulder as Lady Decima continued to speak about the progress happening within Lorceium itself.

"We've managed to find two more pockets," she said as they entered an octagonal room. A stone table had been erected in the middle. A carving of a fox with multiple teeth grinned in the center.

"Where?" Keegan asked.

Lady Decima took a seat in one of the chairs. Everyone else followed suit. "The lower levels of the mountain. Deeper than we'd anticipated."

Cassius's jaw flickered. "You said there was a setback?"

Lady Decima cocked her dark head. "The deeper we dig, the less stable the mountain becomes. There was a cave-in two weeks ago."

Keegan sucked in a sharp breath. "Was anyone hurt?"

Shadows crossed Lady Decima's eyes. "We had a number of casualties. But we cannot keep doing this, Lord Cassius, no matter what your prince says. If we continue, the whole mountain will collapse and the pockets of magic will be lost to us."

Which meant the backup plan to bring the Vampyrs here to escape the creature would be null and void.

"Camilla said the Mages have found something else? What is it?" Cassius asked, his words sharp.

"Perhaps I can explain."

Everyone except Thalia stood as a new person entered the room. Thalia stared in shock at the woman who'd entered.

She was by far one of the most beautiful women Thalia had ever seen. Dark lashes framed her upturned oval eyes, highlighting her silver irises. Her long, straight black hair fell to her waist. She wore a peacock-blue dress of thick velvet, cinched at the waist with a belt of golden brocade.

"Larellia." Cassius inclined his head, and everyone took to their seats. "What have the Mages found?"

It clicked then that this was the head Mage. Larellia took a seat near Lady Decima, folding her pale hands together. "A bitten found its way into the borders of House Olvectus."

Cassius jerked and Keegan cursed. Larellia waved her hand. "Don't be so dramatic. It was dealt with."

"You killed the bitten?" Cassius asked, his words low.

"Not exactly."

"What do you mean?"

"As you know, we've been trying to harness the pockets of magic to expand them to encompass the entire mountain as a whole. It's been slow going, the magic is fickle. It does not like to bend or move in the way we want it to. However"—Larellia lifted her silver gaze—"it can be used to suspend time."

"What do you mean?" Keegan's eyes widened.

"These pockets can hold someone for an indefinite amount of time. They will remain frozen, unaging. Simply sleeping until a Mage pulls them out."

"So what are you saying?" A muscle in Cassius's jaw flickered again.

"We may not be able to house all of Vaccarium, but with the pockets in the mountain, we can bring the bitten here. We can suspend them until a cure is found, without the fear of them waking or retaliating."

Cassius had paled slightly, and Thalia didn't know why. She tried to catch his gaze, but he wouldn't meet her stare.

"This brings us to our second point," Larellia said, nodding to Camilla. "We've been running tests, trying to figure out if the poison in the teeth can be used as a cure."

"And?" Thalia asked, her first word the entire meeting.

Larellia finally glanced at her, surprise flaring in her silver eyes before it was gone. "We believe we have something, but we need a bitten to test it out on. Camilla informed me that your sister was bitten and is staying in the manor by the lake? If we bring her here, we can test out the antidote. If it fails, at least we can suspend her until a cure reveals itself."

Cassius stared at Larellia, his face paling further. His hands clenched on the table, his eyes flashing before he got out, "She won't be of any use." Thalia's stomach dropped as Cassius continued, "She—she is already in slumber."

Camilla gasped, her face morphing in horror. "You drained her blood?"

"We didn't—I didn't know this was an option," Cassius rasped. "I thought I was doing the right thing."

Thalia's stomach twisted in knots. If it weren't for her, his sister would be awake; she'd have a shot at being cured. But because of her—because of her own brash judgment—Sybil would never have a chance.

Bile rose in her throat, and Cassius still wouldn't look at her.

Larellia stared at him. "We shall have to find another bitten, then."

The conversation moved on, Larellia explaining how the cure might work and Lady Decima chiming in every once in a while.

Through it all, Cassius sank deeper and deeper into himself.

Thalia feared he might never look at her again.

Thalia's chamber in the castle overlooked the waterfall. Even so high up, she could have sworn the mist still licked her face. Her room had open archways and no windows to block the mountain air from entering, but braziers lit about the room kept out the chill.

Thalia stared into the night. Up here, the clouds were no more than wisps against the night sky.

She glanced behind her at her closed door. Cassius hadn't found her. Hadn't said a word or looked at her since Larellia said they could suspend a bitten.

And she didn't know if he was angry with her or himself.

Thalia chewed the inside of her cheek. After the meeting, they'd been shown to their rooms. But that had been hours ago. Tentatively, she padded to the door.

She made it all of two feet down the hall before she ran into Camilla.

"What are you doing?" the shifter asked, dark brow raised. She didn't seem to have rested or changed from the day.

"Where is Cassius?"

Camilla's gaze sharpened, something Thalia hadn't been expecting. "His room."

"Where is it?"

"Why? What do you want with him?"

Thalia felt her annoyance rise, but she shut it down. Let it drown alongside her growing guilt. "I want to talk to him."

Camilla's brows narrowed, her golden eyes scanning Thalia. "I don't know if that's such a good idea."

Thalia bit the inside of her cheek, forcing her anger away. "I know. I can assume that you blame me for what happened with Sybil, and you have every right to. I let her out. Practically handed myself to her on a silver platter. I don't . . . I don't know what your relationship was like with her." Camilla looked away, eyes flashing with something that Thalia couldn't place. "But I can assume, given your roles on the prince's council, that you were close. But I—I also know that Cassius blames himself for this. And he shouldn't. I need to tell him that."

Camilla finally looked at her. While her gaze remained guarded, she eventually relented. "He's at the end of the hall."

Thalia nodded her thanks, hurrying to where the shifter had directed her. She knocked on his door. "Cassius?"

No answer.

Thalia swallowed, glancing back, but Camilla had disappeared. She knocked again, then eased inside.

Cassius's room was much the same as hers, open to the elements, but instead of facing the waterfall, it looked out onto part of the mountain, a few snowcapped trees dotting the landscape in the distance.

"Cassius?"

He sat in a chair, his back to her, staring out into the night. He didn't say anything, and Thalia shuffled a bit more into the room, noting the table next to his chair held a decanter of dark liquid and a half-drunk glass.

"Cass?" She moved to his side.

Only when she had moved to the edges of his peripheral vision did he finally look up. His eyes were bleak—dull—the blue so lifeless they were two pools of broken glass.

"This isn't your fault," Thalia got out, sinking to her knees.

He huffed out a dark laugh, grabbing his half-finished drink. He downed it in one go. "I wish that were true."

Thalia swallowed, unsure what to say. His face was a veritable granite mask, one she didn't know how to crack.

She gently grabbed the empty glass from his hands, setting it on the table. Cassius pulled his stare to her. "Talk to me."

"I knew that being in this position, having the chance to change things, it would come with difficult decisions," Cassius finally got out. "Maybe I've made the wrong ones."

"You did what you thought was right. That's all any of us in power can do," Thalia whispered, threading her fingers through his.

Cassius stared at their entwined hands.

"I—I've been thinking about what you said back in Corithian," Thalia began, and Cassius flicked his gaze up. "When you said you wanted the power to not sit idly while those in charge dictate behind their own walls. I was angry when you said that. To know that you may have thought that about me."

"I didn't think that about you. I still don't. You did what you could with what you had. That's always what you've done, trying to better the lives of those in Agripa despite your mother calling the shots."

Thalia swallowed, plowing on. "But you were right to want to change things. To work to get into a position where you could stop this hurt and death that has been lingering for far too long."

"That doesn't change the fact that I made a bad call," he said bitterly.

Thalia frowned. "What can I do to help?"

"Nothing." Cassius stared off, his face once more granite.

"There must be something I can do?" Something to take away that bleak look on his face, to take away the guilt that wrapped around his neck as heavy as millstones. Because no matter what she said, he'd still blame himself for Sybil, still blame himself for Thalia nearly dying. And that just wouldn't do.

"You know, I've been thinking about something else," Thalia started, squeezing his fingers.

"What have you been thinking?" he grunted.

"I've been thinking about the conversation we had back in Irenbis. About how you would go about seducing me."

His eyes flicked up at that, and Thalia shifted so that she knelt before him. "What about it?" he asked gruffly.

"Well, you told me how you might seduce me, but I never returned the favor." She let go of his hand, placing her palm on his thigh.

"Is that so? And how would you seduce me, Princess?"

Thalia shifted forward, rising on her knees slightly. "Well, for one, I would definitely wear that little red nightdress you seem so obsessed with."

"Oh?"

She nodded, leaning closer, one hand resting on his thigh; the other she slid up his torso, resting on the strong expanse of his shoulder. "And I'd weave those little flowers that you picked for me in my hair."

He swallowed, shifting in the seat. "And then?"

Thalia tilted her head, her cheek pressing against his. Her lips brushed his earlobe. "And then I would chain you to the bed."

Cassius's fingers clenched on the arms of his chair hard enough that the wood groaned.

"And you would be utterly at my mercy," she whispered. "Not able to touch me. Only able to watch as I had my way with you."

She took his lobe in her teeth, tugging lightly.

Cassius let out a sharp breath, her hand sliding up his thigh, stopping at the ties of his pants.

"And you would be begging me to touch you," she continued, pulling on the string with her fingers. Her lips pressed against his throat, feeling the roughness of his skin against her mouth.

"Begging me to take you down my throat." The laces loosened, and she leaned back.

His irises glowed brighter than the moon, the bleakness replaced with something much more heady.

She looked down, following the light dusting of hair peeking above his loosened waistband. The outline of his cock pressed against the seam of his pants.

Thalia flicked her gaze back up. "But I suppose it's a good thing I don't have that red nightdress."

Cassius swallowed. Hard. "I suppose it is."

Thalia smirked. "But I guess that means this will just have to do."

She reached inside his trousers, wrapping her hand around his cock, and gave a long, slow tug.

Cassius hissed, watching her hand, fingers tightening on the arms of his chair.

Thalia chuckled, her other hand doing quick work to free him. She'd forgotten how big he was, how her fingers could barely wrap around him.

She gave another pull, and Cassius groaned.

Thalia smiled, and his heavy lids lifted to hers. "Put your mouth on me," he practically growled out.

Thalia raised a brow. "Already begging?"

"Please, Thalia."

Please.

That word, her name on his lips, had her head lowering. Cassius groaned once more as she took him inside her mouth.

She'd missed this.

Missed him threading his hand through her hair, feeling the restraint he kept for himself slowly come undone.

She ran her tongue along the sides, coating him with her saliva. He let out a sharp breath, his hand tightening on the back of her head.

Her teeth grazed the sensitive skin on the top of his cock, just as she tugged downward—

Cassius let out a curse, hips bucking.

Thalia laughed around him. She set to work, using her tongue to swirl up the beads of moisture gathering, her hand working in tandem with her mouth.

"Fuck," he panted.

Thalia flicked her gaze upward. His chest strained against his shirt, his head thrown back. But he wasn't nearly begging as much as she wanted. She needed him undone. Needed him fucking her mouth as if his life depended on it.

She took him deeper, and she choked.

He groaned, his hips moving as he plunged into her. She quickened her pace, her teeth scraping as she pumped him.

She choked again, her eyes watering, and Cassius's fingers tangled so deep in her hair she was at his mercy.

But she relished it.

Relished him as he unleashed himself.

She reached her free hand into his pants and cupped him, squeezing tightly.

That was his undoing.

Cassius roared, spilling himself into her mouth. She pumped him until the waves passed, then she removed herself, swallowing as she went.

He stared at her, chest heaving, his cock still glistening.

She needed him inside her. Now.

Based on the wicked glint in his eye, she knew he was thinking the same thing.

Before either of them could move, a pounding at the door had them both whirling. Cassius shoved his cock back into his pants, grabbing his discard knife.

He motioned for Thalia to get behind him until Keegan's voice yelled between the pounding fists. "Cassius, you need to get out here. Now!"

Chapter Thirty-Five

Everyone gathered at the top of the citadel, staring into the dark city below. Lights twinkled in and out, the expanse of the bridge lit by enough braziers that it seemed to glow.

"What's going on?" Cassius's words were as cold as the wind blowing from the top of the mountain.

"We thought you'd like to see this." Lady Decima stepped forward, her face hard. She nodded down toward the bridge.

Cassius stiffened, and Thalia followed his eyeline. At first she didn't see anything. But then—a flash of white hide gleaming among the flames.

The creature. Or one of the spawn, if she wasn't mistaken, given the size.

Thalia sucked in a sharp breath. *How the hell did it find its way out here?*

"What's it doing?" Keegan asked, his features shadowed.

"A guard told us that it crossed the bridge thirty minutes ago. It's just been pacing there. They weren't even aware it was there until it let out a howl," Lady Decima supplied, her golden eyes flickering.

"Why would it be way out here?" Thalia murmured. Even though they were high above the creature, she could have sworn it turned its eyeless head up toward her. An earthly howl rent the night sky, leaving gooseflesh in its wake.

"Shall we shoot it?" Lady Decima asked.

Two guards standing near drew their arrows, the tips wrapped in oil. Another stepped forward, carrying a torch.

Cassius's fingers clenched around his sword, his jaw tipping—

"Wait!" Thalia blurted out, stepping forward.

Cassius whirled toward her and the soldiers faltered.

"Wait," she said again, staring back down at the creature, its hide gleaming like moonlight.

"That creature needs to be burned," Cassius warned. "It's a threat to us all—"

"I think it came here for something," Thalia said lowly. Once more, she could have sworn the creature lifted its oblong head, focusing on her.

"The teeth," Camilla cursed.

Thalia shook her head, taking a few more steps forward.

Even in the darkness, the creature stared, its snout lifting as if it could scent her on the coasting air.

"No. I think it came here for me."

They all gathered in the same chamber they'd first met in. The only person not present was Larellia, although Thalia had a feeling she was deep in the mountain trying to deal with the pockets of magic.

"What do you mean, it came here for you?" Camilla asked as soon as they'd all sat down.

Thalia shook her head, realizing how utterly insane she sounded. "I—I think I saw it near the lake at the manor. It was on the edge of the barrier, and I told myself it was nothing but the trick of the light. Then everything else happened." Cassius's jaw flickered, but she plowed on. "But that's not all. When I first encountered the creature in Irenbis, it touched me."

"Where?" Lady Decima asked, brows narrowed.

Thalia pointed to her chest. "Right here. And when we tried to extract the teeth, the jaws wouldn't open for anyone, but it opened when I touched it. Then I woke up to it on my chest—"

"Are you saying the creature we killed in Irenbis is the same one down there?" Cassius asked.

Thalia swallowed. "The creature can regenerate; we already know that. When I was leaving the castle in Irenbis, it . . . protected me."

Cassius shook his head. "It was trying to kill you, and Julian just happened to be in the way."

Thalia looked to Lady Decima, who seemed the most inclined to listen to her asinine theory. "I don't think so. It had plenty of time to kill me, and it never did. I don't know why it would be following me, but I think it's here for me."

Lady Decima studied her a moment longer, then her golden gaze slid to Camilla. The two of them shared a look.

"What is it?" Keegan asked, ever watchful.

"You can't be serious." Camilla's eyes widened, turning back to Thalia.

"What?" Thalia shifted, nervous at all the sudden attention.

Lady Decima ran a hand through her curls. "Long ago, the Mages had more of a connection with the creatures of this land. Some even said there were those who were soul bound to certain animals."

Thalia shook her head. "But I'm not a Mage. I don't have any magic."

"I know," Lady Decima continued. "Which is why it is interesting that this creature has decided to soul bond with you."

"Explain what the fuck that means," Cassius said, his voice lethally sharp.

Lady Decima straightened, her golden eyes flaring slightly. "It means, Lord Cassius, that this creature has decided Thalia will be of some use to it. It will serve as a protector to her."

Thalia's stomach churned. "But it tried attacking me in the forest."

"Yes, but after it touched your chest, it stopped. It protected you from Lord Julian. It went to stand watch over you while you slept," Lady Decima said.

"So what does this mean, then? How is it even possible? I thought the soul-bonded creatures and Mages needed to have magic in them," Keegan asked, just as equally confused and horrified as the rest of them.

Lady Decima raised a well-groomed brow. "Perhaps this creature has magic in it."

Thalia glanced at Cassius. They didn't know where the creature had come from, only that it'd appeared in the woods. Chaménos was said to have the same types of pockets of magic as the mountain . . .

"I need to go down there." Thalia stood.

"Absolutely not." Cassius's harsh gaze met hers.

"If it's soul bound to me, then it won't hurt me, right?" She turned to Lady Decima.

Lady Decima inclined her head, hesitating slightly. "Yes."

"That doesn't seem very reassuring," Cassius growled out.

"The soul bond is a capricious thing, but magic is still fickle. I admit it intrigues me that this creature has chosen Thalia, given she has no magic in her." Lady Decima pursed her lips. "Larellia would know more about this than I do. She's the last Mage who was soul bonded to a creature of magic."

"Where is she?" Thalia asked.

"In the mountain, but she's deep below the surface; it will take a couple hours for her to resurface." She nodded to a guard standing watch by the door. He bowed, presumably to go find the head Mage.

"I'm going down there," Thalia said, standing.

Cassius's chair scraped as he rose. "No."

Thalia's brows narrowed. "Step aside."

Cassius's eyes flared, his irises near burning. "I will not let you put yourself in harm's way."

"But you'll allow these people to be put in harm's way?" Thalia said low, stepping into his space. "It is here for me."

Thalia felt it deep in her bones. An inkling she didn't know the origin of; only something deep-rooted inside her told her it was true.

"And what if you're wrong?" Cassius said with equal quiet, harshness clipping each syllable. "What if it's not soul bonded to you? What if it merely got a scent for human blood and tracked you down so it can kill you?"

Thalia lifted her chin. "There's only one way to find out."

Cassius chuckled low. "You have to be out of your mind if you think I'll let you leave this room."

Thalia's anger flared, and she could have sworn she heard the creature howling in answer. "Move out of the way, Cassius."

They stared at each other, each unbreakable.

Keegan cleared his throat. "We'll watch from the parapets. If it so much as looks at Thalia funny, we can shoot it."

Thalia stared up at Cassius, finding the cracks in his granite mask. "Let me do this."

Cassius swallowed, his jaw clenching. "I want fifty soldiers with their arrows trained on that thing."

"That's a bit excessive—" Thalia cut off at Cassius's sharp look.

"We can oblige," Lady Decima said.

"And I'm going out there with you," Cassius said, turning his attention back to Thalia.

"What! No—you're a Vampyr, it will try and kill you. If it bites you—"

"And if it's soul bonded to you, then it will listen to your commands," Cassius countered.

Thalia felt her anger rising, her rage poking its head up. She stepped back into his space, planting a finger straight against his chest. "You stay twenty paces behind me. Don't interfere, not unless it's about to rip my throat out."

Cassius flashed an arrogant smirk. "Of course, Princess."

Thalia stepped back, allowing some of that anger to center her. "Then let's go see what this creature wants."

Chapter Thirty-Six

Thalia stared at the closed citadel gates.

She swallowed, checking the dagger she'd strapped to her side.

"You don't have to go out there." Cassius's low words brought her back. She glanced at him.

His face was in shadows, the strands of his long hair pulled back from his face. He held his sword loosely in his hands, but he'd strapped daggers to every place on his body. Fifty soldiers were lined up above her, all carrying arrows dripped in oil, ready to be placed in the flaming braziers if things turned ugly.

She just hoped Lady Decima was right about the soul bond.

Thalia shook her head. "No. It's fine." She fumbled with one of her straps, trying to tighten it.

Cassius's hands closed over hers. She glanced up, and he said nothing as he tightened the strap for her, checking the other straps along her arms.

They'd dressed quickly, but Camilla had given her some light armor made of pliable leather to cover her chest and braces for her arms. Thalia wasn't sure what it would do against the razor-sharp teeth of the creature, but she was grateful for any sort of extra protection.

"The creature's about halfway down the bridge," Keegan called softly above them. He stood with the rest of the archers, his own bow within easy reach.

Despite her initial reaction, Thalia was glad she had Cassius by her side, watching her back.

She nodded, and one of the guards stepped forward, grabbing the large iron latch that secured the gate.

It creaked open, and Thalia took another grounding breath before she and Cassius slipped onto the bridge.

The gate closed behind them as they walked, and Thalia spotted the creature standing in the middle of the bridge, its hide gleaming in the moonlight.

Thalia glanced back at Cassius, but true to their agreement, he stayed back.

She kept walking, her boots clipping along the stone bridge, the sound near deafening in her ears. The roar of the waterfall echoed, and Thalia stopped not twenty feet from the creature.

She swallowed, sweat dripping down her spine and working into the leather of her armor.

The creature seemed to sense her then.

She hadn't realized it had been lying in wait, because suddenly it stood, rising to its full height.

Fuck.

It'd grown from the size of a dog to the size of a wolf, its head having fully formed back into its strange oblong shape. Its maw was full of wickedly sharp teeth glowing an eerie green color.

Tension radiated from behind her, but she held up a hand, urging Cassius to stay back without turning to face him.

"Did you come for me?" she asked the creature.

It scented the air, its strange nostrils flaring. It took a step toward her.

Thalia held her breath as it took step after step, its claws scraping against the stone like a knife.

Finally it stopped, face inches from her chest.

Thalia stared, trying not to look too long at the rows of teeth or the foaming green saliva dripping from its maw.

It let out a strange chortle in the back of its throat, the same noise she'd heard in the forest.

Then it touched its nose to her chest.

Thalia refused to tremble as it took a deep breath, inhaling her scent deeper.

She raised a tentative hand, placing her fingers on the side of its strange head.

Thalia was suddenly pulled outside her body. Her mind flashed, images taking shape that were not her own. Her mind blurred, flying through the creature's memories, each one passing across her mind faster than she could blink.

She saw herself through the creature's eyes, saw her standing on the bridge, approaching. The memory moved and the creature watched Thalia from the edge of the lake, unable to push past the barrier. Another blink and it was fleeing a burning castle, and then it stood over Thalia as she slept, her features smoothed over by sleep.

They were in the woods, the creature touching her chest for the first time. Another flash had her watching the terror in her own face when the creature knocked her from her horse.

Then the memories moved faster, like sands slipping through an hourglass. Thalia tried to latch on to them.

She saw crimson leaves and gray trunks.

Thalia lunged for the memory, holding on with all her might.

The creature was in Chaménos, staring into a set of corrupted pools. No water flowed into them; no life-giving force bubbled out of them. The springs were covered in a thick layer of bubbling goop.

Thalia would have gagged if she'd actually been there. The steam rising from the pools burped sulfuric acid into the air. Greenish orbs were buried under the slippery, tar-like grime. And there were hundreds of them, all seeming to nestle in the pockets of the corrupted pools.

The creature moved nearer to the cesspits, peering deeper.

Thalia wished she could scream.

The greenish orbs were eggs.

Hundreds and hundreds of eggs, all waiting to hatch in Chaménos. A dark presence came up behind the creature, and Thalia felt the creature bend in submission, turning—

Thalia was yanked from the creature's memories.

She fell down, her heart pounding in her throat, and the creature roared, shaking its head.

Thalia scrambled backward as the creature turned its attention on her. All traces of soul bond extinguished as it opened its gaping maw, ready to devour her whole—

A scream rent the air, and the creature's head was swiftly severed from its neck. It rolled a couple of feet, landing next to Thalia's sprawled form. Its body fell into a twitching, lifeless heap.

Thalia stared in shock at Larellia, the Mage's face set in a deep snarl, the glint of a double-bladed scythe flashing in the moonlight.

Cassius shouted from behind her, and Thalia froze as Larellia pointed her scythe right at her chest. "I'm going to ask you this once, girl. What are you, and how did you create those creatures?"

Chapter Thirty-Seven

"What?" Thalia sputtered, her chest rising and falling rapidly.

Larellia stalked forward, kicking the head aside. Even now, the creature's body was trying to reform, its neck beginning to twine.

"That is no soul-bonded creature." The scythe flashed, and Thalia scrambled backward. "That thing was made. By *dark* magic."

Thalia blanched. "What?"

Before the Mage could question her further, Cassius stepped in front of Thalia, sword drawn. "Back off." His words were lethal.

Larellia stared at Thalia, eyes gleaming. "She needs to explain herself."

"Explain what?" Thalia gasped, finally managing to get her legs under her. "I don't know about any magic or creation or anything!"

Larellia didn't look like she believed anyone until Lady Decima appeared, Keegan behind her. "Perhaps," Lady Decima said, watching the tendrils in the creature's neck stretch and slither toward its head. "We should continue this conversation inside. It seems there's much to discuss."

Thalia decided she'd be living in the strange meeting room in the mountain, given how many times they'd all gathered there since arriving.

The creature's body was splayed out on the table, the head next to it, although Larellia had embedded her scythe in the table so that anytime the tendrils of the neck stretched to join with its head, it would get sliced to ribbons. Already a pile of bloody tendons had gathered like grotesque fallen rose petals.

"Someone want to explain why it keeps doing that?" Camilla broke the silence, staring at the corpse.

"It was made. It was created to be near impossible to kill," Larellia said, her lips twisting. Her gaze landed on Thalia. "The question is why was it made and by whom."

Thalia's anger rose. "I told you, I didn't make anything. I'm *human*."

"Are you?"

Thalia was taken aback. "What's that supposed to mean?"

Larellia's eyes flared. "Made creatures used to be favored amongst the Mages. But it wasn't until one of us created a creature of such atrocity that the other Mages put an end to their creations."

"What was that creature?"

Larellia cocked her head. "The Nestos." Thalia shivered as she continued, "These creatures were meant to serve only their master. They were unstoppable, near impossible to kill. But Klae, the head Mage at the time, saw the danger of using such magic, how the pockets of magic they pulled from had to be corrupted. They had to use the magic and twist it into something other. This creature"—Larellia nodded—"was made."

"How can you be sure?" Cassius countered.

Larellia slowly slid her gaze to him. "Because I was there when the first creatures were made. They have an aura, one that only the most skilled Mage can detect. The symbols of your own Houses were made creatures at one point."

Lady Decima nodded, her golden gaze harsh. "Indeed, I can't put my finger on what it is, but this creature is wrong."

Thalia shook her head, pushing aside the fact that Larellia was hundreds of years old—she'd think about *that* fact later. "I didn't make it."

"Someone close to you did," Larellia said, her silver eyes glowing. "Given it didn't kill you."

Thalia shook her head. "I'm human. No one in Agripa even knows that the pockets of magic left in this world are real, much less how we'd use them to create something like this."

"Do you not have great libraries?" Larellia countered. "You are either ignorant of the information at your fingertips or incredibly stupid."

Cassius let out a low snarl, but Thalia didn't let the insult land. "Our libraries are vast. In fact, before the treaty was broken thirteen years ago, many came to learn from them." She cut a gaze to the others. "But that doesn't mean we have magic."

"There is magic everywhere," Larellia snapped. "How do you think the humans managed to sustain themselves for so long when the world is set to kill them?"

Thalia's anger rose. "Maybe we figured out how to do it *without* magic."

They stared at each other, and something charged the air, the Mage's hair starting to rise on a phantom wind.

"It doesn't matter who created it," Cassius said, breaking the tension like a knife. "How do we stop it?"

Larellia looked like she'd argue but turned back to the creature. "The other spawn that was near Cupisco is already dead, but nothing matters if we don't cut off the head and burn the entire thing. And it's impossible to find its mother in that damned forest."

Thalia gasped. "I—I know where it is."

Everyone turned to her.

"Where?" Camilla's eyes widened.

Thalia shook her head, the memories of the creature coming to surface. With all the accusations flying like arrows, she'd had little chance to dwell on what she'd seen. "When I touched its head, I went into its memories."

She looked to Cassius, if only for some comfort as she plunged ahead. "It showed me a place in the forest. One with five pools of water." Thalia's stomach twisted, nausea rising in her. "There's—there's hundreds of them."

"What?" Larellia paled.

Thalia shook her head, her throat constricting. "It's laid . . . eggs. In the pools. They're corrupted now."

Keegan let out a curse as Cassius turned to her, voice quiet. "Are you sure about the pools?"

Thalia nodded, fighting the growing dread. "Yes."

Cassius glanced at the others, and Larellia let out a bitter laugh. "It's spawned."

"But—but how?" Camilla shook her head, not believing the words. "We went to the pools when the humans finally let loose their rivers. The springs were thriving, nothing was amiss."

It took Thalia a moment to realize that the springs were the ones sacred to the Vampyrs. The very water that seemed to fend off the poison of the creature.

"Did you see the mother?" Larellia directed her sharp gaze.

Thalia shook her head, fighting the sudden panic in her veins. Sweat dripped down her spine. "No. I—something pulled me out before I could see it." At Larellia's mistrusting stare, she added, "But I felt it, behind me—the creature, I mean. I don't think it would leave its eggs unattended."

"So we go, then," Keegan said. "We destroy the eggs, and the mother will come running."

Larellia shook her head, her face hard. "As much as I would like to agree, no."

"What do you mean?" Camilla turned to her, wide-eyed.

Larellia didn't take her attention off Thalia. "We don't know this creature's habits. Whether or not it would even feel sorrow if its young were killed. Even if we managed to destroy the eggs and purge the springs, it could have laid eggs elsewhere. The entirety of Chaménos could be covered by its foul ilk."

Thalia closed her eyes. She didn't want to think about it. The image of the eggs was enough to push bile into her throat. The thought of hundreds if not thousands of those hell-bent creatures waiting to unleash themselves . . .

"What do you propose we do?" Cassius asked. Thalia opened her eyes and found that he'd shifted closer.

Larellia laid her pale-white hands flat on the table. "Trying to destroy the creature and its spawn on our own will be futile. But there might be another way."

Everyone stared at the head Mage, waiting.

Finally, Thalia could no longer stand the silence. "What way?"

Larellia's gaze sharpened like the edge of her scythe. "It is true that the creatures made are meant to be near impossible to kill, but they are linked to their creator. If their creator dies, they will die too."

Thalia blinked. "How is that possible?"

"Magic binds us all. When one takes magic and corrupts it, part of you goes into it. It's a different kind of soul bond. One that can be severed as easily as cutting a string," Larellia finished.

"So how do we find the creator?" Camilla asked.

Larellia tilted her head, something electric pulsing the air. "Seeing as it has some connection with a human, my guess would be to search there."

Thalia barked out a laugh. "You're suggesting you all look for a Mage in the human realm?"

"Not us. You." Thalia's eyes widened, and Larellia lifted her chin. "You have a connection to what's going on, a connection to that creature, despite what you say. Someone very close to you created it."

"How would I even find out?" Thalia countered.

Lady Decima stood, the movement catching Thalia's eye. She placed a dark hand on the creature's hide and it started glowing, marks and whorls appearing before they vanished. Lady Decima turned to Thalia and took a step toward her, and Thalia jerked.

"What are you doing?" she demanded, staring at Lady Decima's outstretched hand. Cassius was tense beside her.

Lady Decima shook her head, not halting her approach. "It won't harm you; it's merely an imprint of the creature. When you are near whoever created it, that imprint will recognize itself. You'll be pulled to the creator." She stopped before Thalia, waiting.

Thalia slid her gaze to Cassius. She took a moment to look at everyone around the room. To read the bleakness and despair they were so desperately trying to fight. Then her mind flashed to the children in the citadel, to the Vampyrs hiding in Irenbis.

Thalia took a deep breath, then nodded. Lady Decima placed a hand on Thalia's chest. Something zapped through her, and she shook her head, trying to get the tingling out of her limbs.

"It is decided," Larellia said, her eyes glinting. "Thalia shall go to the human realm to determine who the creator is."

Dread swirled in Thalia's gut, not because of what she might uncover in the human realm about the creature and its creator but because of who she'd have to face. How she'd have to face the queen knowing that her own heart had begun to pull in a different direction.

"What happens if I can't find them?" Thalia hedged.

"Then we shall prepare the mountain. As best we can." The head Mage cut a look to Cassius, who'd been quiet through the whole ordeal.

"We can send a number of Mages to take care of the pools," Lady Decima said, settling back down. "No need to let that fester any longer."

Camilla and Keegan nodded their agreement.

"But what about the prince?" Thalia blurted out. Everyone in the room froze, all slowly looking at her.

"What about him?" Larellia asked.

Thalia slid her gaze to Cassius. "Shouldn't he . . . I mean, shouldn't he be informed?"

"He will," Keegan said, his golden eyes flashing. "But the courts are already on the verge of collapse. It is better if he distracts them. If they knew that someone from the human realm created this creature and we'd just forged a treaty with them . . ."

"There would be dire consequences," Larellia finished. Her silver eyes met Thalia's. "You are now a part of this world. Whether you like it or not."

Thalia swallowed, feeling the weight of their stares. She had no idea what to think or how to act—only that regardless of her mother's mission, this took precedence. Because this creature was a far greater threat than any Vampyr Agripa could ever imagine.

That was her mission, after all—to keep the people of Agripa safe.

She lifted her chin. "Then I suppose we shouldn't wait."

Chapter Thirty-Eight

The inn at Lekeid was utter shit, and Thalia was already pissed.

They'd left Perden and skirted Chaménos by boat, Cassius navigating the rocky terrain, before they found a small inlet to approach Agripa. As soon as they docked, a summer storm had swept in on a foul wind, drenching them from head to toe.

Thalia scowled at herself in the dirty mirror above the washstand in the room they'd procured. She'd already sent a message to her mother informing her that the prince had allowed her leave to visit but that their transportation had floundered because of the storm and they were in need of a carriage immediately. At least on paper, her mother wouldn't be able to detect the lie.

Just one more day.

One more day until she had to face her mother.

Her stomach churned.

She blinked again at her reflection. Dark circles had appeared under her hazel eyes, a line sketched permanently between her brows. She looked haggard.

Granted, she felt as though someone had wrung her out and left her to dry on a clothesline.

She sighed, peeling off her clothing. She silently cursed, realizing the extra clothes she'd brought along were just as soaked as the ones on her body.

Thalia shuffled to the fire, laying out everything, and prayed it would all dry by morning despite the storm raging hard enough the window rattled.

She grabbed a throw at the end of the bed, wrapping herself in it. Better than sitting naked, waiting for Cassius to come back from wherever he'd gone off to.

The thought sent her blood thrumming.

The door creaking open nearly had her flying out of her skin.

Cassius took one look at her sitting on the bed, wrapped in a blanket, and looked away. The muscle in his jaw flickered as he stiffly carried a tray of food he'd gone to fetch her over to the small dresser in the room.

"My other clothes were wet," Thalia said defensively, unsure why he seemed so ill at ease.

Cassius closed the door behind him, toeing off his boots. "I didn't say anything."

"You're acting weird."

"Forgive me, Princess. I wasn't expecting to find you naked and waiting for me."

Prick.

"You wish," Thalia crooned as Cassius went about taking off his clothes. He let out a curse when he realized his own extra clothes were soaked too.

He looked around, finding another blanket, his fingers clenching in the fabric. Thalia glanced at the tray of food, although the steam coming from whatever stew he'd brought was the least interesting thing in the room. Especially as the sound of his pants hitting the floor brushed her ears.

He moved into her eye line, his lower half wrapped in the blanket, and grabbed the tray. Thalia made room on the small bed as he set it between them. She inhaled the scent of what appeared to be two bowls of rabbit stew, along with two mugs of ale.

"It probably tastes like shit," Cassius said.

Thalia didn't care. She shoveled a spoonful in her mouth, letting the warmth drive out the chill from her bones.

Cassius watched her eat, his gaze intent on hers.

It was only after she'd almost finished the bowl that she realized he hadn't touched his stew. "Aren't you going to eat?"

Cassius shrugged. "I fed earlier on the boat."

Fed. Not *ate.*

It was so easy to forget what he was. Especially in moments like this. When it was almost as if nothing had changed between them.

"I thought you still got hungry?"

"I do, but it usually takes at least a day before my stomach grumbles for actual food."

Thalia set her spoon down with a clink. "Oh."

"I got two"—Cassius nodded to the tray—"because I didn't want the innkeeper to think anything suspicious. You can have it if you want."

"It's fine." Thalia swallowed, the sound audible, and Cassius slid his gaze to hers. "What do we tell my mother when we get to Corithian?"

Cassius raised a brow. "Nothing."

"Please, Cassius. She knows when I'm lying."

"Then don't lie."

"You want me to tell her that the Vampyrs are facing a creature whose bite is fatal, the courts are on the brink of collapse, and their prince seems more inclined to disappear than deal with the actual problems at hand?"

Cassius's eyes narrowed. "Fine, let me do the talking."

"Right, because you're so diplomatic."

"I'm hand to the prince, remember?"

"Right. Right. Sent to broker deals and accept marriage proposals on his behalf. How could I forget?"

His brows narrowed. "What's wrong?"

"Nothing."

"Bullshit."

Thalia turned, her anger rising just as quickly as her dread. Cassius stared at her, his eyes sweeping over her face, seeming to expose every facet of her person. As if he could see right to her heart. She was supposed to kill the Vampyr prince. Supposed to destroy them from the inside out. She was supposed to kill *him.*

And now she was . . . she was *helping* them. Her sworn enemy. The creatures responsible for killing her family.

But it wasn't the creatures who'd killed her sister that she was aiding.

Her mind flashed to Keegan's soft laugh, Camilla raising her brow in approval, Larellia's hard determination as she tried to find the cure for their people.

Her mother would never understand that.

Because while Thalia might hesitate, Helena Cesiaran of Agripa would not.

She didn't realize she'd pressed the palms of her heels into her eyes until Cassius gently peeled them away.

"Talk to me," he said softly, brows furrowed.

Thalia stared at him, her throat constricting like vines around her neck.

She couldn't.

Because he'd never forgive her if she told him her plan. If she revealed the mission her mother had assigned her—the fact that she'd been smuggling intel through her letters so Agripa might better prepare for when she took down the courts and they could sweep in. She didn't think he trusted her, not fully. But a part of her ached for it. For that trust that used to bind them tighter than vows.

But trust had died. It died the moment she'd stabbed him in the back and taken a vow to end him. And it wasn't as if Cassius weren't keeping his own secrets. Secrets about his world, about the prince. She couldn't trust him either, as much as she wished to.

"My mother will ask questions. We should prepare for those answers." Thalia pulled out of his grip, taking a swig of sour ale, only so she'd have something to do.

Cassius watched her with a guarded expression. "The best lies are the ones with truth weaved into them."

Thalia glanced at him over the rim of her mug. "So what should I tell her?"

"If she asks you about Vaccarium, what will you say?"

Thalia set her mug down. "That it's rather like Agripa."

"And if she asks you about the prince?"

"Well, at least I can be honest in saying I don't know much about him and he's hardly around," Thalia said with enough bite that Cassius straightened.

His brows narrowed, but she downed her ale, ignoring the sour taste on her tongue. Each moment she spent dwelling on what was happening in Vaccarium, Thalia felt her composure cracking. Each interaction with the monsters she'd sworn to hate, each bit of light teasing from Camilla or soft word from Keegan, each look of longing from Cassius, created a crack in her meager façade.

"Thalia?"

She ignored him, setting her mug down, heart pounding. Cassius tilted his head, dark hair glinting. His eyes went to her pulse, and she wondered if he could hear it. Hear the conflict spreading through her veins, burning greater than any Vampyr bite.

She looked away, standing up suddenly. She gripped the blanket around her chest, grabbing the tray. "We should go to bed. The carriage should arrive by nightfall."

Thalia managed to awkwardly put the tray on the dresser. Thunder cracked and she jumped, her bicep scraping against the sharp corner of the dresser. She hissed, glaring at the line of red now gleaming on her arm.

"Are you all right?" Cassius rumbled out.

Thalia scowled, making her way back to the bed, ignoring the concern on his face. "Fine."

She didn't look at him as she slid under the covers, her skin pressing against the sheets.

Eventually the mattress dipped.

Thalia stared at the wall, willing the tension to leave. Willing the pressure in her throat to disappear. She shifted again and let out another hiss, her arm smarting.

"Let me see it." Cassius's gruff voice broke through the pounding of the rain outside their room.

"It's fine." Thalia shifted off her hurt arm, facing him.

Cassius's eyes roved over her face before settling on her hair, which splayed around her bare shoulders.

"You'll get blood on the sheets. Let me help you." His words had roughened.

Thalia swallowed. She needed to say no. Because whatever flame was rekindling between them would only burn out in the end. They couldn't be together, not if her vow was meant to be fulfilled. Not if her mission was meant to succeed.

When she said nothing, he scooted closer, pulling her arm out from under the sheets. The scrape gleamed against the shadows of the fire. It wasn't deep, but ruby droplets welled like beads of dew.

She cursed, looking for something she could swipe the blood with, but Cassius shifted even closer.

She froze, heart pounding as his glowing eyes met hers. "Do you trust me?"

Thalia stared at him, unsure what he was asking, only knowing that something else pulsed in his irises, something a part of her ached to discover.

Did she trust him?

Thalia gave the briefest dip of her chin.

Cassius took her wrist in his hand, raising her arm slightly. His thumb brushed along the sensitive inside of her wrist.

Then he dipped his head.

"What are you doing?" Thalia's breath hitched.

Cassius flicked his gaze up, face rippling slightly. "I'm not going to bite you," he said low, a faint hint of fangs showing.

"Then what are you doing?"

"Taking care of that."

A droplet of blood slid down Thalia's arm.

He waited, eyes searching hers. Maybe she'd gone a bit mad, because she gave another nod.

Cassius seemed to shudder as he bent his head once more, his tongue landing on the crimson streak down her arm.

Thalia's fingers curled in the sheets, her heart pounding as Cassius's tongue swept up her arm, following the trail until he got to the cut.

She watched in rapt fascination as his mouth skimmed the wound. She shivered, and Cassius's grip tightened slightly on her wrist. The sharpness of his jaw gleamed, his throat working as he lapped up the small stain of blood on her bicep.

She thought she stopped breathing when he finally lifted his head. His pupils were blown out, a hint of red staining his lips.

"What did it taste like?" Thalia whispered, heat flooding her body.

Cassius took a moment to focus on her. "Like heaven."

A shiver ran down her spine, and she looked away, not able to face the intensity in his face.

She looked down at her arm and gasped. The scrape was gone; only new skin looked back at her. "How did you do that?"

Cassius's thumb swirled along her wrist. "Sometimes, right after a Vampyr feeds, our saliva seems to retain some of the healing properties of blood." At Thalia's wide-eyed gaze, he continued, "Don't ask me how or why. It just happens."

Thalia stared at her arm. Cassius hadn't moved, just kept running his thumb against her skin.

"What are you thinking?" he asked.

That each moment with him felt as though her world were beginning to rip at the seams. That who he was now, a creature with such power—it didn't scare her. Not like she'd thought it would. And a small, terrified part of her wondered what it would be like to feel as he did. To drink from someone and taste their very essence—taste their soul.

"I'm thinking that now I know I can come to you if I ever get a cut," Thalia said, removing her arm.

She turned her back, only so she didn't have to see the disappointment etching itself across Cassius's handsome face.

Chapter Thirty-Nine

Her home seemed drabber than she remembered, the crenellations worn and chipped like old porcelain. It felt less welcoming than the castle at Irenbis. At least there she could count on the comfort of her and Cassius's room, the deep wallpaper and crimson drapes that bled with color. At least, despite all that had transpired, the castle in Irenbis felt as though it had some sort of life. The soldiers standing watch bowed as she hurried into the palace, the steady fall of rain working its way down the back of her cloak.

As soon as Thalia stepped inside, she let out a deep breath.

She wasn't sure why it surprised her that her mother hadn't come to greet her.

Reina waited, her armor glinting despite the darkness. Her hand rested on the pommel of her sword, her gaze wary.

She inclined her head at Thalia's approach. "Princess, we've been expecting you."

"Where's the queen?" Thalia asked, taking stock of the empty halls, the quiet that bled like a tomb.

Reina's dark gaze slid to Cassius, then to the sword strapped to his own hip. "She had to attend to something outside the castle, but she's called for a ball this evening."

Thalia nodded, and they moved through the halls. The banners of Agripa lining the walls all seemed dusty and stained. Had they always looked like that? Was she just seeing it now with different eyes?

She and Reina didn't say anything, Cassius merely a shadow behind them as they reached her old room.

"Is Marcus here?" Thalia turned to her before entering her suite.

Reina's eyes flicked to Cassius. "Yes. Although the queen has kept him busy."

"Doing what?"

Reina shook her head, her cropped hair hardly moving. "I can't tell you."

"Reina—"

Reina straightened, eyes going hard. "Is there anything else I can help you with, Princess?"

Why the hell is she acting like this? Thalia's annoyance spiked, but she pushed it aside. "Tell Marcus to meet me in the library in an hour."

Reina stiffly nodded, then walked away, her boots clipping across the cold floor.

Thalia turned to her room, shoving open the door, and tried to keep her anger from making her do something foolish. Like run down the hall and demand that Reina stop acting so weird.

A quick glance around her room showed that at least her mother hadn't changed anything.

"What do you think the queen is doing?" Thalia asked, sinking to the edge of her bed. She didn't want to admit that she'd missed her mattress.

Cassius looked around the room, his attention lingering on the stained rug before meeting her gaze. "I don't know."

"Was more ore sent to us?"

Cassius leaned against the door. "Yes."

Thalia pursed her lips. Perhaps that was where her mother had gone—to ensure the shipment of ore was properly distributed. But that didn't make sense. Her mother had her advisers do that for her.

She cleared her throat. "I'm going to see if I can find Marcus."

"Do you want me to go with you?"

Thalia hesitated. And maybe it was because he seemed like the only one in the palace acting normal that she nodded.

At least there was Marcus. Reina might not have wanted to speak to her, but Marcus would be willing to.

Marcus couldn't speak to them.

In fact, when they'd gotten to the library, a robed librarian explained that he was not to be disturbed.

Thalia's brows narrowed as the librarian shuffled away, casting a fearful glance at Cassius before disappearing.

"Marcus wouldn't not see me," she said lowly, glancing around the large space. Rain pattered against the high windows. Books stretched far above them for many stories and even down below, the staircase spiraling into darkness.

"Do you think Reina didn't give him your message?" Cassius asked, taking note of everything.

Thalia didn't like the thought of Reina not doing something. Especially given their relationship before she left. Reina had always been loyal to her—a friend, even. Could Reina's sentiments about her have really changed in only a matter of weeks?

Thalia shook her head. "I don't know."

"Any idea on where we might find him?"

Thalia chewed the inside of her cheek, eyes following the spiraling staircase up toward the very top of the library.

"Yes."

Two soldiers stood watch outside the master librarian's quarters.

Thalia frowned as she and Cassius peeked around the corner of the hall from the stairwell.

"He's never had guards before," Cassius murmured in her ear.

"I know." Thalia pulled back into the stairwell.

"Do you want me to take care of them?" Cassius rumbled.

She whirled to him. "I don't want you to kill them!"

A faint trace of a smile curved his lips. "I wasn't going to kill them, Princess. Merely knock them out."

Thalia made a face, looking at the soldiers. They were no doubt under direct orders from the queen to stay put.

"Fine," Thalia got out.

Cassius smirked, then he sauntered toward the guards.

In all of two seconds they'd crumpled to the ground, unconscious.

Thalia blinked at Cassius. He wasn't even winded.

"Shall we?" he asked, brow raised. He gestured to the door.

Thalia swallowed, trying to ignore the sudden heat flooding into her stomach as she stepped over the soldiers. Now certainly wasn't the time.

She knocked on Marcus's door. Nothing.

Thalia frowned, knocking harder. When no answer came, she pushed open the door.

Marcus's room was in disarray. He'd always been messy, but never like this. Stacks of books were piled precariously on everything from the floor to the armchairs, even his bed. Crumpled paper littered the ground like dried rose petals. Trays of food were spread around, some of the contents old enough to have gone green and moldy. Flies buzzed over a tray, the smell ripe.

"What the fuck?" Thalia stepped into the room and accidentally kicked over a pile of books.

Marcus looked up from where he was hunched over his desk. His curly hair was frazzled and unkempt, his normally dark skin wan. He blinked. "Thalia?"

"What the fuck is going on, Marcus?" Thalia's heart began to climb as she moved farther into the room.

Marcus rose, bits of paper falling around him. "What are you doing here?" Then his eyes slid past Thalia's shoulder, and he froze. "What is he doing here?"

"What am *I* doing here?" Thalia crossed the dirty ground. "Why are *you* being guarded? Have you even left this room?"

Marcus scrubbed a hand over his stubbled chin, blinking. He glanced around the room as if noticing how badly it was kept. "Your mother—I mean the queen—she's kept me busy."

"Doing what?" Thalia demanded.

Marcus slumped back into his chair, his desk rattling with the movement. It caused a bottle of ink to spill all over a stack of unorganized scrolls. Marcus didn't move to clean it up. "She's having me research the old trenches of our land."

Thalia glanced at Cassius. "Why?" No one had used the old trenches in years. They'd been dug when the war was first started, because the humans of Agripa thought that if they couldn't go through the forest to get to the Vampyrs, maybe they could go under it. The plan had failed; the soil too difficult to dig. Now the trenches were forgotten, collapsed and caved in.

Marcus ran a hand through his messy hair. "I don't know. She just keeps asking me to get a map of all of them, to see how far we got. With the replenished ore, maybe the soil has become softer—more willing to let us dig."

"How long have you been doing this?" Thalia asked.

Marcus grabbed a mug on his desk and went to take a drink, then frowned at the contents. He set the mug down. "Shortly after you left."

"Why the hell is she wanting to know about the forgotten trenches?" Thalia turned to Cassius.

Cassius's eyes were on Marcus. Thalia could practically see him thinking. "Is there anything else the queen wanted you to research?"

Marcus sighed. "Something about infections? I don't know. She's been rather vague with her requests, and every time I bring her something new, she claims it's not what she's looking for. Hence all this." He waved a hand.

Thalia's stomach clenched as she moved to Marcus's desk, picking up the spilled ink bottle. "You should rest." Marcus stared up at her, his eyes bloodshot. "I mean it, Marcus. Rest. I'll deal with the queen."

Marcus hesitated, but maybe being pulled him from his research-induced stupor had him realizing just how burnt out he was. "All right."

Thalia offered a grim smile, and she squeezed his shoulder before she and Cassius navigated out of his room.

As soon as they'd reached the safety of the stairwell, Thalia whirled to Cassius, her thoughts on the infections that Marcus mentioned. "Do you think she knows about the bitten?"

Thalia didn't know how the queen was so close to guessing what plagued Vaccarium. She'd never sent the half-finished letter to her mother. In fact, it had burned along with the castle of Irenbis.

Cassius's face darkened. "It seems she may suspect. Which means we must ensure your mother doesn't realize how close she is to the truth."

Chapter Forty

Katrina wept when she saw Thalia.

Her old handmaiden held her tight enough that her ribs bleated in protest.

Katrina finally pulled back, tears glistening in her eyes. "They haven't hurt you, have they?"

Thalia shook her head.

"He hasn't hurt you?" Katrina pressed.

"No. The prince hasn't even been around—"

"I meant Cassius."

Thalia froze, eyes lifting to Katrina's. Cassius had left only moments before to go to the soldiers barracks. She wasn't sure what he hoped to accomplish. Perhaps Reina would say something to him, since she seemed inclined to ignore Thalia.

"Cassius—he—I mean, no. Why would you think that?" Thalia sputtered out.

Katrina shook her head, leading Thalia into her bathing chamber. "Because what he did to you was deplorable."

"Cassius never hurt me." Thalia's voice sharpened.

Katrina read her posture and softened slightly. "I didn't mean physically."

Katrina should have just stabbed her. She must have seen the shift in Thalia's face, because she clucked her tongue again. "Get in the bath. And don't get me started on your hair and nails. Do the Vampyrs not know how to treat royalty there?"

Yet as Thalia soaked beneath the suds, scrubbing the days of travel off her, she couldn't quite shake the feeling that she was on the verge of her heart breaking again.

Thalia watched her mother's preening courtiers whisper behind their jeweled fans and glittering glasses of champagne.

Yet the Queen of Agripa was still nowhere to be found.

Kamith was the only one present, his voice booming out across the ballroom despite the music swelling. Reina stood ever watchful near the door, seeming to ignore Thalia's stare whenever she looked at her.

"Was it always like this?" Thalia asked as one of the courtiers said something that had the rest of the gaggle howling. She doubted what the courtier said was very clever.

Cassius was a dark presence at her side. She could smell the scent of whatever soap he'd used in his bath—eucalyptus with mint. Thalia glanced at him from the corner of her eye. He'd pulled half of his auburn hair back away from his face. His doublet was simple, matching his tight-fitting black pants.

"You were usually half drunk by the time this all started," Cassius said lowly.

Thalia whirled to him. "I was not."

Cassius smirked, a hint of fangs showing. His eyes dipped to her own attire as if he couldn't help himself. She had to admit, she'd missed Katrina's attention to detail. She wore a crimson gown of silk, the same style as the one she'd worn when the Vampyrs had come to Agripa weeks ago. It clung to her body, the neckline plunging. She wore a cuff of gold around her bicep, her throat bare, yet her hair hung in waves down her back, one side swept out of the way by a gilded comb.

Cassius finally dragged his gaze to hers, eyes heated. "That or we'd found something else to occupy our attention."

Yes. When she'd tug him down a servants' entrance only so she could feel the heat of his body against hers. When she craved nothing but his strength—his warmth.

But that was a different time.

The conversation with Katrina rang low in her mind. She straightened, stepping away. "I'll be back."

She felt Cassius's stare pinned to her bare back as she wove through the courtiers, ignoring their laughter and the sparkling wine that spilled onto the floor.

Kamith was conversing with a wizened council member whose name she'd forgotten. "Where is the queen?" she asked.

Their conversation halted, and Kamith turned to her, surprise on his handsome face. "Princess, you are looking well—"

"Where is she?" Thalia interrupted.

Kamith straightened, nodding to the adviser, who took that as his invitation to leave. "The queen is indisposed at the moment. But I know she sends her sincerest apologies for missing you."

Thalia didn't believe him. Not for a moment.

Kamith offered a tight smile, inclining his head. "Excuse me, Princess."

She watched him disappear into the crowd. She felt Cassius's stare across the throne room, but she ignored it, aiming for Reina.

"Where is my mother?" she asked.

Reina slid her gaze to Thalia. "Gone."

"Reina," Thalia practically hissed. She stepped closer, ignoring the glinting of her armor. "I don't—I don't know why you won't talk to me, why you're so cold. But please. Please just tell me where she's gone. You owe me that much."

Reina's eyes sharpened into a glittering coin. Thalia thought she'd refuse her until she spoke so softly that Thalia had to lean into her. "The chapel."

Thalia made a face. The chapel? What on earth would her mother be doing there?

Thalia turned away, glancing at Cassius. He'd been approached by Kamith, the adviser quickly drawing him into a conversation.

With Cassius distracted, he didn't notice as she slipped from the throne room in search of the missing queen.

Chapter Forty-One

The chapel was empty. No braziers were lit, nor was there any other indication that her mother was anywhere in the room.

She avoided looking toward the altar where she and Cassius had stood, their hands bound.

It felt like a lifetime ago.

Thalia moved deeper, trying to figure out where her mother could be. Had Reina lied to her? The thought sent a sour tang through her mouth.

She pushed it aside, heading to a door near the back of the space. She knew it opened to a small corridor that led to the priest's rooms along with a few areas to pray.

But Thalia didn't pray to anyone's long-dead gods. She shoved the door open, stepping into the cold hallway.

The priest's bedchamber was closed, but there was a smaller door at the end of the hall that stood ajar.

Thalia walked toward it without a thought, opening it to a small prayer room.

Her heart picked up at the sight of a door in the ground. It probably led to the wine cellar, and Thalia eased it open, pushing aside the memory of the last time she'd ventured down into an unknown space. Lucarius was dead. And no Vampyrs would be in this room. None would be foolish enough to venture this far into Agripa.

She eased down the steps, and faint murmuring drifted up toward her. Thalia stopped at the base of the stairs, light bleeding into the small space.

It was indeed a wine cellar, containing barrels crusted with dust and cobwebs. But in the middle of the stone room stood the queen.

"This won't do, Marcus." The queen's voice wove its way to Thalia, causing her spine to lock up. "I asked specifically which trenches are still usable."

Thalia pressed against the wall, her heart rate starting to rise.

"I've tried, Your Majesty." Marcus's tired words echoed. He sat on a wooden chair, piles of books around him. "But our maps are old—outdated. Perhaps we could ask Thalia? She's traveled all over Agripa; maybe she knows—"

"No." The queen's harsh words had Marcus faltering. "She does not need to get involved."

Marcus sighed, scrubbing a hand through his hair. At least he'd taken Thalia's advice and rested; his face was freshly shaven. "I'll keep searching, then."

The queen nodded. "And the other thing I asked you?"

Marcus shook his head. "It would be helpful to know exactly what you were searching for and how it pertains to this."

Thalia stifled her gasp as Marcus shifted.

She hadn't noticed the iron cage behind him, hidden in shadow. The light from the braziers landed on the person held within.

Not a person—a Vampyr.

She was chained against the stone wall, a mask of iron wrapped around her skull and over her mouth. Her hair was unkempt, her clothing torn and dirty.

But it was her eyes, dull and glassy, the saliva dripping through the corners of the mask and landing in a puddle on the ground, that had Thalia's heart rate spiking.

"This creature is sick," the queen said, a frown pulling on her elegant brow.

"So you're wanting to find a cure?" Marcus asked, his head lifting. The Vampyr tried to surge forward, but given the tight space and her restraints, the chains only rattled.

The queen sighed. "I thought that as head librarian, you would be smarter than this." She stepped nearer to the cage, and the Vampyr jerked. "This Vampyr is sick. And you know what happens with sickness?"

Marcus made a face. "It spreads?"

"Precisely. The question is, how fast can it spread?"

Thalia's stomach dropped. She didn't realize she'd stepped into the room until she blurted out, "You can't."

The queen whirled, and Marcus stared at her wide-eyed. Maybe it was a trick of the light, but Thalia could have sworn her mother had aged at least ten years. "Thalia," she said, displeasure morphing her features. "You shouldn't be in here."

"And you shouldn't have her." Thalia pointed a shaking finger.

The Vampyr lifted her matted head, dried blood crusted around the mask, the clamps squeezing her brain to the point of bursting.

"This creature was captured in Agripa," the queen got out. "As such, it is mine to do with as I wish."

Thalia shook her head, forcing the bile from her throat. "You don't—you don't understand. She has—she has—"

"A sickness?" The queen stepped toward her, and Thalia froze. "What do you know about it?"

"I—" Thalia faltered.

The queen's eyes narrowed. "Thalia, what have you discovered in Vaccarium?"

Thalia shook her head, cursing herself. She should have brought Cassius. Should be better at lying—"Nothing."

The queen paused, tilting her head, the motion making Thalia sick. "Marcus, if you wouldn't mind. I'd like a moment alone with my daughter."

Marcus glanced at Thalia, his hesitancy palpable. But it was clear he had no idea what was going on or what her mother was trying to do. Thalia dipped her chin and Marcus rose, gathering his books before he left up the stairs.

They stared at each other. Mother and daughter. Two halves of a tarnished mirror, reflecting the cracks and flaws in each other's facades.

The queen finally sank onto the seat Marcus had vacated as if it were a throne. The bitten Vampyr behind her shrank back. "Shall we discuss it, then?"

"Discuss what?" Thalia bit out.

"The fact you've discovered a way to destroy our greatest enemy, yet you haven't lifted a finger?"

Thalia forced her trembling hands behind her back. "I haven't had the chance to meet the prince. He's often away from his court."

"Ah yes, how convenient for you."

"I've tried," Thalia said, her heart rate rising further. But her stomach twisted at the halfhearted answer. Because, deep down, she knew she could have done more. "I've tried to find a weakness amongst the courts. Have tried to find out when he might return so I can kill him as you asked."

"But have you?" her mother countered.

"Have I what?"

The queen shook her head, features twisting. "Don't play dumb with me."

Thalia waited, willing the claws wrapping around her throat to leave.

The queen's piercing gaze lifted to hers. "What have you done in Vaccarium to try and save us from this blight? What have you *done* to ensure that what happened to your father, your *sister*, never happens again?"

Thalia's jaw ached from how tightly she clenched her teeth. "The courts do not like the prince."

The queen raised a well-groomed brow. "Yes, your quaint little letters informed me as much." So she had received her daughter's intel and truly hadn't bothered to see how she fared. Thalia's heart stuttered. "And did you try stirring up more discord amongst them? You say the prince is away; surely a lack of leadership would be easy to twist and spread?"

"It's not that simple." Her mind flashed to Lord Adrian and the burning castle at Irenbis.

The queen rose, and Thalia refused to shrink as she stopped in front of her. "I'm disappointed in you, Thalia."

Thalia didn't want to admit how those words sank into her chest, how they started to rip at her already-torn heart. "You don't know what it's like," Thalia got out, ignoring the rattling chains in the cage. "What I've had to deal with, what I've fought—"

"What exactly have you had to deal with?" The queen's words sharpened like a blade.

Thalia swallowed, her eyes darting around. "I—"

Fast as a snake, the queen grabbed her. Surprise flashed through Thalia at the strength she possessed. Her spine locked up as her mother dragged her to the caged Vampyr. "Have you had to deal with this?"

Thalia's feet refused to move as she was shoved toward the cage. Her whole body froze as she met the bitten's eyes. The Vampyr's nostrils flared behind the mask, and she lunged as far as she could with the chains.

Thalia tried to jerk away, but her mother's grip was viselike, pressing her against the cage. "Have you faced this?" the queen hissed, her fingers tightening enough to bruise.

Thalia shook her head, her body trembling.

"Shall I bring Cassius down here? Shall I introduce him to this creature? Perhaps they know each other. Perhaps *he'd* be more willing to talk than my own daughter."

Thalia's cheeks burned with tears. "Please. Don't—"

"Don't what, Thalia? It's clear from your hesitancy that they've wormed their way inside your head. Perhaps I was foolish in thinking you wouldn't succumb to their ways. That your deep-rooted hatred for *him* would have stopped you from falling under his guiles once more. I was wrong."

"No—" Thalia shook her head, willing her mouth to stop speaking. Willing her body to stop acting like a coward.

"No, what?" The queen finally released her, stepping back.

Thalia slumped against the cage, unable to rise, unable to stop the words poised on her lips like a damned confession. "There's a sickness," she finally rasped.

"And?"

Thalia couldn't look at her mother. She stared at the puddle of saliva below the Vampyr's limbs. "It causes madness."

The queen shifted. "How does it spread?"

"Though their bites." Thalia's stomach rolled, but she couldn't take the words back. Couldn't erase the knowledge she'd just handed over to her mother on a silver platter.

"Where did this sickness come from?"

Thalia shook her head, eyes welling, but she pushed the acid aside. "I don't know."

The best lies are the ones with truth weaved into it. Cassius's words rumbled low in her ear. Thalia was going to be sick.

"Is there a cure for this sickness?"

Thalia forced the bile from her throat. She wished she had a blade. Wished she had something so she could slice off her traitorous tongue. She should have just sent the damn letter about the sickness, if only so she wouldn't have to now confess before her mother, who stood above her like a wrathful god. "I don't know."

Thalia finally looked up, finding the queen above her, imperious and cold, nothing like the woman who'd first tasked her with her mission. The woman who'd seemed almost sorry for sending her daughter away like a lamb to the slaughter.

She wished the ground would open and swallow her whole. Wished her mother would just shove her into the cage with the Vampyr, if only so it would save her from the roaring in her head—in her heart.

Icy fingers gripped her chin, and Thalia flinched as her mother lifted her face. "You have done well, my daughter." Thalia trembled as the queen cupped her cheek. "Perhaps I was wrong. You have served Agripa. Far more than I thought."

The queen released her, and Thalia slumped.

"Given this information, I do believe that our enemy is one step closer to their demise." The queen moved to the stairs, her gown rippling behind her.

She stopped before she disappeared under the shadowed archway. The queen looked over her shoulder, and Thalia forced herself to meet her mother's stare. To look at the woman she'd become, who'd poisoned her as thoroughly as a Vampyr bite.

"Agripa will remember your role in this, Thalia. I shall remember."

Then she was gone, leaving Thalia to tremble in her own puddle of bitter regret.

Chapter Forty-Two

She didn't think she could face *him*.

She couldn't bear the thought of Cassius's face when he realized what she'd done—that she'd betrayed him.

So she stayed in the cellar, next to the Vampyr, who every so often tried to lunge at her through the bars. Whose puddle of spit had grown until it threatened to spill out from under the cage.

"Fuck, Thalia."

Thalia slowly lifted her head, finding Marcus on the threshold. He rushed to her, hauling her up.

"I didn't know," he got out, eyes wide. "I had no idea what your mother was trying to do—"

Thalia shook her head, hollowness ringing out like an empty bell. "I know."

Marcus's face fell as he gripped her arms. "You're freezing."

Thalia didn't care.

Didn't care that her touch was ice as Marcus led her out of the chapel.

Didn't care that her feet had gone numb and her wrists were bruised.

She didn't care when Marcus finally left her alone in her room, not even the roaring of the fire able to thaw the coldness that had latched on to her. The horror of what she'd done—what she'd confessed.

The door creaked open, but she didn't turn around. The scent of eucalyptus and mint enveloped her.

"Thalia?"

She didn't deserve her name on his tongue. Didn't deserve the pathetic part of herself that was comforted by it.

"What happened?" Cassius's words rumbled out.

She stood abruptly, walking to the fire. She planted her feet on the stained rug, trying to put distance between them.

Put distance between him and what she'd revealed to her mother.

Because after this, Cassius would never speak to her again. He might even kill her, and she wouldn't blame him for it. Not one bit.

"Look at me." His voice softened.

She couldn't face the look in his eyes when he realized she'd betrayed him. Her mother would use the information she'd spilled in whatever way she could to kill him and everyone else in Vaccarium.

Her eyes blurred, acid working its way down her throat as a gentle hand gripped her arm.

She couldn't do it. Couldn't let him see—

Cassius tugged her, forcing her to face him.

As soon as he saw her face, he stiffened, dropping her arm. "What did you do?"

Thalia could hardly see him through her tears. "I'm sorry," she rasped.

"Thalia, what did you say?" Cassius's words sharpened into a blade.

"She knows," Thalia got out.

Cassius stepped into her space. She couldn't move, couldn't escape him. "What does she know?"

Thalia shook her head, her back burning against the fire. "We were right, she suspected that there's a sickness."

"And?"

Thalia forced herself to meet his harsh gaze. "I confirmed it."

Cassius looked as though he'd been stabbed. "Why would you do that?"

Thalia looked away, her stomach rolling. Silence fell as heavy as a hammer.

Cassius finally let out a bitter laugh. "This is it, then? You get what you wanted."

Thalia's head whipped up. "What I wanted?"

Cassius's face darkened. "Your revenge against the Vampyrs. What you've been seeking for thirteen years."

"I didn't want any of this, Cassius. I didn't want to be forced into marrying a Vampyr. I didn't want to be the reason she now has the power to kill you all. And I sure as fuck didn't want you to turn into one of them!"

Cassius shook his head, his eyes like chips of ice. "At least we're finally being honest."

"Honest?" Thalia gasped. "*Honest?*"

She took a step toward him, fingers curling into fists. "You haven't been honest since the moment you stepped back into that throne room."

Cassius's jaw flickered, but he said nothing.

"You think—you think it was easy for me?" she choked out. "To lie to you? To not be able to do anything as my mother questioned me?"

"What did she do to you?"

Thalia closed her eyes, realizing her slip-up, but she was done lying. He would know if she was anyway. "There's a bitten, below the chapel." She peeled open her lids, throat tight. "She's chained in a cage, her face covered in an iron mask. That's how she knew about the sickness—suspected it. Marcus was there. He—he didn't know what she was asking of him. But I think she wants to use the old trenches to somehow enter Vaccarium undetected and do gods know what." Her breath shook as she finished. "You should leave, head back to Perden and warn everyone."

Cassius's face darkened, and Thalia waited. Waited for him to flee into the night—to disappear just like he had four years ago.

"Come with me," he finally got out.

Thalia let out a bitter laugh, shaking her head.

Cassius took a step toward her. "Come with me," he repeated again.

"And do what, Cassius?" Thalia's eyes blazed. "They won't trust me. Not after they hear about how I spilled your secrets."

"So we won't tell them what happened. The prince already knows the threat of your mother—"

"The prince?" Thalia whirled on him. "The prince who's disappeared? Who I haven't even met? I may have let my secrets spill, but you're still keeping yours."

Cassius's jaw flickered. "I can't tell you what's going on with the prince."

Thalia let out another bitter laugh. "Don't you see that this is hopeless, Cassius? We cannot hope to continue on. To—to be something without trust. And trust does not form from lies." Thalia stepped back toward the fire. "You should go. Before my mother finds you."

"No."

"Don't make this harder than it is, Cassius. Just leave—"

"Not without you."

Thalia stared at him, watching the rise and fall of his chest. The way he seemed to strain against his doublet.

"Did you not believe me when I said I was still in love with you?" Cassius's voice rose. "Did you not think that the idea of leaving here, of returning to face whatever awaits me in Vaccarium, is less terrifying than the thought of you not being by my side?"

"Cass—"

He shook his head. "If you wish to stay here, then I will stay with you."

Anger flared in Thalia's gut. "My mother will kill you, Cassius. Don't you get that?"

"Do you not realize that I'm a dead man without you anyways?" Thalia sucked in a breath as he closed the distance between them. "Do you not think I didn't die the moment I had to flee your presence? Do you not think that I don't die every time I'm not near you? When I'm forced to be away from you?"

Cassius's rough hands cupped her cheek. "I have died every day since that night. Since the moment I was turned. I've been a walking corpse, wandering around in hopes that maybe one day . . . one day you'd finally forgive me."

"Cass—"

"I die every time you look at me, because I know you see me. Through the pain of my betrayal. Through the secrets. You're not afraid of the monster inside me. The thought of you, even far away, is the only thing that has kept this new life bearable. Your presence. Your essence. It consumes me more than the taste of blood. It drives me more than the air I breathe. I'd rather take a stake to my own heart than be parted from you again."

Thalia stared up at him. His eyes glowed, his hands gripping her face as though it were an anchor. "I would rather face whatever dark death awaits me," she whispered, throat tight, "than spend this life without you."

She surged upward, her mouth colliding with his.

Thalia opened for him, her arms threading around his neck as he tugged her against him. She died and was reborn, each stroke of his tongue igniting the embers she'd let burn to ash.

His hands were on her bare back, traveling up to her shoulders, his calluses rough as he tugged the straps of her gown down.

Her bare breasts peaked, and she fisted a hand in his hair as he bent his head, mouth closing around her nipple.

She groaned as his teeth scraped, setting her nerve endings sparking. Her heart pounded in her chest, and his hands pulled the rest of her gown down until it pooled at her feet.

His fingers pressed into her hips, pulling her against him. His clothing frayed against her heated skin.

Her fingers scrambled over his doublet. He only pulled away for a moment so she could yank it over his head before his lips met hers again.

They were a tangle of teeth and limbs.

Thalia hit the edge of her mattress and she sank down, Cassius following. She couldn't get enough of him. Couldn't get over the feeling of his hands running over her skin.

She shivered, his thumb swirling up the inside of her thigh. She sucked in a breath, waiting.

"What do you want?" he whispered, his lips pressing into the innermost portion of her leg.

She nearly whimpered. "You."

Thalia could have sworn he grinned before his lips closed over her. She moaned, hips bucking as he sucked her into his mouth.

His strong hand splayed over her bare stomach, forcing her hips from moving.

"Gods, you taste like a dream. Just like I remembered," Cassius rumbled. Then he pushed two fingers inside her.

Thalia cried out, the sharp pain slipping into pleasure as he worked her with his mouth and fingers.

She came hard and fast, her legs curling around his shoulders. He laughed, lifting his head, then he gently unstrapped her shoes.

Thalia's lungs rose and fell in heavy pants as he unbuckled his trousers, and her mouth dried out as he sprang free. He fisted his cock in his hand, slowly tugging it. Thalia nearly came again at the sight.

Her heated gaze lifted to his. "Get over here. Now."

He chuckled. "Of course, Princess." Cassius crawled over her, kissing up the length of her body, his tongue wet and hot. He hovered above her. "Take off your jewelry."

Thalia slid the arm cuff off, then took off her earrings. She grabbed the comb from her hair and hissed when the sharp prongs pricked her finger.

A droplet of blood welled brighter than a diamond.

Cassius took her hand in his gently, and she didn't protest as her finger slipped into his mouth.

Thalia shivered as his tongue swept over her finger, sucking lightly. But he didn't bite her, just let her blood fill his mouth.

She swallowed as he finished, his eyes glowing, face slightly rippling. "Let me see you," she got out.

Cassius paused, eyes scanning hers, searching for any ounce of fear. Then he changed. His skin sank into his skull, black veins slithering beneath his flesh, eyes burning brighter than the moon.

She cupped his face, feeling the hollowed cheekbones. "You do not scare me," she whispered, pressing her lips to his. Cassius shuddered against her mouth as she pulled away, his skin slowly returning to normal.

"I want to know what it tastes like," she said quietly.

Cassius froze, his pupils nearly devouring the ring of his irises. "Are you sure?"

She nodded, sitting up. Cassius sat back as she grabbed her discarded hairpiece. She took his hand in hers, twisting it so his palm faced up. He didn't react as she pricked his thumb with the prong.

A droplet welled, then she slowly brought his hand to her mouth.

Cassius made a low noise in the back of his throat as her lips closed around his thumb. His blood hit her tongue, a mixture of copper and salt and something else. Something sweetened like a tart berry, and she sucked him deeper into her mouth.

"Fuck, Thalia," he whispered as she fell back against the bed, her tongue running all over the rough pad of his thumb. Thalia's hands wrapped around his arm, holding him to her.

"Thalia?" Her name was a question, one she knew the answer to. She nodded, and he seemed to shudder.

A sharp sting sliced along her fingertip.

Her eyes closed as he took her finger once more in his mouth, moaning as he gently sucked at her skin.

Thalia sucked on his thumb harder, and his own answering groan accompanied hers. The little bit of his blood was overwhelming her senses, making her light and dizzy.

He pulled his hand away from her mouth, and she made a noise of protest—until he took the hand he'd been sucking on and wound their fingers together, letting them rest by her head.

"I would gladly die a thousand deaths . . ." he whispered, his lips bright with her blood. Thalia groaned when he nudged her entrance. ". . . if it meant that I got to do this. If it meant I could be with you. You make all of this worth it."

Thalia's eyes rolled back as he pushed inside her, her fingers tightening around his. "And I'll never get sick of this. The feeling of you. The taste of your blood."

Thalia's hips lifted as an invitation, and he plunged deep inside her.

"The way you're so fucking wet for me, I can hardly think."

Thalia's core tightened as he withdrew, plunging deep inside her once more. She could hardly stand it—the feel of him inside her. How he filled and stretched her as if she had no ending or beginning. It was simply them. Their bodies entwined, fitting into places they'd both thought were forgotten.

Cassius's hips rolled, his strokes coming harder, faster.

Thalia let go of his hand so she could haul his mouth to hers. Her blood on his mouth had her moaning, her tongue stroking with as much fervor as his cock.

"Cassius," she groaned.

His fingers tightened around her waist and he pulled back, sitting on his heels, bringing her with him. She cried out as he reached a deeper angle, pleasure spearing straight to her core.

"Say it again." His rough voice scraped up her neck. He thrust upward just as she sank down and nearly wept at the building pressure, at the bliss that hummed just along the edges of her mind.

"Cassius."

He grunted, his hands tightening on her thighs, his chest brushing against her aching nipples.

"Fuck, Cassius," she got out. She grabbed his hand, shoving his thumb back into her mouth, craving the taste of him one more time just as he hit a spot so deep inside her she couldn't take it.

She screamed around his thumb, her tongue lapping up his blood, and he roared, his pleasure chasing hers.

Their bodies slowed, their breaths hard and heavy. Cassius removed his hand from her mouth, but it didn't go far. He cradled her face, forcing her eyes to his.

They didn't say anything, just stared at each other, as he stayed buried deep inside her.

Her eyes shone, and words gathered on her tongue, but they couldn't push past her tight throat.

Cassius's eyes softened, and he kissed her lightly. "Did you like the taste of my blood?" he whispered. Thalia nodded, and his hands slid down her arms. "There is one good thing about me turning."

"What's that?"

His eyes turned positively wicked. "I can do this all night."

Thalia's aching core turned molten, and she kissed him again, the taste of his blood still a tart cherry on her tongue.

Chapter Forty-Three

"I don't think I can move," Thalia murmured, the rain softly pattering against her window.

Cassius chuckled, his arm a comforting band around her waist. "You were ravenous last night. And this morning."

Thalia flushed, looking over her shoulder. She'd lost track of how many times he'd buried himself inside her. How many times she'd tasted his blood until she was sure she'd gone mad. Only pure exhaustion made them stop. But when morning came, Cassius had woken her with soft kisses along her shoulders, until his tongue had found its way between her legs and she'd screamed his name as she came.

Cassius smirked, a hint of fangs showing. She resisted the urge to prick her finger against them. She cupped his face, feeling his stubble against her palm. "Me? I'm not the one who initiated that." She nodded to her legs tangled in the sheets.

"I told you." His voice turned rough and gravelly. "I'll never get tired of the taste of you."

He kissed her, and she let herself get lost in him before pulling away. "We shouldn't do this right now," she whispered.

Cassius raised a challenging brow.

"I mean it." She tried to be serious, but couldn't stop her lips from twitching as he nipped at her neck.

"Cass?"

"Hmm?"

"What are we going to do about my mother?"

Whatever heat was between them died instantly. Cassius slowly raised his head. She didn't think either of them had really forgotten what had happened the night before.

He sucked in a sharp breath. "We need to take care of that bitten."

And by *take care of*, he meant *kill*.

Dread swirled in her belly, but she pushed it aside. She knew it would be a mercy, but that didn't stop her stomach from clenching.

"It's under the chapel?" Cassius asked. Thalia nodded, and he got up, gathering his discarded clothes.

"What are you doing?" she asked as he tugged on his pants.

"Going to take care of what needs to be done."

"Like fuck I'm letting you go alone."

"You said she's in a cage? I'll be fine."

Thalia's heart leapt. "If my mother catches you—"

"She won't, because you're going to be distracting her."

"How?"

Cassius strapped on his sword, his deft fingers tugging on the buckles. "Tell her there's more she needs to know."

Thalia faltered. "What?"

"Feed her partial truths."

Thalia shook her head. "About what? Cass, I don't know—"

He stepped in front of her, taking her hands in his. "Tell her that you know where the sickness stems from."

Thalia's eyes lifted to his. "Why? She can't know about the creature. She'd try to send her men to capture it."

"I know. But they won't be able to get through the forest. The distraction could give us time to get to Vaccarium and figure out what she wants to do with the old trenches."

Thalia's stomach knotted tighter, but she slowly nodded.

Cassius squeezed her hand, moving to leave, but she held fast. "If the bitten isn't there, you don't go searching for her. You come back here, and we leave."

Cassius's face softened, and he bent to kiss her, his lips seeming to memorize her.

Thalia didn't want to think about whether it was a goodbye or not. "Trust yourself," he whispered. Then he left, and Thalia just hoped his faith in her was well placed.

Thalia knocked on her mother's door.

The white wood gleamed, and she ignored the two soldiers standing watch outside. Thalia waited, picking at the skin around her nails.

Immediately she scowled, but she forced herself to smile as Kamith opened the door.

"Thalia." Kamith inclined his head. "I was just advising your mother."

Advising or fucking?

Based on his disheveled head and the fact that his doublet wasn't buttoned properly, she had a feeling she knew. It made her stomach knot further.

"I'd like to speak to her. There's—there's something she needs to know."

Kamith held up a hand to wait a moment and closed the door in her face.

Thalia huffed, her fingers picking her thumbs, until the door opened again. She glanced at Kamith as he left, then turned her attention to the woman before her.

The queen sat in her sitting area, a set of tea laid out before her. She wore an emerald gown, the color rich on her pale skin. But in the hazy morning light, Thalia noted that her skin appeared even more haggard than the night before. The lines around her mouth were more pronounced, as were the circles under her eyes. She looked old. Far older than Thalia remembered.

"Kamith said there's something you wanted to tell me?" the queen said, her words clipped.

Thalia shuffled into the room, taking a glance around. The last time she'd been in here, her mother had given her the order to take down the Vampyr kingdom.

Thalia swallowed, tucking her hands behind her back so she wouldn't pick at them. "I—I know what causes the sickness."

The queen looked up, interested. "Oh?" Thalia nodded. "And why are you just now telling me this? Had a change of heart?"

"You could say that."

The queen raised an unbelieving brow. "According to the gossiping servants, it seems that your heart hasn't changed at all, given last night's escapades with a certain Vampyr."

Thalia's cheeks heated with embarrassment, but she pushed it aside. "And what of your own escapades with your adviser?"

The queen waved a hand. "Please, don't be a child."

Thalia stiffened but bit her tongue to keep her retort in.

The queen looked at her again. "Well? Get on with it. What causes the sickness you've been so eager to avoid discussing?"

Thalia's fingernails pierced her palms. "A creature."

The queen froze, her eyes slowly sliding to her daughter's. "A creature?" Thalia nodded. "What sort of creature?"

"One that dwells in Chaménos, the forest bordering our realms. It's nothing like anything I've ever seen. It's nothing like anything in this world. They say it was made."

Something flashed in the queen's eyes, but it was gone in an instance. "Made?"

Thalia nodded once more, and something tugged in the center of her chest. A strange pull she couldn't place.

"Something created it. The Mages—" She faltered, then pushed ahead. The Mages weren't a secret, not one whose existence would be threatened, anyway. "They said that this creature was made by magic, that some Mage must have turned to darkness to create it."

Thalia paused, watching her mother. The queen had just sunk against the couch, eyes contemplative.

That tugging was insistent now, as if a string were tied around Thalia's breastbone.

"You don't seem shocked," Thalia got out.

The queen flicked her attention back to her daughter. "The Mages are of no concern to me."

"You know about them?"

"Everyone from Vaccarium knows about them."

Everyone from . . .

Thalia sucked in a sharp breath, the tug intensifying so hard she could barely think. Maybe that was why her mother's words weren't making sense. "What?"

The queen stood, pacing slightly, then she turned suddenly. "And this creature, what does it look like?" Thalia shook her head, mumbling off the description. "And the prince?"

Thalia's head spun. "What about him?"

"You say he's often away from court? That you haven't seen him?"

Thalia shook her head. "No. No there's always an excuse as to why he's gone—"

The queen let out a laugh and clapped her hands, a smile breaking across her face. "How excellent."

"What are you talking about?"

The queen crossed the floor, and Thalia didn't know how to react as her mother gripped her hands, nearly giddy with joy. "You have done very well, Thalia." The queen smiled brighter than the sun. "Very well indeed."

"I don't understand."

The queen shook her head, her hand cupping Thalia's face. "Never mind that. The prince is gone. For good. The courts will soon fall if they aren't already in chaos, based on what you've told me. The creature's poison will spread, especially once I've captured more Vampyrs and turned them thanks to the bitten under the chapel. We've done it, Thalia. We've destroyed them."

Thalia's stomach knotted like a noose. "You mean to send an army of bitten Vampyrs into Vaccarium?"

The queen stepped back, making her way to the window. "I thought that once the prince had been cursed, the lack of rule would lead to a civil war. But I suppose I should have realized that there needed to be more. Then Reina captured that Vampyr, one who seemed . . . different than the rest. I knew it wasn't well; I've been having Marcus look into the old trenches to see if we might continue to push through under the forest."

Thalia had gone cold, her fingertips numb. "There are children there."

The queen turned. "What?"

"Children." Thalia's voice harshened. "In Vaccarium. Innocents. You mean to slaughter an entire populace? For what? Because of what happened to our family?"

"Our family was the least of my worries."

Her words stopped Thalia short. The callousness with which the queen spoke, as though her own husband and daughter were of little consequence, shocked Thalia's senses. "But they—they were murdered."

"Yes." The queen's eyes sharpened. "By the very creatures who killed my own kin."

"What are you talking about?" The tug on Thalia's chest had her stumbling forward. "Your family lives in Mandecium."

"My family," the queen said slowly, "lived in Vaccarium before the prince decided that my father had grown too powerful. Before he decided to have both my mother and younger brother beheaded alongside my father. I fled my home and escaped to Mandecium. I was taken in by a family there who I didn't know were so influential. Who would later pawn me off to your sire like a brood mare in exchange for money," she spat.

Horror mounted as Thalia stared at her mother. At someone she didn't recognize. "What was your father?"

Not who. *What.*

The queen's eyes seemed to glow. "A Mage."

Thalia's throat tightened hard enough that she choked. "Did you make that creature?"

The queen cocked her head. "No. At least not intentionally. I'd hoped to strike the prince down, and in a way, I suppose I did."

Thalia could hardly breathe as the queen ran a hand over her bodice. "It was actually your friend Marcus who gave me the idea. In searching for a solution to the ore, he'd discovered some very interesting books within the library, ones that had been given to us when the Vampyrs and humans of Agripa coexisted. They talked about the magic of the Mages. I'll admit, I wasn't very keen on my father's teachings, and after his murder I'd nearly forgotten everything he'd taught me. But those books opened my eyes to the pockets of magic left over. But using it drained me. Nearly killed me."

Thalia's mind flashed back to five years ago when her mother had gotten so ill Thalia had thought she'd die. She'd always assumed it had something to do with their depleting ore, but now . . .

Thalia was going to be sick.

Everything made sense. The reason the prince had been so absent, why his council kept changing their stories. Perhaps they'd known what had happened but were trying to keep the panic from spreading.

The creature who terrorized them in the woods was their own prince.

"But now we get to sit back and watch as the Vampyrs destroy themselves, as the poison spreads." The queen sank into her couch, triumph flashing across her features. "Thank you, Thalia. I am proud of you."

Thalia felt her whole world shifting.

A knock on the queen's door had her jerking.

Kamith poked his head in. "Your Majesty, I have what you asked for."

"Good, bring them in."

Them.

Thalia shook her head, and her world completely slipped out from under her as two soldiers dragged Cassius into the room and Reina stepped in with the bitten Vampyr.

Chapter Forty-Four

Thalia jerked, but Kamith grabbed her, stopping her from flying across the room.

Cassius's eyes blazed, and a sharp cut along his brow indicated how they must have captured him. There was no other way they could have stopped him. His arms were chained behind his back—unable to fight as they all paused within the queen's sitting room.

Thalia's eyes flew to Reina's. "Reina," she gasped. "She did all this. She's going to kill him—"

The queen laughed. "I'm not going to kill Cassius, Thalia."

Thalia slowly looked to her—heart beating hard enough to crack in two. "You're not?"

The queen shook her head. "No. But I'm rather curious to see how the bite spreads." Thalia's head whipped up, pure terror flooding through her as the queen gestured Reina forward. "Unmask it, but watch out for its teeth."

Reina did as she was told, unscrewing the mask from around the bitten's face. As soon as the metal left the Vampyr's skin, she lunged, teeth exposed. The two soldiers holding her tightened their grips.

"Please," Thalia choked. "Don't do this. You have what you wanted."

The queen frowned. "I thought you would be pleased, Thalia. After all, weren't you the one who wanted to kill him in the first place? Weren't you so eager to go into Vaccarium to seek revenge? To stir up discord and watch the courts fall into ruin?"

Thalia's head whipped to Cassius, her heart threatening to swallow her whole. "Cassius."

He shook his head, eyes blazing. But not at her—not at her secret mission now revealed. His hatred was pinned on her mother, who watched the whole thing with an amused brow.

"Reina, if you please." The queen waved a hand.

Thalia struggled more, but Kamith's grip was iron. She cried, tears streaking down her cheeks, as the bitten was dragged closer and closer to Cassius, spittle flying through the air.

Cassius jerked, trying to fight his restraints.

"Please," Thalia begged. "Please. I'll do anything."

The queen's brows narrowed further with displeasure. "But, my dear, you've already done enough."

Thalia screamed as the bitten lunged, its teeth sinking straight into the strong column of Cassius's throat.

Thalia watched for what felt like a lifetime as the bitten gorged itself on Cassius's blood. His face grew deathly white, his muscles tight enough to snap.

Finally, the queen waved another hand, and Reina and the guards pulled the bitten off. Blood leaked from Cassius's neck, the front of his shirt soaked crimson.

"How long does it take?" the queen asked, eyes darting between them. "For the sickness to set in?"

"Fuck. You." Cassius's lip curled.

The queen flashed a viper smile. "Lock him up, and let me know when he starts . . . reacting."

The soldiers shuffled, ready to drag him out. But Thalia caught Cassius's stare, through the pain, through her own horror.

He mouthed the words *Trust yourself.*

Cold resolve steeled her spine. Cassius started struggling, creating the distraction she needed—

She slammed her boot down hard on the inside of Kamith's foot. Kamith started, and she flung her head back, smashing against his nose.

Thalia used the same maneuver Reina had taught her as she twisted out of Kamith's loosened grips.

Then she pressed her dagger to his lifeblood.

"Move, and I slice his throat," Thalia snarled.

Everyone froze.

The queen slowly rose, eyes widening. "Thalia—"

She tightened her grip on Kamith, pressing the dagger hard enough that blood welled. "I mean it. Take one more step, and you'll watch him bleed out."

The queen held up her hands, her face slowly hardening. "What do you want?"

"Unchain him." She jerked her head to Cassius. She could have sworn pride shone in his eyes as the queen jerked her head. His chains fell off.

"Everyone back off," Thalia growled.

Kamith shifted, but her blade pressing hard into his neck stopped him. Cassius slowly eased away from the soldiers, eyes on the bitten, who foamed at the mouth. The soldiers holding her struggled.

"We're going to walk out of here." Thalia angled herself toward the door. "And you're going to let us go."

The queen's eyes blazed as Cassius took a step toward Thalia.

"I don't expect we'll see each other again," Thalia said, taking another step.

"I am sorry," the queen said, her face hard. "I wanted better for you."

The soldiers released the bitten.

It lunged toward Cassius. Thalia moved, her knife slicing across Kamith's throat, and her mother screamed.

Cassius's hand punched through the bitten's chest. It froze, eyes flickering, before he ripped out its heart, letting it splatter to the ground. The soldiers charged. Thalia tossed him her knife, and he plunged it into the neck of the first one before his hand punched through the armor of another, ripping his spine in half. The other two were quickly dispatched.

Thalia's heart pounded as Cassius arrived at her side, hands dripping. The queen stood by Kamith's body, her gown soaking up his blood. Reina stood in front of her, sword drawn.

Thalia stared at her mother, at the woman she'd never really known. *Kill her,* her mind screamed.

But staring at her mother, at the woman who stood in the growing pool of her lover's blood, she couldn't. And perhaps she'd just damned all of Vaccarium because of it.

"I wished better for you too," Thalia choked out.

Then she grabbed Cassius's hand, and they fled.

Chapter Forty-Five

Thalia finally pulled her horse to a stop.

They'd left Corithian behind, nothing but blood in their wake.

She half fell off her horse, whirling to Cassius, who dismounted clumsily. "Tell me what to do," she rasped, hands clenching in his bloodied shirt. "Tell me."

He shook his head. "Nothing."

"There has to be something. Feed from me; that will help you—"

"Thalia." He gripped her face. "There's nothing to be done."

She didn't realize she was crying until his thumb swept over her cheeks, catching her tears.

"It will be okay," he whispered.

She shook, gripping his hands. "Cassius—"

"We need to get back to Vaccarium. We need to tell them everything."

She fought past the bile in her throat, the acid burning her cheeks. She forced herself to mount her horse, to keep it together as they rode hard toward the forest stretching in the distance.

To not sink into despair as Cassius's hands tightened harder around her waist as if afraid to let go.

Chaménos was quiet.

Eerie silence bled into the air as they traveled through the forest. The gray trees reached their skeletal limbs together, blotting out the sky above their crimson leaves.

Thalia's heart didn't stop pounding.

"How long do we have?" she whispered, even though there was no need to be quiet. No one was in the forest, and if any creatures attacked . . . well, she hoped they did.

Hoped something would come at her so she could sink her blade into them as opposed to letting herself drown in despair.

"It will take a few days," Cassius said, his fingers tight on her waist.

They'd already spent days getting to Chaménos. They'd hardly rested, only switching out horses when needed.

Thalia blinked the tears from her eyes.

"You have to promise me something," Cassius said, his words in her ear.

"What?"

"After . . . after I say goodbye to them, you need to kill me."

Thalia jerked, her breath catching. "Cass—"

"I don't want to become one of them," he continued, undeterred. "I don't want to be suspended in a state of sleep wondering if I'll ever wake up."

Thalia started crying, her tears splashing onto their joined hands.

"Keegan won't do it. Camilla will try and suspend me. I—I need you to kill me." Thalia shook her head, but Cassius's grip tightened. "Please, Thalia. You need to do this for me."

She twisted, finding his gaze hard on hers. His eyes glowed with such pain and sorrow that she wished she could stab her own heart.

"Promise me," he whispered.

Thalia swallowed, eyes blurring. "I promise."

He seemed to relax, brushing his lips across her brow. "Thank you."

They continued on, and Thalia could have sworn she was hallucinating when something orange blurred in the distance through the trees, a smoky haze that made her vision fuzzy.

"What's that?" She squinted.

Cassius stiffened behind her. "I don't know."

Thalia urged their horse, heart pounding.

The orange glow spread, and the scent of smoke hit them in full force.

"It's a fire." Thalia's throat closed. She twisted in the saddle, looking back the way they'd come. Horror rose at the orange closing the distance.

"Go!" Cassius yelled.

Thalia kicked their horse and they took off, the sounds of crackling and burning logs falling behind her.

The smoke grew thick enough to choke, and Thalia's eyes watered as she urged her horse deeper into the forest.

"Which way?" she shouted. Creatures moved by in a blur, trying to escape the flames.

Cassius gripped the reins around her fingers. He didn't say anything as he urged their horse faster, trying to escape the fire that'd turned into a blaze. The trees seemed to cry out, their shrieks piercing her ears.

The horse whinnied, pulling to a sharp stop as branches fell in their path.

"Fuck," Cassius cursed, before whipping their horse, spurring it toward a different path.

The fire was all around them. Thalia could hardly see the ground, couldn't see with the fire closing in around them—

They broke through the trees, and Thalia's eyes widened.

Five pools of water stared at her. Or what had been five pools. They were no more than scorched patches of earth. The Mages must have come and burned the eggs, but the rivers had obviously not reached the springs yet.

Thalia's eyes widened even more as Keegan stumbled into the clearing, along with Lady Decima and Larellia.

"What the fuck are you doing here?" Cassius shouted.

Keegan's eyes were as wide as saucers. "What the fuck are you doing here?"

"Escaping this!" Cassius shouted.

"We're trying to stop it," Larellia said. She raised her hands, and something cold whipped past Thalia's ears. She turned just in time to see a flaming branch aimed for their head get knocked aside.

"How did this start?" Thalia shouted.

"We don't know," Keegan ground out, his brows narrowing. "We took care of the eggs days ago. We just got word that a fire was seen in the forest not an hour ago. Rumors are that the humans sent soldiers. The other Mages are on their way; with enough of them, we should be able to stop this."

Thalia swallowed, the heat of the flames licking at her back. Her mother must be trying to drive the creature out so she could capture it herself. That or she'd set the fire to stop her and Cassius.

"Well, don't just stand there," Larellia yelled. "Move!"

They did, moving away from the fire, which seemed to have hit an invisible wall. In fact, the entire area was blocked off by a hard wall of air, protecting the springs.

"What do we do?" Thalia asked as Cassius dismounted. He grabbed Keegan in a tight hug. The golden-eyed Vampyr looked stunned for a moment before he returned the embrace.

Cassius turned to Thalia. "You need to get the fuck out of here."

"Like hell I will."

He ignored her, turning to Larellia. "Make a path for her through the flames. Get her out of this forest."

Larellia gritted her teeth, sweat beading along her brow. "I'm a little busy at the moment."

Thalia slid off her horse, gripping the reins tight. "I'm not fucking leaving you. Not now. Not when we only have hours left."

"What is she talking about?" Keegan asked.

Cassius's eyes flared. "Thalia—"

"I can't," she choked. "I can't do it."

"Cass?" Keegan questioned. "What happened in Agripa?"

Thalia quickly explained her mother's vendetta against the Vampyrs. How she somehow was from a line of Mages and had used her lost power to curse the prince. Thalia added her suspicion that the queen had caused the forest fire.

"Fuck," Keegan said, running a hand over his hair.

"Did you know?" She turned to Cassius. Now wasn't the time, but she had to ask. "That the creature was the prince?"

Cassius swallowed. "We had our suspicions, but nothing confirmed. He disappeared when the creature appeared. We thought perhaps he was killed, but . . ." He cursed.

"It doesn't fucking matter," Larellia said over her shoulder. The entire forest was now a raging inferno. Even if Thalia wanted to flee, she didn't think Larellia had enough strength to provide her a safe way out. "Did you kill the queen?"

Thalia looked at Cassius. "No."

"Why the fuck not?" Larellia whirled to them, and the barrier around them wavered. Lady Decima grunted, trying to replenish Larellia's magic.

"Cassius—" Thalia's throat tightened.

"'Cassius' what?" Larellia stalked forward.

"They had a bitten," he said softly.

Keegan's face drained of color. "Did it bite you?"

Cassius nodded.

Larellia's eyes flashed, but she slowly looked at Thalia. "If this creature escapes this forest, if it heads into Vaccarium and spreads its poison, this is on you."

Thalia's throat tightened. Then movement caught the corner of her eye.

The blood left her face. "Cassius."

He turned, his own face slowly slipping as something emerged from the inferno of the fire.

The creature—the prince—whatever it now was—had somehow survived the flames. It was the size of a horse, far bigger than its offspring. Its claws dug up the ground, turning the trunks into smothered ash. Its silver hide was covered in scorch marks, holes burned through its white, leatherlike flesh. And next to it was her mother.

"What the fuck?" Thalia couldn't make sense of it, couldn't believe her mother was standing next to the creature, seemingly unharmed.

"Get behind me," Cassius breathed, but his hands trembled. Something wasn't right.

The creature let out a chortling sound in the back of its throat, its strange nostrils flaring.

"You can't escape this, Thalia. The Vampyrs were always meant to fall," the queen yelled, fire flaming behind her.

Lady Decima glanced nervously, the barrier wavering, and heat blasted into the space.

"Keep it up," Larellia growled, drawing her scythe. Keegan's blades flashed. "You have no business here."

"Here I thought the Mages stuck together." The queen smiled.

Lariella snarled, everyone taking position against the creature and the queen.

"My mother may have created it," Thalia got out. "But maybe it will listen to me like its spawn—"

The creature shrieked and charged.

Cassius shoved her out of the way just as it flew between them. Someone screamed, and the barrier faltered even more.

"Keep it up!" Larellia roared as she turned to the queen. Tendrils of darkness shot from the queen's hands, and the head Mage cut them apart with her scythe.

Thalia turned, her knife in hand, as the creature shook sparks from its skin. It rumbled, its jaws snapping, before it charged at Keegan.

Keegan swiped his sword, the blade bouncing off its hide. Cassius attacked with his own weapon, but his movements were jerky, his eyes widening and unfocused.

Thalia's heart clenched and Larellia screamed, raising her scythe against the queen, but she was blasted back by the queen's own power. Keegan sliced his sword along the creature's side, but not even the sharpened blade could penetrate its thick hide.

The barrier faltered once more.

Thalia glanced behind her. Lady Decima was on her knees, sweat pouring from her as she tried to keep the fire at bay.

"Thalia!" Keegan shouted as the creature charged her.

Thalia rolled out of the way, her chest catching. She turned, sword ready.

The creature had found another prize.

Cassius was distracted, shaking his head as if he were trying to shake dots from his eyes. He stumbled about, his sword falling from his hand. He scrabbled at his head, and Thalia's heart broke in half as she realized what was happening.

Thalia screamed, but it was too late. The creature launched itself, jaws dripping, as it slammed into Cassius. He disappeared under its white hide and slicing claws.

Thalia forced her legs to move, to unstick herself from where she'd been frozen.

Rage like she'd never known slammed into her. It fueled her steps as she roared and charged.

She didn't look at Cassius's shredded form as she slammed into the creature, her limbs reverberating as she tried to strike it with her knife.

The creature turned, and quick as an asp, its jaws sank straight into her arm.

Thalia screamed, pain blinding her as the creature lifted her up.

She was going to lose her arm—

It froze, shuddering, as its jaw opened and dropped her to the ground. Thalia hit the dirt, moaning.

The creature screamed, shaking its head. Its mouth began foaming quicker, spittle flying.

"Thalia!" Keegan grabbed her uninjured arm, hauling her up.

The world swayed.

The creature stumbled, shrieking as its mouth started to steam. It fell into one of the craters, beginning to twitch.

The queen screamed, stumbling toward the creature, clutching her chest as though she were being burned from the inside out.

Then the queen looked down, watching the metal of Larellia's scythe embed in her chest. She looked at her daughter. Blood dribbled from her mouth. "Thalia—"

"Now!" Larellia roared, pulling out her scythe, and the queen collapsed, staring unseeing at the trees. Keegan left Thalia's side and they surged to the creature, their blades sinking into its armored hide like moss.

The creature continued to shriek, its lips steaming and peeling back from its mouth. But Larellia and Keegan didn't stop.

"Wait—" Thalia stumbled to the pool.

Larellia chopped off its head, and they waited, hardly daring to breathe. The tendrils in its neck stretched toward its body, but whatever was happening in its mouth was spreading.

Its skin was decaying, falling apart at the seams. The tendrils from its severed neck withered into nothingness.

It seemed as though the whole forest let out a collective sigh and the rest of its body slowly flaked away, until it was nothing more than a pile of ash.

Chapter Forty-Six

"What happened?" Keegan panted, eyes wide. He directed his question at Thalia, but she'd already stumbled away.

"No, no, no," she cried, falling to her knees by Cassius's broken body.

His chest was a gaping hole; part of his hip was missing. She knew he wasn't dead, not wholly.

She cradled his head with her good arm, the other still leaking blood.

Tears streaked down her cheeks, and Keegan came up, sinking beside her. Larellia and Lady Decima appeared too; the other Mages must have arrived and begun holding the fire at bay, trying to stop it from destroying all of Chaménos. But she didn't care.

Thalia raised her bleeding arm.

"Thalia—" Larellia cautioned, and she paused. "Cassius was bitten. Even if your blood heals him, he will be turned into something else."

"I don't care," Thalia snarled.

"He could bite you," Keegan warned, his voice hoarse. "You could turn into one of us. He has the poison in him. If you turned into a bitten, he'd never forgive himself for it."

"I don't *care*." Thalia's tears dripped onto Cassius' face. His face was so cold and pale it was as if he'd become a corpse.

Before anyone could stop her, she shoved her ruined arm against his mouth.

Nothing happened.

Thalia counted in her head, barely breathing, as time moved so slowly. She started crying again.

He couldn't be dead. He couldn't.

Because she hadn't gotten the chance to tell him that she loved him. That if he died, she was as good as a ghost. That this life meant nothing without him in it.

She cursed her mother, who was dead behind her.

Cursed whatever death god watched from the shadows, wishing to steal him.

She wouldn't let them take him.

Cassius was good, and kind, and strong. He deserved more than to succumb to madness.

Thalia grabbed her dagger, slicing her arm to the bone.

Someone started, but she shoved her arm back against Cassius's lips, forced his mouth to part so her blood trickled into his throat.

Slowly, like watching morning dew dry up in the sun, color began to bleed into his face, like an ink stain spreading across water.

Her tears mixed with her blood, but his skin began knitting itself back together, muscle and sinew pulling itself by the seams at his hips, then his gaping chest.

Her head lightened, but she ignored it. Ignored the way her vision blackened around the edges.

Cassius's chest rose, a breath stuttering out.

Then his hand gripped her wrist, his tongue poking into the cut along her arm. His throat worked as he took drags of her blood, as she willed it to move into Cassius's body, to fix what was broken inside him. Thalia ran her hand over though his hair, fingers snaring on the strands.

Her heart rate was slowing, each beat shorter than the last.

She didn't care.

Because he would be alive, and that's all that mattered.

"Get ready," someone murmured, perhaps Larellia. "We'll need to suspend him the moment he wakes."

Thalia's fingers were slowing their strokes, her vision spotting with darkness.

Cassius's eyes flew open, the irises glowing.

"Now—"

"Wait." Keegan's harsh voice halted the command. "Just wait."

Cassius focused on her, his pupils blown out, his fingers pressing gently into her wrist. She was nearly slumped over him, her braided hair brushing against his cheek.

Finally, he pulled his mouth away, just as Thalia's vision went black.

"Shit." Keegan caught her, and she fought hard to keep her eyes open. Someone touched her arm, a curly head out of the corner of her vision. Blinding white seemed to glow around her forearm, but she couldn't tell what was happening.

Cassius lay there, his eyes open, although he didn't seem to focus on anything. Merely stared up at the broken canopy of leaves above his head.

His chest rose and fell, but it didn't seem like he was even really breathing. That any oxygen was getting down into his lungs.

Lady Decima stepped away; whatever she'd done to Thalia's arm had healed it. Or at least patched it up enough that she was able to weakly shove herself out of Keegan's hold.

"Cassius?" She crawled over to him.

She half lay across his body, running a hand over his face. "Cass?"

He stared at nothing, his eyes unseeing, although they were just as open as hers.

"Come back to me," she whispered. "Please come back to me."

Minutes dripped by, but still he lay there.

"What is going on?" Keegan got out.

Thalia shook her head, crying. She'd healed him, but something wasn't right. Maybe because he'd been bitten . . .

She gripped his face in her hands. "You can't leave me, you prick." Tears splashed onto his cheeks. "You can't leave me. I will not allow it."

She pressed her lips into ice-cold ones.

She shuddered, willing him to feel her. Willing him to wake. To hold her. To yell at her. She didn't care.

Thalia pulled away, running a hand over his face. "Come back, you asshole, so I can tell you that I love you."

Cassius took a deep, shuddering breath. It blasted through him with enough force that Thalia rose as he inhaled.

Then he blinked, slowly focusing on her. They stared at each other, his chest rising and falling with such beautiful breath that Thalia cried harder.

His brow furrowed, hand reaching up to cup her face. His thumb swirled along her cheeks. "Did you just call me an asshole?"

"I love you," she choked out, pressing her lips to his. Cassius kissed her back, gently.

Then he grunted. "What the fuck happened?"

Thalia pulled back, and dizziness racked her despite Cassius's steady grip. Everyone around them seemed to be in varying degrees of shock.

"Are you feeling . . . well?" Larellia asked, her hands raised as if ready to blast him with her power.

Cassius's brow furrowed further. "I feel like half my body was torn off. But yes . . . well."

Keegan shook his head, his eyes glistening. "You were . . . Cass—you started showing symptoms of the poison. You were beginning to turn."

Cassius glanced at Thalia. "Is that true?" She nodded, and his eyes flashed. First with anger, then relief, then back to anger. "I told you to kill me."

"Well, I was trying to kill that thing." She pointed behind her to the pile of ash that was the creature. Already some of it had drifted away, picked up by a fell wind.

"What happened to it?" he demanded.

Thalia shook her head, just as confused as everyone else, until Larellia gasped. "Your blood."

Thalia stared at the Mage. "What?"

Larellia's silver eyes flicked between her and the creature. "When it bit you, its mouth began to steam as if your blood was the poison instead."

"How is that possible?" Lady Decima asked.

Larellia shook her head, her eyes landing on the dead queen. The forest was forming around her—as if the wild magic in Chaménos had formed a pocket in that spot. Roots from the trees wrapped around her body as she sank into the earth, covering her over in moss and rot. "I do not know." Her gaze landed on Thalia. "But perhaps there is hope for a cure after all."

"Are you okay?" Cassius gripped her face, but Thalia just stared at the place where her mother's body had been. The forest had taken her, no doubt retribution for all the harm the queen had done. Harm that Thalia would have continued if she'd let her hate rule her heart.

Thalia glanced at Cassius—at the man who'd never faltered from his path, even when hers had led her astray. "I can fix this. I can fix Vaccarium."

Chapter Forty-Seven

"Are you ready?" Camilla asked, her eyes steady on Thalia's.

Thalia nodded, holding her hand out.

The shifter carefully sliced along her heart line with a sharpened blade. Cassius tensed beside her, and she resisted the urge to glare at him.

The shifter allowed the blood to well, then slowly tipped her hand over the jar of teeth.

As soon as Thalia's blood hit the poisoned teeth, they began to bubble. They popped and hissed, burning away until there was nothing but a pile of ash.

"I think your blood is the cure." Camilla looked up, eyes wide.

Thalia turned to the others around the table. They'd all gathered back in Perden. The Mages had managed to put out the fire in Chaménos, but most of it was lost. Over half of their sacred forest had gone up until nothing remained but crisp, charred earth.

"Do you think it's because Thalia's mother made it?" Keegan asked, the golden-eyed Vampyr watching with his ever-calculating eye.

"It would seem the most likely cause," Lady Decima said, her curly hair catching the light.

"But how is that possible?" Thalia asked, after Camilla had bound her hand. She directed her question at Larellia, who sat opposite her.

Larellia's lips pursed, her silver eyes flashing. "I admit what happened was strange, something I still don't understand. Your mother told you that her father was a Mage?" Thalia nodded in confirmation. "As far as I know, there is no magic in the human realm, no pockets for your mother to have pulled from. That is why our forest is so sacred. It protects the magic from the mundane. It acts as a barrier to keep the wild magic from running loose."

"Are you sure there aren't pockets of magic there?" Thalia pushed.

Larellia shook her head. "No. But seeing as none of this should happen, seeing as your blood is the cure we've all been praying for, anything is possible. At least with your mother now dead, we have no fear of more creatures spawning and creating havoc."

Silence fell, until Thalia asked quietly, "And the Vampyr courts?"

Cassius stiffened once more beside her.

Since coming back from the brink of madness and death, he hadn't left her side. Not that she'd been inclined to leave him either. At night his unseeing eyes would flash in her mind, and he was driven out of sleep as much as she was.

She didn't know what sort of nightmares terrorized him, but she'd hold him closer. Let the steadiness of their breaths anchor them until they both drifted back to sleep.

"Lord Adrian has slunk back to House Gallinus now that the cure for the sickness has been revealed," Cassius finally said.

"He is being watched," Camilla added, settling into her seat. Indeed, the shifter had taken it upon herself to fly back and forth to ensure that he stayed there.

"And the prince?" Thalia asked. Everyone glanced at each other. "What have the courts been told?"

"They were told that the prince perished slaying the creature," Larellia said. "He, at least, is now seen as the savior to his people. A tale is already being spun about how he's spent months trying so desperately to slay it."

"Has that stopped the unrest?" Thalia pushed. The issues of the Vampyr courts all linked back to the sickness and the missing prince. But the prince was dead now.

"The unrest has paused, especially with Lord Adrian no longer whispering in the other Houses' ears," the head Mage started. "But I do fear that, once the relief of the creature being dead and a cure being found has passed, the unrest will resurface."

"Why?" Thalia asked.

"Because a human princess now rules the Vampyr kingdom." Larellia met her stare.

Thalia straightened at that. "Would they even accept me as ruler, considering the marriage between the prince and me was never finalized? We never consummated anything. Does it even count when he was turned into . . . that?"

Cassius cleared his throat. "The law of the Vampyrs is black and white. Marriage is recognized during an agreement, when a ceremony is performed and vows are taken, including blood sharing, even by proxy."

"That's the real reason Lord Damien wanted me to take your blood in Agripa when we were first bound," Thalia breathed. "Because it would have solidified the line of rule right then and there."

Cassius nodded. "Yes. Blood is stronger than ink. "

"So, I am the ruler of Vaccarium?" Thalia said.

Cassius nodded once more, his face becoming hard. "Yes. The courts, the Mages, and the shifters—we are bound to serve and protect you."

Thalia felt the weight of it settle over her shoulders.

Everyone began to trickle out, Camilla promising Thalia that she would begin to take her blood to start working it into a cure. It had taken her being nearly drained for Cassius to come back, perhaps because his injuries had been so grave.

But she'd gladly drain her blood if it meant that her mother's wrong could be righted.

Thalia found herself standing in the inner courtyard of the castle, looking out past the bridge suspended over the waterfall and into the pine forest, almost as if she could see the manor nestled near the lake.

A dark presence came up beside her.

"We'll still save Sybil," she said, eyes out in the distance. She might have been drained of blood, but Sybil wasn't a bitten anymore. Not with Thalia's blood in her serving as a cure for the poison.

Cassius's arm slipped around her waist, tugging her close. "I know."

She leaned into him, her chest tightening as she whispered, "I should have just killed her back in Agripa." Thalia's mind flashed to her mother buried in Chaménos. While their relationship had been strained, she was the last of Thalia's kin. Thalia hoped she found peace, wherever she went. That maybe in the next life her hatred wouldn't bind her the way it had in this one.

Cassius's fingers clenched on her waist. "You did what you needed to do to get us out of there."

Thalia shook her head, throat tight. "If I'd just killed her, the creatures would have all died right then. Who knows if the fire would have even started. You wouldn't have gotten hurt. You wouldn't have—have died—"

Cassius gripped her chin, lifting it to his. "Don't dwell on the past or what might have been." His thumb swirled over her cheeks, catching the tears. "We are both here. We are both *alive*. That's what matters."

Thalia nodded, her head going to press against his chest. She could hear his heartbeat, feel the rise and fall of the breath in his lungs.

Alive.

"But it won't be easy," Cassius said. "With the courts."

"I know. I don't expect it to be."

"You being the cure should help," Cassius mused, running his fingers through her hair.

Thalia huffed out a laugh. "I should hope so."

She pulled away slightly. "I want to start over, with the courts." Cassius raised a brow as she plowed on. "I want to earn their trust—for real. No matter how long it takes, no matter how much pushback there is. I want to see this world—I want to see Vaccarium thrive. I want to see Agripa thrive."

Although Thalia didn't know if Agripa would recognize her rule, seeing as she'd had a hand in killing her own mother.

But despite the uphill battle she faced with the courts, some of the weight around her shoulders lifted.

This was what she was meant to do. This was how she'd fulfill her vow—not with revenge but by living to see what Ariadna had wanted to see: their two realms enter into a time of peace.

Thalia turned to Cassius suddenly. "But I'll need your help."

Cassius offered a small smile. "You always have me. No matter what."

Thalia lifted her chin. "And if it comes to it, will you fight for me if I ask?"

"I will die for you."

His lips pressed into hers, and she let herself sink into his kiss.

She pulled away, her hand resting against his chest. "We have our whole lives ahead of us. Let's not try and die anytime soon."

"Agreed."

"When you agreed to step in as proxy," Thalia said, staring at the ring on her finger, "you were agreeing to marry me yourself, given the fact the prince never could?"

Cassius swallowed. "Yes. I always—I always knew it would be you, no matter what."

Thalia's throat tightened, and she flicked her gaze to his. "Shall we take the vow, then, officially?" At Cassius's raised brow, she continued, "Go to the springs and vow that no matter what darkness comes, even if we become darkness ourselves, we shall be by each other's sides? That we'll face whatever trials this age brings—together, two souls entwined."

Cassius gripped her chin. "Princess, I would like nothing more."

Thalia grinned, sealing her lips against his, their silent vow stronger than iron.

Epilogue

Three months later

"I swear, are you even listening?"

Thalia jerked, banging her knee against the top of the desk in her office. She hissed, shaking her head to try to clear her thoughts. But it was rather hard considering the sensation currently traveling up her thighs. "What?"

Camilla stood before her, golden eyes narrowed. She held a cream letter in her dark hand, but Thalia couldn't make out the wax seal. "I said that House Gallinus will not be attending your coronation."

Thalia shook her head once more, trying to calm her rising heartbeat. "Oh." She ignored the huff coming from between her legs. Her heart rate spiked.

"How do you want me to reply?" Camilla tilted her head.

Thalia paused, chewing the inside of cheek. House Gallinus seemed more opposed to her upcoming coronation than any other House. After Lord Adrian had slunk back to Cupisco, he'd been . . . quiet. But that didn't mean winning over the other Houses had been easy, even with the cure now spreading throughout Vaccarium and the bitten Vampyrs being cured. It had taken months and countless meetings with the other Houses to regain some degree of their trust. At least for now they seemed resigned to the fact that she'd be ruler of

Vaccarium, but she still had a long way to go if she ever hoped to be seen as their true ruler.

Later. She'd deal with that later.

"Just leave it," Thalia finally said. "I'll figure it out—" She sucked in a sharp breath, fingers tightening on the arms of her chair. Tiny fires erupted along her skin, setting her core molten. She tried to clamp her thighs together, but there was a pressure currently keeping them open.

Camilla raised a brow but set the letter on the desk. Before she left, the shifter turned. "Oh, tell Cassius to hurry up. The Houses will be here tomorrow, and we still have a lot to prepare for."

She left, closing the door to Thalia's new bedroom behind her.

Thalia shoved back her chair, yanking up the hem of her dress. "You couldn't have waited until after she was gone?"

Cassius sat back on his heels, a faint hint of fangs gleaming. "And waste what little time we have before the shitstorm arrives?" Thalia glared at him, and he smirked. "Forgive me, Princess, for wanting to ensure you're entirely relaxed and taken care of before your coronation."

He leaned forward once more, blue eyes set with such intent that Thalia resisted the urge to open her legs again.

"Camilla's right," Thalia got out, staring at the letter on her desk. Cassius paused. "There's still so much to do before the rest of the courts get here."

Cassius flicked his gaze up, challenge evident on his handsome face. "Good thing I work fast."

Thalia couldn't help the smirk that came to her lips. Cassius started pushing the folds of her gown aside, but she stopped him. "How do I reply?"

"Don't."

Thalia gripped his wrist, forcing his attention back to her. "I can't *not* reply, Cass. All the Houses were summoned. House Gallinus is choosing to ignore it—ignore me."

Cassius's brows narrowed, but he rose, grabbing the letter Camilla had left behind. He leaned against the desk, scanning the contents.

Finally, he said, "Well, Lord Adrian was at least . . . polite in his refusal to show. I doubt he wrote it, given the flowery prose."

Thalia snorted, but all humor died as she stared at the wax emblem of a stag with eight legs on it. "The other Houses will recognize this as an act of defiance."

Cassius set the letter aside. "The other Houses are not as stupid as House Gallinus. They know you are the reason we have a cure."

Except they didn't know to what extent.

Having to explain to the other Houses that the only reason Thalia was the cure was because her mother had dabbled in dark magic and created the creature in the first place wasn't something that she, or the prince's former council, was keen to experience. Especially with the tentative peace between the humans of Agripa and Vaccarium still on unsure footing.

As if Cassius knew where her mind had wandered, he asked, "You still haven't heard from them?"

Thalia chewed the inside of her cheek. "I sent a letter. To both Reina and Marcus. But there's been nothing."

Cassius shifted. "Have they tried to stir up anything in Agripa?"

Thalia shook her head. Before the queen had gone to Chaménos to try to stop Thalia and the Vampyrs, she'd spun a web of lies about Thalia murdering her adviser and attempting to take the crown by force. But the queen was gone—dead. Buried in Chaménos along with the creature.

The remaining members of the queen's council didn't really know what had happened when Cassius and Thalia went to the castle three months prior. Only Reina and Marcus knew the true extent of what had gone down in the queen's sitting room. Yet the lies that Thalia's mother had spread went deep.

And even though by birthright, Thalia was the next ruler of Agripa, that didn't mean she could waltz back to Agripa and take the throne. Agripa was being ruled by the remaining members of her mother's council, but Thalia continued to send ore. Continued to keep up the treaty her mother had signed when she bound her daughter to the prince of Vaccarium.

"I thought that Marcus would be more inclined to listen to my side of things." Thalia pinched the bridge of her nose. "I don't know what sort of lies my mother told Reina for her to . . . act the way she did."

Her mind flashed back to that day, to the way Reina stood protecting her mother against her. The memory made her sick.

Cassius gently grabbed her hand, pulling it away from her face. "They can't ignore you forever."

"It feels like they will," she muttered.

Cassius made a face. "Once all of this is over, we'll go back. Explain ourselves."

"And if they don't accept me as ruler?" Thalia flicked her gaze to his.

Cassius threaded his fingers through hers. "At least they'll know the truth. At least they'll know that Vaccarium has no desire to further the war between our peoples. Agripa can rest easy knowing that the Vampyrs will continue to send ore and leave them be."

Thalia sighed. Yes, she supposed Cassius was right. But one problem at a time. "Are the rooms set up for everyone who will be arriving?"

Cassius nodded, squeezing her hand. "Yes. Keegan and Lord Damien have it all sorted. Don't worry about that. The Houses are spread out throughout the castle to avoid . . . any future disagreements."

Thalia snorted. House Lorenzia had been rebuilt in a short few months in the aftermath of Lord Adrian's attack. She supposed the magic the Mages wielded was good for one thing: speeding up construction so that she and the prince's former council didn't need to stay in Perden with the rest of the Mages and shifters.

But it would be the first time in months that all the Houses saw House Lorenzia. Saw that the prince and his home had not died within the fires set by Lord Adrian but had risen from its ashes.

Thalia had her work cut out for her.

"I suppose I should see what else needs to be done," Thalia grumbled, preparing to stand. There'd be a whole week of feasting and dining before the coronation, which would happen during the full moon. She was still confused on all the customs that would go into a Vampyr coronation, but she figured she should find Camilla so they could review it all . . . again.

"Or we could do something . . . else," Cassius said.

Thalia raised a brow. "We don't have time for something *else*."

Cassius smirked, the sharp point of his fang setting a fire in her belly. "I'm not referring to *that*. Although, glad to know where your priorities lie, Princess."

She huffed out a breath. "Then what are you referring to?"

"The courts won't be here until tomorrow. But there's something I think we should do first. The rest of the council agree."

Thalia made a face. "What is it?"

Cassius held out a scarred hand. "Let me show you."

Thalia wasn't sure how long she sat in the carriage as it rumbled away from the castle of Irenbis, but all of a sudden it rolled to a stop and Cassius pushed the door open, hopping out before he offered her a hand.

Thalia sucked in a sharp breath. "Why are we here?"

Chaménos stretched before her, its silver trunks and crimson leaves twining together to create a wall of impenetrable forest.

Cassius met her stare. "Do you trust me?"

Thalia nodded without hesitation, even though the forest sent a chill down her spine. "Always."

Cassius offered a small smile, although he seemed to fidget as Feryena was brought forward. "Good."

But he didn't say anything more as she mounted and he swung up behind her. He clicked his tongue, and Feryena set off, heading into the tree line.

Thalia grew tenser the deeper they went.

She could practically smell the smoke from the fire her mother had started, feel the heat of the flames as they licked at her and Cassius's heels. As the poison from the creature slowly began driving him mad—

"Easy," he murmured, his lips brushing against her temple. "Nothing bad is going to happen. I have you."

Thalia swallowed, forcing herself to relax into him. "I wish you would just tell me what we're doing here—"

Her words died as they broke through the trunks and Cassius pulled Feryena to a stop.

Five pools stretched before her. But instead of remaining dry patches of earth scorched from the burning of the creature's eggs, they were full of glittering water. The incinerated trees had re-formed, either from the Mages' help or the forest's own pockets of wild magic. Flowers had bloomed, white and full petaled, each one nearly as big as her head. They hung from the branches of the trees like dewdrops, their fragrance tickling her nose.

"What the hell?" she got out as she realized they weren't alone in the forest. Keegan appeared, as did Lord Damien and Camilla. They all stood around a pool whose surface sparkled like liquid starlight.

Cassius dismounted, grinning up. "You told me that you wanted to take the vow a few months ago. Seemed like a good enough time to do it."

Thalia huffed out a laugh as Cassius helped her down, his fingers twining through hers. They moved toward the trio, a few petals falling from the trees, brushing against Thalia's cheeks as though to caress her.

"You all knew about this?" Thalia said as they stopped before Keegan, Camilla, and Lord Damien.

The shifter rolled her eyes. "Of course. Who do you think suggested it?" Thalia laughed as Cassius faced her, still holding her hand.

"Are you ready?" Cassius asked. "Do you still want to do this?"

He looked nervous, as if he was afraid Thalia would suddenly refuse him. She softened, stepping into him, and planted a kiss on his lips. "I'm always ready for you."

Cassius seemed to sag in relief, his lips firm against hers.

Keegan cleared his throat loudly and Thalia pulled away, laughing even as Cassius growled at him.

"Then step into the water," Lord Damien said, the red-eyed Vampyr gesturing toward the pool before them.

Cassius's fingers tightened on hers as they both stepped into the pool, the water surprisingly warm and light. She glanced around, her eyes lingering on a spot that stood out from the environment around them.

Just like the blooms in the trees, a bunch of flowers seemed to have sprouted from the ground in only one particular spot.

Thalia's eyes burned, her throat tightening.

"Thalia?" Cassius's words were soft.

She turned back to him, reading the concern in his eyes, but also the understanding . . . the love that not even the taint of the creature or the actions of her mother could dim.

"Let's do this."

He offered a small smile as Keegan stepped forward, wrapping their bound hands in a length of shimmering white ribbon.

"As your hands are bound together by this ribbon, may your souls be bound as one," Keegan said, tying a knot. "May you share your lives as one, both bound in love and loyalty until the end."

Camilla stepped forward with a jar of golden liquid. "May these hands always hold each other. May they have the strength to endure whatever darkness awaits them, or whatever light dares to shine upon them." She tipped the jar, its contents spilling out over their joined hands, coating them with sticky residue. "May their love be as sweet as this honey, and their hands remain tender and gentle as they carry each other through this world."

Thalia didn't realize she was crying until her tears splashed onto their bound hands, Cassius's own eyes bright.

"Iron may kill us," Lord Damien said, stepping forward and holding two bands of iron in his pale palms. "But by wearing it, we defy its power to destroy. Instead, this iron is a symbol of a new beginning. Of the hope that you both carry for each other into the years to come."

Cassius grabbed the smaller band with his free hand. He met Thalia's gaze. "I have loved you since the moment I first laid eyes on you," he said lowly, his words just for her. "And no matter what darkness comes, no matter if we become darkness itself, that love will never fade."

He slipped the band on her ring finger, nestling it below the one already there.

Thalia grabbed his ring, holding his fingers tightly. "There is no one I would rather face this world with. No matter what darkness we have to face, no matter who we have to become, I choose you."

She slipped the ring onto his finger, and the whole forest seemed to hold its breath as Lord Damien stepped forward once more, her jeweled dagger in his hands.

"You are bound by earth." He nodded to the pool that they stood in. Then he grabbed their joined hands.

Thalia didn't even flinch as he slid the dagger, cutting through the ribbon and honey and into the flesh of their palms.

Cassius cradled her cut hand, his eyes near glowing. "I love you," he whispered, then brought his palm to his lips. Thalia shuddered as his tongue lapped up the blood along her heart line.

Then Thalia raised his hand to her face, his blood bright against her lips and sticky with honey.

"You are bound by blood," Lord Damien finished. "Your souls are bound through darkness and light. May you never forsake the other."

The whole forest seemed to let out a sigh as the words rang out, settling into every hollow corner of Chaménos.

Thalia twisted, looking around at her court—her council—her friends. "Thank you."

The three nodded, their smiles brighter than the stars beginning to peek through the leaves.

"What happens now?" Thalia looked at Cassius.

His eyes seemed to glow brighter, and he wrapped his arms around her waist, pulling her flush against him. "Now we have to consummate this union."

"Wait, right now?" Thalia gasped.

Cassius smirked, and the trio all seemed to disappear, leaving them alone. "Would you rather wait, Princess?"

Thalia grinned as he gently laid her on the soft earth, flowers raining down around them. "I'm done waiting for you."

"Good." He pressed his lips against hers. "Because I plan to do this all night."

Acknowledgments

Writing a book is no easy task. Countless hours, tears, blood (pun intended), and sweat go into creating something like this. I could probably fill an entire ten-book series thanking every single person who helped me on this journey, who impacted me in the years that I spent querying, editing, creating, living. But that series wouldn't be enough to truly articulate how much this means to me. All of this couldn't be possible without you, the reader, and I am forever grateful that you took this journey with me.

I would first like to thank my agent, Grace Milusich, for your constant support, reassurance, and everything in between. Thank you for taking a chance on me. Thank you for always pushing me to be the best writer that I can be. I wouldn't want to do this journey with anyone else. To my editor, Melissa Rechter, your enthusiasm and vision for this book helped shape it into the best version of itself. I'm so grateful and humbled that you chose me and this story; thank you for believing in Thalia and Cassius. To my wonderful copy editor Eve Keith-Henningsen, thank you for your sharp eye. To the entire team at Alcove Press—Rebecca Nelson, Thai Fantauzzi Pérez, Dulce Botello, Mikaela Bender, Bethany Pullen, Lexi Baker, Julia Abbott, Megan Matti, and Stephanie Manova, among others—you are all amazing, and I could not have asked for a better home for my debut. To my cover artist, Olivia Hintz, thank you for such a beautiful piece and for bringing my book to life.

To the Gayngels group chat, I cannot express how much I love each and every one of you. You are all the bright spot in my life, and I am so proud to call you my friends. To Megan and Monique, thank you for your friendship, which goes far beyond our little books. Norees, thank you for reading the first draft, for being a cheerleader, and for loving Cassius as much as I do! To everyone across all the Discords, I love you all, and I am so blessed to have you on this journey. Shout-out to my amazing Vampyr Street Team! Thank you to every single one of you for supporting me, and getting the word out about this book! It's been such an honor and a privilege having you along for this journey. To #QuestPit, who created the event that landed me my agent. To every single person I've built friendships with in the book community, both inside and outside of social media, your unwavering support and encouragement mean the world.

To my family and friends, countless mentors at school, and the big dawgs at work, for pouring so much life, wisdom, and grace into my life—thank you. Thank you. Thank you.

To my parents, who always told me to pursue what makes me happy, even if it's unconventional, and who have provided more support and encouragement than can ever be counted, I love you both so very much, and I share this accomplishment with you.

To Taylor, my dearest friend, I could not have done this without you. From brainstorming sessions to first feedbacks to sharing our lives together, none of it would have been possible without your help. I cannot wait to see where we go and the stories we create. Thank you for believing in me and encouraging me when I didn't believe in myself. Thank you for sharing your beautiful family with me. I love you to the moon and to Saturn.

Tito (Penelope) and Tommy, your furry butts and paws have tried to delete this book and countless others a million times. But you are my heart, and I love you so much. Please never stop trying to crawl into my lap for cuddles.

Christian, you are forever my person. My rock. My home. I know you don't care for flowery words or long-winded statements, so I'll simply say thank you. Without your support, I wouldn't be doing this. I love you.